Surprise Me

Surprise Me

A NOVEL

Deena Goldstone

NAN A. TALESE | DOUBLEDAY
New York London Toronto
Sydney Auckland

www.nanatalese.com

DOUBLEDAY is a registered trademark of Penguin Random House LLC. Nan A. Talese and the colophon are trademarks of Penguin Random House LLC.

Jacket design by Emily Mahon
Jacket photograph © Enric Montes/Millennium Images, UK

LIBRARY OF CONGRESS CATALOGING-IN-PUBLICATION DATA
Goldstone, Deena.
Surprise me : a novel / Deena Goldstone. — First edition.
pages ; cm
ISBN 978-0-385-54123-7 (hardcover) — ISBN 978-0-385-54124-4 (ebook)
I. Title.
PS3607.O48595S87 2016
813'.6—dc23
2015027280

MANUFACTURED IN THE UNITED STATES OF AMERICA

1 3 5 7 9 10 8 6 4 2

First Edition

For Alvin,

who first told me that "it's okay to get lost."

Surprise Me

Contents

Illustrations   ix
Introduction by John Keegan   xi
Acknowledgements   xiii

Prologue   1

PART ONE:
FATHERLAND/GERMANY, 1866–1933

1 Breitenheim   13
2 Ultra-Dada Days   31
3 'Once You Had Berlin, You Had the World'   47

PART TWO:
FALSE SANCTUARY/HOLLAND, 1933-42

4 The Long Mirage   65
5 Shadowland   87
6 The Decision   103

PART THREE:
DIVING UNDER/HOLLAND, 1942-44

7 Submerging   129
8 'My Name is Toni Muller'   151
9 The Girl Next Door   169

PART FOUR:
THE HUNGER WINTER/HOLLAND, 1944-45

| 10 | The Raid | 183 |
| 11 | Holland SOS | 203 |

PART FIVE:
SAFE HARBOUR/HOLLAND, USA, 1945-49

| 12 | To See the Sky | 231 |
| 13 | Wonderful Town | 249 |

	Epilogue	259
	Afterword	265
	References	279
	Bibliography	295

On January 17, 1994, at 4:30:55 a.m. Pacific Standard Time, a 6.7-magnitude earthquake jolted most of Southern California awake. It lasted twenty seconds but felt interminable, a blind thrust quake producing the highest general ground acceleration ever instrumentally recorded in an urban area in North America.

Although the epicenter was in the San Fernando Valley, about twenty miles northwest of the center of Los Angeles, damage occurred up to eighty-five miles away.

Isabelle Rothman, a senior at Chandler College, located several miles east of downtown, and at least thirty miles away from the quake site, was tossed out of bed, onto the floor of her bedroom, books and a dresser tumbling around her. Immediately she saw it as the wakeup call she needed: Life is unpredictable, have some courage.

A few blocks away, Daniel Jablonski, starting his fourth year as some sort of ill-defined visiting professor at the same college, woke to the sound of a freight train rushing through his rented campus house. It took him all of the twenty seconds of shaking and rocking to realize he was in the midst of one of California's legendary earthquakes. And not much more time than that to understand that here was the consummate confirmation of what he had come to believe in his life: that all is unstable and there is no safety.

Opposites attract.

Part One

JANUARY 1994 – MAY 1994

I sabelle strides across the beautifully manicured Chandler campus lost in her own internal, and achingly familiar, monologue of indecision. The subject matter varies according to the problem at hand, but the need to mull over, argue with, and second-guess herself remains the constant. How many hours of her life has she wasted this way? she wonders. More like days, months, even years. Does she ever make a decision without this particular form of agony? Does she ever make a decision at all? is probably a better question, or does she simply throw up her hands and slip into change?

The dilemma for today is whether she's done the right thing by signing up for a tutorial with Daniel Jablonski. The campus wisdom on him, given freely by everyone she consulted, was unanimously some version of *Jablonski, he hates doing these one-on-ones, so mostly the guy doesn't show up for meetings.* Or, even more ominously, *The guy's been known to sit there the entire hour and never say a word. Not one word! He'll stare at you, that's it.* What will she do if there's nothing but an hour of staring ahead of her? She has no idea.

And yet . . . and yet . . . there are his two early novels, published almost twenty years ago, which Isabelle has read and reread and reread again, and they are luminous. If only she could learn to write like that. That's her secret hope, told to no one and barely acknowledged even to herself: that Daniel Jablonski might lead her to that rarefied place.

Even that wish feels like a sort of heresy to Isabelle. Nothing in her background or the very clear expectations given to her by her parents has pointed her toward a career as a writer. Her father would be horrified—there's no stability there. And her mother would be incredulous—Isabelle a writer? Not remotely possible.

Teaching—that's the profession they had all agreed upon. And it had seemed, when she started college, to be exactly the right choice. In love with literature, Isabelle envisioned a life of losing herself in the endless pages of very long and distinguished novels and communicating the wonders of other people's minds to young, hopefully eager students.

Then, on a whim, she took a class entitled "The Psychodrama of Drama," taught by a visiting professor who was both a psychiatrist and a published novelist and who required all her students to keep a journal. They were to write for twenty uninterrupted minutes per day, every day, without correction or rereading. For Isabelle, it was as if the gates of Hoover Dam had been blown open. To her astonishment, torrents of words and memories and then, finally, exaltation cascaded out. Until that moment, she had never known she had anything to say.

Head down now on this bright and brisk January morning, gesturing to herself from time to time as each new thought occurs, Isabelle passes the student union and the bookstore, built around an outside quad in a style that mimics the historic California missions—thick white walls and red tile roofs. All the buildings at Chandler owe a debt to the Spanish architecture of the early days of the state.

And along every path, California native plants have been

arranged in complementary combinations. Within a few short weeks, because February brings spring to Los Angeles, the California poppies, which are just beginning to sport tight little nuggets of buds, will bloom a buttery, golden yellow and all the salvia will send up thin wands of pink or red or purple bells held high above their gray-green rosettes of leaves. But Isabelle notices none of it.

Is it possible for her to learn something from a man everyone describes as a recluse? Who will show up this morning in his office, the Jablonski who wrote those two stunning, emotionally raw books or the taciturn eccentric everyone describes? Or maybe . . . oh my God, a new thought . . . maybe they are one and the same!

As Isabelle climbs the stone stairway that leads to the upper campus, she joins the tide of students rushing to their ten o'clock classes. Through the heavy wooden door of Lathrop Hall and into the classroom building they go, en masse.

It is at the second-floor landing that Isabelle pauses. Here are the professors' offices. Here it is quieter. She reminds herself to take a few deep breaths as she contemplates what's in front of her. The hallway is long, with many tightly closed doors on each side. The wooden floor is worn from a hundred years of students' feet shuffling along its narrow length. The old-fashioned ceiling globes, positioned every fifteen feet, are impossibly dirty and give off a weak light. She hears a male voice loudly imploring someone to "hold on a minute . . . Now hold on!" and as she nears the fourth door on the right, the door she needs to knock on, the raised voice gets louder. That must be him. He must be yelling at someone. Not a good start. She wants to turn around and leave.

DANIEL JABLONSKI IS ON THE PHONE with his second ex-wife, and they have reached the point in their habitual conversation that they are shouting over each other. Why is it that his divorce from Cheryl seems to fill up more of his life than their short, misguided marriage ever did? Why can't she be more like his first wife, Stephanie, who transferred another man into the slot labeled "husband." Simon Bannister is a man better suited to Stephanie, Daniel readily admits, although he isn't sure his children felt the same way years ago, when Simon entered their lives.

"Old news," Daniel manages to interject as Cheryl rants on about how their marriage blew her life off course and how she's never been able to regain her momentum, which of course is all his fault.

"Why are we *still* having this conversation?" he asks Cheryl, but she doesn't even miss a beat. Her diatribe continues. She's crazy, he now believes. And he was crazy to marry her. Desperate is more like it, fevered to believe that love or something like it would jump-start the engine of his writing career, which, after the success of his first two novels, had rapidly descended into oblivion.

Daniel has a great fondness for his third and fourth novels, but apparently no one else does, neither the critics nor the book-buying public. He has no idea why. Writing for him is a mysterious process, and he has no explanation for the fact that it yielded first two books of wondrous reviews and respectable sales and then two books that fell off the face of the earth.

ISABELLE STANDS OUTSIDE HIS OFFICE DOOR and contemplates the etiquette of knocking. On the one hand, the man inside seems entirely preoccupied by a very personal conversation and it would be embarrassing to interrupt. On the other, she doesn't want him to think she's late for their ten o'clock meeting. After several minutes of debating and realizing that the argument inside isn't subsiding, Isabelle knocks loudly. Should she now call out his name?

But she doesn't have to. Daniel, pacing as Cheryl's list of grievances continues to grow, hears Isabelle's knock. Seizing on it, grateful for an excuse to end the conversation, he tells Cheryl, "I've got a student here," and hangs up without waiting for her response.

"All right!" he calls out, and Isabelle opens the door.

Of course she's seen his picture on the back of his two books, but that picture is hopelessly out-of-date, Isabelle now sees. It has done nothing to prepare her for the man who stands across the room from her.

It's his physical presence that stuns her. He's so much bigger than she imagined, maybe six feet three or four, and fleshier. Unlike most of her male professors, who seem suddenly, now that she's standing in Daniel's office, smaller and more cerebral, as if their bodies were an afterthought, this man takes up space.

"We have a ten o'clock," Isabelle says. "Isabelle Rothman."

"Yep. Sit down."

There's only a worn couch against one wall and a club chair of dubious color and condition in the corner. It probably was yellow once but now hovers somewhere between gray and beige and holds the imprint of a large man's body in its cushions. She quickly chooses the sofa. The armchair seems too intimate. As she moves the books and papers from one small corner of the couch, piling them up on the middle pillow, he doesn't attempt to help her.

She puts her hands in her lap, draws her long legs up, knees touching, the toes of her shoes on the floor, not the soles. Neither one of them says anything. She's waiting for him to speak. He's too busy watching her.

There are two large windows behind Daniel as he stands by his desk, and the bright morning light coming in behind him makes it difficult for Isabelle to read his face. Why isn't he saying anything? Is he annoyed that she's here? He read the first three chapters of her novel in progress and agreed to take her on, didn't he? Maybe he didn't. Maybe he doesn't remember what she wrote.

"I sent you the first three chapters of my book. About the girl who commits crimes." She can't bring herself to ask, "Did you like them?" so she waits again.

"Right," he says as he rummages through the papers on his desk and on top of the table behind it, which runs underneath the windows. "Here they are!" he says triumphantly, as if he is totally surprised the pages exist.

" 'Outlaw,' " he reads on the first page. "Pretty bold title," he says, almost to himself, as he scans the pages.

"She breaks into houses and steals things."

Daniel looks up at her in surprise, and Isabelle knows in that instant he hasn't read her pages. And then she doesn't know what to do. Should she call him on it? He's had all winter break to read them. She dropped the chapters off in his campus mailbox weeks ago. Oh, why didn't she listen to everyone and choose someone more dependable?

Daniel unclutters the other end of the couch and sits down, her pages in his hand. They look at each other, and Isabelle has the uncanny feeling that the weight of his body has tipped the sofa on an angle and she's having to work very hard not to slide down its length into his lap.

Up close, Isabelle has redeeming features, Daniel sees. Her skin is beautiful, even as it flushes now in embarrassment at their predicament, or maybe in anger. She wears no makeup, he can tell, and hides her eyes behind bangs, which her long fingers flick away from her forehead from time to time. There's nothing about her that says, "Look at me," but he finds himself looking anyway.

"Why this particular girl who takes this particular action?"

Isabelle has no idea. "She came to me," is what she says, and

Daniel knows immediately what she means. He can write only when something comes to him.

"Ah ..." And then there's silence as he quickly turns the pages, hoping for some clue.

"You didn't read them, did you?" Isabelle can't believe she's confronting him, but she's angry. Furious, really—an untamed emotion she rarely feels. But how long does it take to read forty-seven pages? Isn't the six weeks of winter break long enough?

"I left them here, in the office," he says, as if that's an explanation. "By mistake."

She wants to say, *And you couldn't come get them?* but she doesn't. Instead she gets up, and so does he. Now they're facing each other, and he sees that she's tall for a girl. Isabelle, standing less than three feet from him, suddenly, gratefully, doesn't feel too tall at all.

"I'll come back next week. Maybe you'll have had a chance to read them by then."

He nods once, rakes his fingers through his hair, the color of beach sand. Doesn't apologize. Doesn't promise. And she walks out of the office with his eyes following her.

DANIEL COLLAPSES INTO HIS ARMCHAIR as the door closes, overcome with regret. But there was no way, simply no way, that he could tell this girl that the walk from his house to his campus office was too difficult for him to navigate, that even the contemplation of it produced anxiety too great for him to handle. It's a miracle that he made it today. Well, that's how he feels every time he makes it—that it is only through the grace of God that he manages the ten-minute walk.

He knows what his condition is called: agoraphobia. When the thought of walking outside his front door began to give him sweats and heart palpitations, he went to the doctor. And after all the requisite tests for heart disease and endocrine problems and whatever else the doctor had to rule out, the proper diagnosis was given to him. The problem is, the cure is iffy and involves therapy, which he refuses to consider, and medication, which he's afraid will interfere with his work. It's a humiliating problem and he keeps it to himself.

"I'M NOT GOING BACK," Isabelle spouts suddenly into the muffled air of Brighton Library. It's late afternoon; the library is crowded but very quiet—the scrape of chairs being pulled out, the soft plop of a book being dropped onto a wooden table, even the slight snoring of a boy at the next table whose head is pillowed by a well-used backpack.

Her boyfriend, Nate, sitting next to her highlighting his criminology textbook, shrugs and whispers back, "Okay," and returns to his book.

"He made me *ask him* if he'd read the pages!"

"Right, then find someone else to work with." He's really not interested.

"It was degrading. The whole thing." Isabelle is fairly hissing her opinion. An older man across the table wearing half glasses and a pained expression shushes her.

Nate points to the textbook, the man watching them. "Work to do. This is a library. We've talked about this already."

"Okay." She's quiet for ten seconds, fifteen. Then: "But I mean it."

Nate pretends she hasn't spoken.

AT THE END OF THE DAY, as twilight creeps into his office, Daniel stands at one of the large square windows and watches the campus empty out. He knows that if he were outside and the day were clear enough, he might be able to see the Pacific Ocean in the far distance as it absorbs the last rays of the lowering sun, but those days appear to be over—the days when he feels comfortable outside.

Once the old-fashioned lampposts lining the major campus walkways have switched on and the foot traffic of students has diminished to a trickle, Daniel begins to argue with himself about walking home. He knows he has to do it. He can't sleep here. It's ridiculous, but he's broken out in a cold sweat, and no matter what he tells himself, he can't seem to make his large body move toward the door. If his son, Stefan, were coming today, that would help, but he isn't. He has a job interview, and if the planets are aligned just right, he might get hired to do something.

Then his eye falls on Isabelle's pages and he sees them as a reprieve. He has to read them, doesn't he? He owes it to her. He'll read them first and then he'll walk home.

The armchair beckons, just waiting to embrace his out-sized body, and he sinks into it gratefully, puts "Outlaw" on his lap, and begins reading. After the first page he sighs—he was so hoping he'd find even a modicum of talent. The second page doesn't change his mind, but on page 13 there's a scene between the girl and a hitchhiker she picks up that brings him a surprise. Something unexpected. Thank God—there's something to work with here. He settles in, stretches his long legs out in front of him, crossed at the ankles, and reads on.

A WEEK LATER ON A TUESDAY morning, eight minutes before their ten o'clock meeting, Isabelle is crossing the hilly Chandler campus, rehearsing the speech she will give Daniel Jablonski, preparing to do something that will be hard for her.

"It would be better," she's going to say, "if I worked with another professor." She will make no mention of the fact that he never read her pages, that he lived up to his reputation of being unprepared, of not caring about his students, of being just plain weird. No, she won't say any of those things. She'll simply say with as much poise as she can muster, "It would be better," so that there's no room for discussion.

She carefully chose boots to wear today so that she's even taller—her beautiful, handcrafted, caramel-colored boots with a singular, lyrical vine etched along the outer edge. She loves these boots and they give her confidence and she's at least six feet tall when she's wearing them, and maybe Daniel Jablonski's height, his just plain mass, won't seem as intimidating.

Isabelle takes the stairs to the second floor of Lathrop Hall, the staccato sound of her boot heels on the wooden floor announces her approach, and her rapid knock punctuates her arrival. She opens the door without waiting for an answer.

Daniel is sitting behind his desk as she enters. He doesn't stand up.

"Professor Jablonski," she begins, "I think it would be better if—"

"I like the blackbirds," he says, watching that simple sentence drain all the starch out of her stance.

"You do?" she says, and sinks down into the corner of the couch.

"I wasn't expecting them," he says. "It's always a gift to read something you're not expecting."

He thinks *my* writing is a gift?

"Here's what I learn about Melanie." He rummages for her pages, somewhere on the mess of his desk, and pulls them up, scans the page in his hand. "It is Melanie, right?"

She nods.

"When she won't let that boy, that wreck of a boy that she picks up hitchhiking, throw those stones at the birds, I see something in her worth paying attention to."

He gets up and takes his place on the opposite corner of the couch. "I want you to surprise me some more."

"Okay."

"Good. Rewrite the pages up to that scene and bring them next week."

He stands up. Her comprehension lags a moment. Oh, the meeting is over. That's all? It must be, because he's walking back to his desk and she understands she's supposed to leave. She does.

ISABELLE STANDS OUTSIDE Daniel's closed office door, motionless. She's trying to figure out what just transpired. Was she given the brush-off? Was he truly complimenting her work? Is that all he's supposed to do—tell her to rewrite and leave her to it? She's mystified. He didn't exactly teach her anything, but still, she feels like she was given something. In less than five minutes. How is that possible? What is it? Maybe his expectation that she can do it. Is that it? She almost turns around to go back into that office to ask him, "What just happened here?" but she doesn't. She walks away down that long hall much more slowly than she arrived.

DANIEL JABLONSKI IS PLEASED with himself. He feels the meeting with Isabelle went well. He could honestly compliment her work. He gave her direction. *Now let's see what she comes up with.* He has no idea how mystified Isabelle is by their interaction. Being a self-taught writer with nothing but junior college classes, which he rarely attended, in his background, he has no idea what a writing mentor does. He thinks the whole idea of teaching someone to write is a fool's errand. Writing is mysterious and mercurial and maddening, and he certainly has no idea how to help someone do it better.

He can't even help himself. He settles his large body into his desk chair, turns on his computer, brings up his working file, and stares with dismay at what he wrote yesterday. And he groans. It's bad. It's awful. It's irredeemable. He deletes two and a half pages with ruthless abandon, feeding his secret terror that he will never finish another book. Each day as he turns on his computer and faces the words he wrote the day before, he wants to weep. Sometimes he does.

His last novel was published over eight years ago. When it sank like a stone in water, the depression and anxiety that he had been trying to hold at bay for almost a decade washed over him, sweeping away his marriage to Cheryl (a good thing) and rendering him agoraphobic (a bad thing) and hopeless about his work (a devastating thing).

This novel in embryo, his fifth book, refuses to gain viability. He prods it each day nonetheless. He doesn't know what else to do.

IN THE RAMSHACKLE WOODEN HOUSE she rents on the edge of campus with Nate and her other roommates—Jilly, who barely makes it out of bed each day, and Deepti, who rarely lifts her head from her books—Isabelle also stares at her computer screen. Rewrite the first twelve pages so that they surprise Daniel Jablonski. *What the hell does that mean?* No answer comes to her. Nothing. And then, gratefully, a distraction. She hears the front door slam shut and she knows Nate is home. Neither of the girls announces her presence with a preemptive slamming of the front door.

"Nate?"

And he's there, leaning against the doorframe of the dining room, which they've designated the communal study area, his long, somber face almost as familiar to her as her own. They've been together since high school, nearly six years, primarily because, even though Isabelle didn't want him to, Nate followed her out to California for college. She never found a way to tell him not to come.

"What surprises you?"

He hates these open-ended questions, she knows, and she can see it on his face—the furrowed brow, the exasperation, the indecision.

What he'd like to do is sidestep the question. The conversation Isabelle wants to have is guaranteed to waste precious minutes.

He tries for diplomacy. "I'll think about it and get back to you."

"No, I need a jump-start here. I have to write something that surprises Daniel Jablonski."

"Then ask him."

Isabelle is exasperated. "I can't. It doesn't work like that."

"How does it work, then?"

"He tells me to surprise him and I have to come up with something by next week that does."

"That's fucked," Nate says as he pushes himself into motion and out of the room. "You want lunch? I'm heating up the leftover soup."

"No," Isabelle says, staring at the empty computer screen hopelessly. "I've got to manufacture something startling, and don't roll your eyes," she says, even though Nate is in the kitchen now, banging pots around, and she can't see him. It doesn't matter. She knows that rolling his eyes is exactly what he's doing.

And then she hears him walk into the living room and turn on the TV, ignoring the fact that she's trying to work in the next room. He likes to catch up on the noon news while he eats and calls out random bits of information he thinks are noteworthy every few minutes.

"Izzy, Tonya Harding's husband, Jeff something or other, took a plea for whacking Nancy Kerrigan's leg."

"Really?" is all she needs to say to satisfy him.

"Whoa, that Tonya's in trouble now."

"Nate, I'm trying to work here."

Thankfully, he's quiet, and after forty-five minutes of staring at her computer screen, she hears Nate leave the house. He has an afternoon seminar, she knows, on drug policy and criminal intent. "Later," she hears him yell as the back door slams shut. Always so noisy, as if every action has to be punctuated by an aggravated sound. And then the house is quiet. Perhaps she is the only one home, but she doesn't think so.

The kitchen is empty; the dented tin pot he used to heat up the soup is still on the stove. They rented this old shingled house knowing there was no microwave or dishwasher, but somehow that hasn't translated for Nate into the idea that he has to wash his own dishes.

She turns to the living room, where Nate's soup bowl rests on the floor next to the couch, and paces from the fireplace they've never used to the large windows that look out on the front porch, which they do once the weather turns warm. She's totally lost. She knows it. How can she come up with something that surprises Daniel Jablonski when she has no frame of reference? What would he consider startling? She has no idea.

Down the hall she goes, to the back of the house, and stops outside Jilly's room, ear to the door. She's trying to figure out whether her roommate is home and sleeping. Jilly has opinions about everything. Maybe Isabelle can borrow some surprising data from her. Quietly she turns the doorknob and peeks in. There Jilly is. Well, there is the top of her very messy, curly hair above the mass of sheets and comforter. How can one person sleep so much? She closes the door softly.

Deepti, Isabelle thinks, maybe Deepti is home. It's hard to know, because when Deepti studies, it's always in her room and she's quiet as a mouse. There must be many surprising things she could say, coming from another culture to go to college. She knocks gently on the last door at the end of the hall.

"Deepti?"

"Yes, Isabelle? Come in."

And Isabelle does. It's like taking a step into another country. Immediately the vibrant, hot colors of Indian prints assault her eye. There are the patterned silk curtains at the windows, a batik bedspread, and Deepti sitting cross-legged on her bed in a green and pink sari, her chemistry books spread out around her in one circle and her class notes spread out in another.

"I have a question."

"Okay." Deepti puts her highlighter aside.

"What surprises you?"

"I am surprised that I ended up in Los Angeles."

"Yes . . . but what surprises you about life in general?"

"Ahhh, a deeper question." Deepti looks out the window to the side yard, where a star jasmine vine is in the midst of winding its way around a chain-link fence, obliterating ugliness and replacing it with beauty. Soon the jasmine flowers will perfume her room, and Deepti can hardly wait. Now she takes a quiet moment to contemplate Isabelle's question.

"That people sometimes act kindly," Deepti says finally.

"I used that already. Unfortunately."

"What is this for?"

"Daniel Jablonski."

"You have to give him the gift of surprise?"

"Yes! Exactly!"

"Then it has to be from you."

Isabelle groans. "I'm the least surprising person alive."

And Deepti laughs, a soft, rounded series of chuckles that always makes Isabelle smile, too. "Maybe not."

By four o'clock Isabelle has managed to write not one word.

She thinks it's safe to call home now. It will be seven o'clock in Merrick, Long Island, and her father should be there, back from the train that takes him to the city each day and brings him home. If she had called his law office in Manhattan, he wouldn't have had the time to hash out her question. And if she called home before he got there, her mother would be no help at all.

It is Ruth Rothman's opinion, communicated to Isabelle in ways both subtle and overt, that her daughter is far too dependable to be original—she lacks the temperament. In their family, Ruth long ago claimed the mantle of "creative spirit." During her long quest to find her particular métier, Ruth has tried painting, photography, ceramics, fiber art, and jewelry making. With each obsession, Isabelle dutifully stepped in to care for her three younger brothers, and when Ruth retreated to her bedroom—her latest passion sputtering out—drew the curtains, and took to bed, Isabelle picked up the slack then, too. Ruth's migraines are legendary.

"Dad," Isabelle says when her father, thankfully, answers the phone.

"There's been another earthquake?"

"No, Dad, but I have a question."

"Shoot." She can hear the relief in his voice. He can deal with a question but not another natural disaster.

"What surprises you?"

"Give me the context." Her father, always the lawyer.

"I'm taking this writing tutorial—"

"You are? What for? You write fine."

"It's creative writing."

"Same question."

"There's a man here on campus"—Isabelle is wary, trying to explain something to her very practical father, who she fears won't be able to understand it—"a published novelist, a wonderful writer actually, and every semester he takes on a student or two to mentor."

"And?"

"And this semester it's me."

"You've finished all your other courses? You don't have any requirements to take so you can fool around with creative writing?"

"Actually, yes."

"Hmmmm." And there's silence while her father digests this.

Isabelle figures she'll try once more. She's desperate. "So, Dad, I have to come up with something that surprises him when I hand in my work next week, and I'm drawing a blank."

"Well, of course, that's a stupid assignment."

Now it's Isabelle's turn to be silent. Her father sounds too much like Nate for her to continue this conversation.

"Here," her father says, "say hello to your mother." And Ruth gets on the line.

"Hi, Mom."

"What's wrong?" are her mother's first words.

Isabelle sighs. "Nothing."

"Then why are you calling?"

"I thought Dad might be able to help me with an assignment."

"And did he?"

"No."

"I could have told you that."

"Okay, Mom, how are you? How're your headaches?"

"They're there. It's what I live with."

"I know. I'm sorry."

"Wait a minute, your father wants to say something."

And Isabelle waits while her mother hands over the receiver. She hears Ruth questioning her father—"Didn't you just speak with her?"—when they all know he just did. Then her father has to explain *why* he needs to talk to Isabelle again. Through it all, Isabelle waits. She's used to the constant dissension between them. Finally she hears her father's voice.

"Use your imagination," he presents to her.

"Okay, Dad, thanks, I'll try that."

And her father is pleased, she can tell. He thinks he's come up with an idea to help his daughter.

But of course Isabelle has been trying to use her imagination all day, with no success.

CHAPTER TWO

S tefan Jablonski is sitting high up on the steel bleachers inside Townsend Gym watching the Chandler Coyotes at their basketball practice—passing, dribbling, shooting, a slam dunk every once in a while from their very tall center, Marcus Mohammed. He could play with them, Stefan thinks, although his only basketball skills are those honed on playground courts. He checks his watch from time to time. He knows he has to be at his father's office at 5:30.

That was part of the deal they made when Stefan showed up with no warning at his father's house two months ago. He could stay, but he had to have responsibilities. The first: he had to get a job, which so far he hasn't managed to do. And second, he had to walk his father to and from campus.

Stefan readily agreed. He had no choice. His mother, Stephanie, and his stepfather, Simon, had kicked him out. They'd had enough of his drifting, they said. He wouldn't go to college, even community college. He wouldn't work at any of the menial jobs open to him. And they would no longer put up with a twenty-three-year-old who was quite content to stay in his room playing music and increasingly violent video games.

Stefan has never lived with his father. Oh, the first two years of his life don't count, because he can't remember them. And once his father left, two days after his second birthday, when his sister, Alina, was five, they saw each other sporadically, only when Daniel was in town. Of course. Even Stefan understands that nobody stays in Erie, Pennsylvania, who doesn't have to.

What he doesn't understand is what's wrong with his father. How can a grown man, a man who's lived more than fifty years and been successful—hell, he's written four books—be afraid to walk outside his door? His dad told him what it's called, this thing he has, but Stefan lacks the empathy to truly understand it. And Daniel doesn't like discussing it, so it's there, in the middle of their lives together—immutable, it seems, and confusing.

At a quarter to six Stefan still hasn't arrived. *Goddammit, the kid's always late.* Daniel turns from the window where he's been keeping a vigil and tries to calm down. *He eventually gets here,* Daniel reminds himself. But then: *What if he doesn't?* It infuriates him that he has to rely on his less-than-dependable son to get home. But there it is—his life as it's now configured. Daniel paces, and suddenly Stefan is opening the office door with his customary "Hey, Dad," and Daniel grabs his jacket. It's late January, and contrary to his expectations before he arrived in Southern California, it can get cold in winter.

They walk across the rapidly darkening campus, two tall men keeping pace, Stefan thinner and rangier than his father. Daniel walks with his head down, concentrating on his feet. The last thing he wants is for some student to stop and talk to him. That would be a disaster, Daniel believes. The kid would be able to see the panic in his eyes, fear that has no cause he can pinpoint, no cure he can find.

"So I was like, killing time, you know," Stefan tells him tentatively, still unsure how to relate to this large presence walking beside him, "before five thirty when I had to be here, and

I went in to watch the basketball team practice, and here's the thought I had, Dad—I could play with them."

"You'd have to attend college first. Something you refuse to do."

"No, I'm just saying that I'm like . . . well, good enough to play with them. Well, maybe except for that Mohammed guy. He's awesome. He'll be drafted first round for sure."

More walking. More silence from Daniel. Stefan steals a sideways look at him and ventures a suggestion. "Maybe we can take in one of their games."

Daniel looks up at his son and his expression says it all: *Are you crazy?* And Stefan immediately understands his mistake and backtracks. "Oh, okay, right, too many people at a game. I get it."

Daniel nods and grunts. He quickens his steps. He wants nothing more than to be inside his house.

"When are you going to get done with this thing, Dad?"

"When are you going to get a job?"

Stefan shrugs. He has no idea.

"And there we have it—two unknowables."

THE NEXT TUESDAY MORNING Daniel finds himself eager to get to campus, a feeling he can't remember having had in the more than three years he's been at Chandler. He has a hunch, or maybe just a gleam of a hope—something that's in short supply in his life—that Isabelle will bring him pages he'll be glad to read.

"Let's get a move on," he tells his son, who is hunched over, elbows on the kitchen table, reading the sports section of the *L.A. Times.* It's basketball season, and there's plenty to read.

Stefan glances at the clock above the stove. "We've got time," and goes back to reading all the box scores of all the basketball games played anywhere across the country.

Daniel doesn't argue. He simply takes the paper from his son's hands, folds it, puts it on the pile of the rest of the unread paper, and says calmly, "Time to go."

ISABELLE CAN'T MAKE HERSELF LEAVE the bathroom. She hates the way she looks this morning. Well, okay, she hates the way she looks most every morning. She's too tall, ungainly, she thinks. She wishes her hair weren't such a nondescript brown and that it was thicker. She'd kill for some natural highlights. Her mother is beautiful. Every relative from the Abramowicz side of the family, her mother's side, will sooner or later come forth with the same sentence: "Oh, Isabelle, your mother could have been a movie star!" But Isabelle came out looking like her father. *Yes,* Isabelle tells herself as she stares back into her own brown eyes, *you look just like a tax attorney.*

She pulls her hair away from her face and wraps it up against the back of her head. No, she decides, and brushes it back into its customary curtain, which hugs both cheeks and is her fallback position. More hair, less face—much better.

You've got to get out of here, she tells her reflection. *You're going to be late.*

The last thing she wants to do today is face Daniel Jablonski. She is certain, absolutely certain, that although she's rewritten the first twelve pages, she hasn't come up with anything that will surprise him, and the idea that she may, almost certainly will, disappoint him is unbearable to her.

Only Jilly, knocking on the bathroom door, forces her out into the hall. Jilly, whose attire of choice seems always to be pajamas, is half asleep as she brushes past Isabelle, muttering, "Gotta pee," and closes the bathroom door.

In the kitchen, Nate is peeling an orange, drinking a mug of coffee, and studying. He says "Hey" to her without looking up from his book. "I'll be ready in, like, five minutes."

And suddenly Isabelle can't bear the thought of walking to campus with him, listening to him talk about the test he's studying for, because she knows Nate well enough to know that if there's a test waiting for him, that's what he'll talk about. She needs to get her head straight before she enters Daniel Jablonski's office.

"I've got to go now," she says without waiting for his response and is out of the kitchen, down the hall, out the front door.

DANIEL IS READY FOR ISABELLE, sitting at his desk, when she knocks lightly and walks in. He watches her come in, does a quick inventory of how she looks. Without a word from either of them, she hands him the new pages, his eyes eager to read what she's brought.

It's beyond unbearable, but she has to stay in his office as he reads the pages, so she begins to walk around it. Her back to him, she pretends interest in the books in his bookshelves, the view outside his window.

It's only twelve pages, but he takes forever to read them. Maybe he's reading them more than once. Isabelle doesn't know, because she's consciously not looking at him. Finally, her curiosity gets intolerable and she finds herself turning around.

The pages are on his desk. As he finishes one, he carefully picks it up, turns it over, and places it in another pile. His concentration is total. She could disrobe and he wouldn't even see her. *Now why did I even think about that?* Isabelle asks herself, mortified and already blushing at her own thoughts.

She sits on the couch, in her place at the corner nearest his desk, hunched over her drawn-up knees as she was the first day, and watches him read her work. She can't help it. She watches. It's excruciating.

Daniel is focused so intently on the pages that he doesn't even feel her eyes on him. At long last, he takes the last page, picks it up and lays it on the pile of read pages, and looks up at her.

"I like what she says to the hitchhiker when he gets into her car." And here Daniel picks up page 4, which he's dog-eared, and reads from it: " 'You talk to me while I'm driving, I'll stop the fucking car. Middle of traffic. On the highway. I don't care.' "

And Isabelle finds she can breathe again. "It's Melanie being tough."

"I see that, but it's just over the top enough for me to understand she's working herself up to it. She's talking like some stiff from New Jersey, so she's probably scared of this kid."

"Yes, she is! You got that?"

"And she wants to set the dynamic—'You better watch your ass with me.' "

"She behaves the opposite of what she's feeling."

Daniel nods. He knows something about that. "You let us see that. That's good."

That's good, he said. What I wrote is good. Isabelle smiles and leans back, puts the soles of her feet on the floor, unclenches her hands and lays one on the armrest of the sofa. Something has loosened within her. He's validated her instincts—how amazing is that!

Daniel pushes away from his desk, opens a lower drawer with his foot, and props both feet on it. They look at each other. There's a lull, but the tension has drained from the room and each can take a deeper breath. This is going to work. They've both decided at the same time without a word being spoken about it.

After watching her in silence, Daniel finally speaks. "No boots today?"

Isabelle looks down at her Nike sneakers and says the first

thing that pops into her head. "Today I was beyond help. Even my boots wouldn't have made me feel like an equal." And then she looks directly at him. "Today I was throwing myself on your mercy."

"And how did I do?"

"You surprised me," Isabelle says with a smile, and Daniel grins back at her, appreciating this tall, lanky girl who has filled his office with something like a sensation of pleasure long missing from his life.

"TELL ME MORE ABOUT MELANIE," Daniel says when Isabelle walks into his office the next Tuesday. He doesn't read the pages she hands him, the rest of Chapter One. He lays them on his surprisingly neat desk, pushes back in his rolling desk chair, thumps his feet onto his opened drawer, laces his fingers behind his head, and waits.

"Aren't you going to read the pages?"

"Not right now. Now I want you to talk."

Isabelle wasn't prepared for this. Is that the point? she wonders. Has he calculated a way to catch her off guard?

"She grew up with a lot of expectations."

"Such as?"

"Oh, the usual."

"I don't know 'the usual.' My expectations, I guarantee you, weren't yours."

Isabelle finds her spot on the couch, moves a basketball out of the way so she can sit down. She wants to ask him what his expectations were, but she's not sure that's allowed. In a rush of courage she does it anyway. "What were yours?"

And he answers without hesitation. "That I follow my father and older brother into the trades. They were ironworkers. Do you know what that is?"

Isabelle shakes her head.

"Every bridge you see, every skyscraper, the skeleton was

forged by ironworkers. Men who don't need to be especially smart, but they sure have to have a strong back and be built like an ox." Daniel looks at his own large body, now gone to flab, and shakes his head. "Once I fit the bill."

"And so you did that?"

"Anything but. I loaded cargo onto and off the ships on Lake Erie. I painted houses. I hung drywall. None of that much better than being an ironworker, but at least I could say it was my choice." Daniel shakes his head at his own youthful naïveté. "Even though it wasn't, of course. No skills, no choices."

"Sometimes you can have skills and it can still seem like there are no choices."

"We're back to the expectations again."

"Yes. The expectations Melanie had laid on her made her rob houses."

Daniel laughs out loud, a big whooping laugh. He's delighted at her complete lapse in logic. "You'd better explain yourself."

"That doesn't make sense to you?"

"No."

"Okay." Isabelle pushes herself off the couch and begins to walk around Daniel's office. Sometimes she needs to move to think. Daniel watches her, silent. He knows how to do that. The student gossip on that score was right—sometimes he lets an entire hour go by without speaking.

Today Isabelle is wearing a Chandler College hoodie zipped up over a T-shirt. The school colors are orange and black, and Daniel has never been able to get over the perception that the whole campus is perpetually celebrating Halloween. She pulls the hood over her head, encasing herself in black cotton knit and hiding her face. She needs to shut him out to be able to organize her thoughts.

"It's different being female," she begins. "You've got society's expectations of you, which are really rigid, and your parents' expectations, which can be idiosyncratic, but still, and sometimes the only way to break through those two strait-jackets is to burst out of them, do something so dramatic that there's no going back. That's what Melanie does. She doesn't want to become the person everyone else sees."

"Which is?"

"Oh, I don't know—good, kind, responsible, predictable . . . boring."

"Nothing worse than boring." Is he teasing her gently? She thinks so but doesn't know him well enough to be sure.

She stops her pacing and faces him. "Melanie wants to shock everyone into backing off."

"So that she can be . . . what?"

"Free," jumps out of Isabelle's mouth.

"Being an outlaw makes her free?"

"She chooses it."

"No," Daniel says slowly, "she is acting in reaction to, just the way I ended up loading ships. It's not a free choice, a choice that comes from the core of a person."

"Like?"

"Like writing."

"Oh."

He watches her face as she attempts to sort through what they've just said. Such an easy read, all the emotions flitting across her face in rapid succession. He's sure she has no idea.

"Writing is a sort of freedom?" she asks finally, tentatively.

"At its best, it can be."

And there's silence. What they've just said feels so intimate that Isabelle doesn't know how to proceed. *How do you get there?* she longs to ask but can't. *How do you get to be free?*

"Melanie robs houses for the same reason some people join the Peace Corps." She expects Daniel to laugh again at her logic, but he doesn't.

"She needs the space." He completely understands.

"There are so many people hovering."

"Expecting things of her."

"Yes!"

"Okay, that makes sense."

And Isabelle beams.

"So now you need to get that into the pages."

And the smile vanishes. "How?"

"How indeed," he says.

"HE SAID, 'HOW INDEED'? REALLY? HE DID?" Jilly's voice rises in an incredulous crescendo. The four roommates are sitting around their kitchen table drinking beer (Nate and Isabelle) and wine (Jilly) and eating pretzels (Deepti), along with sliced salami, which everyone but Deepti is eating as their dinner.

When Jilly isn't sleeping she tends to be assertive or, to be less charitable, aggressive. Her opinions are always stated at high volume and with no ambiguity. Deepti often watches Jilly openmouthed and fascinated.

"Isn't he supposed to be telling you 'how indeed' to do it?" Jilly won't let up. "Isn't that the whole point of an independent study?"

Isabelle shrugs. "I have no idea how this one-on-one is supposed to work. I've never done it before."

"I'm with Jilly," Nate chimes in. He loves living with three women and listening to them talk. Guys don't talk the same way. Hell, guys don't talk much at all, and he's a verbal guy. He likes the give-and-take. He likes the arguments, but he especially likes to *win* the arguments, and with three women he usually does. He's supremely confident that he's going to make a very capable criminal attorney.

"Chandler is paying him, right? His job is to teach you to write better, is it not?"

Isabelle shrugs. *Is it not?* When Nate starts using phrases like that, she knows enough not to engage. Inside his head he's playing out some kind of game, and she doesn't want Daniel Jablonski to be the football they kick back and forth until Nate wins his point.

"That's all you've got, a shrug?" Nate leans forward, his body in what Isabelle has privately labeled his attack mode, index finger pointing. "You know he's on thin ice already? He's got a reputation as a slacker, you know that, and you're having the exact fucked-up experience you could have predicted, right?"

"He wrote two amazing novels, Nate." Isabelle can't help herself. She has to say it.

"Like maybe twenty years ago. They don't count."

"Of course they count. He wrote them."

Nate sits back in his chair now, crosses his arms. "Circular logic."

Isabelle should let it go, she knows that, because Nate will never understand why she is desperate to work with Daniel Jablonski—the reward-to-effort ratio doesn't pan out for him. But there she is, with the need to defend him, Daniel, as she now thinks of him.

She starts talking quietly and slowly, as if her tone and pace can lower the agitation level in the kitchen to a simmer. "Maybe when he says, 'How indeed?' what he's really saying is that writing is baffling." Isabelle looks first at Deepti, the most sympathetic listener at the table, then Jilly. She doesn't look at Nate. "That he has as much trouble doing it well as anyone else." And then Isabelle lays her fledgling hope on the table. "And that maybe he sees me as part of the group . . . as a writer."

There, she's said it, and nobody is laughing, not even Nate, and so she's emboldened and she continues. "Maybe what he's saying is that we're all trying to find the exact words to convey what we need to say, even if we don't exactly know what that is until we write it."

"Well, there's a recipe for success." This from Nate as he gets up. The sarcasm in his voice ends the conversation and makes Isabelle feel dismissed and stupid. Did she really think he was hearing her?

"It works for me, Nate."

He stops at the doorway and looks at her. "Really? And you got all that from a 'how indeed?'?" He shakes his head. "A little creative writing going on in your explanation, maybe?"

And Isabelle has been shamed into silence.

"I've got a real paper to write." And he's gone.

"Men," Jilly says, "they're all bullies." And that assessment sits on the table among the three women until they hear Nate go into the bedroom and close the door.

"You understand something about this professor, Isabelle, and he understands you, no?" Deepti's voice is quiet, to keep Nate from hearing, to soothe Isabelle a little, because Deepti can see she is agitated.

"Sometimes it feels like that, which is weird, because we barely know each other."

"In this life, perhaps."

"Oh, Deepti." And Isabelle smiles at her, shaking her head; they've had this discussion of reincarnation and karma and old souls before.

"There is more than we know," is all Deepti says now, with a shrug and a small smile, and to Isabelle's surprise, Jilly agrees.

"There better be more than we know or else what's the fucking point?"

At that, both Isabelle and Deepti laugh, Deepti hiding her grin behind her hand, slightly scandalized still by Jilly's language. And Nate is forgotten as the women sit in the warm kitchen and begin telling stories to each other.

Deepti tells Jilly a bit more about reincarnation and how she sat beside her grandmother's bed and watched her die. And about how she could actually feel, almost see, the life force escaping from her body at the moment of death. "One moment she was breathing and she was my grandmother, and then the next it all stopped and she became something, someone, else. Her face altered immediately. I can't tell you how exactly, but her face in death wasn't my grandmother's. Something was gone from her. That's the soul, I believe, and it will go on living somewhere else."

"Maybe," Jilly says, and Isabelle looks at her sharply. Jilly, who tends to be so skeptical and caustic, isn't dismissing the notion out of hand.

"You really believe that—that the soul migrates?" Isabelle insists.

"I don't know. I've never witnessed a death. Have you?"

Isabelle shakes her head.

"So let's go with Deepti's version—you and this professor of yours knew each other in a previous life, or your souls did."

"Oh, Jilly, please."

"Maybe he was your neighbor and you saw him coming back from the market every day with onions and carrots sticking out of his grocery bag."

"Much too mundane for the connection we have." Isabelle is teasing, but not completely, and Deepti watches her banter with Jilly without saying anything.

"Okay, maybe he was your teacher in a past life and that relationship shadows this one. That's what you feel."

Isabelle shakes her head.

"What do you lose by believing that?" Here is Jilly beginning to push her point of view again for the sake of winning the debate. This Jilly, Isabelle recognizes.

"It's comforting," Isabelle says finally, because she doesn't want to argue with Jilly or because she'd like to believe it, or both. She doesn't know.

MUCH LATER ON, WHEN THE HOUSE is that stark quiet of 3 a.m. and the three women are sleeping, Nate gets up from his laptop and slips into bed beside Isabelle. He gathers her warm body into his arms and she stirs, hardly awake, and then settles back into sleep.

"I just don't want you to be disappointed," he says very softly into her ear.

"Mmmmm." She has no idea what he's talking about, but she wants nothing more than sleep.

"That whole business about Jablonski and you—it's a setup for disappointment, and I'm trying to prepare you."

He's apologizing, Isabelle understands immediately. This is his way of doing it, obliquely, never head-on, but still . . .

"Okay," she says, and burrows deeper into his arms. That's why she's with him, she tells herself, because he cares about what happens to her. All the rest doesn't matter.

Daniel gets up early on Tuesday morning and rereads Isabelle's pages from the week before. They never got around to discussing them because Isabelle, emboldened by their discussion of writing and freedom, asked Daniel about his first two novels. How he came to write them. And how much he took from his personal life, since the first one was about a man coming to terms with his difficult father's death and the second about a divorce.

"Everything," Daniel told her. "I stripped my life bare."

"Without regard to the people you might hurt?"

"My father was dead and my ex-wife thought I had been overly kind to her in the book. Not in real life, I might add."

"Don't you have a responsibility, though, to the people who care about you?"

"Don't you have a responsibility to the work you are doing?"

"Which is?"

"To tell the truth, as you see it."

"Despite—?"

He cut her off. "Despite."

Today he has to talk to her about the pages that complete Chapter One. What he realizes as he rereads them in the tiny back sunroom that he's turned into his home office is that she has to get out of her own way. When she does, her writing is interesting; when she doesn't, he feels like tossing the pages in the trash bin.

STEFAN, QUIET THIS MORNING, walks his father to campus. Daniel is grateful for the lack of strained conversation. The silence allows him to focus on his rising tide of panic, the tingling he feels along both arms, his ragged breathing, the sweat accumulating under his arms and across his palms, the certainty that he's building up to a heart attack, the terror that he's going to pass out here, on campus, in full view. *Breathe in,* he tells himself with one step, *breathe out* with the next.

"It's a waste of time, you know," Stefan says finally as they're passing in front of the science building, Dunham Hall, and Daniel looks at his son, really for the first time this morning. That's the thing about a panic disorder: it tends to fill up a person's consciousness. Now he sees that Stefan is dressed in a button-down shirt and jeans without holes in them, a miracle in and of itself. He must have yet another job interview.

"You go in with that attitude, you're guaranteeing it's a waste of time."

"You're telling me it's mind over matter?"

"Something like that." Daniel can't have this conversation now, out in the open, while he's walking. It takes too much concentration simply not to pass out.

"I just walk into the interview with a positive attitude and everything works out?"

Daniel grunts, puts his head down, walks faster. They cross the quad in front of the student union, only the stone steps— there are twenty-seven of them; Daniel counts them every time—to go before they're in front of Lathrop Hall.

"Why don't you try that yourself, Dad, and tell me how it works out?"

Daniel hears the anger in his son's voice but he can't deal with it now. Nothing matters except getting to his office. He opens the heavy door into Lathrop—finally, inside!—and takes the stairs with long strides.

The two men reach the second-floor landing together, anxiety fueling the father, anger fueling his son. Daniel doesn't stop; his focus is lasered on his office door, midway down the hall on the right. If he can get inside, he'll be fine, he'll be able to breathe, this thumping of his heart will quiet. He doesn't see Isabelle leaning against the opposite wall, waiting for him, two white Starbucks cups in her hands.

But Stefan sees her. "Hey—you waiting for my dad?"

Oh, his son, of course. Isabelle can immediately see the resemblance—the high cheekbones, the blond hair that furrows away from a broad face. And the ice-blue eyes.

Isabelle nods, but Daniel can only concentrate on getting his key into the door and the door open. He fumbles with it. Of course he does—his hands are shaking. Stefan doesn't help; instead he directs his attention to Isabelle.

"Stefan Jablonski," he tells her.

"Isabelle."

"You a writer?"

She hesitates, then: "Your dad and I are trying to sort that out."

"Oh, you're in trouble, then." Daniel disappears into his office, gone from sight, so Stefan can say, "Can't you find someone else to help you with that?"

Isabelle looks at him, stunned. What a strange thing for a son to say. "I don't want to find someone else."

"He's got writer's block, you know. He can't help himself, so good luck with his helping you."

"Are you coming in?" Daniel bellows out the office door.

Stefan turns to go. "Don't say I didn't warn you."

Isabelle watches him walk down the hall, his shoulders

hunched against some private trouble she doesn't want to even think about now. *Wow, angry kid.*

"Isabelle!" Another summons from inside the office, and she takes a deep breath, gathers her courage—it's always hard for her to begin these meetings. What is he going to say? Did he like her pages? Does she have it within her to be a writer? Will he give her what she needs? All those questions are swirling in her brain as she forces herself to walk into the office, the two cappuccinos in hand. She finds him in his customary place, sitting behind his desk.

"You drink coffee?"

"I'm not supposed to," he says as he reaches for the white cup.

She settles into her corner of the couch. They look at each other. Each samples the coffee. She waits. He pulls her pages from his briefcase and puts them in front of him on the desk. All eating up time. It feels like he doesn't want to begin, and Isabelle tenses in anticipation.

"You need to get out of your own way."

"Meaning?"

"Too much head and not enough heart."

"Oh."

And she's wounded. He can see that. She flicks her bangs over her eyes, a cover-up, and he curses himself silently. How can he put it so she understands? He tries again. "You need to stop thinking so much when you write and let your instinct take over—that's when your writing takes off." And then, more gently: "That's when you have a voice."

She shrugs her shoulders. "I don't know. I wouldn't . . ."

"Here," he says, "this is good. 'She chose each house by its degree of difficulty. The more impenetrable, the bigger the high. The house on the corner had bars on its windows and a sign outside that read "Armed Security Detail." Bingo! The jackpot!'"

He looks at Isabelle, who seems to have been swallowed up by the corner of the couch. "I like that," he tells her again, because she looks so miserable, "but not this." And he pushes ahead because he wants her to see what he sees. " 'The moon cast a hoary glow across the backyard pool, turning it into quicksilver. The black branches of the apple tree waved in the wind like witches' fingers pointing the way to the cellar door.' " He looks up again. Now she looks even more inconsolable.

"Do you see the difference?"

"I'm not sure."

He's exasperated. It's so clear—the first is interesting, the second is derivative and overwritten. "Well, think about it," he says, without a note of kindness in his voice.

"You give me all these tasks and I have no idea how to accomplish them."

"You'll figure it out."

"Is that supposed to make me feel better?" Maybe everyone is right. Maybe he isn't up to it. Maybe she shouldn't be here.

"Well, yes, it's a sort of . . . vote of confidence."

"It doesn't feel that way."

"Well, that's your problem." What does she want of him?

"It feels like a cop-out."

He starts to redden, a flush working its way up his neck. He's trying with this girl, he really is, and she won't meet him halfway.

"Take a leap, dammit, Isabelle!"

And she flinches at his tone—frustrated, angry, maybe dismissive.

"You want to be Melanie, be Melanie."

And the lie comes flying out. "Who said I wanted to be——"

"Have some guts!" he almost shouts, piercing her at the core of her worst and most shameful flaw.

And now they've both said too much. She wants to scream

at him, *How am I supposed to do what you want?* He bites his
tongue to prevent an inappropriate apology from spilling forth,
asking forgiveness for transgressions well beyond the scope of
this student, this room.

God, he wants it to be different with this girl. He pushes
back from his desk. He can't look at her. It's better to stare out
the window and let a cavern of silence swallow up their heated
emotions.

He hears her get up, walk to the door, open it. Then: "Why
do writers have writer's block?"

He turns quickly, caught off guard as she had hoped, but he
doesn't hesitate. He tells her what he believes. "Self-loathing."

REMORSE. AS FAMILIAR TO DANIEL as his own hand. A neat,
smooth package with no corners or edges he can use to pick
it open and air it out. A tight, hard ball of regret he turns
over and over as the shadows lengthen in his office and he sits
marooned in his dilapidated easy chair.

ISABELLE SWIMS LAPS IN THE campus pool. There's no sound
but the muffled slap of her arms through the water, no expectations beyond hitting each of the walls and turning toward
the next. Whenever she wants the noise in her life to stop,
Isabelle gets in a pool and does laps.

In the middle of an unexceptional Tuesday morning, there
are only a few other dedicated swimmers, as determined
as Isabelle to finish their laps. She registers their presence
peripherally, but the last thing she wants is to acknowledge
any of them. She needs the isolation of the water. She needs
to stop thinking.

When she's done, when she can no longer lift her tired arms
one more time, there's a calm that comes. And from that calm,
she hopes, a sense of what to do.

Walking home, her long hair wet and dripping, her body humming quietly with exhaustion, Isabelle realizes she has to apologize. He doesn't deserve her anger.

THE NEXT DAY FINDS ISABELLE EXAMINING the dusty bookshelves of Seaman's Rare and Used Books on Lorenzo Street, close to school. Unlike UCLA, which has transformed the part of Los Angeles known as Westwood into a college town, Chandler hasn't managed to do much to gentrify the streets surrounding the campus.

As beautiful as the college itself is, up a gently sloping hill from the urban sprawl, the city streets below it are a mixture of small appliance shops, fast-food restaurants—Popeyes, Burger King—and one sprawling mall anchored by a Food 4 Less and a 99 Cents Only Store. Here and there on the side streets are a few shops and a café or two which cater to the students and professors up the hill. Seaman's is one of those.

It is a tiny place, jam-packed with books stacked in piles on the floor and on chairs and crammed tightly onto flimsy shelves. The only way to find something is to devote several hours to browsing or ask Oscar, who is permanently installed, it seems, behind the front counter. He must be in his eighties, but it's hard to tell. It's entirely possible he's in his sixties or even younger. He has the look of a person who never sees the light of day. Pasty skin, thinning white hair, rail thin, spine curved like a C, chain smoking. And always reading a book in poor light.

There's little light throughout the store. Isabelle can barely read the titles in the poetry section, which takes up a back corner of the store, but finally she finds what she's looking for, a copy of Philip Levine's *What Work Is*.

She wants to take Daniel a small present, a way of apologizing for yesterday, and she remembers from an interview he once gave that Philip Levine, a working-class poet from Detroit, had had a huge influence on his decision to become a writer. If Daniel could write about what he knew—his own hardscrabble neighborhood of Erie, the men who broke their backs doing manual labor and broke their families with the resentment that kind of life causes—well, then, maybe he could become a writer, too.

Finally she finds the slim volume with its brown cover and simple black-and-white photograph of a child at work in a factory and takes it to Oscar at the front desk. He never rings up a purchase without commenting upon it. He may well have read every book in his store.

"He won the National Book Award for this collection, did you know?"

Isabelle shakes her head. She doesn't much like poetry; it seems a code she hasn't yet cracked. "It's a gift."

"So you want it gift wrapped?"

She looks around the dusty counter with its ashtrays, cigarette butts, stacked books, and old magazines in teetering piles. "You gift wrap?"

"Are you kidding me?" And he grins, his yellow teeth stained from decades of smoke poking through his thin lips. "I always ask just for the reaction."

"You're a mean man, Oscar," Isabelle says as she takes the small paper bag he finds for her book, and he chuckles.

SHE KNOWS WHERE DANIEL LIVES. In the small community of Chandler College, things like that are common knowledge. There's a row of houses bordering the campus that the college rents out to professors at a much-reduced rate, and with a couple of questions to the right people, it's easy for Isabelle to find out which one is his.

She walks there now. Her plan is to leave the book in his mailbox with a little note she's already written. It simply says,

Next Tuesday can we start over? Isabelle. She spent more than an hour trying out different messages, everything from an out-and-out apology to a note that didn't mention what had happened between them at all. She feels guilty for exploiting what his son told her—that he has writer's block—to wound him. She has no idea what he's feeling—disappointed in her, probably, ready to wash his hands of her; she's not sure. It never occurs to her that Daniel's guilt may be exponentially larger than hers.

He doesn't have a mailbox, not the kind that stands on a post near the curb. He has a mail slot in his front door, which means she has to walk up the front path of his house and try to slip the book in silently.

The problem is, there's Daniel, watching her from one of the living room windows. So now what should she do? She realizes she has to ring the doorbell. She has to have some sort of interaction, which is the last thing she wants. *Keep it short,* she tells herself. *Don't make conversation. Leave quickly.*

When her foot reaches the doormat, a black rubber number with the school crest on it, Daniel opens the door. He's barefoot, wearing old jeans that sag even on his ample frame, and a rumpled striped sweater with a tear along the neck seam. He hasn't shaved and his beard is laced with white. He looks terrible. Older. He doesn't say anything, simply waits for her to start.

"I was at Oscar's bookshop, you know, on Lorenzo, and I saw this book of poems, and I remembered that you said in some interview that Philip Levine was a strong influence for you, and I thought I'd pick it up and give it to you ..." She trails off. He still hasn't said anything. "You've probably got it anyway," she says as she hands it to him.

He shakes his head, then opens the door wider. "You want some coffee?"

She doesn't. She wants to go. This was a terrible idea, but

she finds herself saying, "Sure." Trapped again by indecision, by her inability to state what she'd like, she finds herself closing the front door behind her. She sees his retreating back off to the left, entering a room she assumes is the kitchen. He hasn't said another word but she follows him.

In the kitchen, he's pouring two cups of coffee from a large, old-fashioned metal percolator which sits on a very dirty stove.

"You take sugar? Or milk? I may have some in the fridge."

She shakes her head, and he hands her an orange mug with the Chandler coyote on it, drawn in cartoon style, faintly reminiscent of Wile E. Coyote. He sits down at the large kitchen table and she sits opposite him.

He pulls the Levine book out of its brown paper bag as she sips her coffee and avoids eye contact with him. Her note is stuck in the book, and he finds it and reads it while she surveys the dirty dishes in the sink. Several days' worth, it looks like.

"Yes," he says simply in answer to the question on her card—*Can we start over?*—and now she can take a breath and look at him. When she does, he's smiling.

"I was sure you'd had enough of me," he says.

She shakes her head.

"Well, I'm relieved," he tells her.

"Me, too."

He lays the small book of poems gently on the wooden table between them and attempts to give her the gift of Levine's wisdom. "What Philip Levine taught me is that what you've lived, what's inside you, is worthy enough to write about. You need to believe that." And then he says her name, "Isabelle," with so much tenderness in his voice that it sounds like a prayer.

"Can I do it?" They're looking at each other now, across the table.

He nods.

"But do I have something to say?"

"I think so."

"Will you help me?" she finds herself saying.

He bows his head over his large hands, wrapped tightly now around his ceramic mug. He doesn't want her to see his face, to detect in it the struggle going on to remain steady. That this girl believes he can do it despite the wreck she must see in front of her. That she trusts what he doesn't even trust about himself.

"Yes," he says finally, and only then can he look up into her expectant, hopeful, very young face.

ON THE NEXT TUESDAY it's as if they've crossed some invisible bridge. The air is clearer on the other side. More supple. There's laughter, even.

During the previous week as Isabelle worked, her spirit grew lighter. She tried more things, took some risks, and she suspects her writing got better. *Daniel said I can do this,* she told herself whenever her nerve failed, and his belief in her led her forward.

When she walks into his office at ten o'clock, eager, even excited, she holds two sets of the rewritten pages, the end of Chapter One again. One for him and the other for her. The plan is to read aloud as he follows along. That way, she tells him, they can hear the words together.

She paces as she reads, and Daniel finds it hard work to follow the words. He's drawn to watch her cross and recross the worn floor of his office. She's performing for him, and he appreciates it.

He likes these pages better, he tells her. Maybe it's because she's reading them to him. He tells her that, as well.

"You've got an unfair advantage," he says. "You read well."

"Part of my plan." She's still walking around his office, not able to light anywhere.

"To do what?"

"Bring you over to my side," she tells him in an offhand way, gently teasing. They both feel so relieved today. So glad to find themselves in this uncomfortable office, so comfortable with each other.

"Isabelle, can't you tell by now? I am *by* your side and *on* your side. Don't you know?"

"I do," she tells him as she stops pacing and looks directly at him. "I know."

And that's enough for his face to fold into a grin. "And you know I'm going to reread these pages later tonight, alone, by myself, to see what I think of them then."

"But you'll hear my voice in your head as you do."

"Probably," he admits. Then: "You stay with me."

You stay with me, too, immediately leaps into Isabelle's mind, but all she says is, "I hope so."

LATER THAT NIGHT, he does just that—he rereads her latest pages. The house is quiet. Stefan is out somewhere. He often leaves without telling Daniel where he's going, and Daniel doesn't ask. His son is twenty-three. It's not Daniel's job to ride herd on him. What his job exactly is in terms of his son, Daniel hasn't quite figured out.

Outside the small sunroom, the backyard is full of darkness, and with the one small table lamp alight beside him, the room feels cozy and cocooned.

As Daniel reads, he of course hears Isabelle's voice reading the words and sees her striding around his campus office with some kind of newly acquired confidence. Did he give her that? Maybe. But how? Another one of those mysteries that Daniel accepts without questioning, as he accepted his writing gift when it came and mourned when it left him.

The pages are verification—they're better than any she's given him. He relaxes into the old-fashioned wing chair, his head resting against the high back, and sees his image reflected back to him in the glass walls of the room. He's grinning stupidly. The girl is learning. Somehow he is teaching. Amazing, an outcome he never expected.

When Stefan comes home sometime after midnight, he finds his father fast asleep in his chair, his jaw drooping open, snoring slightly, Isabelle's pages spread across his lap. *He looks pathetic,* Stefan thinks, *like some kind of old guy.*

"Dad . . ."

Daniel doesn't stir.

"Dad," Stefan says much louder, but that doesn't wake him, either. He has to walk into the room, shake his father's shoulder, and finally Daniel rouses.

"You oughta be in bed."

Daniel mumbles something that sounds like "shit." He's half asleep as he pushes himself up from the chair, Isabelle's pages floating from his lap to the floor like settling birds. Stefan kneels and picks them up.

"These that girl's? The one I met in the hall?"

"Isabelle," Daniel says as he makes his way out of the room, his hips tight and aching from hours of sleeping upright.

"Are they any good?"

"Finally, yes."

"I told her not to work with you," Stefan says to his father's retreating back, and that stops Daniel. He turns around so that Stefan will hear him clearly.

"Well, you were wrong. She should very much work with me."

CHAPTER FOUR

During the spring months, Isabelle lives with a constant commotion inside her head. She carries on conversations with Melanie and her other characters, sometimes arguing with them, often rewriting dialogue or even paragraphs of prose. The process feels as though she is running a low-grade fever, just enough to make her normal reality seem glassy and unreal. It doesn't matter. All Isabelle cares about is the world she is creating with her words, the one she shares with Daniel. Everything else falls away. Waking up, eating, sleeping, are only valuable because they enable her to write and then deliver those pages to Daniel on Tuesday mornings.

One hour a week, and yet each week whatever occurs in that room sustains her, pushes her, and finally rewards her. She doesn't stop to examine the mechanics of how that happens. She only knows the whole transaction feels private, her words almost a transfer of a secret language that only Daniel will be able to decipher. Pure in a way nothing else in her life has ever been.

And yes, there's a freedom she's never known. Daniel was right: the freedom to express exactly what she wants to say without a filter, and the freedom to be received with generosity, because Daniel is capable of great generosity, at least with her.

Each Tuesday session begins with Daniel behind his desk as he always seems to be, reaching out and telling her, "Hand 'em over," as she steps into the room. No preamble. No *How are you, how was the writing this week?* Simply his large, open hand reaching toward her, a gesture of giving—*Here is a place for your words*—as much as asking—*Tell me, tell me what's in your heart.*

"Be kind," she wants to say, and sometimes does as she hands over her pages.

"I will not," Daniel tells her.

"Then be honest."

"That I can do."

And she sighs with relief—that's exactly what she wants to hear, and he knows it. They are united in common purpose; they are on a mission and they've set a goal. She will have the first three chapters finished to his satisfaction and hers by the time she graduates in May.

Nate has no idea what has become of the calm, steady, reliable Isabelle he's known since high school, but he particularly doesn't like how unavailable this new Isabelle has become. She no longer listens to the stories he wants to tell her, has no patience at all if he begins to complain. She cuts him off when he wants to discuss the pros and cons of the various law schools he's applied to. She needs to work. She has to finish these chapters before graduation.

"What difference does it make?" he asks her, annoyed, one night over dinner, which *he* has had to make because she's been too busy to shop or even think about what he might like to eat.

"I made a promise to Daniel that I'd be finished by graduation, finished so that he agrees it's finished."

"And if you don't?"

"That's not an option. I promised Daniel."

"So fucking what?"

"So honoring that promise means more to me than any-thing else." This is said very calmly. She's not baiting him. She's simply stating what is.

"There's something whacked about this."

She stands up, plate in hand. She's had enough of him and this conversation. "I'll eat while I'm working," and she leaves him alone at the kitchen table.

"We're having dinner! Hey, Isabelle, we're eating here!" He's yelling. She can hear the exasperation in his voice, but she ignores it as she closes the bedroom door, settles herself on their unmade bed, laptop in front of her, her half-eaten din-ner forgotten on the nightstand. If he comes in after her, she'll pack up and go to the library. But he doesn't.

ISABELLE DELIVERS THE LAST PAGES of Chapter Three the Tuesday before graduation. She comes into Daniel's office, her long legs in denim shorts, her feet in flip-flops, her hair brushed away from her face into a high ponytail, commenting on the unnatural heat of this early May day. "They say it's going to be a hundred and one today." Daniel's first thought is that she looks maybe ten years old, but he doesn't tell her that. Instead he extends his hand as he always does.

And she gives him what she sincerely hopes will be the final pages and situates herself on the floor, her back against the sofa, bare legs stretched out in front of her. She takes from her backpack Cormac McCarthy's *All the Pretty Horses*, a novel she picked up solely because she felt Daniel would like it, and begins reading.

When Daniel finishes her pages, he says, "They're good."

"They are? I thought they were! Oh my God, I'm finished!"

"Not yet."

And she groans. "Daniel, graduation is Saturday."

"You have four days, then."

"What's wrong with them?"

"Nothing's wrong with them. They just can be better."

"You know," she tells him, but there's none of the anger of their early interactions, "nobody but me would put up with that kind of vague directive."

"Isabelle," he says very quietly, "you know exactly what I mean."

She sighs dramatically for his benefit as she drags herself off the floor, stuffs the novel in her backpack. "Unfortunately, I do. You're going to tell me that Melanie is too intimidated by the cop."

"Where's her famous attitude in that scene?"

"Okay, okay."

When she's at the door, a thought occurs to her. "Come to graduation. Will you, Daniel?"

He shakes his head, not looking at her, his hands busy on his desk, his eyes there.

"You could meet my parents—not that that's any big inducement, but you could see me up there. You could see me walk across that stage and graduate."

"I wish I could. I do. But I just can't."

"Okay." And she shrugs as if it doesn't matter, but of course he knows it does. He watches her face close up; her tone of voice become impersonal. "I'll try to give you these last pages by Friday, but if I can't, I'll bring them by—"

He interrupts her. "I can't go anywhere."

She shakes her head. She has no idea what he's saying. "You're here."

"Here and my house, that's it, and if Stefan didn't show up most days to walk me to and fro like a goddamn preschooler, I probably wouldn't make it to either place."

She walks back into the room, drops her backpack, takes her

customary seat on the couch. They're maybe three feet apart. "What is it?"

"It's called agoraphobia. It means literally 'fear of the marketplace,' only for me it's fear of every place that isn't this office or my house."

There—it's out. She's the only person besides Stefan he's ever told, and he watches her face for a reaction. If she's repulsed by such weakness or flooded with pity or—

"I know what it is," Isabelle says with the same matter-of-factness she used earlier to comment on the weather. "My aunt Sarah has it. She can't even walk out into her backyard."

Daniel nods.

"People get over it," Isabelle says.

"A few."

"There's medication and therapy—"

He stands up behind his desk. "It's not your problem, Isabelle." He won't discuss this any further. "These last eight pages are your problem."

She's preoccupied with what he's just told her. "That's why people say you're not engaged or why you don't even show up for meetings or why you didn't—"

"Stop!"

She does.

"Bring the pages to my house when you're done."

"Okay." She stands again, slings her backpack over a shoulder. "Well, I guess I don't have to ask if you'll be home."

He looks up at her. What?

"Any old time should work out fine for you, don't you think?"

"Isabelle." It's a warning, which she ignores.

"Here's the thing—I won't have to call first or make an appointment."

As her hand flies to cover her mouth, he sees the smile anyway. "You're totally outrageous."

No one has ever said that to her before. She's thrilled. "Good," she tells him as she walks out.

THE LATE-ARRIVING PARENTS FILE INTO Kellman Amphitheater, an arena carved out of the hillside which college legend has it mimics the ancient theater at Delphi. Struggling in the heat, the middle-aged people climb the stone steps higher and higher to reach the last few vacant seats at the top. All graduations at Chandler College are held in this outdoor venue, the likelihood of rain in May in Southern California being quite remote. Historically, May is mild, but this year, for some reason, the temperatures are soaring and the sun is brutal.

Despite the 95-degree heat, many families have been sitting in the unshaded venue for hours, laying claim to their spots. Every parent has a camera in hand, ready to capture that one moment they've anticipated for the past four or five or six years, that instant when their graduate reaches out and takes his or her diploma from the hand of the president of the college.

Isabelle's father, Eli Rothman, sitting midway up the steep semicircle, wishes they had arrived earlier so they could have gotten better seats, but Ruth takes forever to get herself ready, as if each event they attend is her opening night. And he is worried about Isabelle and this unseasonable heat. How long do they have to be in those heavy black robes? Has she made sure to drink lots of water this morning and slather her face with sunscreen? He would guess not. He glances at his wife, who is fanning herself with the program and scanning the crowd, looking . . . well, dissatisfied is the best way he can describe it. The three boys sit between them. It is always the way—the children between them, even though the children are practically grown. Aaron is seventeen and will graduate from high school next year, and the twins are almost sixteen.

He has one of those moments when he looks at his wife

and honestly can't remember why he married her. Whatever was he thinking twenty-two years ago? He knows Ruth has those same moments, only probably many more of them. If she hadn't gotten pregnant on their honeymoon, would they still be together? He doesn't know.

Thank God Isabelle turned out to take after him. She looks like him and her temperament is like his. He worries about Ethan, one of the twins, because he seems to have inherited Ruth's self-aggrandizing dramatic flair. No good can come of that.

He spots Nate's parents in the crowd, much closer to the stage, of course. Sharon and Greg Litvak are beaming with self-congratulation. Here it is—the graduation, magna cum laude, of their brilliant son, whose future is limitless and who has no stumbling blocks to his success. Eli truly wishes he liked these people better, since it seems their children are moving in lockstep into the future.

And now, thank goodness, the music starts and the audience begins to settle, although he sees that every mother continues to fan herself with the program. As the graduates file in, it is Aaron who spots Isabelle first. "There she is. Do you see her, right behind that big guy with the ponytail?" And Eli does. He points for Ethan and Noah. And finally Ruth, who has to rummage around in her purse for her glasses, which she refuses to wear unless it's absolutely necessary, spots her, as well. So they all see her and they can settle back for the speeches and the awarding of the diplomas.

John Liggins, the president of the college, a large, imposing black man known for promoting diversity and thinking outside the box—Daniel owes his stay at Chandler to him—starts his welcome by thanking them all for coming, acknowledging the unseasonal heat, congratulating the graduating seniors, and then, switching gears, he tells the still settling crowd that he feels it is incumbent upon him to acknowledge the history-making event that occurred on May 10, just a few days earlier, in Pretoria, South Africa: Nelson Mandela's inauguration as that country's first black president.

"President Mandela had much to say that would apply to our graduates," Liggins tells the audience, "but I would like to quote you all one particular sentence from his inaugural speech: 'We enter into a covenant that we shall build the society in which all South Africans, both black and white, will be able to walk tall, without any fear in their hearts, assured of their inalienable rights to human dignity—a rainbow nation at peace with itself and the world.'"

The crowd has grown silent; the dignity of Mandela's words has compelled them to quiet and listen. John Liggins tells his graduating seniors, "All of you would do well to take the same pledge, to strive to build exactly the same society here in our country.

"There is, of course, a great deal more to say, and under normal conditions I would be saying it. Probably too much and too long." There's a ripple of laughter from the students. John Liggins is a very popular president. "But I made a promise," he continues, "given the unseasonable heat, to cut my remarks short today." There's a scattering of applause, particularly from the graduates, and Liggins laughs and says, "I guess I made the right decision."

And then he introduces the commencement speaker, some Los Angeles official—is he the mayor?—who begins his speech by assuring the audience that he will make no such concession to the weather. Standing at the podium, multiple white pages of his speech fluttering in the hot Santa Ana wind, this small, trim Latino man promises (threatens?) to give the whole speech and nothing but the whole speech. This is a once-in-a-lifetime moment for your graduates, he tells the parents, and what he has to say may well change their lives. A groan escapes from the audience, but he ignores it and begins talking . . . and talking . . . and talking. After forty minutes, with no end in sight, Ruth leans toward Eli, across the boys, "I'm going to faint. I've got to find some shade."

Aaron gets up with her without being asked, to take her arm, to help her out of the amphitheater.

"You're going to miss Isabelle," Eli warns, but all Ruth does is wave her hand as she makes her way out of their row. He looks at the twins, Ethan and Noah, and shrugs. "Your mother can't take the heat."

"Neither can I," Ethan shoots back, "but you don't see me leaving."

"You're fifteen and she's . . . well, a lot older."

"Yeah, Dad, so what?"

Eli doesn't have an answer to that. And Ruth and Aaron don't come back. It is only Eli and the twins who see Isabelle walk across the stage, radiating happiness, take her diploma, and stride with purpose into the rest of her life.

AFTERWARD, AS THE FAMILIES AND GRADUATES mill about outside the arena, Eli finds Ruth sitting at a small table under a tree. Her sandals are off, her eyes are closed, and she's fanning herself with the now very rumpled program. Aaron stands miserably by with three bottles of water in hand.

"Well, you missed her."

"Eli, I had a throbbing headache. I was dizzy and nauseous. My heart was going a mile a minute. Do you know what those are symptoms of? They're symptoms of heatstroke. Should I have stayed in my seat? Is that what you wanted, your wife dead at her daughter's graduation?"

Eli considers this question. For a split second it sounds good to him, and then he says, "Of course not, but Ruth, we came all this way to see her graduate, and you missed the moment when—"

"How did I know it was going to be this hot? Is that my fault? You know I can't stand the heat."

And Isabelle, pushing through the knots of people, spots them. "Hey, Dad! Mom!" They watch her come to them, grinning, relieved, riding a bubble of celebration.

Eli embraces his daughter and whispers in her ear, "My beautiful college graduate," and the boys mumble, "Congratulations." Aaron manages an awkward arm around her shoulder, a halfhearted hug. And then Ruth and Isabelle are facing each other.

"It's bloody hot." Ruth doesn't get up.

"Oh, I know. I'm so sorry, Mommy, I know how much you hate the heat."

"I was sitting there and suddenly I knew I was getting heatstroke!"

"Ruth." Eli's tone an admonishment to his wife, which she ignores.

"The problem is they don't have any other place to hold graduation," Isabelle explains.

"Well, could they have handed out water or hats or something?"

"I'm so sorry," Isabelle says again, as if the heat and the amphitheater, the lack of water and hats, were all her fault.

"Isabelle was sitting in the same heat as you, only in that long black robe, which must have upped her internal temperature at least ten more degrees."

"So it doesn't matter what I was feeling? Is that what you're saying?"

Isabelle and Aaron exchange a look: *Here they go.* The twins melt into the crowd. They don't want to witness what they've seen countless times before: their parents, with over twenty years of resentment built up, going at each other until her mother starts to cry and her father apologizes.

"Of course that's not what I'm saying. What I'm saying is that today is Isabelle's day and you should have—"

"What? Died? Because it's her day?"

"Mommy, nobody said that."

"Your father did—I just heard him."

"Ruth, that is not at all what I said."

"There's nothing wrong with my ears!"

"Why do you persist in attributing to me things I never said, things I never in a million years would say?"

And they're off. Only today Isabelle can't take it. Isn't it possible to put all this aside for one day? Her day. The day she's so happy. Do they have to ruin it? Well, she won't let them. She'll flee the train wreck piling up in front of her. It feels very daring.

"When they stop fighting," she says to Aaron, "tell them I'll see you all later at the hotel."

"You can't leave." Aaron is panicked. "It'll only get worse if you leave."

"See those steps over there, the ones in the shade? Go sit there and wait it out."

Aaron doesn't move. He looks wretched.

"I have a paper to turn in, A."

"Can I come with you?"

"Not this time. I'll see you later, okay?"

There's no way out for him. Not now, not for another year, until he goes away to college and never comes back. "Okay," he says finally, and Isabelle is gone, swallowed up by the crowd.

She pushes the guilt down, away, away from her just for today as she weaves through the milling families, recognizing somewhere inside her that she made the decision to leave without any of her habitual agonizing. Should she have stayed and mediated her parents' argument? Should she have tried harder to head it off? Should she have stayed to protect Aaron, as she has countless times before? Should she have been a better daughter? Those questions would have trapped her into indecision if not for Daniel, who is waiting for her.

And then her eye is caught by a swirl of primary colors shimmering in the heat: Deepti's extended family—her mother in a rose-colored sari shot through with gold thread, her older sister in shades of green and blue, Aunt Priya, the doctor, dressed in bright yellow silk. And in the middle, startling in contrast, is Deepti in her long black gown and tasseled cap. Her father, Ajay, stands proudly on the periphery of all these colorful women in his woven sandals and starched ocher shirt, content to watch them flutter around his beaming daughter.

"Isabelle!" Deepti calls to her, and the two roommates embrace. "We did it!"

"We did!" And suddenly, in that split second, Isabelle is overcome with a sense of loss. "I'm going to miss you so much!"

"I know. I know!"

"I won't see you every day. How can that be?"

"You'll visit me in the Bay Area. Promise me?"

"Of course I promise," Isabelle says, because she wants it to be true—that she will take a trip to San Francisco sometime soon, even though the days and weeks past graduation are a fuzzy blur to her now.

And then she spots Nate and his parents and grandparents, Rose and Bernie, and a couple of aunts and uncles and their children, all of whom Isabelle knows. So many Litvaks have come out from Long Island for this. Isabelle waves to them over the heads of the people.

"I've got to go." Isabelle gives Deepti one last hug, her eyes on the fast-approaching Nate as she takes off in the opposite direction. "I will come!" are the last words Deepti hears.

"Isabelle, wait!" Nate calls out.

"See you at dinner," she shouts to him as she slips through the crowd and is lost from view. The last thing she wants to do now is acknowledge her connection to the whole Litvak clan.

THE WALK FROM THE AMPHITHEATER to Daniel's house is quick and smooth. As soon as Isabelle is down the hill, the campus empties out, the way it does on any Saturday. And walking through the shaded groves of ancient oaks and eucalyptus feels good after all the hours of sitting in the sun. It's only when the buzz of voices recedes and the quiet beauty of the Chandler campus reinstates itself that Isabelle can allow herself to realize that this is the last day she will walk these paths, see these buildings, live here . . . see Daniel.

She stops in front of Lathrop Hall and fixes it in her mind's eye. *Remember the twenty-seven steps you took every Tuesday. Remember the red tile roof and the elegant arch over the front door. Here is where your life changed, on the second floor, in that derelict office Daniel keeps for himself.*

Something extraordinary happened, she knows it. Somehow Daniel guided her toward a vision of herself that is singular, unique, divorced from everyone else's expectations—a writer. She has to let him know how grateful she is.

DANIEL HAS BEEN WAITING ALL WEEK. He really didn't expect her on Wednesday, or even Thursday. He knew it would take longer than a day or two to rewrite the pages. But Friday he was at the living room window every few hours, and when she didn't show up, he knew it had to be Saturday, even though Saturday was graduation. Sunday she was leaving with her parents, back to Long Island for a summer job in her father's law firm, she'd told him. And then? She doesn't know.

All morning he waited for her. Maybe she'd come with her pages before the ceremony. But she didn't. So he knew that somehow she'd come after. And it is late afternoon and he is pacing in his living room and then he sees her, flying down his front path. She's still wearing her long black robe, and it's flapping open to reveal bare legs and sandals. She isn't just coming to him, she is rushing toward him.

He opens the door and she sails through. "Daniel ... Oh, Daniel ... How can I go back to Long Island with *them*? They're already driving me crazy! My mother's sure she has heatstroke and my father is yelling at her and the twins are mortified and Aaron, poor sweet Aaron, is beside himself and I left! Can you believe that? I ran off and left them all there to sort it out!"

"Good." Daniel says this unequivocally, and it immediately calms her down.

She tosses her body into a living room chair and a small smile starts. "It is good, isn't it?"

He nods. He knows something about dealing with selfish parents.

"If it had been any other day, I would have pleaded with them to stop arguing, begged my mother not to misunderstand, pushed my father to apologize ..."

"Sounds exhausting," Daniel says, his tone mild, neutral. He doesn't want to encourage a conversation about her parents.

"Don't you think they could have held it together for one day?"

"Apparently they didn't want to."

Apparently not. A sobering thought. She reaches into the pocket of her gown and takes out the much-folded eight rewritten pages and hands them to him.

"Come into the kitchen," he says. "I have lemonade."

"You do? You bought lemonade for me?"

"Yes. Well, Stefan did. I don't go to the market."

"Oh, right," she says, and now she's openly grinning, simply entirely happy to be here. "Did he get a job?"

"Not that I know of."

"Wasn't that part of the bargain?"

"It was."

"Are you going to send him back?"

Daniel looks stunned. "No, of course not. He's my son."

In the kitchen he pours her a glass of cold lemonade and sits down at the kitchen table to read the pages. All the windows in the room are open to catch whatever breeze might be brave enough to come, and the door to the backyard stands open, as well. Isabelle walks to it as Daniel reads.

What she sees is a large and overgrown space, but there are old fruit trees struggling along at the back of the lot and a flagstone patio that would be welcoming when the weather was cooler.

She doesn't turn around. She knows that behind her Daniel is reading her work, but the two of them are very far from those beginning days when she needed to monitor his reactions.

Daniel reads quickly. He's mainly interested in the scene between Melanie and the motorcycle cop who stops her just minutes after her last robbery. Isabelle hadn't paid enough attention to that scene. It was an opportunity to see Melanie scared and then rising above it, using all her moxie to take control of the situation. And this time, in these pages, Isabelle has done it.

Melanie's car is pulled over. The cop approaches. Her heart is thumping through her chest. This is it, she thinks, this is where it all ends, but no, the cop is talking to her about a non-functioning rear taillight. He tells her he has to write her a "fix-it ticket." And that would be the end of it, she would be off the hook, but Melanie can't leave it be. She provokes. *Ah, good*, Daniel thinks as he reads. This is what he had been hoping she'd do.

Isabelle stands in the doorway and sheds her heavy robe. She's supposed to turn it in, she knows, along with her cap, which she thinks one of the twins took from her, but in her hurry to get to Daniel, she didn't do it. Under her robe she wears the thinnest of sundresses and a pair of bikini underpants and that's all. She knew it was going to be blisteringly hot. The hem of the dress barely covers her thighs, and the top looks more like a chemise with ribbons for straps.

Daniel focuses on the expanded final scene Isabelle has written. Melanie gets out of her car and asks to see what the cop is talking about. They walk around to the rear and he points to the left taillight. The red plastic is cracked. The light doesn't work. Does she see? The trunk, just inches away, is filled with objects stolen less than ten minutes before, objects taken at random—a set of steak knives, a quilt off one of the beds, a crystal pitcher, two dresses. Small and useless things.

The adrenaline rush, perversity, heedlessness, push Melanie on. She brings up the robberies with the cop. Everyone in the neighborhood is talking about them. Who could be doing this, robbing all these houses?

"Professionals," he tells her, head down, writing out the ticket, paying little attention. "The jobs are too clean for amateurs."

"Maybe it's just a really smart amateur," Melanie finds herself saying for the thrill of it, to see if she can teeter on the edge and not fall off. "Maybe it's somebody with a point to make. Or maybe it's an act of desperation from someone who feels like he has no other avenue. Maybe these robberies are saving someone's life."

The cop looks up at her quickly. Has she said too much?

Crossed the safety line? His eyes don't leave hers, and she makes herself stare right back at him as if the secret she owns wasn't pushing against the back of her throat, desperate to leap out.

"You've been watching too many cop shows," he tells her finally, and smiles.

She smiles back. "I guess so."

Yes! Daniel is pleased: so much better. He looks up from the pages to see Isabelle standing there, her back to him, her body outlined against the flimsy cotton of her dress, which has all but disappeared in the light and the breeze from the back door. His breath catches and he has to wait a minute before he can say, "Isabelle . . ." And she turns around and looks at him. "The pages—they're very good."

She nods, taking it in. "That's all I've ever wanted," she says softly, "for you to say that. For you to believe I could be a writer."

"You have to believe it."

"I do now. You gave me that."

She walks back into the room, closer to him. "Daniel, I don't know how to tell you how much this has—"

He stands up. He can't tolerate a long speech of thankfulness. He doesn't deserve it. "You did the work."

"But without you . . ." She shakes her head at the thought, understanding somehow that she must be quiet, that he can't accept what she wants to give—her enormous gratitude. But he must.

She moves closer to him, and they stand less than a foot apart. Silent. Anything might happen now. They both know it. She reaches up and puts her arms around his neck and moves her body to his and lays her head in the curve of his shoulder.

He's conscious of the girth of his stomach in contrast to the slender young arms she wraps around him and the lean, eager body he feels along the length of his. He holds her and finds himself doing something he hasn't thought to do in thirty years: he prays. Then he puts his lips on her bare shoulder and tastes salt from her perspiration and smells something young and floral and utterly mesmerizing—Isabelle.

She slips the strap of her dress from her left shoulder, her head pressed against his chest as she does, her eyes closed, and he gently, tenderly, carefully allows his lips to travel across the perfect flesh of her collarbone, down to her breast and then her nipple. Her hand goes to the back of his head and time stops, and then he straightens up and so does she.

He steps back first and they look at each other. He lifts the strap back onto her shoulder. It may be the most selfless gesture he's made in a decade.

Carefully, she says what she came to say. "Without you, Daniel, I would have been lost my whole life."

And he nods, acknowledging, accepting finally what he has meant to her. Only then can she turn and go.

Part Two

That summer back in Merrick, Long Island, after graduation felt like a creeping suffocation to Isabelle, a slow slide into death. And the person who was dying was the Isabelle Daniel had nurtured in his own idiosyncratic way from January to May.

Having made no plans beyond receiving her diploma, Isabelle told herself she would spend the summer, and only the summer, working in her father's law firm. It would give her some breathing space to figure out her next move.

But that's not what happened. As soon as she read the expressions of expectation on her parents' faces, she turned back into the dutiful daughter she had always been astonishingly quickly. And Daniel's vision of her as an unique person, ripe with possibility, faded into insubstantiality.

Maybe they hadn't had enough time together. Or maybe it had only been the alchemy between them that had allowed her to write freely and, finally, well. In her most fragile moments, Isabelle believed that Daniel may well have conjured that eventually confident girl, who strode into his dingy office in Lathrop Hall eager to get to work, from his own wishing.

It is a stifling summer in New York, each day blooming hotter than the last, and every morning as Isabelle takes the train into the city with her father and returns home at the end of the workday, she feels Daniel's Isabelle disappear a tiny bit more into the humid, noxious air.

At the beginning she held on. That first week, as she and her father settled into seats on the Long Island Railroad, lucky if their car had some degree of air conditioning, Isabelle would take out her laptop and enter Melanie's world. She would make notes, try out bits of dialogue, talk to her characters. Eli, sitting next to her reading *The Wall Street Journal*, would glance over from time to time but not intrude.

Or she would write postcards to Daniel, quick notes as the train sped toward Manhattan, telling him she was working, planning her next chapter. Once in a while she'd get a cryptic card back with no salutation or signature—*What if Melanie used a horse for her getaway instead of a car? A horse so black he couldn't be seen in the night?* Isabelle laughed out loud as she read that one—a horse in the middle of the city?

At her desk, in her father's sterile law offices, when she felt stupefied by the statistics she was compiling for some case or another, she would log on to the office's AOL account and e-mail Daniel. Stefan, who still had had no luck finding a job, turned out to have the savvy to set up an e-mail account for Daniel (and not coincidentally himself) at the house. *Don't worry*, Daniel wrote to her after she had complained one day that she was stuck, at sea with Melanie's story, *it's okay to get lost.* She contemplated every sentence he wrote because she knew he was trying to nudge her toward the unexpected. *Surprise me.*

How is it possible to know someone so well, as she now feels she knows Daniel, and know almost nothing about his life? Of course, she knows his son and that Daniel suffers each day with his agoraphobia, but outside of that she knows nothing.

Does he have other children? What happened to his marriage? Why was he at Chandler? Was he working on another book? Whom did he vote for in the last election? She couldn't have answered one of those questions, and yet there is a certainty within her that she knows him.

At the beginning of their second week of travel, her father puts aside his paper and begins to talk. Anyone watching the two of them sitting side by side in the crowded, stuffy, rapidly warming train car would have easily guessed they are father and daughter, the resemblance between them so apparent— the same light brown eyes that are almost hazel, the same long limbs, the same graceful hands, the same air of apology which hangs from their shoulders and hunches them inward. Ruth's constant admonition to "stand up straight" throughout Isabelle's childhood never really took. She is her father's daughter and has learned to bow her shoulders against all possible onslaughts, just as he does.

That morning at breakfast Eli and Ruth had made sure to flagrantly ignore each other, the air between them sizzling with more resentment than usual. Isabelle and her brothers ignored the ignoring.

"Your mother's having a hard time right now." Eli starts the conversation as the train gathers speed away from the Rockville Centre station.

Isabelle mumbles, "Hmmmm," and continues typing, her laptop angled so her father can't read the screen.

"I'm worried about her."

"Oh, Daddy."

"No, really, this is different."

And at that Isabelle feels compelled to close the computer, turn, and have a conversation she doesn't want to have.

"She's a creative person, Isabelle, and she doesn't have an outlet."

So am I! Isabelle wants to yell but doesn't. Being home in the Rothman realm, she feels as though some entity is holding a hand over her mouth, muzzling every sentence she longs to shout.

"That's why she gets depressed, you know. And snappy. She's been searching so long without finding the right thing."

"Maybe she *isn't* a creative person, Dad." Isabelle knows she sounds snappy herself. She tries harder to be gentle. "Maybe she wants to be but really isn't."

Eli thinks about that for a moment as the train stops at the Valley Stream station and he watches crowds of men, already sweating through their light-colored shirts, their suit jackets over their arms, push into the aisles, raising the temperature in the car just by their bodily presence.

"Well, that would be worse, then, wouldn't it?" Eli finally says. "That would mean she'd be perpetually unhappy."

"Dad, she is!"

"No, no, you mustn't say that. That sounds so hopeless."

Isabelle studies her father's earnest, guileless face and realizes there's no getting out of this conversation, which they've had countless times before, and that there's no good resolution to it. They will discuss Ruth's dissatisfaction and her struggles and her migraines and her "courage," as Eli calls it, to forge ahead to find herself until the train pulls into Penn Station. And they will get nowhere. They never have.

The forty-minute ride each morning gives Eli the opportunity to vent. Isabelle is relieved to discover that he seems too caught up with workday events to continue the conversation on the way home. He has set aside the morning commute to unburden his heart.

At first his comments are all couched in concern for Ruth, but after not too many days the morning monologues become laments about his own lost life, his bad choices—marrying Ruth being one of them.

"Why did you, then, Daddy?" Isabelle asks one morning, when she can't bear the thought of his laundry list of could-have-been's and should-have-been's gathering steam.

Eli doesn't answer right away. He stares out at the landscape whizzing by, baking in the already brutal sunshine. His voice is tinged with wonder and a certain pleasure as he tells Isabelle, "I couldn't believe this amazing creature who was your mother back then would even look at someone like me. But for some reason—and I still don't know what it was—she saw something in me." For an instant he seems proud of the younger Eli. "So I threw away all judgment and let passion have its way."

In the sweltering train—no air conditioning today—Eli shakes his head at his own foolishness. "A big mistake." And then he repeats it to drive home the point. "*Big* mistake. And I've been paying for it my whole life."

Isabelle turns away. She so doesn't want to hear these things from her own father.

"I should have chosen someone solid. Someone steadfast." Eli looks at his daughter's profile as she feigns interest in the passing terrain, anything to avoid eye contact, anything to discourage these inappropriate revelations. But her father isn't done. "Someone like Nate."

Isabelle shrugs. He's right. Nate is steadfast. He calls her daily from Washington, D.C., where he's gone to establish himself, working as an intern in the Justice Department before law school at Georgetown in the fall. "Good contacts," he explains to Isabelle, and she's sure he's right. He plans ahead; his life all carefully mapped out, with her participation already drawn in. All she has to do is acquiesce and all the moving parts will glide effortlessly forward. He's guaranteed her that—success, security, predictability. Why doesn't she come down to D.C. and work at something—"It doesn't matter what," he tells her—while he goes to law school? That question has become the daily refrain. She's not doing anything that she can't leave behind, is she? What's stopping her?

She finds she can't answer him. And she hates this about herself, that she clings to the well-worn path of least resistance. All those years of refereeing between Eli and Ruth have robbed her of the ability to speak her mind, deference a habit so deeply ingrained in her now that she can't find a way to say to Nate, "You. It's you that's stopping me," without sounding cruel. And so she listens to his monologues and pretends interest and deflects his questions. One thing is clear to her, though: after talking with Daniel for five months, she no longer wants to talk to Nate at all.

"Yes," she tells her father now, "Nate is steadfast"—to stop the discussion, to have that agreement between them so that Eli will feel he can stop talking. But he's not done yet. He needs her to know that it is important—no, crucial, because she is on the cusp of all things bright and beautiful—that she make the right choices. Everything hangs in the balance, as Eli knows. Everything.

"Don't live a life of regret," he tells his daughter.

"How do you avoid that?" Isabelle finally asks him one morning when she's heard the same admonition many times.

And all Eli can say is, "Be careful."

And of course that's the last thing Isabelle wants to be, because it is the one thing she always is.

And then she meets Casey.

When the blistering summer finally cools and the first sharp edge of autumn marks the early mornings, Isabelle faces the fact that she's still in New York, still without a plan of action, still fending off Nate's campaign to have her move to Washington, and that she has to do something about it all. But being home has resurrected the vacillating Isabelle.

And then a thought: Deepti! She promised Deepti, didn't

she? It is so much easier to fly to San Francisco and visit Deepti, who's in medical school at the University of California, San Francisco, and who has been pleading with Isabelle all summer to come.

On Isabelle's first morning there, a Sunday, Deepti takes her across the bay to Berkeley for breakfast. They sit at a small square table on Buon Mangia's tiny front patio, really just a part of the street corner that the restaurant has appropriated for its own use. No one seems to mind that the sidewalk is marked off as an eating area by cement planters filled with lavender and sage and that everyone must walk around them to cross the street.

They've landed in the Gourmet Ghetto on the north side of the university campus, and people come here primarily to eat. Chez Panisse, the mother of the American slow food movement, is just down the street.

"Local farmers, local flavors—I guess that's the best way to describe it," Deepti explains to Isabelle as they eat their blueberry pancakes and homemade maple syrup and drink their delicious freshly roasted free-trade coffee. "Sort of the antidote to fast food."

The weather is perfectly sweet—in the high sixties, with a faint breeze carrying the scent of the bay. Somehow Deepti, sitting across the table in her rose-colored sari, fits into the landscape here. In college, in Los Angeles, she always looked a bit exotic, but not in the eclectic mix that is Berkeley.

Isabelle turns to see, up and down Shattuck Avenue, scores of people eating, talking, idling, with nowhere pressing to go. She realizes suddenly, with a deep sigh, that she hasn't felt this relaxed all summer.

"Yes," Deepti says, acknowledging the relief in Isabelle's sigh, "the whole Bay Area, there's something gentle about it."

"Do people really live like this?" Isabelle asks, watching

parents leisurely stroll the sidewalks with chubby-cheeked children riding high on their shoulders in baby backpacks. On the patio of the café across the street college students are grouped together at a round table, talking, endlessly discussing, and laughing, and ordering more coffee. At the opposite corner barefoot children splash in a shallow fountain as their mothers sit on the tiled edge and gossip. No one seems to have a sense of urgency. "Where are all the unhappy people?"

Deepti smiles. "All around you."

Isabelle shakes her head. "It doesn't seem like it." Then she has to tell Deepti about her summer, even though the telling brings angst into this sanguine day. "My father and I took the train into the city every morning, and there usually wasn't any air conditioning, even though there was supposed to be, so the train was a sauna, and my father had this campaign going to spend each morning commute unburdening himself about twenty-two years of misspent life. Every morning. All summer. Every day added up to *Look how miserable I am.*"

"No," Deepti says, dismayed. She can't imagine her own father ever complaining, let alone unburdening himself. "Once my father broke his foot tripping on a concrete step and he never said a word about it. Just used a cane and limped around the house until it finally healed."

"One of his revelations was that he made a mistake marrying my mother."

Deepti nods. She's not surprised. She remembers graduation. "And yet they stay together, even though in America it's so easy to get a divorce."

"I know. It's their addiction, I think. Their unhappiness."

"People expect too much of marriage here."

"To be happy together?"

"Contentment comes—if your expectations are in the right place."

"Oh, Deepti, that's so Indian of you."

And Deepti laughs. "But I am Indian."

"Don't you want love?"

And here Deepti blushes.

Isabelle sees it immediately. "What? What is it?" And then she knows. "You met someone!"

"That's all. I met someone."

"And?"

"And we're going to go watch him play soccer after we finish breakfast."

"Oh, good."

"We can walk there. It's just down Shattuck at Bancroft."

"See," Isabelle insists, "we don't have to cram ourselves into stifling public transportation. We can just stroll like all these other happy people."

Deepti smiles at her. "He's a resident in emergency medicine, and his name is Sadhil. It means 'perfect.' " And here Deepti giggles.

Isabelle stares at her openmouthed—Deepti giggling? "I can't wait."

But it is Casey Isabelle sees as soon as she and Deepti are seated on the sun-warmed bleachers of Goldman Field, part of the university campus. Casey kicking the ball so hard it is a missile into the net. A goal!

And then he is racing up the field, arms streaming straight out behind him as if he were a 747 about to launch itself airborne. And then he is jumping, screaming in triumph, his fist in the air, his teammates mobbing and embracing him. Years later Isabelle understands the irony in her first sighting of Casey, but at the time all she sees is golden limbs, streaming blond hair, and joy. Unfettered, unquenchable joy! It is thrilling.

"What just happened?" Isabelle asks Deepti without taking her eyes off the field.

"Casey made a goal."

"You know him?"

"He's on Sadhil's team."

"Casey." Isabelle tries out the name and that's all it takes: she is lost.

The rest of the game is a blur to Isabelle, because she doesn't understand a thing about soccer and because her eyes never leave Casey's long, tanned body as he runs and runs and attempts another goal, which is blocked, and runs some more. *Doesn't he ever get tired?* He doesn't.

Deepti points out Sadhil, dark and lean, standing in front of the other large net. He's the goalie for their side, Deepti explains, and his job is to keep the other team's ball from going into the net. Even from this distance, Isabelle can tell how intense he is, how focused on his task, and she wants none of it. Her eyes won't stay on him. She wants the speed, the motion, the abandon of Casey as he flies up and down the grass field in endless pursuit of the ball.

When the game is over and the spectators mingle with the players, Deepti leads her to the sidelines to meet the very serious Sadhil. His team has lost, 2–1, and as the goalie, Sadhil holds himself responsible for those two points.

"You mustn't," Deepti tells him. "No one, not even a professional soccer player, could have blocked those shots."

Sadhil tilts his head toward Isabelle and says with a smile, "Your friend is a bit biased, I think."

And Deepti blushes again and Isabelle feels she should be somewhere else. These two people want to talk only to each other, and then she spots him, Casey, at the end of the field, next to the net. He has an arm around a teammate's shoulders. They're laughing, the game over, the loss absorbed, it seems. And then she watches Casey grab his duffel bag, sling it over his shoulder, and begin to walk across the grass toward the Bancroft Avenue exit.

He's leaving! No! Not yet! And Isabelle acts without even a split second of contemplation. All she knows is that if Casey reaches the street, he is lost for good. And so she sprints across the grass, feeling the spongy thickness beneath her sandals, and then the dry, hard cinder of the running track that rims the field. Oh, no, he's too far ahead of her. She won't reach him before he walks through the gate and is gone forever.

"Casey!" She has no idea who this person is inside her who's yelling at a perfect stranger.

He turns around, a puzzled look on his face. "Hey," he says, but he waits. Then, as she comes closer: "We know each other?"

"You made my first goal. I mean, I'd never seen a soccer game before and we walked in and there you were kicking the ball into the net. And I was . . . well, overcome." Did she really just say that? She cannot believe she's standing there having this conversation in which she knows she sounds like a complete dork. But it is as if her volition has been taken over by a tyrant who wants what she wants: Casey.

"You seemed so . . . oh, I don't know . . . filled with joy." And now she's totally embarrassed and desperate to back away before she says another stupid thing.

But Casey is listening to her, for some odd reason taking seriously what she has just said. "When I make a goal, it's like . . . like every cell in my body explodes into this manic happiness."

Tears spring into Isabelle's eyes. "How lucky you are," she says softly. He has to lean forward a little at the waist to hear her. If only . . . if only she could feel like that just once in her life.

"Yes," Casey says quietly, "I know."

She goes home with him then. She has just enough presence of mind left to tell Deepti where she is going and then she is gone.

Casey lives in a tree house built of unpainted cedar shingles and situated high up in the Berkeley Hills on a narrow, winding street overgrown with pines, red maple, and California sycamores. Isabelle's first thought is that she may well be entering a fairy tale, because there they are, the many, many steep steps that the princess must master to reach the tower and her prize. As they climb upward, each step a railroad tie anchored into the hillside, Casey explains that the house isn't his, that he is house-sitting for a professor on sabbatical leave. When they arrive, finally, at the front door, hand in hand, Isabelle is out of breath, but Casey is not even winded.

The view through the living room windows is breathtaking—San Francisco Bay and the city skyline. She recognizes the Transamerica Pyramid with its needlelike spire and the blockish Bank of America Center from the pictures Deepti has sent. Below the house is a panorama of green, the tops of hundreds of trees leading down to the campus.

Casey hasn't let go of her hand, and she doesn't want him to.

"Do you want something to drink or—?" he starts to say, but she shakes her head before he can finish. She wants him. That's all.

"Well, we can sit out on the deck. The sunsets are amazing."

She finds herself putting a hand on the side of his face, her thumb across his beautiful lips to silence him, and he understands. He doesn't say another word. He brings her to him— his arms are strong and muscled, his body warm from the exertion of soccer—and gently kisses her.

"Yes," she whispers.

In the bedroom, he watches as she undresses, and she finds to her surprise that she wants him to. And then he can't watch anymore and comes to her, touching her bare skin, bringing her to the unmade bed, apologizing for the mess, but she shakes her head—she hasn't even noticed.

She reaches for him and pulls the weight of his body onto

hers and now they're gone, consumed by what their bodies want and nothing else. So this is sex. She wants to weep for the person she used to be. What if she had never known this? What if she had gone her whole life thinking that what she and Nate did in bed was all there was?

Isabelle is all feeling and no will. She cannot utter a single word, and she doesn't need to. Casey knows. Somehow he knows what she wants, what she needs. And somehow she knows the same about him. They have been bewitched, and they flow into their enchantment, greedy and reckless.

AS THE AFTERNOON LIGHT BEGINS TO SOFTEN, Isabelle and Casey lie side by side, naked and silent. The trees outside the bedroom windows sway in the perpetual breeze off the bay. Neither of them has spoken a word. Their breathing slowly quiets, and Isabelle can now hear the campus Campanile strike the five o'clock hour. She waits until the last tone has thinned into nothingness and then, finally, she's able to say, "What's your last name?"

Casey laughs, delighted. "That's your first question after all that?"

"I want to know who you are."

"Mendenhall."

"Tell me something else."

"I sorta thought that was amazing."

She turns on her side so she can look at him. "About your life."

He runs his hand from the curve of her hip down the long bone of her thigh and cups the back of her knee. "Was that just *my* opinion?" he asks softly.

She can't answer. He's touching her. The warmth of his hand on her leg renders her mute. "More . . ." she finally murmurs, and as he envelops her body with his, words flee again.

Isabelle wakes some time later to find herself alone in the bed. She hears the shower going in the bathroom. Outside it's finally dark. She has no idea what time it is and no desire to find out. The only time that matters is the moment she's in, here, in Casey's bed. She is frankly astonished at herself, but she doesn't want to think about that now. She doesn't want to think about anything ever again. She's never before understood that life can be pure feeling.

When Casey comes out of the bathroom, naked and so gorgeous that she can't believe he's real, she finds herself asking, "Are you married?"

And he sits down on the bed and grins at her, shaking his head. "No."

"Do you have a girlfriend?"

"Not at the moment."

She considers these tidbits of very reassuring news, then: "Do you want to ask me something?"

"Will you stay?"

And so she does.

She doesn't call her parents until the day before she is supposed to return to Long Island. The week she spends with Casey only reinforces her decision to stay. He is kind and funny and, most astonishing of all, he finds reasons to be delighted at the offerings of the world. She wants to understand those reasons. She wants him to teach her to live in the moment and be happy.

She places the call when he isn't home. She has no confidence that the Isabelle who is Eli and Ruth's daughter won't be battered back into existence by the conversation she knows she is about to have with her parents. She doesn't want Casey to witness that transformation.

Her parents, each on a phone extension, are, of course, "shocked, simply shocked" that she isn't coming home, her mother furious and her father puzzled. She offers them little explanation beyond one sentence: "I found out that this is where I want to be." She knows if she offers specifics, if she tells them about Casey, arguments will follow. So she is cryptic and unmoving.

"I'd appreciate it if you'd send my clothes out, but if it's too much trouble, no worries."

"And where exactly should we ship them to, Isabelle? A P.O. box?" This from her mother.

"If you send them to Deepti's, that would be fine."

"So you're staying with Deepti?"

"No."

"Isabelle," her father pushes into the conversation, his voice tight with worry, "it doesn't sound like you've given any careful thought to this move. The best thing to do would be to come home, discuss it all with your mother and me, and then see what makes sense for you."

"I don't care what makes sense, I'm doing what I want."

"But—"

"No regrets, Dad."

And at that he is silent, but her mother isn't done. Not once have any of her children defied her in such an egregious way.

"Isabelle, people your age make all sorts of mistakes with their lives because they're flailing around. This is what happens the year after college."

"I'm not flailing."

"All right, but you're not thinking clearly, either, and you're too far away for me to figure it out for you. So come home tomorrow the way you planned and then we'll see."

"No," said simply again, without anger but also without equivocation. Her refusal hangs in the empty air between them. Then: "If it's too much trouble to send my clothes, forget it."

Her mother's voice is low and hard-edged. "I want to see you get off that plane at JFK tomorrow afternoon, Isabelle, do you hear me? And if you don't, don't bother to come home later."

"Ruth!" Eli is frankly shocked. "Your mother doesn't mean that."

"Don't tell me what I mean or don't mean."

"It sounds like you're telling your daughter she's not welcome to come home."

"She can come home tomorrow the way she's supposed to."

"But you're threatening her."

"Your poor choice of words, Eli, not mine."

And Isabelle has disappeared off the radar screen again. Eli and Ruth are at it, and Isabelle knows the trajectory of this fight will be like all the others. Quietly—she's not sure they've heard her—she says, "I'll be in touch." And she hangs up.

Her hands are shaking, but she is proud of herself. She didn't give in—a victory! Now the harder call: Nate.

She's ashamed of herself; that's what makes the call to Nate so much more difficult. Ashamed that she let this relationship continue on well past the time she wanted to be in it. Ashamed that it became a habit, a sort of annoying habit which was more trouble to stop than to continue. In that thoughtlessness, she understands now, she gave false hope. And the time has come: she's going to have to pay the price of her own cowardice.

Nate is disbelieving. Her precipitous move across the country is so unlike the Isabelle he's known since high school that he feels like he's talking to a stranger.

"You're doing what?" is the first thing he says after she tells him she's staying in Berkeley.

"Staying here. Not coming home—well, not coming back to Long Island."

"But you said you were coming down to D.C."

"No, Nate, you said I should come down. I never said I would."

There's silence on the line.

"You do that a lot. You assume what you want is what I want."

More silence. She can almost hear his brain twisting itself into knots trying to figure out what she is telling him.

"You're where you should be—in law school. And I'm where I should be—the Bay Area. And we should be separate."

She waits. He doesn't say anything.

"It's better."

"How is that better?" comes out of a strangled voice. "It's not better, Isabelle, it's not what we planned at all. It's a curveball thrown into the works and it fucks up everything."

"Your plans, you mean."

"Yes, my plans. Our plans."

"No, Nate, my plan is to stay right here."

They go round and round with this until finally Nate is screaming at her that the only explanation is that she's gone nuts! They made plans. They're practically engaged.

"No, we're not, Nate. I never said I'd marry you."

"You never said you wouldn't!"

"I'm saying it now."

And there's an intake of breath, as if suddenly he believes her, as if suddenly his whole world tilts on its axis.

"Why are you doing this to me?" It's a whine.

"You'll be better off. I promise you, Nate, in the long run, you will."

"Don't you condescend to me!"

"I'm sorry, Nate." And she is. Sorry for how long it took her. Sorry for letting him think what he wanted to think. Sorry for disrupting his plans. But not sorry for making the call. She puts the receiver gently back onto the phone and stares across the treetops to the bay and the city on the hills. And then it all hits her—a sharp slice of fear that cuts through her happiness. What has she done? Thrown away everything that kept her steady and anchored. And unhappy and dull, she reminds herself, but still her anxiety grows. Can she do this? Does she have the courage to grasp and hold what her heart wants?

Daniel. She'll e-mail Daniel. He saw her as a person with possibilities. He'll tell her she has a future. Somehow. Somewhere. Daniel.

CHAPTER SIX

D aniel Jablonski gets Isabelle's e-mail as he's packing up his campus office. Over the summer the board of trustees ousted John Liggins. The word around campus was that he should have spent as much time fundraising as he did raising the diversity profile of the school. With Liggins's departure came Daniel's notice that the Visiting Scholars' Program was being terminated. He was out of a job. And, not inconsequentially, a house.

"But where are we going to live?" Stefan's voice spirals upward into a twirl of anxiety. He has thrown in his lot with his father, and now it looks like they are being tossed out onto the street.

Daniel shrugs. This latest development has come as a complete surprise. Just getting through each day takes all of Daniel's concentration. Contemplating the future isn't even on his radar screen.

"You can always go back and live with your mother. All you have to do is get a job."

"That's not so easy! Why do you think that's easy?"

"Millions of people do it every day, Stefan," Daniel says reasonably, and that only ratchets up his son's panic.

"And maybe I don't want to go live with Mom! Maybe that's like . . . going back! Maybe I want to live with you!" Stefan spits these words at Daniel as they stand in the kitchen, his angry tone almost managing to eclipse the tender sentiment: *It's you I want.*

Daniel is struck once again by evidence of the anger running hard and deep beneath his son's seemingly benign exterior. Stefan will go weeks barely speaking, hardly interacting, treating Daniel as if he were an annoying impediment, and then suddenly, *boom!* An explosion of feeling, usually anger. It's like living in the middle of the siege of Sarajevo.

"You can stay with me," Daniel says calmly, "wherever I end up."

"But where?"

"I don't know right now, Stefan."

"But you have to! I don't want to end up in, like, a homeless shelter!"

"Really? My guess is even homeless people don't want to end up in a homeless shelter."

"Dad!" is fairly screamed at Daniel.

And then Daniel smiles, a small grin that lets Stefan know he is playing with him just a little, and it defuses the anger instead of escalating it.

"Okay," Stefan says, "I get it. Calm down."

"If we're lucky, I might just be able to find us somewhere to live."

But first Daniel has to pack up his campus office. He's been putting it off—that walk to campus—and Maintenance and Housekeeping has been reminding him daily, with less and less civility, of his responsibility to "vacate the premises."

Because he never put any effort into making his office comfortable or even serviceable, the packing up takes no time. A few books, the handful of acceptable pages of his woeful novel, his computer. It's as he opens his e-mail that he sees Isabelle's note, sent the day before.

Daniel,

I've done something completely out of character…

A good start, Daniel thinks as he sits down to read the rest. She needs to shake up her life. Maybe she has.

I went to visit my friend Deepti in the Bay Area, and I met a friend of her boyfriend's and decided to stay here and not go back to Long Island. I've known him for a week.

Daniel leans back in his desk chair and contemplates these last two sentences. He doesn't like them, but he doesn't know exactly why. Perhaps he's being parental, he tells himself, not happy that she's made such a precipitous decision based on a few days. As for the spark of jealousy fueling his disquiet, Daniel doesn't move in that direction.

But, oh Daniel, I've been suffocating all summer at home and I haven't been able to write at all. Now I will, I know it. Berkeley is an amazing place and Casey is this amazing guy who makes me feel capable of anything!

"Shit," Daniel says in his empty office, and he gets up and begins to pace the perimeter. She's having great sex. That's all it is. Well, of course, at her age, there's little else. He remembers great sex. He remembers he would do most anything at Isabelle's age to have it. He remembers feeling he had invented it. He must have. No one else could be experiencing what he was; otherwise, they'd be doing it twenty-four hours a day and the world would grind to a halt. So he understands, but he doesn't like hearing about it.

He makes himself sit down and finish reading the e-mail.

Now I can continue Melanie's story. Now I feel I can take all that you've given me and go forward and write. There's only one problem. And Daniel, you're the only one I can say this to—I'm terrified. Does all this make sense or am I being completely insane, as my parents have said?

Isabelle

Daniel hits Reply and then takes a minute to stare out his window. He will miss this view. The Chandler campus is beautiful, stately and very reminiscent of Old California—lacy jacaranda trees that bloom shocking lavender flowers in the spring, Engelmann oaks with ten-foot-tall camellia bushes in their shade, Mission Style buildings, gentle hills, and views to the ocean. He has no idea where he (and he supposes Stefan) will end up, but he has to address Isabelle's question first. He starts typing.

Isabelle,

Terrified isn't so bad. Terrified tells me you're taking a leap. Use those long, strong legs and jump.

Daniel

He hits Send, pleased with his response, and has a quick visual memory of the last time Isabelle marched into this office. The day was unbearably hot and she was wearing shorts. Her legs were gorgeous.

Enough of that, he tells himself as he sits back in his chair. He needs to be facing the very real question of what to do next. Is there someone, at some college, who will take him in? And then he sees Isabelle's response pop up in his in-box.

Daniel,

Terrified isn't so bad as long as it isn't "terrified to leave the house."

Daniel grins in his empty office. Okay, she's cheeky. She's called him on it. But there's more.

I don't want to be afraid. I know you don't either. What we would give to be free of it!

Isabelle

Oh, Isabelle—how does she manage to see into his soul so effortlessly? Because of course she's right. Fear has become his constant companion. When did it first show up? He remembers a boyhood laced with fear, but that was of a whole different order, that was fear with a clear cause.

His father, already disappointed with life by the time Daniel was born, had a temper, was a screamer, and Daniel and his older brother, Roman, would find ways to stay out of his path. They became practiced disappearing artists who slipped between houses, ran the alleys, hid out in the comfort of other people's families. This was the early 1950s, and everyone they knew in the Polish section of Erie, Pennsylvania, had lots of children. When Gus Jablonski was "in a mood," as Daniel's mother called it, his two sons would seek shelter at someone else's dinner table. And be welcomed.

But then, when Daniel was eight, there was his father's accident. A load of steel rebar. A surface slicked by overnight rain. One second with his mind elsewhere and Gus Jablonski slipped, crushing three lumbar vertebrae. The subsequent spinal fusion yielded only chronic pain. "An ironworker's lot," his father always said, still proud of his profession, the buildings they created, the bridges that stood only because some arrogant, foolhardy men were willing to put their bodies on the line for them.

After that, things got particularly bad at home. Some days Daniel would see his mother dressing his large, barrel-chested father the way she had dressed the boys when they were toddlers. There's the memory of Gus sitting on the edge of the bed, wincing, as his wife slowly guided each of his arms into its shirtsleeve. Next she would kneel in front of him, working the buttons of the shirt closed, buckling his belt, and tying his shoelaces. Sometimes Gus would place a hand on her head—in gratitude or subjugation, Daniel was never sure.

After the beginning months of false hope yielding little improvement, there were the years of frustration and fury, accompanied by bouts of drinking to dull the pain. Those were the years that Daniel practically lived at Benny Janusz's, his best friend's, house. The nights with Benny's family helped him weather the worst of Gus's alcohol-fueled despair. More times than not, when morning came and Daniel warily reentered his own cramped kitchen, he would find his father at the breakfast table, head down, reading the paper. And his mother always gentle, always there, calm now to match the calm in the kitchen. Something would have transpired during the night to make his father subdued and penitent. Even as a child, Daniel could tell the storm had blown over.

On those mornings, Roman, a grin on his face, would throw Daniel his catcher's mitt—"Let's go, Dan-de-lion!"—and the boys would escape into the neighborhood streets, sure to be able to scrounge up enough boys with a quick tour of the surrounding blocks to make their version of a baseball game. Suddenly all seemed right with the world. There was enthusiasm and silliness, the blessed release of physical exertion, and often happiness. So that was different, Daniel understands, because the fear didn't stick around. It didn't invade his very spirit.

But this fear that has taken up residence now is as much a part of his cellular being as his DNA. Daniel remembers it crept into his life surreptitiously around the time he was contemplating his fourth novel. The writing of it brought him no joy, and he had the nagging suspicion that it would fare no better than his third, which was roundly panned by the very same critics who had praised his first two.

He'd lost his gift, he realized. Lost his compass, which had been unerringly true. Lost the ability to write from a sacred place within him. Lost his way. That's when the fear began to seep in—when he didn't know in which direction to turn, when he married Cheryl on a desperate whim, hoping that her crazy life force might jolt him back to himself.

And then the fear just grew and spread like a malignancy. At first it showed up occasionally, attaching itself to public events like book readings, when there was still hope for his fourth book, or parties. Then it piggybacked onto whatever trip Daniel had to take. Getting on an airplane became agony. Braving crowded spaces like an airport or a mall or even a supermarket became next to impossible. Finally, when he landed at Chandler College and settled into his perfectly adequate rented house and campus office, he thought maybe familiarity and routine would beat it back into hiding, but no, the fear exhaled and spread out even further, across every mundane aspect of his life. Why? He doesn't know.

How do you combat something that won't show its face, something that won't stand up and declare itself, something that will only insinuate itself and slither soundlessly as it strangles the breath and twists the heart?

Daniel feels entirely defeated by this form of fear. *Terrified isn't so bad,* he wrote to Isabelle. Can't he be honest even with her? *Terrified is crippling.*

And that thought stops him cold—the word he chose, *crippling,* because the memory he has is of his father attempting to stand up straight, attempting to walk out of their house under his own power, existing only for the relief his pain medication would bring. "A cripple," self-declared when he was drunk and reveling in his own pathos.

Daniel picks up the phone. Anything's better than following that line of logic. He may have his own trouble leaving the house, but there's something he still can do. He can talk, schmooze, call in a favor without groveling. There must be some college somewhere that will take him in. It takes an afternoon of talking to people he used to know, but finally his phone calls lead him to Harry Axelrod, fellow failed novelist, former drinking buddy from his early years in New York, and current chair of the English Department at Colorado Plains College in Colorado Springs, wherever that is. Harry can offer him a spot for a semester—one of his teachers is out on maternity leave.

"Sold," says Daniel, grateful. He'll worry about the semester after that when it comes.

He tells Stefan they're moving to Colorado.

"How are you going to get there?" is his son's first question. "I mean physically get there."

"You'll drive me."

"Whoa! Road trip!"

"Exactly," Daniel says grimly, anticipating the fifteen hours alone in the car with his son as Stefan fairly dances around the room in anticipation of the same.

CHAPTER SEVEN

September melted into October, then November began, and Isabelle was afraid of the amount of happiness she felt. *Can this be real?* she asked herself at random quiet moments. Often, while watching Casey sleep beside her, sprawled on his stomach, his face stripped of all but his innate sweetness, she felt compelled to put the flat of her palm on his warm back in order to feel his breath flow into and out of his lungs. *Is this real?*

One early morning as they were hiking through the centuries-old redwoods of Muir Woods, Isabelle simply stopped, needing to look around her, needing to see so she could remember. Arrows of sunshine, shot from hundreds of feet above them, pierced the haze that clung to the tops of the trees. A living cathedral. Hushed. Simple.

"What is it?" Casey asked her.

"I need to remember how happy I am."

"Oh, baby," he said and took her hand, "there'll be lots more."

On a Sunday morning in early November, bundled in sweaters over pajamas, their feet in heavy wool socks propped up on the deck railing, sipping their morning coffee, waking up slowly, not a word being spoken, their eyes watching the fog lift across the bay, Isabelle felt it again—*Can this be real?*

Everything else had fallen away, and rather than feeling unmoored, she felt weightless, able to skim along air currents and never fall.

Casey was a revelation to her. The men she was used to talked and talked. They complained and needled and pugnaciously pursued arguments. Nate would never stop his relentless words until she had agreed that, yes, he had a point, yes, he had figured it all out. And her father, who had spent the summer constructing one long monologue, was always talking, always making his case, always needing her to listen. Even her brothers, whom she adored, created constant noise, shouting over each other, the twins in some kind of inexhaustible contest of one-upmanship since the day they could talk until Aaron, patient Aaron, would shout at them, "Shut up! Shut up! Shut up!"

Words all around her—male sounds, arguments, and grievances. The static of her life. But Casey could be quiet. He could use two words where others would need a paragraph. He would rather touch than talk. Suddenly life was quieter. Peace crept in and took up residence inside her, a tiny corner of stillness, and she was grateful.

What she didn't realize until it was too late was that there was a price to pay for all this tranquillity. There was a list of things Casey had neglected to mention—that he had no home, that they soon had to vacate this hilltop cottage they were living in, that he had no clue where he was going next. But more important, what he didn't tell her was that he could be whisked away in a heartbeat, out of the country, across the world for months at a time. He didn't talk about that possibility until the call came on November 15.

Of course Isabelle had asked Casey about his work. He was

proud to tell her about Global Hope, about how they were among the first responders when any disaster struck—when earthquakes devastated villages or hurricanes swept away houses or floods wiped out farmland or famine threatened children. The nonprofit was homegrown, started in Berkeley in the 1960s, when everyone believed they could make the world a better place. Casey believed it still, he told Isabelle. He believed in his obligation to do so.

"I was raised that way," he says simply one Sunday morning as they are making their way from their tree house down the hill, crossing College Avenue to Bancroft and then down to Goldman Field for one of Casey's soccer games.

As they walk, Casey has his duffel bag slung over his left shoulder and holds Isabelle's hand in his right. He doesn't continue. "I was raised that way" seems enough of an explanation for him.

But Isabelle wants to know more. "Your parents?" she prompts.

"My parents walk the walk," he says with a shrug. "My dad runs an alternative school in Oakland. Very progressive, sort of Montessoriesque without the dogma."

"And your mom?" Isabelle thinks quickly of her own mother, who had never been "well enough" to hold a job, the threat of a migraine always hovering somewhere behind her disillusioned eyes.

"She teaches English as a second language at a night school for migrant workers. During the day she lobbies for immigrants' rights."

"Wow," Isabelle says quietly, frankly intimidated. These people all do such good in the world. What has she or anyone in her large, extended, rowdy, raucous Rothman family done that approaches the good Casey's family does?

"On the other hand . . ." Casey adds with a grin, to let her know his next comments are meant benevolently, although Isabelle would have taken them that way. She hasn't experienced a moment yet of meanness or pettiness from Casey.

"You walk into their house and it's like you're having a flashback. I mean, you will see actual tie-dye and a framed Woodstock poster and a lava lamp in the bedroom. The sixties have never ended as far as my parents are concerned."

"But that's not a bad thing, is it, if they do such good in the world?"

"My sister, Mimi, thinks all three of us are embarrassing."

"She does?"

"Yep."

And Isabelle has to ask, "Because of the tie-dye?"

"She thinks we've drunk the Kool-Aid or something. That we're mouthing platitudes. Like we're as cringe-worthy as recycled clothes or something." He stops talking, and then the sly grin starts again and Isabelle has no idea what he's going to say next. "She married an investment banker. They live in Connecticut, and she voted for George H. W. Bush in the last election. My parents had apoplexy. I think that was the point."

When they reach the soccer stadium, Isabelle spots Deepti immediately. Although she sits demurely in the bleachers, hands folded in her lap, waiting for Isabelle and the game to begin, her aqua sari, the only pop of color amid the steel-gray slats, screams "Here I am!"

Casey seems to stand taller as they cross the grass field, to smile more broadly, to fill up with expectation. Isabelle can tell how eager he is for the game to start.

"I'll see you afterward," she tells him, preparing to slip away, to join Deepti and the scattering of spectators in the bleachers, but Casey grabs her wrist and brings her to him. They stand face-to-face, their bodies touching in all the right places, and Isabelle feels a surge of heat.

"Wish me luck?"

"Do you even need it?"

Casey puts his arms around her and kisses her with real hunger. And she kisses him back, her arms around his neck, her hands in his long blond hair, matching his eagerness. She doesn't care who sees. And then they smile at each other, because they share the only secret worth having in the whole world—that love is wonderful!

"Now we'll win," he tells her.

Isabelle, with Deepti beside her, settles in to watch the teams play. Paying attention is serious business for both women, and their eyes never leave the field. They might miss something otherwise—a play, a clue about their men, a secret revealed only through the immediacy of the game.

"How constant he is," Deepti murmurs as Sadhil blocks his second goal attempt.

"Yes," Isabelle agrees. "Sadhil was made to be a goalie." To stand and protect.

"And how fast Casey is," Deepti adds, to be evenhanded.

"Exactly!" That's what Isabelle wants—the thrill in her blood as she watches Casey fly down the field as if his life depended on his team's next goal.

After the game, which the Berkeley Breakers win by a score of 1–0, Sadhil as proud of his stops as Casey is of passing for their one goal, the two couples walk to the Indian Oven Café, a few blocks away on Shattuck, for an early dinner.

It is only on these Sunday nights that Isabelle feels the least bit in touch with the rest of the world. As they walk, she's reminded that there are other people talking, laughing, pushing their children in strollers, going about their lives—the rest of humanity she hasn't given even a fleeting thought to in the intervening week. They pass a copy store, a Laundromat, a small grocery with pears and apples mounded in symmetrical piles out front, an Italian bakery closing for the night. Making a left turn at the corner newsstand, Isabelle catches glimpses in the Sunday papers of the fallout from the congressional elections. Newt Gingrich and his "Contract with America" had swept Republicans into the majority in both houses. Bill Clinton's policies had been repudiated, but right now, in this bubble she's living in, Isabelle isn't interested. Casey has his arm around her shoulders. She's watching his animated face as he and Sadhil recap the game they just won. There's a whole world in that lovely sunburned face.

Deepti and Sadhil, Hindu and vegetarian, order eggplant bharta, dal makhani, naan, and aloo gobi. Isabelle orders tandoori chicken for Casey and herself. She's learned that Casey will eat anything, or rather, that he doesn't care what he eats. Many days, she now knows, he would forget to eat if she didn't remind him, or he'd have cereal for dinner, standing up in the kitchen, shoveling it into his mouth quickly so he can get on to something much more interesting—a movie they want to see, or a friend who's playing at a coffeehouse in Oakland, or the 49ers game on TV. Anything to do with sports takes precedence over eating.

So Isabelle has begun to cook for him, something she did for Nate but only with a secret resentment. With Casey it feels as natural as waking up next to him each morning and curling into his body to fall asleep at night. The two of them in an effortless rhythm, Isabelle has come to feel, of give-and-take that forms a perfect circle, smooth and continual and impenetrable.

At dinner, Casey and Sadhil talk about their Global Hope trips. It's the only time Casey builds paragraphs of long sentences leading to the next paragraph, as though the ardor he feels for his work fuels his tongue.

Isabelle listens as Casey explains how he and Sadhil

met—on a mission to Erzincan, Turkey, in 1992 after a 6.9-magnitude earthquake had killed hundreds and injured thousands and created 50,000 homeless people.

"All across the city there was nothing but concrete rubble, some pieces as big as this table, piled up on top of each other. Apartment houses, office buildings, so we knew there were people underneath all that, but we didn't have much equipment. This was less than forty-eight hours after the quake."

"Everywhere you looked, men were pulling at the boulders with their bare hands," Sadhil adds.

"I was working at this four-story apartment building that had been totally destroyed. You couldn't even see what the building had once been."

"There was snow on the ground. It was so cold," Sadhil interjects, "and these men didn't have gloves or shovels or any kind of equipment. Just their bare hands. And they were bloodied and raw and nobody cared, they just kept digging. Casey was right beside them."

"And then I heard it, or I thought I heard it." Casey takes over the telling. "A faint sort of moaning coming from somewhere underneath all that debris."

"A child," Sadhil says.

Deepti looks at Isabelle, her expression suddenly troubled—a child buried alive in stone.

"We started to open up a small hole where we thought we had heard the sounds. It seemed to take forever, but we had to be careful. We didn't want to start a slide." Casey shakes his head as he remembers, not liking what he's about to say.

Isabelle's breath catches—she doesn't want the child to be dead, but Casey's face, as he remembers, is somber.

"We unearthed a hand. A tiny hand, the whole thing smaller than half my palm." He shows them his palm so they can envision just how tiny the hand was. Then he continues the telling.

"It didn't move. The men were talking to the child in Turkish, but we heard nothing back, and the hand didn't reach for us or grab on. And my heart dropped. We had taken too long. We had been too careful. A minute sooner, maybe thirty seconds. When did the child stop moaning? It was impossible to know."

Both men are silent. In their memory, they are back in that rubble as Casey reached into the hole and brought out the limp body of a three-year-old boy. Impossibly dirty, dried blood covering half his face. Absolutely still.

"He was dead?" Isabelle whispers, terrified of the answer.

"We pulled him out dead," Casey confirms.

"No . . ." from Deepti, a soft moan.

"And then this guy here"—and Casey grins at Sadhil—"comes from I don't know where . . ."

"From the other side of that pile of rubble," Sadhil adds.

"And he checks the kid's pulse, puts two fingers on his carotid artery, and starts breathing air into the kid's body. He's calm—you should have seen him, so calm—and he forces life back into that boy. Really, he brings him back from the dead."

And Casey sits back in his seat, pleased with the story, pleased to be able to present Sadhil to the women as the hero Casey believes him to be.

"That's how we met," Sadhil says, modest, matter-of-fact.

When they're alone, Isabelle asks more questions about Casey's missions. She wants to understand this part of his life. And he tells her, but they seem like stories of people and places so far away, so peripheral to the immediacy of their lives, because here Casey is, naked beside her in bed, stroking her skin, or beside her in his Jeep, driving with his hand on her thigh as they travel north to Mount Tamalpais State Park, or here is Casey with her in their secluded tree house as they build a fire in the living room fireplace and stretch out on the rug and undress each other and move into that unreal space where everything they do to and for each other is right. So she can delay comprehension, refuse to understand what his commitment to Global Hope means for her.

And then there is a 7.1-magnitude earthquake which creates a tsunami which devastates Mindoro Island, part of the Philippines, and Casey has to go.

It's as if he's vanished off the face of the earth. That's how Isabelle feels. There is no way to get in touch with him once he's on Mindoro. Seven hundred and ninety-seven houses have been totally destroyed, 3,288 have been damaged, 19 bridges have been washed out. The power supply throughout the province has been cut off, and the power barge of the National Power Corporation was washed away by the oversized waves.

Isabelle knows all this because she has been watching CNN obsessively in the hope of catching a glimpse of Casey amid the raging floodwater, the rivers of cars and trees and parts of houses that pour over the land. The network runs the same loop of grainy footage over and over and repeats the same disaster scorecard, because that's all it has.

Isabelle has even less. Casey left so quickly they barely said good-bye. Once he got the call from Lester Hoffman, the head of Global Hope, Casey was a laser beam focused on stuffing his backpack with underwear and making the 5:47 plane out of San Francisco airport. She watched and stayed out of his way. She'd never seen him so single-minded and so closed off.

He kissed her good-bye as they pulled up at the airport curb and told her he loved her and then was out of the Jeep and gone before she could say, "I love you, too."

She went home to their tree house, which felt startlingly empty, and turned on the TV and never turned it off until she heard a key in the front door five days later.

She is in her pajamas, wrapped in a blanket she took from their bed, huddled on the living room sofa even though it is the middle of the morning, watching CNN in the faint hope that it will report something new. Since Casey left she hasn't felt well, as if she is coming down with the flu, but she reasons that it is only loss—the absence of the body and spirit of the person who had sheltered her and nourished her and led her into the light.

And suddenly a small, tidy man is standing in the doorway. He is maybe five feet five or so, impeccably dressed: expensive wool slacks, a cashmere sweater, a beautifully tailored black trench coat draped with an alpaca scarf in subtle shades of plum. His salt-and-pepper hair is cut close to his head, and his face, with its small, regular features, is distinguished only by deep bruises of exhaustion under his eyes. He has two large suitcases with him and looks astonished to see Isabelle there, as astonished as Isabelle is to see him.

After surveying the rest of the room, the man sighs, as if he has figured it out. "Casey?" he asks.

Isabelle points to the screen, to the footage of toppled buildings and flooded streets. "There's been an earthquake and tsunami in the Philippines."

The man sits down on the nearest chair. "I heard."

"That's where he is."

"And he didn't tell you I was coming home today." It's not a question.

"He left so suddenly, you know. The phone call came and he was gone. I'm sure he would have if—"

"Right," the man says, without much conviction. And then he looks at Isabelle, really looks at her, and she grabs the blanket around herself more closely.

"Orson Pratt," he tells her.

"Isabelle Rothman. I'm a friend of Casey's."

"I figured." Then: "Well, this is awkward."

"No, no." Isabelle gets up from the couch, clicks off the TV, trails the blanket as she quickly moves out of the room. Orson winces as she drags it, bites his tongue so he doesn't bark at her to pick up the end, for God's sake. "I'll be out of here in five minutes," she says as she makes her way into the bedroom and closes the door.

Orson sighs again. With Casey there's always one surprise or another.

Isabelle surveys the bedroom and is overcome with embarrassment. It's a wreck—the bed unmade, clothes everywhere, plates of half-eaten food. She's lived here and in the living room since Casey left, trailing morosely between the two rooms. Now she sees it with Orson's eyes and she's frankly horrified. If she were the owner of this house and in her right mind, as Orson seems to be, she'd be furious.

The owner of the house walks into the kitchen and averts his eyes; nobody's cleaned up for days. It must be the girl. The last time Casey house-sat for him, he had the decency to clean and spruce and leave the house spotless.

He pushes up the sleeves of his cashmere sweater, turns on the water, starts to rinse the dishes and load the dishwasher. It's the last thing he wants to do. He's been on a fifteen-hour flight from Rome and he wants a hot shower and a long nap.

In the bedroom, Isabelle packs like one of the three Furies, flinging everything she owns into her one suitcase and cramming it shut. Luckily, her mother never sent her clothes—one more dramatic show of anger from Ruth: *You choose to defy me, you cannot have anything that resides in this house, including my love.* Isabelle hasn't spoken with her mother since that unpleasant phone call home to announce that she was staying in the Bay Area. She's called her father at work several times, but she hasn't given him the phone number at the house. She doesn't have any confidence that he wouldn't bend under pressure and divulge it to her mother.

Now Isabelle is glad her mother has been so vengeful. There's so much less to pack. She looks around the room in distress. What to do with all of Casey's things? He's lived here far longer, and his clothes and shoes and soccer balls and papers for work and his hiking boots and his yoga mat and his general *stuff* is everywhere. She does the best she can. She piles up everything of his neatly in a corner of the room. She strips the bed of their sheets—this last act like peeling off a layer of her own skin—and remakes it with fresh linens. There, that looks a little better.

When she sees Orson in the kitchen, washing her dishes, she's mortified. "Please," she says as she stands in the doorway, dirty plates in one hand, suitcase in the other, laptop in its case slung over her shoulder, "let me clean up the kitchen before I go."

Orson shuts off the water, finds a towel to dry his hands, and turns slowly to look at her. "The best thing you can do," he tells her as he takes the plates from her hand and adds them to the pile next to the sink, "is just go." He wants his house to himself. He wants her to disappear.

She nods; there's nothing to say to that. And she turns and walks across the living room, toward the front door, when he adds one more sentence. He can't help it. "And if I were you, I'd ask Casey why he didn't tell you that I was coming home today."

"Oh, because it was all so sudden——" Isabelle begins.

"He knew that." Orson cuts her off, too tired for politeness. "He's been doing this work for years, this relief work, and he left you holding the bag, young lady." And Orson turns away from her, back to the sink, back to the dishes and the pots that have to be scrubbed, and Isabelle opens the front door and is gone.

It's only when she hits College Avenue that she realizes she doesn't know where she's going. The only person she knows is Deepti, but she's in San Francisco. There's nobody on this side of the bay, and she can't go into the city; she can't be that far away. *From what?* she asks herself. Well, from Casey when he returns. And then another slap of recognition: he won't have any way to contact her. He had the phone number at the house, but that's all. Wherever she ends up, he won't know.

And that realization causes her to sink down to the curb, at the intersection of College and Durant, as the gravity of the situation settles in: she's homeless and alone and has no way to get in touch with Casey.

There's too much to figure out, so sitting on the curb, her suitcase beside her, idly watching the hordes of students pass her on their way to class is the most she can manage. Nobody takes much notice of her. She looks like she could be one of them, a Berkeley student who's stopped for a minute or is waiting for a friend. It's the suitcase at her side and perhaps the look of hopelessness on her face that prompt a boy riding a skateboard down the incline that is Durant Avenue to yell at her as he whizzes by, "The hotel's one block down!" and he's gone.

Isabelle cranes her neck and there it is—the Hotel Durant, an old stone building on the corner of Bowditch and Durant. It even has a long vertical sign on the edge of the building with the word *HOTEL* spelled out from top to bottom in very large white letters against a slate-blue background. A hotel! A place she can stay until she figures out her next move.

When given a choice at the front desk, she chooses a room on the fifth floor so she can look out across the beautiful Berkeley campus and maybe capture some of the lightness she felt when she and Casey were cocooned in their tree house.

And then she falls asleep. She's exhausted. The last two months have been the happiest of her life, but they've also worn her out. All that defying her parents' expectations, her own reticence—a history that reads to her now like a playbook for misery. This, all that she's experienced with Casey, is life full to the brim.

It's when she wakes up, just as the Campanile is striking four o'clock, that she immediately realizes she has to go back to Orson Pratt's house. Now that she has found a place to stay, she has to give him the number so he can give it to Casey.

She arrives at Orson's door with an enormous bundle of flowers, winter blooms bought at a shop on Telegraph Avenue—giant snapdragons with stems two feet long, magenta stock with the musty smell she loves so much, interspersed with sprays of prickly pink Australian heather, all cushioned by shiny green leaves and wrapped in clear cellophane, finished off with a purple bow. She knocks and waits and no one comes. She knocks again with the same result. Just as she's laying the flowers down on the doorstep, her note of apology tucked into the foliage, Orson opens the door. He's wearing a silk robe over bare feet and white shins and looks furious to be awake.

"Oh, no." Isabelle is dismayed that yet again, despite her best intentions, she's annoyed him. "I woke you. I'm so sorry. I just . . . well, take the flowers and go back to sleep." And she puts the bouquet in his arms and starts down the stairs.

"Is that all?" he finally says to her retreating back. "The flowers?"

And she turns around slowly. "Well, no, actually, it was to bring you the flowers, yes. To apologize, really, there's a note in there . . ." She comes back up the steps and fishes the small white card out of the mass of flowers, shows it to him so he won't miss it. "But also . . . I wrote down the number of where I'm staying—it's on the back of the card—in case Casey calls. Do you think you could give it to him?"

"All right," he says. His voice is weary.

Isabelle wants to add, *Promise me you won't forget*, but of course she doesn't. Instead she adds, "As soon as they have some phone lines up on Mindoro, I'm sure he'll call."

Orson stares at her. "How long have you known Casey?"

"About two months."

"So you've never been through one of his trips?"

"No."

"They can take a long time." He puts it as delicately as he knows how. He's not a delicate person.

"I would suppose."

She's not quite sure what he's getting at. And he sees that, sees that she's not processing what he's trying to tell her, and he sighs. There's something compelling about this girl. She looks so lost and so hopeful at the same time.

He sits down on his doorstep, wraps the silk robe around his legs, puts the flowers down next to him. "There's always a flood somewhere or a hurricane or another earthquake or a famine that's reached the tipping point."

Isabelle sits down next to him on the step, folding her long legs under her, settling in. He seems to be inviting her to talk about Casey, and she wants nothing more in the world than to do that. She hungers to do that. "That's why I admire what he does so much. There's all this need and he doesn't just brush it aside. I mean, some people give money when there's a natural disaster, but really, how much effort does that take? And then there's Casey, who sees a crisis and is there!"

"Every time," Orson says pointedly.

"Yes! He's amazing, isn't he?"

Orson nods grimly and stands, the flowers in his arms. "There was no need, but thank you for these."

Isabelle stands with him, suddenly realizing that she towers over him, both of them awkward now. "I'll just go."

He nods, then watches her make her way down the railroad-tie steps. She's almost skipping until she stops midway down the staircase and turns to him. "You won't forget?" She couldn't stop herself from asking.

Orson shakes his head: no, he won't. If Casey ever calls, he'll tell him where Isabelle is.

CHAPTER EIGHT

Daniel surveys the faces of the students in his creative writing seminar, English 452 in the catalog, and despairs. None is Isabelle's. Of the nine people sitting around the worn conference table in Room 17A of Holmes Hall (named after Julia Archibald Holmes, the first woman to climb Pike's Peak, in 1858) on the campus of Colorado Plains College, eight look bored and the remaining one looks terrified.

Corinne Berlinger, in honor of the upcoming holiday Sunday, wears a red sweatshirt with Christmas bells ringing across her chest and the words to "Jingle Bells" floating beneath in wavy script. She's the terrified one. He's giving the class back their final stories today, and she seems to be the only one who cares what he thinks of them. Too bad she writes like an inferior Hallmark card. She's not going to be happy with his comments.

The rest of the students have placed their backsides on their chairs in the spirit of doing time, like prisoners on a lengthy sentence. And none of them can write, either. Daniel chalks up the lack of talent to the preponderance of military bases in the Colorado Springs area—Peterson Air Force Base, Fort

Carson, Falcon Air Force Base. He's sure that the present or former military personnel who somehow end up in his classes haven't the imagination to write creatively. That was his prejudice before the semester started and that's his conclusion now as the semester limps toward its finish.

Daniel knows he should be grateful for this teaching job. He was desperate when he accepted it, but right now, after three months of reading his students' work, he'd prefer to put a gun to his head than continue on. But he has to. He's been offered a second semester, and since he has no alternative, he gave himself a stern talking to and found the appropriate answer: "I'd be glad to."

And then there's Stefan, who has stuck to him like flypaper, flapping around him constantly, never leaving him alone the way he used to when they lived in Los Angeles. It's as if the drive to Colorado cemented some kind of attachment for his son that he'd been missing for the twenty-one years Daniel was absent from his life. *You always pay for your mistakes,* Daniel reminds himself. And now he's paying for abandoning his two children as part of his first divorce.

Of course Stephanie was furious at him when he first left her. And when she kept the kids away as punishment, he wasn't surprised. Even before the separation, his wife had watched the undeniable connection he and five-year-old Alina shared with a jaundiced eye. "Two peas in a pod," Stephanie would say with alarm, as if it were a problem that had to be solved. Stefan, three years younger, Stephanie kept close to her before Daniel left—almost in counterbalance—and even closer after.

But he could have demanded to see them, could have stayed in Erie and fought for that right. Maybe even hired an attorney. Another man, a better man, would have. But he didn't. He escaped to New York, where he could pretend to be someone else, a promising young writer, and never looked back. The least he can do is be honest about his own culpability. He chose the path of least resistance years ago, selfishly, and now he has Stefan mooning over him, trying to make up for all the years of drought.

And mistake number two: never finishing his much-maligned, rarely-worked-on novel in progress so he has to make his living teaching these Colorado dolts. Oh, where is Isabelle when he needs her cheeky attitude, her *engagement?* Still in Berkeley, he supposes, although he has no way of knowing, because once she announced via e-mail that she was having great sex, her communications with Daniel ceased.

Well, that tells you something, Daniel admonishes himself, *about just where you fit on the sliding scale of important people in her life.*

So instead of Isabelle's eager face in front of him, he has Corinne Berlinger and her jingle-bell sweatshirt and eight other faces that could be mug shots for terminal boredom.

Of course, when he's not facing these nine objectionable faces, he wonders if the fault might be in him. How do you teach writing when you don't believe writing can be taught? That's the dilemma. That's probably at the root of the problem, more than the sort of students he has before him. The blame, Daniel confesses to himself in his solitary moments, in all likelihood is his. But the result is the same: his students don't want to be here and he doesn't want to be, either. Pitiful. He's landed himself in a pitiful situation.

"There are two grades on your papers," Daniel tells his class as he passes back the short stories, "one for the story and the one underneath is your class grade. If you want to discuss either, you know my office hours—Fridays from two to four, although I suspect that most of you will be on your way home for Christmas by tomorrow afternoon." Daniel grins at his students. "It almost seems like I planned it that way." But not a one smiles back at him. Nobody is interested in his small joke. Isabelle would have responded. She would have tilted her head to her left shoulder, a small grin playing at the corners of her lips; on to him, understanding immediately his desire not to discuss grades ever, at any time. He hates summing people up by a letter. She knows that.

But none of these students understand irony. *Oh, kill me now*, Daniel thinks as the members of English 452 push back their chairs, gather their backpacks and puffy down jackets, and leave the room without looking at him. Only Corinne has something to say.

"Merry Christmas, Mr. Jablonski."

"You, too, Corinne."

"I'm going to look at my grade after Christmas. I do that with all my grades, because there's the chance, you know, that they might ruin my holiday."

Daniel nods. He thinks that's a good idea. He should say something encouraging to her, he knows, even if it's a lie. It's the holiday season after all—"Good will to all" and the rest of those sentiments. But he can't. She's a nice girl but a terrible writer, and he can't bring himself to lie. She leaves empty-handed, empty-hearted, and he knows it and she knows it.

It occurs to him as Stefan walks him home across the campus, past the many massive red brick buildings, that he has become an even lesser version of himself. More judgmental, grumpier, far less hopeful than he was that last semester at Chandler, when he had Isabelle's visits to look forward to once a week and her ever-evolving and finally lovely prose.

The two men are bundled against the Colorado cold. It's the week before Christmas and the gray sky promises snow that may or may not get there—the weather so unpredictable every season of the year here. The temperature is plunging as the day wanes, and both wear heavy jackets and wool scarves wound around their necks and hats in deference to the stiff wind. The trees are leafless and stark against the rapidly darkening sky, and Daniel wishes briefly and intensely for the bright, warm Southern California December days when the light is sharp-edged and challenging and the temperature might reach 80 degrees, even in the depths of winter. Better to count his steps than wish for what he cannot have, and so Daniel does. He puts his attention on his heavy boots as they crackle the brittle leaves underfoot and take him closer to the one place he can draw a real breath: his apartment.

At his side, Stefan chatters nonstop. He's taken to having opinions about everything, and he gestures widely and often, flinging his arms out, a maestro conducting an imaginary orchestra. It's as if the majesty of the Rocky Mountains edging the skyline to the west and the vast high plains to their east have translated into an expansiveness in Stefan's attitude. Gone is the sullen kid who showed up on his doorstep in L.A., the one who could spend days not talking, then explode into bursts of anger and accusation. Now Daniel is living with Arsenio Hall—glib, hyper, relentless.

Although Stefan can't quite put all the pieces together to explain why he feels so much better living in Colorado, he knows it has something to do with his dad. Daniel needed him to drive across the deserts of California and Nevada and up the six thousand feet onto the plain where "the Springs" is located. And his dad relies on him to do anything that happens outside their apartment—go to the market, the bank, walk to campus, pick up dinner most nights. Although Stefan wouldn't use the word, it is accurate to say that he feels competent for the first time in his life. And he has convinced himself that he is crucial to his father's well-being. "Let's face it," Stefan has even said to Daniel, "where would you be without me?"

And although Daniel felt the accurate answer to that question was, "With maybe some peace and quiet in my life," he didn't, of course, say it. Instead he replied with as much equanimity as he could muster. "I don't know, Stefan. Up shit's creek without a paddle, I guess." And Stefan grinned, delighted.

Their only bone of contention is the fact that Stefan still hasn't managed to get himself a job in Colorado, either. *But I have a job,* Stefan thinks but doesn't say. *I take care of you.* Instead he tries to be practical.

"Yeah, but Dad, your schedule is so, like, erratic. I couldn't really work a job around your comings and goings to campus. You've got three classes and they meet on different days, at different times, and then there are your office hours and—"

"Erratic?" Daniel is amused by Stefan's choice of word.

"Yeah, you know, like not the same every day."

"I know what *erratic* means, Stefan. I'm just surprised you do."

And Stefan is stung, hurt, and Daniel sees it and tries to backtrack.

"It's just not the sort of word you normally use."

"You think I'm stupid, don't you?"

"No," Daniel says slowly, although he's not sure he's answering honestly. "I think you have untapped potential." It's the kindest thing he can think of to say about his son.

"Yeah, I do." Stefan is practically glowing. "I've got untapped potential."

They reach their apartment just as the twilight disappears into night. It's in a squat brick building four blocks from campus, constructed over a hundred years ago. Square, utilitarian, the architecture far less interesting than the elaborate brick buildings on campus, bleak now that the trees which surround the perimeter are lifeless and bare, but Daniel doesn't care. For him it is a fortress where he can be safe from the dread that accompanies him anywhere outside its strong walls.

All Daniel wants now is to be inside his little piece of it, his small, badly furnished, barely clean apartment. Tonight, as Stefan pushes the button for the elevator, Daniel finds he can't even wait for the old and lumbering machine to descend to the lobby.

"Taking too long," he throws over his shoulder as he makes for the stairs, and Stefan immediately turns and follows, concerned because most days Daniel is able to wait.

"Is it bad today, Dad?"

Daniel doesn't answer. He's concentrating on scaling the last set of stairs and flinging open the door to the third-floor hallway.

"Dad?"

Daniel is fumbling with his keys, struggling to open the door to their apartment. There's no way he's answering Stefan. There! He's in, his son behind him watching with worried eyes as Daniel attempts to slow his breathing to a normal level. Stefan has become an expert at reading body language and nonverbal cues that tell him what his father refuses to—how he's doing, how consumed he is by his own panic.

"Stop hovering," Daniel manages to say.

Stefan takes the hat off Daniel's head. "Give me your coat." And his father complies. "Now your scarf."

But Daniel is halfway down the hall. Stefan knows where he's going: into his bedroom, where he's set up his desk, where his computer is, where somehow Daniel feels he can breathe.

Okay, Stefan knows he's got maybe half an hour before Daniel comes out of his room, calmer, ready for a beer and the dinner that Stefan has to go out and get. He does so most nights without a murmur of protest. He likes walking the streets. That's his newest occupation during the days, and almost every day he ends up at the High Plains Ice Hall. Sitting high up in the bleachers, Stefan watches the Olympic ice skating hopefuls who come from all over the world to train there. For hours on end he doesn't move until she—Mitsuko Kita—skates onto the ice. It's only then that Stefan makes his way closer to the rink so he can watch her spin and swoop and jump and glide with a grace he finds mesmerizing. Often he's late to pick up his father because he can't tear his eyes away from her tiny figure on the vast white ice—so singular, so determined, and so vulnerable all at once. Stefan feels he could watch her forever.

That's his skill, he's decided. He's a watcher. He notices everything. Every wrong turn of a shoulder, every tight twirl that lasts a split second too long, every toe pick that is an inch off its intended target. He's taken to bringing a notebook with him and recording all Mitsuko's triumphs and mistakes, day by day. He has no idea what he'll do with the results, but his note-taking increases his pleasure in watching and so he continues.

Of course he hasn't told his father what he does with his days. He knows him well enough now to know Daniel would have something harsh to say—something about voyeurism, about time wasted, about one more detour Stefan has chosen instead of the right road to success. Especially if Stefan told him that some days, when he can't stop himself, he follows Mitsuko through the streets of town as she walks home beside her coach, a ramrod-straight Japanese man in his fifties. Every day the older man talks to her during the walks, rapidly, sometimes hitting the palm of one hand with the fist of the other as he explains a point. The young girl listens respectfully, her head dipped in deference, nodding from time to time.

Stefan doesn't like this interaction at all. It verges on something unsavory to him, and so he walks behind and makes sure Mitsuko arrives safely at her apartment. Only when her coach leaves her there and continues on, only when the glass front door of the building closes behind the tiny skater and Stefan considers her safely inside, only then does he move on.

Stefan keeps this private pleasure to himself—the watching, the note-taking, the following. He's not hurting anyone, is he? And maybe sometime he could even present Mitsuko with his notes. They might help her. They might even add to the likelihood that she will make the Olympic team in 1998, the Nagano Games. That's all he wants. To be some kind of help.

On this Thursday night, the pregame show is on for the Denver Nuggets, and Stefan settles himself on the living room couch, a beer in hand, to prepare for the game, which will fill his evening. The play-by-play guy, Drew Goodman, is talking about their rookie guard, Jalen Rose, first-round pick out of the University of Michigan. The Nuggets' record is nothing to write home about, perched at the break-even mark, but this Rose guy is going to be good, Stefan thinks. He can't wait for the game to start so he can watch him. Maybe his dad will do delivery tonight so he can watch the whole game without interruption. Yeah, that would be sweet—the Nuggets game, another beer, Chinese food from the Lotus Blossom, and Stefan would be set. He easily acknowledges to himself, if not to his father, that he's happier than he's been in a long time.

Daniel, in his bedroom, sits upright in his desk chair and breathes deeply. Some doctor somewhere, when he was still consulting doctors about his condition, told him he might be able to quiet the panic attacks by deep breathing. It doesn't work, but Daniel, in desperation each time one hits, tries it anyway. He has no other solution.

As a distraction he turns on his computer and scrolls through the in-box of his e-mail. Ruthlessly he deletes every message without a familiar name. Some of the deletions could be students whose names he never bothered to learn, but he hasn't the patience to open each one to find out. And then, in the midst of the spam about refinancing your home and enhancing your penis, he finds Isabelle's e-mail. The subject line is "Merry Christmas," and so he almost deletes it. But he doesn't. He recognizes her e-mail address and opens it instead.

Daniel,

I don't know where you are but that's the beauty of e-mail. I don't have to know in order to write to you. I'm thinking of you and hoping that you will have a happy Christmas. My life has taken an unexpected turn. I'm trying to see it as a positive, but I have to confess (especially to you, since I only tell you the truth) that it's a struggle. I hope you're not alone this holiday season. It's the time for family, isn't it? And I hope you have someone with you.

Isabelle

What a melancholy Christmas message. So different from her last e-mails to him, in September, when she seemed to be flying high with optimism and fervor. It's probably the guy, he thinks. He probably dumped her. That's what it sounds like to him. The "unexpected turn" part of her message. And the worry that he not be alone, as she probably is.

Well, that's what happens in your twenties. You often make a mess of things. He certainly did. Marrying Stephanie because she was available and there and wanted to marry him. Having two children he wasn't ready to raise. Drinking too much, working construction, on a path to copy his old man's miserable existence. Desperate. And then finally, when he hit thirty, beginning to write, a decision that saved his life. Too bad the writing can't save his life now.

He should tell Isabelle some of this, he thinks, but how to

say it so he doesn't sound condescending? And she didn't ask for advice. Maybe he should just wish her a merry Christmas and be done with it.

But he doesn't want to be done with it. He wants her back in his life, with all the attitude and sauciness and appreciation she brought to him. He wants to matter to someone.

He hits Reply and begins his e-mail. His breathing slows, his panic recedes.

Isabelle,

I'm in Colorado Springs, Colorado, teaching a bunch of dolts. There isn't one student who can hold a candle to you. My son, Stefan, is with me and he can't find a job in Colorado either, although to be fair, taking charge of his old man, as he seems to be doing, could be described as a full-time job.

What happened to that guy you met? The one you wrote me about the last time, who convinced you to stay in Berkeley?

Daniel thinks about that last paragraph. Is that overstepping some invisible line? Does he have the right, the standing even, to ask her that? He stares out his bedroom window as he ponders. There's another brick building right next door. Nothing to look at. Nothing to help him decide. Oh, what the hell—he wants to know the answer to his question, so he's going to leave it right there. She can answer it or not. It's up to her.

I hope the Bay Area has turned out to be the place that encourages you to write. Don't let your gift slip through your fingers.

Merry Christmas,
Daniel

And he hits Send before he can reread it and delete the question he's dying to have answered.

Almost immediately he gets Isabelle's response.

Daniel,

There's been a 7.1-magnitude earthquake and subsequent tsunami in the Philippines and Casey is there saving lives.

Isabelle

Well, that doesn't tell him what he wants to know, but Daniel leaves it there, already a little embarrassed he asked the question in the first place. Too revealing. Her life has moved on. She's involved with a guy who sees himself as a hero. Why does Daniel think she'd want anything to do with an old, broken-down writer who can't even save one life—his own?

CHAPTER NINE

Isabelle rented half a bungalow in the flats of Oakland with the last of her summer salary, eking out just enough to cover first and last month's rent and the security deposit. She found an old wooden house on Marston Street, built in the 1920s and reconfigured into two side-by-side apartments sometime after that. With its requisite low-pitched, gabled roof and horizontal wood siding, it is a perfect example of the California Craftsman Style which peppers the state. Each unit has its own small front porch held up by stone pedestals. That was the selling point for Isabelle, that quaint front porch with its white wooden railing, sitting four wide steps up from the street.

The living room overlooks the porch and has a large fixed window bordered by two smaller double-hung windows that open from the top and bottom. There is an eat-in kitchen with a window along the driveway, two small bedrooms, and a pink-and-black–tiled bathroom on the other side of the house. Isabelle and the tenant in the other unit, Mrs. Hershfeld, share the backyard, but so far Isabelle has seen her neighbor only when she hobbled out to hang a few pieces of hand-washed underwear on the ancient clothesline positioned behind the garage.

"It's for you, too," the older woman called as she struggled up the back stairs, her shockingly bright orange hair set in curlers, a cigarette packed into a lip so she can use both hands to haul herself onto the back stoop. Isabelle waved from her bedroom window, the one that overlooks the backyard, and smiled. They hadn't yet formally introduced themselves, but Mrs. Hershfeld wasn't standing on any ceremony. She wanted Isabelle to know she was welcome to hang her dripping intimates on the two skinny, sagging lines.

It took Isabelle about a week at the Hotel Durant without any sort of communication from Casey to realize she'd better make some decisions on her own.

I have to find us somewhere to live—that's how she thought about it, without ever discussing it with Casey. *Where can the two of us live?* The classic bungalow on Marston, much rented but still adorable as far as Isabelle was concerned, would do perfectly.

Once her telephone service has been activated, Isabelle makes her way back up the hill to Orson Pratt's house to give him the new, and now permanent, number. She knows she could simply call and deliver the information, but there's a pull toward that house. She was so happy there. Bits and pieces of her life with Casey still reside there. She decides to walk up the hill. Seeing it all again, being there, will reinforce the necessary belief that it was all real.

Isabelle is immediately struck with the sense that climbing the steep stairway of railroad ties up to Orson Pratt's house takes much more energy than she remembered. With Casey by her side, she would float upward to the front door, but today it's hard work. Everything seems harder without Casey. She admits this to herself, but she won't be undone by it. She'll just tackle each thing as it comes along, she tells herself. And then he'll be home and everything will ease into effortlessness again.

"This is the last time I'll bother you," Isabelle says as Orson opens the front door. His expression is hard to read. Is he annoyed with her still?

She hands him a small slip of paper with her new information carefully printed on it. "Here's my new address—I've rented a duplex—and my phone number."

"No more Hotel Durant?"

"God, no." And then Isabelle adds, as if she's made an unprecedented discovery, "Hotels are expensive."

"No kidding?" And he's smiling.

"Obvious, I know," and she smiles back. A small détente.

"Oakland?" he asks her, looking at the address.

"Yes, but it's just off College, not too far away. In Rock-ridge."

"Did you walk?"

"Yes."

And then Orson has an idea. "Wait a minute," he says, and disappears into the house. He's back immediately, a set of keys in his hand. "Take Casey's Jeep. It's just sitting in the garage taking up space. Along with all his other things," Orson adds tartly and unnecessarily, despite his best intentions of holding his tongue.

"I don't know."

"Couldn't you use a car, now that you've moved?" He watches her eyes fill with tears. "What's the matter?"

"It's just so kind of you to think of it." Why is she crying? She has no idea. All she knows is that she's embarrassed in front of this man she hardly knows.

"Are you all right?"

And now the tears won't stop. She's not sobbing or hysteri-cal, she's just awfully tired and worn-out and feeling alone and she can't find the off valve for the tears.

"Come in," Orson says.

"No, I couldn't . . ."

"Just until you stop crying." What else can he do? Send a crying woman away to weep alone?

He opens the door wider and Isabelle steps into the familiar living room, only now it looks like a photo from a home improvement magazine, everything dusted and cleaned and in its place. Perfect Iceland poppies, tissue-thin orange petals crinkled and curved into cups of color, sit in a crystal vase on the coffee table. All the throw pillows are plumped and arranged by contrasting colors on the neutral couch.

Isabelle sinks into a corner of the soft sofa and Orson sits at the opposite end, back straight, hands on his knees, watching Isabelle try to get a handle on her tears.

"I'm so sorry," Isabelle says as she rummages in her large, satchel-like purse for a Kleenex. "I never do this. Really, I can't remember the last time I cried. It's just that . . . oh, I don't know, maybe because I haven't heard from Casey yet . . ."

"Uh-huh." Orson is biting his tongue so he doesn't say, "I tried to warn you" or some other harshness.

"It's been over three weeks. And CNN isn't interested anymore and so I really can't get any information about what's happening over there . . ." Isabelle trails off, heaving a big sigh. And then she squares her shoulders. "This is all so pathetic. Every time I see you, I'm one big pathetic mess, which is really weird because in my family, I'm the one who always keeps everyone else going. My mother is usually the mess, although she'd die before she accepted that label, and I'm the one who gets her through whatever crisis is causing the uproar, and here I am dissolving into tears for no reason whatsoever. I am so sorry."

And then there's silence—Isabelle has run out of apology, and Orson has no idea what would be an appropriate response to her confession.

"Well," he says finally, in order to move her up and out of

the house, "here are the keys to the Jeep. I'm sure Casey would want you to have it." And he stands, places the keys in her hand to indicate that now that she's no longer dripping tears his intervention is over, but Isabelle isn't getting up.

"How do you know Casey?"

And Orson sits back down. "Casey and my son went to school together, from preschool through high school."

"You have a son?" Isabelle is stunned. Orson seems such a singular presence, it never occurred to her he had children, a wife. There's no trace of either in his house.

"All grown now, same age as Casey. Luke lives in Detroit, where he is attempting to resurrect the downtown—a hopeless mission if there ever was one." And then Orson adds, proud despite himself, "But that's my son."

"What was he like as a child?"

"Luke?"

"No, Casey."

"Pretty much the way he is now, only smaller."

And Isabelle laughs. "I can see that. I can definitely see a tinier Casey"—and she takes both hands and holds them about two feet apart—"behaving exactly as he behaves now."

"Lots of energy," Orson says, nodding.

"Happy if the sun was shining."

"Yes. Whatever was in front of him was pretty much it."

And Isabelle is silent. Then: "Not much good at long-term planning."

"No. Not his strong suit."

"Well," she says as she stands and he does, as well, "that's what I can help him with." And she finds that she's lightheaded, dizzy, and she sits back down again.

"I'm sorry." God, she must have said that ten times already to this nice man. "I'm a little light-headed. In fact, I haven't felt well since Casey . . ." And then she stops herself, because she knows instantly what's wrong. How could she have been so clueless? Of course it's been crazy since Casey left, and she's been worried about him and worried about where she was going to live and how she was going to pay for it all, but to completely skip over the missed period, even though she's never been exactly regular so it wasn't such a big deal, but still, the queasiness alone should have told her. Oh my God.

"I'm pregnant," simply springs from her mouth before she can censor herself. Then, more slowly, with real wonder: "I just realized I must be pregnant."

Orson sits back down for a second time. Obviously this girl isn't leaving anytime soon.

"What a mess," she says, and he would concur if it weren't cruel to do so.

They look at each other, neither knowing exactly what to say now, Isabelle gradually coming into complete embarrassment. And with her face flushing red, she stands up again, car keys in hand, and makes for the door.

"Thank you," she says as she crosses the living room. "I can't thank you enough," is lobbed over her shoulder as she reaches the front door, opens it, and is gone.

ISABELLE SITS ON HER TINY front porch and stares out at the stillness of Marston Street. Up and down the block are small two- and three-bedroom wooden houses similar to her own. The old maple trees planted at the curbs, probably when the houses were built seventy years ago, are huge and leafless in the December air. Christmas is less than two weeks away.

It's the middle of the day. The kids who live on the street are in school, and it's so quiet Isabelle can hear the occasional squeal of car brakes on College Avenue several blocks to the east and the faint music of a guitar trio that often positions itself outside the Rockridge Café, playing for change.

Stupid. Could you have done anything more stupid? The words run through her head in an endless loop. She knows it's her mother's voice accusing her—she hears the harsh tone and staccato cadence, exactly as if her mother were sitting beside her—but she has no defense. She agrees. She can't think of anything more stupid.

And then comes her father's sorrowful voice from one of their morning discussions on the Long Island Railroad, when he fervently admonished her not to "live a life of regret." "How do you avoid that?" she remembers asking him, and he responded, "Be careful."

Well, she wasn't. And now what? *You can have this baby,* she tells herself, *or not.* That's the first choice she has to address, and she prepares herself for endless agonizing bouts of indecision which will tie her up in knots. But to her amazement, the "or not" of her choice seems like an impossibility. It is crystal clear to Isabelle that she will have this baby. No, she tells herself, she and Casey will have this baby.

That rock-solid belief is a revelation to her. Where did that certainty come from? She has no idea. Maybe pregnancy carries with it this gift of clarity. Maybe she's gone slightly crazy. All she knows for sure is that it feels amazing to be so unequivocal.

"Well!" And she says this out loud to the quiet street, frankly astonished at herself.

Mrs. Hershfeld, dragging a wire shopping cart loaded with groceries behind her and smoking, as she always seems to be, hears the loud and self-satisfied "Well!" as she nears the bungalow and takes it as a greeting.

"Fanny Hershfeld," she says from the bottom of the steps. She could climb them to be more neighborly, but it would kill her knees.

"Isabelle Rothman," Isabelle says as she gets up and walks down the steps to shake Mrs. Hershfeld's hand.

"Rothman," the older woman says with a knowing nod. "Good. Things will be fine between us."

Isabelle has no idea what she means and it shows on her face.

"The Jews—we know." And with that Fanny turns, grabs her shopping cart, and slowly begins to maneuver the four stone steps to her front door.

"Here, let me help you." And Isabelle easily carries the cart onto the porch. And then, she can't resist: "What do we know, Mrs. Hershfeld?"

"More than most," she says with a sage nod of her head. She bumps the cart into her open doorway, then turns to give Isabelle the rest of her wisdom. "The Safeway—may they rot in hell for the produce they put out." And with that, Mrs. Hershfeld maneuvers herself and her groceries through the front door and closes it with a slam of her foot.

CASEY CALLS ISABELLE THE FRIDAY BEFORE Christmas from Subic Bay International Airport in the Philippines. She's had well over a week to make some kind of sense of her new state. The first thing she did was call Deepti and make a doctor's appointment and take Deepti with her to ask the questions she wouldn't think to ask. And the doctor confirmed the pregnancy, even though Isabelle didn't need any medical test to verify what she knew, absolutely, in her bones.

What she wasn't sure of was how Casey would take the news. She realized that no matter how many hours they had spent together, no matter the whispered conversations that often took place as they lay naked in each other's arms, no matter the complete and easy intimacy she felt between them, she had no idea what he was going to say. How could that be? She felt she knew with more certainty what Daniel would say if she told him than what Casey's reaction would be.

When she thinks of Daniel now, she always pictures him in the messy kitchen of his rented house in Los Angeles, sitting at the large wooden table pushed against a wall, the way he was the day she took him the Philip Levine poems. Something changed that day for both of them, she believes, and it is that morning that she goes back to in her mind.

If she went to him there and told him she was pregnant, he would lean back in his chair, cross his arms against his broad chest, narrow his light-blue eyes, and appraise her, trying to discern how she felt about it. Then he would ask her, and she would tell him that she was terrified and excited and committed in a way she had never been before in her life to anything, except maybe her writing.

"What about your writing?" he would say. And she would reassure him that she wouldn't give it up. That she would manage to do both—raise this child and continue to write. Lots of women did it. She could, as well.

"Hmmm," he would say, coming forward and leaning his forearms on the table in front of him. "Hard to do."

"Yes," she would admit, "but I think I can."

And then Daniel would smile and say, "Keep me posted," and she would know that he was on her side, as she had felt from that day in the kitchen with the book of poems and his explanation that "what's inside you is worthy enough to write about." Such a powerful statement. Contained within it was the assurance that he had seen her essence and judged it worthy. What greater gift is there, except maybe his declaration that he would help her find a way to get the words on paper?

Why was she able to imagine Daniel's reaction to the news so clearly, but not Casey's? Was Casey the sort of person whose presence made all the difference and Daniel was not? How did that work? Why was her connection to Daniel still strong despite the months and months of absence and her connection to Casey, gone simply a matter of weeks, already feeling threadbare and thin?

Despite the questions Isabelle spends most of her days mulling over, when she hears Casey's voice on the phone, her legs give out and she has to sit down. Simply the sound of his voice overwhelms her.

"Casey, oh, Casey, where are you?"

"In the airport, near Mindoro."

"You're coming home! Oh my God!"

"Well . . . not quite yet."

And Isabelle is silent, flooded with disappointment. She has no idea what to say next.

"Isabelle, there's a famine in South Sudan. Eight hundred thousand people are in danger of starvation. Can you imagine? In Bor, where I'm headed, a hundred people a day are dying— children first, of course, always, but the whole population, they're walking skeletons."

"That's awful," Isabelle manages to say, just barely.

"So you can understand why I'm not coming home just yet." His voice is strong, urgent. She thinks she might detect some glee in it.

"Yes, but . . . Casey, there's something else."

"The World Food Program, that's part of the United Nations, said that nowhere else in the world are people in such dire straits. The situation's beyond a crisis. Global Hope's got two planes loaded with food, basic stuff like powdered milk for the kids, beans and rice, essentials, and they're on their way even as we speak, and I'm going to meet them on this dirt landing strip outside of—"

"Casey!" And Isabelle feels like a horrible person. Selfish. Superficial. Why is she making such a personal fuss when scores of people are dying? But she has to tell him. "Listen, there's something we have to talk about."

"Okay, shoot."

And then Isabelle finds she can't get the words out. She's practiced this moment many times in her head over the past ten days, but now that she has to speak the words, she finds she can't.

"Isabelle, what is it? They're calling my flight."

"When will you be back?" is what she is able to manage.

"Jeez, I don't know. It depends on what we find when we get to the Sudan. And how much relief work they'll let us do there. There's a civil war going on, that's a huge part of the trouble, and the government—"

"Casey, I'm pregnant."

There's an immediate black hole of silence, sucking out all of Isabelle's hope, and then a very soft "Wow" from Casey.

"Is that a good wow or a bad one?"

"I'm just sort of shocked."

"Me, too."

"What do you want to do about it?"

"I'm having this baby." Isabelle says this quietly, resolutely.

Casey says nothing. Isabelle can hear in the background, behind his silence, a muffled voice calling for passengers to board a plane, probably Casey's.

"Shit, I've got to go. I'll call you again. As soon as I can. All right?"

"Yes, but—"

"I love you." And then there's a dial tone.

CHAPTER TEN

By the time Isabelle gives birth to her son in late July 1995, just days after her twenty-third birthday, Daniel is in Iowa. He doesn't tell Isabelle about this move, and she doesn't tell him about the baby. Since the summer of her graduation and his exile from Los Angeles, they have e-mailed each other only sporadically—their exchange of Christmas messages, an e-mail from Isabelle when she found Daniel's third novel, long out of print, in a used-book store and he made her promise not to read it. But primarily Isabelle has been consumed with the life taking shape within her and Daniel has become more and more disgusted with himself and his vagabond existence, this begging for academic scraps and babysitting a son who refuses to grow up.

Isabelle names her son Avi, which means "my father" in Hebrew, a name carefully chosen. It is a talisman, one more way of tying Casey to a child he professes to love.

After their initial stunted conversation from Subic Bay Airport, Casey called a second time, when his plane landed in Khartoum. He had minutes before he had to board a much smaller plane, which would land on the dirt airstrip outside the town of Bor.

In this phone call, Casey sounds excited about the baby—that's Isabelle's sense of it, and her heart soars. He's had time to think about her news on the plane ride, she decides, and he's gotten over his shock and has come down on the side of excitement. She tells him her due date, July 21, and he promises to be home for the birth.

"But Casey, that's seven months away. You'll be back before that, right?"

There is a microsecond of hesitation and then Casey answers, "Sure. Probably. I should be. Once we finish giving out the foodstuffs here and see what else we can do, then I should be coming home."

And Isabelle's whole body relaxes into relief. She hears what she wants to hear: Casey is coming home. She can hold it together until that day.

"I wish it were tomorrow," she tells him.

"Me, too," he says before he gets off. And she believes him—he wants to come home.

But in January there is a 6.9-magnitude earthquake in Kobe, Japan, that kills 6,425 people, injures 25,000, and renders 300,000 people homeless. It is the worst Japanese disaster since World War II, and Global Hope sends Casey immediately.

"I don't have control over all this," Casey informs Isabelle in an early-morning phone call that wakes her up. "They need every able body they can get to Japan, fast. It's better that I go there than come home. You can see the sense of it."

Isabelle is silent. She doesn't see the sense of it, not at all, but she also doesn't feel awake enough to present a cogent argument. It's dark outside her uncurtained window, just a few minutes past four o'clock, and her mind won't work. Only her emotions are awake, and they are screaming, *No! No! I want you with me!* But she knows she can't say that. Even to her ears it sounds too selfish to voice.

"I'll be home as soon as I can." His tone isn't placating or the least bit guilty. It's matter-of-fact and firm.

But what Isabelle hears is *home*. He considers her home.

Five months later, it's spring when Casey returns to Oakland and moves into Isabelle's half of the Craftsman duplex. With Casey's unerring instincts, he arrives in time for her birthing classes, to pick out a crib, and to marvel at the physical changes in her body. How beautiful she is. How beautiful their baby will be. He can't get enough of placing his large, warm hand on the tight basketball she carries proudly in front of her. He wants to feel the baby stretch and kick. "I *need* to," he tells Isabelle, as if his desire to connect with their child were a physical ache. All of it delights him, and his happiness lulls Isabelle into thinking that somehow everything will be all right. Casey loves her. He's excited about the baby. He's here now. The possibility of his going away again she banishes from her mind. No, the three of them will be fine, she tells herself every day.

But before he comes home, Isabelle has to fend for herself. She's proud of how she manages to find a job, which pays the rent and the necessities, just barely, but that's all right. Lots of people in Oakland and its neighboring city, Berkeley, live the sort of frugal life she is crafting. People make do. They tend home gardens, shop at thrift shops and co-ops, buy secondhand books, and barter services for goods. They help each other out.

Isabelle never once considers asking her parents for money. She understands without needing to have the conversation that the support would come with demands—*Come back, leave Casey, play by our rules.* So she waits until she knows Casey is coming home to her, until she has found a job and can pay her rent, until she can speak calmly and firmly, until her pregnancy is well advanced and she's sure she won't buckle, to call her father at work. He tells her mother, of course, and her mother calls and says all the things Isabelle knew she would: *How could you be so stupid, Come home immediately, There's no way you can manage by yourself, Whatever were you thinking, getting pregnant?*

To the last question, Isabelle answers simply, "I wasn't," and hangs up.

Mrs. Hershfeld turns out to be her inadvertent guardian angel, inadvertent because her neighbor is not in the habit of being especially benevolent. Fanny Hershfeld's preferred stance toward the world has always been a slow, simmering indignation, but as she tells Isabelle the long-running story of her estrangement from her brother, Meir, Isabelle sees a possibility.

They are in the backyard, their common space, their only meeting place, since Isabelle hasn't accumulated enough furniture yet to invite Mrs. Hershfeld over for coffee, and Mrs. Hershfeld never invites anyone into her half of the house. It is her domain and she doesn't want it invaded. But the backyard, that's where she allows herself a few minutes to stop and talk.

Years ago, a long-forgotten tenant left behind a tiny, circular wrought-iron table and two lacy chairs. The white paint has chipped and blistered, but the wrought iron underneath is sturdy, and Isabelle often finds herself walking out and sitting there at the table, under the one tree in the yard, a persimmon tree, which hangs its globular orange fruit on leafless limbs from October through January. Organic holiday ornaments.

It is the week between Christmas, which Isabelle spent with Deepti and Sadhil in San Francisco, and New Year's, and Mrs. Hershfeld is shuffling out with a wad of dripping-wet cotton support hose to hang on the clothesline. Isabelle is bundled in a heavy sweater—the sun is out but gives little warmth this far into the winter—reading *The Simple Truth* by Philip Levine, which had been published earlier that year. She has set herself the task of trying again to understand the poetic form, to discover what speaks so strongly to Daniel.

"You like to read. Every time I see you—here, the front porch—you're reading."

"It's poetry," Isabelle tells her, holding up the book so Mrs. Hershfeld can see the front cover.

"Ah, Levine," the older woman says as she lowers her aging body into the other chair and gingerly straightens out her aching knees. Fanny Hershfeld reminds Isabelle of a pouter pigeon, all billowy chest and skinny, birdlike legs. Rarely has she seen her out of a housecoat—this current one is printed with a green-and-yellow pineapple pattern—and Isabelle watches as Fanny smoothes the cotton down over her naked legs.

"Do you know him?" Isabelle asks.

"I know he's Jewish and writes about the working man. What else is there to know? He's on our side."

Isabelle is struck again by the dichotomy Mrs. Hershfeld insists upon. The Jews over here, everyone else over there. Gingerly she says, "I guess I never thought about the world as our side or their side."

"That's because you're too young," Fanny Hershfeld shoots back. "What year were you born?"

"Nineteen seventy-two."

Fanny utters something that sounds like "Pssshaw," and Isabelle is chastised, dismissed by her youth and inexperience.

"Try the thirties and the forties, when anti-Semitism grew like baker's yeast. And the fifties, when that megalomaniac Joe McCarthy saw a Communist under every bed. People were *blacklisted*." Fanny turns and stares into Isabelle's eyes as if to burn in her message. "Jewish people. Their lives were ruined. Permanently." And now the older woman turns away from Isabelle and stares out over the overgrown backyard. "Sometimes they even became other people."

"You mean they changed their names?"

"I mean they changed their souls!"

"Oh."

And a silence hangs between them. Fanny isn't looking at Isabelle. The rough turn of her shoulder and the deliberate twist away of her head make Isabelle hesitate to say anything, but it feels like there's a story to be told. Just as Isabelle is gathering her courage to ask, Fanny begins to talk again.

"My husband and I were both blacklisted. Why?" She shrugs. "We were clerks at city hall. Nothing important. I did real estate deeds, that kind of thing. Saul, he was in the parks and recreation division. We filed things. We helped people out when they came in. It was fine. It paid the bills, but our lives were elsewhere. What we did for a living, that was just to have our lives."

Now she turns to look at Isabelle. This part of the story she will address head-on. "Okay, we were Communists, but so what? We weren't going to burn down the government. We wanted fairness, that's all, fairness for the working man, and when that *paskudnyak,* holding his Senate hearings and sweating and yelling and pointing his finger, accusing all sorts of people of being traitors, when he got on TV, well, we were fired and then we couldn't get other jobs. People were afraid to hire us. We were branded. Achhh, there was so much fear.

"And what did my husband do? He blamed me. 'You're the one who got me into this,' he told me. He meant the Party. 'You're the one who insisted.' As if he had no will of his own."

Fanny stops talking, lost in remembering, and Isabelle feels she has to say something. "That must have been a hard time."

"Hard?" Fanny shrugs again. "He was a weak man, Saul Hershfeld. How did he fight back against the evil of Joe McCarthy? He found a *shiksa*—stupid, with two stuck-up parents—and married her."

Mrs. Hershfeld has found her groove. She doesn't stop talking, and as her stories evolve, it becomes clear to Isabelle that this woman doesn't have much use for men. Each story she tells has at its root some condemnation of a man's ill-conceived action. It is when she is talking about her brother, Meir, that Isabelle pays better attention. He took the wrong path in life: he became a capitalist, although he would never admit to it. He bought and sold things to make a profit. He skimmed and scammed and kept on making more and more money.

"But is he happy?" Mrs. Hershfeld asks, and then answers her own question. "Not on your life. So what difference does it make that he owns a block of College Avenue?"

"He does?" Isabelle is frankly impressed. College is one of the main commercial streets flowing from Oakland down through Berkeley to the university. Long stretches of it hold small and interesting shops and restaurants and fresh-produce markets and craft shops. And then there are the seedier establishments, often interspersed here and there.

"So what good does it do anybody that he keeps a tattoo parlor going and a place that sells T-shirts and some hamburger joint?"

"Bluto's?"

"Yeah, that one."

"Oh, their hamburgers are delicious."

Mrs. Hershfeld looks at her as if she's committed treason. Us versus them again. Isabelle realizes her mistake immediately and her first impulse is to apologize and placate, and then she thinks better of it and forges ahead.

"And then down at the corner of that same block is a wonderful old bookshop, Noah's Ark—right, Mrs. Hershfeld? It reminds me of a shop I used to go to all the time when I was in college—Seaman's, it's called—where the books are piled up everywhere and you can spend hours just browsing until you find this hidden gem, a book you've heard of and always wanted to read but never could find. Oh, I love stores like that."

"Well, the next time you're in, tell Meir you live next to me and see what you get. He spends his days sitting at the front counter pretending he's one of us working people, but all he really does is get fatter and fatter by the day."

And the next day Isabelle walks into the bookstore to find part of Mrs. Hershfeld's rant to be accurate. Her brother, Meir Schapiro, is a very large man. And he's sitting at the front counter, reading a book and working his way through a bag of Doritos. To the right of the front door, in a shallow alcove, are a secondhand sofa and two easy chairs around a small steamer trunk serving as a coffee table—somewhere to rest and read and fall in love with a book.

Meir looks up when he sees Isabelle come in, says, "Welcome," as if he means it, and goes back to his book, leaving Isabelle to browse and dawdle.

She makes a tour of the shelves lining the walls, then repeats the walk around, only this time she edges closer and closer to the center. It's all here, everything she loved about Seaman's: stacks crammed with secondhand books, volumes on esoteric subjects—witchcraft, Malaysian basket weaving, American foreign policy in the Depression—and early, out-of-print novels by established writers. It's here that she finds Daniel's third book and takes it to Meir at the front counter.

"Ah, Daniel Jablonski," Meir says as he looks over the book. "Not one of his best, I'm afraid."

"But still worth reading, don't you think?"

Meir lifts his shoulders in uncertainty. "The first two— gems."

"I know!"

"But this one . . ." Meir shakes his head.

"Yes?"

Meir thinks for a minute. He wants to get this right. The girl seems so eager for his opinion. Or maybe just eager in general, full of life. Attractive, very attractive to a man who's eating himself into a certain grave. "The first novel, about his father, was like spun gold. Shining, as if each word had to be there, in that order, making those sentences. There wasn't a false step."

"And tough, too, don't you think?"

"Honest, I would say."

"Very," Isabelle agrees.

"And the second book, about his marriage dissolving, it felt just as raw."

"But the writing was even better."

"You felt he'd hit his stride as a writer."

"Yes!" Isabelle is so happy to be exchanging praise about Daniel with this complete stranger, she's slightly giddy.

"But when he decided to write this one," Meir says as he picks up the book, "I don't know. It's about Harry Bridges and the San Francisco longshoremen's strike of 1934. Did you know that?"

"Not until I saw it here."

"Maybe he thought it would elevate his game, you know, historical subject, but instead it just shouts *Look at me, I'm trying to be significant.*"

"And that's so unlike him."

"The critics hated the book."

"I've heard that."

"And they were brutal—'self-important,' 'stillborn,' 'life-less,' they called it. And even worse. So"—and here Meir smiles at her—"read it at your own peril. Either you will see some glimmer of his early brilliance in it or you will be disillusioned with Jablonski for good. Risky business, reading it."

"I'll take the risk. I'm inclined to see the glimmers."

"A hopeful girl," Meir says, "I like that." And he's smitten.

And from that first conversation about Daniel's work comes Isabelle's job at Noah's Ark, Used Books.

CHAPTER ELEVEN

When Daniel and Stefan leave Colorado Springs, their exit has nothing to do with Daniel's disdain for his students. They leave to keep Stefan out of harm's way. All through the winter and early spring, on the days that Daniel teaches, Stefan continues to haunt the High Plains Ice Hall.

Over the months he has honed his routine to a tight choreography. And he never deviates from it. There is immense satisfaction for him in the repetition of predictable events. He enters from the same glass door every day, farthest left of the four that make up Gate B. With purpose he makes his way up to the very top row of Section 210, where he waits patiently for his reward, the first sighting of Mitsuko Kita as she floats onto the ice to begin her practice. The despicable coach (and jailer, as Stefan thinks of him) is always there, as well, stern-faced, punitive, from time to time calling out abrupt and harsh instructions, but Stefan tries to ignore him. If he dwells too much on the small Japanese man, it ruins his day.

Instead Stefan goes to work: he makes his way down to the third row of section 109, mere feet from the ice, takes the first seat on the aisle, and assembles himself for his task. He pulls a spiral notebook from his backpack, its green cover curling from extensive use, and then a series of pens, which he lays across his lap. The red one is for mistakes and errors of judgment, the black for moves Mitsuko has mastered. Here Stefan's comments are cut-and-dried. What is working, what isn't. Every move is given a numerical value. But the purple pen—that is for his personal observations. And here he allows himself more leeway. His system is meticulous and foolproof, he feels. He secretly hopes that one day Mitsuko will be able to take a look at his immaculate charts and know exactly where she is—her strengths, her weaknesses, even the path to perfection.

There are other people in the arena watching the skaters as they work through their practices, so Stefan's observation and recording garner no scrutiny. He stays put in his seat on the aisle and doesn't raise any kind of alarm. He never approaches the skater. He never intrudes.

It is as he follows Mitsuko home to her apartment that he gets into trouble. Even though he walks at least a block behind, hoping to blend in with the rest of the pedestrians, it isn't long before both the tiny skater and her coach, Hideo Suzuki, begin to notice him. He's always there. He takes the same position every time, across the street from her apartment house, leaning against a leafless tree, to watch her walk into the building, waiting for the glass door to click shut behind her so he can experience that moment of exquisite relief—she's safe for now! And then he waits for the Japanese coach to move off down the street and turn the corner and be gone.

But Hideo Suzuki has taken to circling the block and surreptitiously watching Stefan watch Mitsuko's building, making sure the large young man doesn't make a move toward his skater. And Stefan doesn't. He's not ready. His notes aren't complete. His courage hasn't been gathered yet, so he simply stands across the street, his eyes on the second-floor window where sometimes, if he's lucky, he can catch a glimpse of Mitsuko as she walks through her living room.

"You're six-foot-four!" Daniel roars at him some weeks later, when he has made his way, somehow, to the police station to claim his wayward son. "And you dress like a homeless person! Didn't it occur to you that someone might notice you?"

"I was making sure she was all right." Stefan is unrepentant. "That coach of hers is a wild card, I can tell."

"Why is this your job?"

"I take care of people. That's what I do." Stefan is belligerent as he confronts his father. *That's what you've made of me,* he wants to say to Daniel, but doesn't.

The two men stare at each other in a small windowless interrogation room in the Colorado Springs police station, the fluorescent overhead lights buzzing and flickering sporadically. A fleshy uniformed cop, close to retirement age, his arms crossed against his bright blue shirt, watches from his spot near the door, saying nothing.

Ron Sessions has been doing police work for almost thirty years, and he's learned a few things. Sometimes stepping back from the problem is more powerful than stepping in. He's never actually articulated this philosophy to other officers— their work, after all, is almost exclusively about active engagement—but he has learned that there are times when waiting has its merits. And this is one of them. He wants to see if this father can get control of this son. Maybe then they can all avert a problem.

"She is not your responsibility." Daniel lowers his voice, understanding Stefan's unspoken accusation even though his son hasn't voiced it.

"But you are, is that it?"

"God, no, Stefan."

Ron has heard enough. This is going to devolve into family issues that aren't going to be solved in a police station, so he pushes his shoulders from the wall, grabs a chair, and sits down at the table where Stefan and Daniel look away from each other in misery.

"Gentlemen," he says, "let's take stock. You, Stefan, are on the verge of something we take very seriously here—stalking. Nobody wants to deal with that possibility, am I right?"

Daniel looks at Stefan, waiting for his son to answer. Out comes a mumbled "No."

"All right, son, then listen to what your father is telling you, because if we catch you back at the Ice Hall or on any of the streets surrounding Miss Kita's apartment, you'll be in serious trouble. You get that?"

Stefan nods but doesn't say anything.

"He understands what you're saying," Daniel volunteers.

"Don't talk for me! Goddammit, I'm not a mute."

"Then tell the officer that yes, you understand, and you will stop what you've been doing."

"I just did."

Ron stands. "Okay, we'll all take this conversation as the one warning you're gonna get." And he opens the door to the hallway.

Stefan slouches through the doorway, but Daniel, following him, is stopped by a hand on his arm.

"Take this," Ron says, handing Daniel his business card. "I raised two like him, both almost thirty now, and I know sometimes you might need to call somebody. That could be me."

"Thank you," Daniel says, humbled, grateful. Obviously, whatever he's been doing with Stefan isn't the right thing.

"Did you hear him?" Daniel asks his son as they walk out of the station, a squat brick fortress with no windows on the lower floors. "Were you paying attention?"

"I wasn't doing anything wrong," Stefan answers, sullen.

"Stefan, that girl is fifteen years old!"

"They start them skating at, like, four."

"No, that's not the point!" Daniel is struggling to stay on the rational side of his anger. "You were making that little girl and her coach—"

"Who's a fucking asshole—"

"You made them afraid of you, Stefan!"

Stefan shrugs as they walk. There's a lot he could say in his own defense, like *The coach turned me in, she never would,* or *She's afraid of her own coach because he yells at her all the time.* But he's done talking. His dad isn't listening, and besides, he'd never get it. He hasn't seen her skate. He hasn't held his breath as she launches herself into the air and lands on the toe of one tiny skate. He hasn't watched her spin endlessly into a whirling dervish of color and sparkle and silken black hair that wraps around her head like a velvet cloud. So he stops talking altogether. But he won't stop watching. Only now he has to be craftier about it.

Daniel knows he should talk to his son about his behavior—it's not normal—but he has no idea what words to use. All he has to do is look at his own behavior, which is equally far from normal, to know that he has no ground on which to stand if he decides to lecture his son. What can he say? *We both had ruinous fathers who failed us?*

He tries a variation of that. "I should have been around more when you were growing up."

Stefan shrugs. "Whatever." Then: "How are we getting home?" And another thought: "How did you get here?"

"I took a cab."

"You did?"

"What was I going to do, let you stay in jail for weeks until I could make myself drive over here?"

"You called a cab and stood outside and waited for it and then got into the car? By yourself?"

"Yes, Stefan, I did."

"Wow . . . We gonna take a cab home, then?"

"I guess we have to."

"Cool." And Stefan finds one for them.

As they sit in the backseat of the moving taxi, Stefan watching the bleak and chilly streets of Colorado Springs out his window, Daniel tries again.

"What exactly did you think you were doing with that girl?"

Stefan gives his all-purpose shrug, his eyes on the scenery, hoping that if he doesn't turn around, his father will just shut up.

Daniel waits a minute. He's trying very hard not to start yelling again. When he finally speaks, he makes his voice as soft as he can. "Did you consider how it might look, your following her?"

Stefan shakes his head.

"You need to."

"I'm sick of other people," Stefan mumbles, not looking at his father, but Daniel hears him, and despite himself, his face softens. There's a sentiment he can embrace.

"Me, too."

And that turns Stefan around to stare at his father's face. Did his dad just agree with him?

"But mostly," Daniel says in a rare moment of confession, "I'm sick of myself."

Some things change after that. They never discuss the incident again—what does Daniel have to say that he hasn't already?—but he keeps his son as close to him as possible. It's the best he can do. He insists that Stefan come into the classroom with him whenever they walk together to campus and stay for the entire hour, right there in a seat where Daniel can keep an eye on him. Stefan's expression says it all: *I am going to die of boredom here.* And on the days Daniel doesn't teach, he keeps his son in the apartment with him.

Stefan idly wonders how many hours of daytime TV it is possible for a person to watch without losing IQ points, because he feels he's crossed the line. His mind has become logy and slow and his body loose and sloppy from hours sprawled on their broken-down couch.

It's only in the evenings that Daniel lets his son out of the apartment, to pick up their dinner. For the first week or so after their unplanned visit to the police station, Daniel called for dinner to be delivered, but it soon became apparent how expensive that was, and so the Jablonski men returned to their previous habit: Stefan walks to one of the many restaurants close to their apartment and picks up their food.

What Stefan doesn't tell Daniel is that often, when he feels he can get away with it, he jumps in the car and makes a quick trip to Mitsuko's apartment and stands across the street, pleading with the universe to allow him a glimpse of her through the second-floor window.

He keeps a disguise in the trunk of the car—a battered fedora which he's convinced hides his face, a Denver Nuggets jacket bought expressly for this purpose and which she's never seen. Even if she looks out the window and sees a guy leaning against a tree, barely lit by the streetlight several feet away, she has no way of knowing it's him. That's Stefan's firm and deluded belief, which is completely shattered one late March evening. There he is, in his disguise, gazing longingly up at Mitsuko's brightly lit window, and there she is, standing at the window looking right down at him! And suddenly there's another girl by her side, taller and probably older but looking so much like Mitsuko that she must be her sister. What happens next makes him so happy he feels he might just levitate right up to their window. They both wave. They giggle behind their hands at their audacity, then clutch each other's shoulders in embarrassment, and then pull the drapes tightly closed. Stefan is left limp with happiness and wonder.

That night when he returns home and encounters Daniel's questions about how long it's taken him to bring back dinner—questions that he's heard on previous nights—Stefan tells him the restaurant was really crowded. Sometimes he'll say that they messed up the order and he had to wait while they remade it or that they were training a new chef and the guy was way slow. Stefan makes sure to rotate his excuses. Does Daniel believe him? It's hard to tell.

Daniel wants to believe him. It's easier for everyone if Stefan is behaving himself. And shouldn't Daniel be exhibiting some trust in his son? Shouldn't he be treating him more like a man and less like a child? Stefan was in that interrogation room with Daniel and the cop. He heard the warning. He understands what will happen if he doesn't leave this girl alone.

"Look," he says to his son, "you've got to act like an adult here."

You mean act like you? Stefan is desperate to say but doesn't.

"You've got to stay away from that girl. Can't you find something else to do during the days?"

As if that's the point.

Stefan mumbles, "Okay," his eyes on his feet. He doesn't like lying to his dad, but there's a bigger principle involved here.

Daniel chooses to hear that barely audible *okay* as a promise, and so, after several weeks, he loosens the reins a bit. Given the extra freedom, Stefan hatches a plan. He knows he can't go to the Ice Hall anymore. Even with a disguise, he's pretty sure the coach, that asshole, will spot him. So his days of watching practice and taking notes are probably over. But he has the notebook. He wishes he'd been able to complete it, but it still contains gold as far as Stefan is concerned. If Mitsuko could read it, it would help her. It might even make the difference between her making the Olympic team or not. So he will present it to her.

That decision necessitates a lot more watching. And several changes of disguises. He goes to the Salvation Army store and buys whatever he would never wear in his real life—an army fatigue jacket, a Yankees baseball cap, a Stetson and a fringed jacket, a ski cap and goggles, a red nylon jacket with a hood, and several pairs of large, dark sunglasses. He will mix and match.

First he stays away from her apartment for two weeks. It's agony, but he wants to lull the coach into complacency—*Okay, the kid has given up.* And Stefan's far more regular habits also serve to reassure Daniel that his son has stopped his nonsense with the skater. But all Stefan is doing is biding his time.

One day in late April, the crabapple trees begin to bud, purple and red swellings that burst forth into pristine white blossoms laced with pink, and suddenly spring is thrust upon them. It's wondrous how, overnight it seems, change is palpable and possibilities are poised on tiptoes after the cold, harsh winter. Now, Stefan thinks, he has to make his move.

The dilemma is how to get Mitsuko away from her coach but outside her apartment. Even if Stefan could get into her building, which is locked and needs a key code, he feels he shouldn't walk in and knock on her door. If he gets into trouble for this—and he might—he wants to be able to minimize the damage. He wants to be able to say to Daniel, *I just ran into her on the street. An accident. It was a public place. There were people around. Nothing bad could have happened.*

So he has to see where she goes after the coach drops her off. Does she leave the apartment, go out to eat with the other girl? Her sister, he's sure. To a movie? Shopping?

On Friday afternoons, when Daniel has office hours, Stefan takes to waiting in his car, slumped down in the driver's seat, watching the door to Mitsuko's apartment house from under the brim of his cowboy hat. He discovers that the coach, the despicable one, lets her come home early from practice on Friday afternoons, and then one day Stefan gets lucky. He sees Mitsuko and her sister exit through the glass front door and walk down their street to a minimall two blocks away. He follows them in his car, creeping slowly behind them, and parks across the street.

All the tiny stores are eating establishments—Jamba Juice, a KFC franchise, a Thai restaurant, and a Yuzu Yogurt shop, which has a sign out front in both English and Japanese and a tiny patio with a few white plastic chairs and tables. He watches the two girls come out of the shop with their cones and sit there on the patio, eating and chattering.

Most Friday afternoons, he soon learns, now that the weather has turned more temperate, this walk to Yuzu Yogurt, this sitting on the patio and eating their cones, is their routine. Now he knows where he will approach Mitsuko, but first he has to make sure the notebook is as complete as he can make it and he has to write a note to go with it which explains the significance of it. All of this takes time, the note particularly, because he doesn't know exactly what to say. He doesn't want to brag, but he does want to let her know how important his notes are. How they might make the difference between going to the Nagano Games and not. He wishes he could ask his dad for help, because the one thing his dad knows how to do is write, but of course he can't. So he struggles on his own and comes up with this note:

Dear Mitsuko,

I have spent many hours watching you practice and taking notes. What is in this notebook will help you make the Olympic team, which you truly deserve. It is a record of every hour of every practice I have been at. The black ink is for routines you have mastered, the red is for mistakes (not as many of those by far!), and the purple is for some personal comments of mine that might help you—all positive, don't worry!

I did this only to help you know where you are at because I think you are amazing! Even though I am not a citizen of Japan, I will be rooting for you.

Sincerely,
Stefan Jablonski

Stefan reads the note over so many times he has it memorized. Is it exactly what he wants to say? Not even close, but he feels it's as nonthreatening as he can make it. He knows it's inappropriate to tell her how he feels watching her skate or how his heart beats more quickly when he sees her set foot on the ice. He's not some weirdo, after all. He was engaged in a helpful mission, using his unique gift—his powers of observation. That's the message he wants to get across to her.

Now that the note is done and he's reread every entry in his notebook, there's nothing to do but give her both. He makes his plan. On a Friday afternoon, he will wait until Mitsuko and her sister are sitting on the Yuzu Yogurt patio. He will approach and take a seat at their table—better to be sitting down than looming over them. (He's proud that he's thought all this through so carefully.) Next he will put the notebook on the table and explain what it is and that there's a note inside, and then he will get up and leave. Simple. Nonthreatening. Mission accomplished.

The next Friday he makes sure to wear clean jeans and a simple white T-shirt. He combs his hair, something he rarely thinks about doing. He makes sure to shave that morning, and when he gets out of his car and crosses the street to the yogurt shop, his spirits are soaring.

The two girls look up at him as he approaches, breaking off their conversation abruptly. It's obvious that they both recognize him, but instead of the anticipation and smiles he'd hoped for, he sees a flash of fear across Mitsuko's face.

"No, no," are the first words out of his mouth, not at all what he had planned to say.

When he sits down at their table, the sister stands up, grabs Mitsuko's arm, and pulls her up to standing, as well.

"Please," Stefan says, "I just want to give you something," and he lays the battered green notebook on the table. "To help you. I want to help you," he says again in desperation, because both girls look terrified.

The sister says something in Japanese to Mitsuko, something terse and anxious, and pulls her sister into the shop and attempts to close the glass door behind them. But Stefan is there, worried now that they've misunderstood.

He pushes the door open, to explain, to put the notebook in her hands, and that's when everything goes wrong. The Japanese owner screams at him from behind the counter, in broken English, to get out of his shop. Stefan screams back that this is none of his business. The girls cower in a corner by the counter, the sister yelling something over and over in Japanese and wrapping the tiny Mitsuko in her arms, protecting her from whatever harm is coming.

In the midst of all the chaos, Stefan suddenly understands that he left a crucial element out of his planning: Mitsuko doesn't speak English. There is no way she can understand what he is offering. How could he not have realized that? How could he have been so stupid again?

Frantic now to right his wrong, Stefan approaches the girls again with the notebook and they scream and he tries to put it in Mitsuko's hand. And then he'll go. He tries to tell them that—"Just take it and I'll go!"—but they don't understand a word. They sink to the floor, trembling, and he's heartsick and desperate, standing over them, pleading with them, the notebook thrust toward them.

And then suddenly four strong arms are dragging him away. Two big cops he didn't even see enter thrust him out of the shop and slam him up against the hood of their patrol car, knocking the air out of him, twisting his arms behind him so they can snap on a pair of handcuffs. And Stefan doesn't utter a word of protest.

Through the back window of the cruiser, as he's being driven away, Stefan spots the tattered green notebook spread-eagled on the parking lot asphalt, and at that moment he understands that all is lost.

TWO HOURS LATER DANIEL AND STEFAN are sequestered in the same shabby, sterile, windowless room of the same Colorado Springs police station, waiting. Today one of the fluorescent lights has given up the ghost and half the room is in murky light. But where they sit, across from each other at the square table with the scarred top, the light is irritatingly bright and still flickering from time to time.

Stefan says nothing. He sits with his hands lank in his lap and stares at somebody's initials—B.R.D.—gouged into the Formica with a pen. He is working on emptying his body of every emotion he possesses. It's a tactic he's practiced since childhood. If he doesn't feel anything, nothing can hurt him.

Daniel's hands are clasped in front of him on the table, his eyes fixed on the dark corner of the room. He's frightened in a way that's new to him. This isn't fear of leaving the house, or fear of being trapped in a crowd, or fear of having a panic attack. This is the very real fear that his son might be taken away from him.

How did he let this happen? How did he fail to protect his son? What can he do now?

"Stefan . . ." he says tentatively.

"Don't you say anything," his son spits at him. "You don't know. You have no idea."

"Stefan," Daniel says again, quietly, "I've been in love."

"That has nothing to do with it!" And Stefan's voice mounts into hysteria. "I was helping her! I was making sure she got into the Olympics!"

Daniel is completely nonplussed. Is his son crazy? At the very least he's delusional. How has he missed all this in his child?

"The notebook," Stefan says as he scrubs his knuckles across his face. Again and again. "The notebook . . . the notebook . . ." It's a kind of keening.

Daniel doesn't respond. He looks away. He has no idea what Stefan is talking about, and he's not about to ask.

While the men sit in the airless room and wait, both hopeless for different reasons, the green-covered notebook at the center of this debacle is finally in Mitsuko's hands. As Stefan laments its loss, the skater is carrying it into the police station, her sister on one side of her, Hideo Suzuki on the other. It was Mitsuko who picked the fluttering pages off the parking lot surface after the police took Stefan away. Even though she couldn't read a word of it, she understood enough to know that Stefan valued what was in the book. She's in the police station to return it to him.

Her sister wouldn't let her go without her coach, and Suzuki agreed to take her only so he could talk to the policemen himself. The boy is a distraction. His presence, his antics, have pulled his student's focus away from her skating, and he can't have that. Stefan must be gone. Gone from the Ice Hall, gone from the streets of Colorado Springs. Gone from the planet, if that were possible.

Hideo speaks enough English to say "the tall boy," and he points to Mitsuko. The station is small, and the day has been slow enough for the desk sergeant to know that this is Ron Sessions's case, so he calls him to the lobby.

As the substantial officer enters the room, Mitsuko steps forward with the notebook held out in front of her, an offering. She's as tiny as a bird, Sessions sees, a hummingbird. Not even five feet tall. No wonder the looming presence of the boy, who is well over six feet tall, frightened her. And she is shy, tentative, as she stands in front of him, but, he can also see, determined. She says something in Japanese to her coach and he translates it roughly: "For the boy. It is his."

Mitsuko nods and places the notebook in Sessions's hand. "Please," she says in English.

"Are you here to file a complaint?"

No one answers. None of the three of them understand enough English to translate *complaint*.

Sessions tries again. "The boy—he committed a crime. You are here to tell us that?"

There is a rapid discussion in Japanese, with Mitsuko's face coloring with emotion as she says something over and over again to her coach. He keeps shaking his head and arguing with her. At least that's how it seems to Sessions.

Finally the coach turns to him. "No crime," the Japanese man says, shaking his head as if he doesn't agree with the words coming out of his mouth. "No crime," he says again, and looks directly at Mitsuko, who nods and then says something very quickly in Japanese.

"She didn't understand," Suzuki tells Sessions.

"What?"

"The boy."

Sessions heaves a sigh. They aren't getting much of anywhere. The language barrier. The girl is so young.

Again Mitsuko tells her coach something and he translates. "He did not do anything."

Now Sessions gets it—they're not going to press charges, although he suspects that the coach would like to. But the man wasn't there. It's the word of the two girls, and they've decided it was a misunderstanding. Their position doesn't give him much room to maneuver with the father and son waiting in the interrogation room.

"He go away," Suzuki says, "right now."

"I'll see what I can do," Sessions tells them all.

"Thank you," Mitsuko says, and lowers her eyes. "Thank you," she says again.

Sessions brings the notebook with him when he opens the door of the interrogation room to find Daniel and Stefan sitting motionless, staring at nothing. He tosses it onto the table and Stefan sits up straighter.

"How did you—?"

"She brought it in. The girl."

"But it's for *her!*" And now Stefan puts his head in his hands and moans. He's fucked this up, like he has fucked up everything in his life.

Sessions and Daniel look at each other. The moaning from Stefan fills the small room, and each man, a father, is moved by the hopelessness in it.

"Look, son," Sessions says as he pulls out a chair and sits down next to Stefan, "you're in trouble."

Stefan doesn't raise his head, doesn't remove his hands.

"Look at me!" And all traces of compassion are now gone from Sessions's voice. If he's going to get anywhere with this kid, he's going to have to scare some sense into him. "Sit up straight and look at me when I talk to you!"

Stefan does, reluctantly.

"What did we agree to the last time you were here? You tell me. I want to hear it."

Stefan mumbles something that Sessions finds unacceptable. "What? You need to tell me what our bargain was, son. What you were going to do so that there wouldn't be any more trouble. Say it. Tell me."

Stefan mumbles a few words. "Stay away" is what it sounds like.

"What? I can't understand a fucking word you're saying! What was our agreement?"

"Not bother . . ."

"Speak in goddamn sentences!"

And as the duet of mumbles and shouts plays out across the table from him, Daniel picks up the notebook and opens it. There it all is, the whole story of his son's futile, clueless life. Endless pages in Stefan's meticulous, tiny script. In black ink he has carefully created charts with a place for the date, then the skating move, and then a number grade based on a 1–5 scale: *double axel, triple toe loop—4.75; triple flip . . . great speed coming out—5; triple lutz . . . you nailed it—5!* Every turn, every spin and leap and dip, has been noted and graded. Pages and pages and pages of observations. And in red pen Daniel sees Stefan's notation of mistakes: *under-rotated triple axel . . . insufficient speed on triple lutz to permit triple toe loop . . . head angle tucked down.* But it's the lines of purple ink that crack Daniel's heart open, because they contain so much longing: *lovely, gentle quality . . . soaring jumps . . . I saw 4 minutes of joy.*

Only from a distance, hidden behind these supposedly objective comments, can Stefan allow himself to love this girl. When Daniel reads, *You skate like an angel from heaven*, he closes the book. He can't read any more, because it's too revealing. Here is a boy who sees himself as the damaged goods Daniel feels him to be. And Daniel is ashamed of himself for communicating all this to his child.

"And what did you do?" Sessions is now shouting. "Did you leave her alone?"

"For a while," Stefan manages.

"Not good enough, Stefan. I said permanently. Leave her alone *permanently*! You remember that discussion? Do you? Answer me, son!"

But Stefan is gone. His eyes on his lap, he shakes his head, doesn't speak, doesn't look up. Everything is lost. What difference does it make where he ends up—jail, his father's apartment, which feels like jail?

And Daniel can't bear it anymore, the cop browbeating his son, the hopelessness weighting Stefan's shoulders. "We're leaving," he says as he stands up.

"That's up to me," Sessions says. "Sit down."

Daniel doesn't. "No, we're leaving Colorado."

At that Stefan raises his head.

"If I guarantee that we will move to another state? In another time zone, somewhere back east, say. If I'm responsible for him, if I tell you that he won't leave my side, will that do it? Will that solve the problem?"

"But Dad, where would we go?" Stefan is panicked. He can't be that far away from her. From Mitsuko.

"If you tell the girl that? If you reassure her? Would that solve the problem?"

Sessions shrugs.

"He fell in love and lost all judgment." Daniel is speaking to the father inside Ron Sessions, to the man who gave him his card and told him he understands about raising sons. Very softly Daniel says, "Haven't you and I done pretty much the same at one time or another?" He shows the cop the open notebook. "He meant well. Look. He wanted to help. It's all here."

And Stefan presses the heels of his hands over his face. His father understands. He never thought he would. But he does.

Daniel watches the cop scan Stefan's pages, and when Sessions's face settles into surrender, Daniel knows that their flight from Colorado is what he can do for his son. Perhaps the only thing.

It is the action that keeps Stefan out of jail, Daniel believes. And so, in early May, father and son are on the move again, across the high plains of Colorado on I-76, through the entire state of Nebraska on I-80, and then into Iowa, past Des Moines to Grinnell College in the center of the state, halfway between the capital and Iowa City. It isn't the East Coast, but it is where Daniel can find a job. And it is far enough.

CHAPTER TWELVE

By the end of the academic year Daniel is in New Hampshire, the southwestern part, just over the Massachusetts state line, in a tiny town called Winnock, population 394. His stay in Iowa, at Grinnell College, lasted two semesters. He experienced it as a year of polite, well-mannered students overshadowed by Stefan's constant, unrelieved anger, all of it directed toward him.

Stefan blamed Daniel for their flight from Colorado, convinced somehow that his father could have negotiated a better outcome than the one he did, that there was a way to keep Stefan out of jail and remain in Colorado Springs, close enough to Mitsuko Kita that he could have found a way to see her again.

During one of their endless arguments, Daniel finds the legal definition of stalking in one of the criminal law books he had Stefan bring home from Grinnell's library for just that purpose—to scare some sense into his son: " 'Stalking involves severe intrusions on the victim's personal privacy and autonomy, with an immediate and long-lasting impact on quality of life as well as risks to security and safety of the victim even in the absence of express threats of physical harm.' " Daniel reads that last part out again, but Stefan is pacing through the apartment—long, irate strides, head down, hands stuffed in his jeans pockets—and appears not to be listening.

"If someone 'repeatedly follows, approaches, contacts, places under surveillance, or makes any form of communication with another person,' then they're stalking." Daniel is shouting now. "And it's a class five felony! A felony means jail time, Stefan! That's what was waiting for you in Colorado if we had stayed!"

His son yells right back—"You're crazy!"—and slams out of their apartment. Every fight is some variation on the same theme, until twelve months of unrelenting battle culminate in Stefan's driving Daniel to Winnock to deposit his father with his sister, Alina.

In counterpoint to his son's relentless demands—Stefan's caretaking and anger two sides of the same filial imperative: that his father pay attention to him—Daniel's daughter seems to need nothing from him. Or from the world around her, either.

When asked, Alina always maintains that she chose this remote town in New Hampshire, almost an hour northwest of Boston, for its beauty. But Daniel suspects that Winnock's isolation is a key factor. Here Alina can go for weeks without seeing or speaking to anyone. And she is content, or at least she insists that she's content. The arrival of her father is not welcome, that much is clear. She has no interest in him. She has no need to mend what was irrevocably broken back when she was five.

She takes him in because Stefan delivers him and she loves her brother and can see that he is at the end of his rope.

"Your turn," is what Stefan says as he deposits Daniel on the gravel driveway of what looks like a small barn. "We're going to kill each other if you don't take him." And Daniel didn't dispute those words. In fact, he says little. By this point he has come to see himself as a piece of unwanted luggage handed over from one child, who is done with him, to another, who has no need for him.

The barn Alina stands in front of has been rehabilitated—a coat of deep red paint, new windows, and a black shingled roof. And the main house, which is just visible on a slight rise to the left, is a sprawling, stately white clapboard structure with a deep front porch.

Daniel faces his two adult children and waits for his fate to be decided.

"You can't stay here," Alina tells him, gesturing vaguely to the structure behind her. "There's only one bedroom."

"All right." Daniel looks at Stefan. What next?

"Not all right," Stefan says. "What about the cottage? Where I stayed that time. That's what I thought—the cottage."

Alina shrugs. "If he wants to."

"He has no choice," Stefan insists.

"All right, then, let me get the key."

And although uninvited, Daniel follows his daughter through her open front door. He's curious to see how she lives.

In front of him is a spare and pristine living room, everything in it white—the walls, the planked ceiling, the intricate lace curtains at the windows, the slipcovered sofa. That is why his eye is drawn to the large blue-and-gray fieldstone fireplace, which bisects the right wall, and its white-painted mantel, where found objects are grouped in threes and fours. Seedpods. Twigs. Stones. The skeletons of several small animals, white and brittle. A bird's nest. The display is simple and beautiful, composed by a sure hand. Through an open doorway Daniel can glimpse a tiny jewel box of a kitchen. More white—cabinets, sink, refrigerator. The entire effect is both restful and austere.

There's a closed door to the left of the front door.

"The one bedroom?"

"Where I work."

"I thought you were teaching."

"I was. Not anymore."

"And now what do you do?"

She opens the door so he can see what lies beyond. The space is large and open. It is easy to see the barn that this structure used to be—a tall, pitched roof with heavy wood struts criss-crossing beneath the roof, a concrete floor, windows high up in what must have once been the hayloft.

One wall is lined with crude shelves made of bricks and wood planks. They are crowded with salmon-colored bowls and dishes, vases, goblets, whatever can be made of clay. There's a large structure of stacked cement blocks, looking like a small fortress, which Daniel understands is a firing kiln, and there's a potter's wheel under a window.

"These are yours?" Daniel asks. The bowls are delicate and willowy, with rims that undulate. The vases pour upward at their edge like outstretched arms. Everything is delicate and beautiful even in this primitive, unfired state.

"That's what I do now," Alina says. "I take care of the O'Malleys' land and they let me stay here and work." She turns, looks at Daniel, appraising him. "And now you're here." The last thing she wants is this problem that Stefan has dumped in her lap.

"You don't have to—" Daniel starts, without really knowing what the end of that sentence is going to be, but his daughter interrupts him.

"The cottage is only one room."

"Okay." Daniel is determined to be agreeable. What choice does he have?

She shrugs and grabs a key from a nail by the door. "Come on, then," she says, and tromps out in her heavy boots, Daniel following.

His daughter is formidable, Daniel sees. She wears jeans

caked with dried clay, a torn T-shirt with *The Vagina Mono-logues* in faded script across her breasts, and those hiking boots that lace all the way up her shins. Her honey-colored hair is pulled back into a low ponytail and tied with a length of twine. Her hands are callused and look supremely capable. She seems so strong and self-reliant. And Daniel is immediately jealous. To be as at home in the world as she is, marching quickly ahead of him now across a meadow bursting on this June day with wild lupines and woolly-headed lavender bergamot and milkweed plants crowned with vivid yellow-and-black Monarch butterflies.

Alina's destination is a small stone building with a low door and a roof of charcoal slate, situated on the edge of a pond.

"Foyle's Pond," she tells him, keeping her sentences short and factual. "And this was once the springhouse for the farm."

With a copse of birch trees creeping up behind the building and large granite blocks in shades of gray and amber making up the walls, Daniel can see that it must have been an ideal spot for keeping perishables cool.

Alina hands him the key. "The O'Malleys remodeled it some, but it isn't much."

Daniel shrugs. He doesn't need much. Four walls. A door he can close to keep the rest of the world at bay.

"Two miles farther down the road you came in on is the town. Winnock." She points him in the right direction. "I work during the day. Every day. You'll have to fend for yourself." And with that, she turns and walks back across the meadow, the way they came.

Daniel watches her strong strides quickly put distance between them, and then a high-pitched tone, a whistle, cuts through the quiet air. And immediately an image flashes across his mind of a five-year-old Alina, lips pursed into an *O*, the tip of her tongue lodged against her lower teeth as he taught her, struggling to push just the right amount of breath out to make that whistle. Nothing, for days and days, but she didn't give up. They practiced together for weeks, in the car when he drove her to school, on the sofa after dinner, her determined little face bunched with concentration, fierce even then, until she finally got it. Surprised at herself, but oh, so proud. And then, less than a month later, he was gone. Left: he should be clear. Less than a month later, he left.

Now she whistles a second time, and a medium-sized mutt, a blur of white and brown, shoots out of the trees, bounding toward her and circling his daughter with leaps of happiness as she walks back to her barn. To Daniel, it feels as if Alina has forgotten him as soon as her back is turned.

From across the meadow he watches Stefan open the trunk of the car, take out his three boxes of books and two suitcases, put them on the gravel, get into the car, back it up, and head down the driveway toward the main road. On the drive from Iowa to New Hampshire, Stefan made the case, relentlessly, that he needed the car more than Daniel did. Daniel is afraid to drive, Stefan reminded him, and, besides, where was there to go? The car would just sit there rusting out and being wasted, while he, Stefan, already had plans for it. Daniel, exhausted from all the years of arguing and opposing his son, agreed to let Stefan take the car. Which he is now doing. Down the driveway, almost to the end, and then the car stops abruptly and Stefan gets out and lopes across the meadow to Daniel.

"This is for the best," is his parting statement.

Daniel shrugs. "I don't see much alternative."

"Right, that's what I mean. We wore out our welcome."

With each other? Daniel wants to ask but doesn't. No need to start all that up again. He simply nods, raises a hand to rest across Stefan's shoulder in parting. "Son—" But Stefan has already turned and is now sprinting through the wildflowers, desperate, it seems, to get in the car and be on his way.

And then Daniel really is on his own, the next chapter of his life in front of him, inside the stone cottage. He stoops a bit as he opens the heavy wood door to see a small room with thick granite walls—the kind of walls that weep with moisture in the winter. A basic, unfinished wood floor. Through a door to his left he can see a serviceable bathroom. There's a small fireplace in the rear wall, its stone blackened from use and never cleaned, a simple wrought-iron bed to its left, and an old stove, an older refrigerator, and an enameled sink along the right, open shelves with a few mismatched dishes above it. Two easy chairs, looking like garage-sale rejects, upholstered in a faded stripe, are positioned to face the fireplace; a braided rag rug in autumn colors spans the floor between the chairs and the hearth. A simple wooden table, maybe four feet long, and two straight-backed chairs are angled next to the stove. Four long, narrow windows, two on either side wall, reach almost to the floor and are curtainless.

So this is where he has landed. Fifty-four years old. Homeless, disdained by his children, unemployable. Besieged by panic attacks. Without any skills. And feeling sorry for himself, he has to admit, which brings a grin at his own predicament, there in this barren room which is to be his home for the foreseeable future. Life does a number, doesn't it? There's nothing to do but grin at that. He's living out an appropriate retribution for his acts of selfishness in his thirties—leaving Stephanie and his kids—and his self-centeredness in his forties—drinking too much, enjoying the literary acclaim too much, marrying Cheryl when he shouldn't have.

He puts his laptop down on the wooden table; somehow he hasn't let go of it since stepping out of his car. Does that tell him something? That he's pathetic? That he still clings to the illusion he's a writer?

He sits down at the table and surveys the room again. It will do. Maybe it's all he deserves right now. Maybe he'd better unpack. He goes out to Alina's driveway and begins carrying in his boxes and suitcases. His daughter is nowhere to be seen.

It's while he's unpacking his books that he finds the crumpled eight pages that Isabelle gave him that day two years ago when it was so hot and she took off her graduation robe to reveal that gossamer sundress, almost like wearing nothing. And then she took the strap off her shoulder and then he . . . And he stops himself. He shouldn't be going there.

He smoothes the pages flat and reads her words again. About Melanie. And needing to be an outlaw. About sass and meeting life head-on. He's missing Isabelle's spirit in his life. That's the deepest sadness of all.

He opens his laptop and begins an e-mail to her that he knows he will never send. It contains too much longing. And besides, he hasn't heard from her since she was having great sex with some guy who was saving the world. She had found Daniel's disgraced third novel in a secondhand shop, and he had made her promise not to read it. By now she probably doesn't even remember him. But still he writes.

CHAPTER THIRTEEN

I sabelle's son has night terrors. When they happen, Avi bolts upright in bed, eyes open but still deeply asleep, and screams. On particularly bad nights, he darts through the house as if being chased by demons.

"Three is a common age for night terrors to begin," Deepti tells Isabelle calmly one mild September evening, "and there is no reason to be overly concerned."

The two women are sitting on the front porch of the Craftsman duplex, Isabelle in an ancient rocker found at the Berkeley Flea Market whose contours fit her lanky frame perfectly, and Deepti in a wicker chair. They're sipping chai tea that Deepti made for them, sweet and aromatic. Fanny Hershfeld's side of the house is quiet, with only the blue light from the television screen flickering in the living room darkness. Isabelle knows that in all likelihood her neighbor is fast asleep in her Barca-Lounger and that the television will be droning on till the early-morning hours. Usually Fanny manages to rouse herself, turn off the TV, and hobble to bed before the sun rises, but not always. How much you know about someone living in such close proximity, Isabelle has discovered—things you would never know about friends, who feel much closer to your heart.

"In the transition from REM sleep to the deeper non-REM sleep, the central nervous system of a child can become overly aroused, and it responds with a sudden reaction of fear." Deepti is patient and careful in her explanation. It is easy to see the excellent physician she is preparing to be.

"But he looks terrified," Isabelle whispers into the soft night air, as if it were a shameful secret.

"Yes, children do, but he's fast asleep. He doesn't know, Isabelle. It's only you who sees the terror."

Isabelle nods, is quiet for a moment, then adds in a rush, "I was afraid it was something I've done. Something emotionally damaging." Her greatest fear, spoken to Deepti, whom she trusts completely.

"No, it's a neurological phenomenon."

"Meaning it's physical, not psychological?"

"Yes, so simply hold him so he doesn't hurt himself and wait. That's all. There is no comfort you can give. Just wait."

Wait while her child is inconsolable? Wait and do nothing? "That's torture in itself."

"It passes, Isabelle."

"Yes," Isabelle agrees finally and sighs. "It does."

With her foot Isabelle pushes the ancient rocker lightly back and forth against the weathered stone porch and watches the flickering light coming through Fanny's front window. There's a pool of quiet between the two women, comfortable, familiar.

"I wish . . ." Deepti starts, and then pauses.

"What? I love any sentence from you that starts 'I wish.' So rare, Deepti."

Deepti blushes in the dim light, but Isabelle can't see it. "I wish . . ." Deepti says slowly, trying to find exactly the right words, "I wish you didn't have to deal with this problem by yourself."

"Yes," Isabelle agrees. Just that one word, afraid if she doesn't stop there, she will say too much.

"That is the unfortunate part."

And I am furious about it, Isabelle wants to say. *Where is Casey? Why is some child in Indonesia or Senegal more worthy of his attention than his own? And why do I feel like such a horrible, uncaring, selfish person whenever I even entertain these thoughts?*

"As long as Avi is all right," is what she says instead.

"Avi is fine," Deepti reassures her again.

What Isabelle doesn't tell Deepti that evening, or anyone else, is that she is afraid to fall asleep, afraid her sleep will be shattered by Avi's screams. Better to stay awake, be alert. Better to hold his tiny body and lull him calmly back to sleep with all her wits about her.

So she's become a night troller, surfing the Internet for clues, corresponding with other wide-awake mothers across the country whose children cry out in the night. Modifying the loneliness as she can.

There's something about the early-morning hours, about the tension of waiting for the screams to pierce her heavy quiet, about the harshness of her solitude, that feeds her need to feel connected to somebody. One night she finds herself writing to Daniel.

Where is he now? Still in Colorado? Does he even have the same e-mail address? Will he even remember her? Will he answer?

Daniel,

I think it's been over three years since we've been in touch. I have no idea if this will reach you or whether you'll even want to respond.

You must think I've dropped off the face of the earth, if
you've thought about me at all.

It's been a pretty life-changing three years. I had a son in
July of 1995. An amazing, wonderful, funny child named Avi.
We live in Oakland and I work at a bookstore that reminds
me of Seaman's. Do you remember Seaman's, near the Chan-
dler campus?

Avi's father works for a nonprofit called Global Hope and
he spends most of his time saving people's lives. We're not
married but we're a couple, sort of. It's complicated. Actually,
life these days is complicated.

I think about you often, but I'm afraid that you will be
disappointed in how my life has turned out.

Isabelle

She clicks the Send icon and closes her laptop, dispatching
the bedroom into complete darkness. Now the whole house
is dark and quiet. Peace ... there should be peace now, but
Isabelle doesn't feel it. She gathers the quilt from her bed and
drags it into Avi's room.

First a hand to cup the curve of his head, to feel the warmth
of him, the steady draw of his breath in and out, then Isabelle
lays the quilt on the floor and curls up beside his bed. It's only
here that she can sometimes fall asleep.

DANIEL RECEIVES ISABELLE'S E-MAIL first thing the next
morning. He's become an early riser now that he's settled in
the New Hampshire countryside. With no one to wake him
and no morning responsibilities, he's still out of bed by six.
By seven o'clock he's at Bev's Bakery, where Bev makes cappuccinos for the Boston weekenders and strong, simple dark
coffee for the locals. He takes his with a cinnamon bun and

an Internet connection. By nine o'clock he's back home at his kitchen table to begin his day's work.

He has become regular in his habits, and he's writing, but he has no idea what. It started the day he arrived, when he found Isabelle's eight pages about Melanie, and before he even unpacked, he sat down and began an e-mail to her. Of course he's never sent it or any of the others he's written since. But he's found himself writing more, bits and pieces, then scraps of ideas that have nothing to do with Isabelle, nothing ever fully realized, but he continues on.

At first he thought he was wasting his time, but that notion no longer bothers him. With no real hope of publication— where is his book agent? he has no idea; would his last publishing house even read a new manuscript he submitted? who knows?—Daniel is free to write whatever comes to him. And he finds the isolation of his cottage and the lack of demands coming from the rest of the world, particularly his daughter, as a sort of tonic—they spur him on to write. The act of doing it is what matters to him now, he has come to realize, not the finished product.

There is something about this time in Winnock that is reminiscent of the first time he began to write, more than twenty years ago, when he had left his first marriage (and his children, he reminds himself) and lived alone on the top floor of a rooming house, in that shabby room with the peeling wallpaper and the bathroom down the hall, and worked sporadically hanging drywall. He had totally fucked up his life, he felt, and no one would have disagreed with him then. Or now.

Out of that nadir came his first book, the one about his father, the one he had to write before he could move on. He sees now how freeing that feeling of hopelessness was. He could write because no one would ever have expected it of him and because he expected nothing to come of all the hours he spent in front of the typewriter.

Two years now living in Winnock, he is a familiar figure at the bakery's round window table, head down over his laptop screen, a thick white mug of Bev's arabica coffee at his elbow. People refer to him as "the writer," or "that writer fella," but nobody is really interested in what he has written or might be writing now. People mind their own business in New Hampshire. Their state motto is "Live Free or Die."

When Daniel sees Isabelle's e-mail in his in-box, he sits back in his wooden chair, surprised, and suddenly awash in rusty emotions. He contemplates the screen for several minutes. It really is from Isabelle, even though he's never sent even one of the scores of e-mails he's written to her over the past two years. Oh, Isabelle—she remembers him! She's written!

A large, handsome woman, chestnut hair mixed lightly with gray, cut chin length and pushed behind her ears, a white apron tied around her ample waist, coffeepot in hand, refills Daniel's mug without being asked. Bev knows his likes and dislikes by now, at least when it comes to his morning routine, and she is in the habit of quietly pouring his coffee, nodding but not speaking, not intruding. For all she knows, he may be in the middle of creating.

What little pride Bev allows herself rests with her ability to sleuth out her customers' needs, to listen, to observe, to make the bakery a welcoming place. Her women friends would say she carries that kindness into the rest of her life, as well, but Bev isn't so sure of that. She has a kind of New England reserve, she knows, a strong spine that has seen her through the chronic depressions and early death of her husband. She fears that sometimes what she calls her "Yankee backbone" gets in the way of her softer instincts.

This morning Daniel is sitting back in his chair, a look of surprise, then pleasure, on his face, and he glances at Bev as she tops up his coffee. "One of my former students just e-mailed me."

"Good for you," she says, pleased for him. He seems so solitary; a communication from someone, anyone, can only be positive.

"Yes," Daniel says quietly, "good for me." And he leans forward and clicks on Isabelle's name. Whatever she has to say, he is eager to read it.

Daniel,

I think it's been over three years since we've been in touch. I have no idea if this will reach you or whether you'll even want to respond.

Daniel stops reading and looks up, out the window of the bakery to the empty sidewalk. Directly across the road is the Winnock Arts & Craft Gallery, and he can see a set of Alina's wine goblets featured prominently in the window display.

Could Isabelle seriously think he wouldn't respond to her? He can't think of anything he'd rather do. How could she doubt that? Human relationships are baffling and impossible, he concludes again, for at least the hundredth time in his life. Navigating them is a skill he has never been able to master. Not with his children or his ex-wives or his former students. All except for Isabelle. She was different, so how can she start her e-mail with that statement? He shakes his head and continues on.

You must think I've dropped off the face of the earth, if you've thought about me at all.

Bev gives him privacy, remains at her spot behind the bakery counter, watching as he reads the entire e-mail and begins typing a response. Daniel is endlessly fascinating to her—a writer, with a lifetime of interesting stories in his face. Over the past two years his early-morning visits have become the highlight of her day.

THAT SAME MORNING IN ISABELLE'S Oakland duplex is as hectic as every morning seems to be. She has overslept again. Her late-night vigils often translate into mornings conducted in overdrive, Isabelle behind the eight ball before the day has even begun.

Her first task is to get Avi up and dressed, which usually includes coaxing—he doesn't like to leave the warmth of his Power Rangers quilt—and a lengthy discussion about what he will wear. The child has clear preferences in almost every arena of his life. Some days everything must match—blue jeans, blue shirt, blue sneakers. Some days he decides he has to have shorts, even though all his shorts are in the hamper, casualties of finger painting or mud play or who knows what. Lugging the laundry to the Laundromat is Isabelle's least favorite household chore, and it is only when the choice is a trip to Washworld or a nudists' colony that Isabelle manages to get them some clean clothes.

This morning there are no clean shorts—no surprise—and the discussion turns to what would be an acceptable alternative. Finally, in desperation because they're going to be late, now very late, Isabelle takes scissors to a pair of Avi's old jeans, and he is thrilled.

"Awesome!" He is beside himself. "Wow, new shorts!" All day he will tell anyone who will listen, "My mommy made these shorts with scissors!" as if Isabelle is a wizard to have accomplished such a feat.

Isabelle, exhausted already at 7:55 in the morning, feels only relief to have solved the problem. "Okay, into the car. Grandpa is waiting for you." Even though Isabelle doesn't have Casey on any sort of regular basis, she has Art and Lou-

isa, Casey's parents. And Art's alternative school, A Circle of
Friends, where Avi spends the day and thrives.

"And Dylan," Avi reminds her. His best friend in Miss Dor-
othy's class, Dylan, makes everything okay, and Avi knows he
is already at school waiting for him.

"And Dylan," Isabelle agrees as she shepherds her son into
the Jeep, pulling on a sweater as she does, barefoot, her shoes
stuffed into her purse, handing Avi a granola bar and an apple
for breakfast as she buckles him into his car seat.

"Mommy, put on your shoes."

"I will, pumpkin."

"Right now or your feet will catch a cold."

And she has to stop and show her conscientious son that she
has in fact put on her shoes.

As she maneuvers the Oakland streets from Telegraph Avenue to 51st Street to Broadway, and then a right turn onto 41st,
where Art's school is located, she wonders, as she has many
mornings before, when her son started taking care of her. And
how she has become such an incompetent person.

She glances into the rearview mirror to see Avi eating his
breakfast in a sort of rhythm of his own making—one nibble
of apple, one bite of the granola bar, one nibble of apple. His
attention is focused on whatever game he has made up for
himself, and he doesn't look up to meet her eyes. He's never
bored, her son. In that way he carries his father with him, even
though he looks like Isabelle: long-limbed (he will be tall) and
brown-eyed, with a cap of straight blond hair rapidly darkening to match Isabelle's color.

Art is waiting for them as they pull up at 8:25, late again.
Seeing him standing calmly beside the wooden gate painted
with stars and the moon—a tall, angular man with a strong
profile and a shock of gray hair—Isabelle marvels yet again at
how the perpetual motion that is Casey came from the steady
serenity that is Art.

"Just making sure you guys got here all right," Art says with no judgment in his voice as he opens the door of the Jeep. Quickly he unbuckles Avi from his car seat, swings him up and out of the car, and deposits him safely on the sidewalk. "My man!"

"We had a shorts crisis," Isabelle tells him from the driver's seat.

"Mommy made these with scissors!" Avi is bursting with his news. "Come on, Grandpa!" he yells as he runs up the cement path, more painted stars leading the way like stepping-stones to the front door of heaven. "School's started *already*!"

"Sorry," Isabelle mumbles. "The mornings get away from me."

"No worries."

"Have you heard from him?" She knows she shouldn't ask. Art would tell her if Casey had contacted them, but she can't stop herself.

"Papua New Guinea, you know." Art shakes his head. "Halfway around the world. The earthquake and then the tsunami . . ."

"All the thousands of people left homeless and all the vil-lages washed out to sea and all the little old people floating dead and bloated in the water like guppies at the top of a fish tank."

"Isabelle," Art says kindly, in the gentlest of admonitions.

And she stops. She knows her comments offend Art's Quaker sensibility, but she's so deep-down mad at Casey, and Art and Louisa are the closest things she has to him.

"He'll call when he can, I know," she backtracks now. She appreciates Art, loves him really, for stepping in and being present every day for Avi, and so there are conventions they must observe: no criticisms of Casey, who's doing God's work; no airing of her own trouble with it, because her unhappiness tests Art's loyalties. She smiles now and Art smiles back. Better this way; harmony is restored.

On to Full of Beans on College, where amid the hordes of Berkeley students, who look twelve to her—so young, when was she that young?—she gets a large cappuccino and a bagel. And then on to Noah's Ark, where she usually opens the bookstore by nine o'clock.

It's too early to have many customers. She's told Meir that—nobody comes in until almost eleven—but he likes the idea that the store is open at nine just in case, and Isabelle manages to do that for him most days. He arrives after lunch, and that is Isabelle's favorite time of the day. They sit behind the counter together and talk about the books they have read or what they hope to be reading, or Isabelle will tell an Avi story because Meir is such an eager audience. Or he will tell Isabelle what happened in the store after she left the day before or what he's planning to cook for dinner. Anything and everything is fair game for conversation, except Casey, because Isabelle already knows without a word being spoken how Meir feels about that subject.

As they talk Meir eats junk food—Doritos and Mallomars, most days—and Isabelle pours one cup of coffee after another from the Mr. Coffee they keep going on the counter. Each tells the other to take it easy on their vice of choice, but neither acts on the suggestion, their conversations too engrossing to pay much attention to curbing appetites.

Yesterday during a midafternoon lull, while they were sitting at the front counter on their tall stools, Isabelle relayed the conversation she had had with Deepti about Avi's night terrors.

"It's a neurological condition, fairly common, that will resolve itself as he grows."

"That's a relief." In his heart of hearts, Meir claims some small familial connection with Avi—an older uncle or a surrogate grandfather—although he would never presume to voice it.

"A huge one."

"You guys got used textbooks?" a Berkeley student, long hair tied in a ponytail, wearing sandals, calls from the half-open front door, not willing to commit to coming in if the answer is no.

"Back wall." Meir points as he tells him, and the kid saunters in.

"We were sitting on the porch last night as we were talking," Isabelle begins again. She has an agenda here. Meir can feel it. "It's quiet on our street, you know."

"I do."

"And the only sound was the television going in your sister's half of the house."

"Isabelle . . ." he says in warning. Meir knows where this is heading and doesn't like the destination, but Isabelle plows ahead.

"She falls asleep in that BarcaLounger every night, Meir, all alone in there, watching one stupid television program after another. Nobody visits. I hardly ever hear the phone ring—"

And a customer stops them, bringing a Moroccan cookbook up to the counter, which Meir rings up.

"Do you carry any new books at all?" the woman asks. "I'm looking for *Summer Sisters* by Judy Blume."

Meir and Isabelle look at each other. This has been an ongoing debate for years; she thinks Meir should expand their inventory and he is reluctant to make any change.

"It's on the *Times* bestseller list!" the customer adds, as if she's announcing the Nobel Prize. "She's written an adult novel. Interesting, don't you think?"

Bestseller list? Judy Blume? What does Meir know about the bestsellers, or current authors? The past is where he is comfortable.

"We're thinking about expanding into that area," Isabelle says pointedly, her eyes on Meir.

"Yes," he says, "we're *thinking* about it."

"Oh, that would be wonderful! Then I could get everything I need right here!" She takes her used cookbook, slips it into her cloth bag.

"Thank you for coming in," Meir and Isabelle say in unison, and smile at each other. "She's making me redundant," he adds, pleased nonetheless.

And their customer, with her heavy gray braid swinging across her back, pushes open the front door, the welcome bell jingling as she passes through, and is gone.

"Popular fiction!" Meir says with a tinge of horror, but Isabelle is not to be derailed. She picks up their previous conversation right where they left off.

"Why don't you just pick up the phone and call her?" She is fed up with this brother-sister feud.

"Call Fanny?!"

"Or come over. I'll make dinner for the three of us—you, me, and Fanny."

"Oh, heavens, no! She's the most disagreeable of women. I don't even want to talk to her—why would I want to eat with her?"

"She's your sister."

"An accident of birth I try to ignore."

"Meir!"

"When was the last time you called your mother?"

"That's a completely different situation. She stopped talking to me."

"Bingo!"

"But Fanny is all alone."

Meir shrugs.

"What is it about Jewish families?" Isabelle asks sincerely. "There's always a feud somewhere."

"At least one a generation."

"An uncle who hasn't talked to his brother in forty years,

a cousin who's disowned a son for some long-forgotten transgression. Why do we hold such grudges?"

Meir shakes his head at the vagaries of family. "You can't tell the heart whom to love, I guess." He looks longingly at Isabelle, whose back is turned as she rings up another customer's purchase. "It goes its own way, however inconvenient."

This morning Isabelle takes her customary place behind the front counter, alone until the afternoon. She spreads cream cheese on her bagel, takes another large shot of caffeine—oh, if only she could mainline the stuff—and opens her laptop. And there it is. A response from Daniel.

Isabelle,

What happened to Melanie? Are you writing?

Daniel

That's it. That's all. Not *How nice it is to hear from you after all these years* or *Tell me about your son* or any other pleasantry. No, he cuts to the chase. Well, that's Daniel, isn't it? When has he ever made small talk? Should she tell him the truth? Will he disown her? Be disgusted with her lack of dedication? But then she remembers what Stefan told her that morning in Lathrop Hall when she was waiting outside Daniel's office with cappuccinos: *He's got writer's block, you know. He can't help himself, so good luck with his helping you.*

Maybe there will be some compassion there for her lack of productivity. Maybe . . . She deliberates, but in the end she answers Daniel because she wants him back in her life, however peripherally. And she answers honestly, because there has always been that between them—honesty—and she honors it, however difficult.

Daniel,

Sometimes I write a little. But not very often and never about Melanie. She is an outlaw and I shop at the co-op, stack books during the day, and play Chutes and Ladders. How can I begin to understand Melanie?

My son often wakes up screaming at night so I don't sleep much now. It's called "night terrors" and it will pass as he gets older, but right now there's always the possibility that this night will be the one. And so I stay awake and wait.

It feels like I'm on watch, and writing feels to me like disappearing into another world, and so they are in conflict. Right now it has to be that I am in this world, our world, with my son. He's only three.

Isabelle

DANIEL HAS COME BACK TO BEV'S for lunch. He couldn't stay away. He needs the Internet access. He needs to see if Isabelle has answered his question—*Are you writing?* And she has! With a hunger that animates him, he reads her answer. Ah, her life is all about her son. He knows what to say. He writes:

Isabelle,

Having spent the past several years with my son—my clueless, hopeless, unhappy son—I realize I sacrificed him to my ambition to write. It's a loss I mourn every day.
I know you will do better with your son.

Daniel

Daniel,

Are you telling me not to write?

Isabelle

Isabelle,

Of course not. Just not to be stupid about it the way I was. Selfish. Heedless. Unconscious, really, I now see.
   But I know you won't be. You're made of better stuff.

Daniel

Isabelle reads that last e-mail between customers. *Oh, Daniel, I am not. Look at what I did—got pregnant when I didn't want to, tied myself to a man who has no need of home, who flees into danger rather than away from it.*

But she writes none of that to Daniel. If she puts it on paper, then it's tangible and she'll be forced to face it. If she doesn't actually say it—to Daniel or Deepti (who already knows it, Isabelle suspects) or to Meir (who is waiting for her to say something along those lines, she is sure)—then there's still hope that one day Casey will tire of this life, one day he will want them, his small family, more than he wants to fly off to Mongolia.

Instead she writes:

Daniel,

I think you have a completely skewed idea of who I really am. You remember that eager, hopeful, yearning student who

knocked on your door many years ago, the one who blossomed
because you believed in her dream to write.
  But something happened to that girl.

Isabelle

Daniel answers her immediately.

Isabelle,

What happened?

Daniel

And alone in Noah's Ark—no customers at the moment,
Meir's presence several hours away—Isabelle ponders Daniel's question. How to explain what has happened? She starts
typing without thinking, without allowing her better judgment to stop her.

Daniel,

  It's not just Avi's birth, although that changed everything.
  Being a mother shifts all the priorities. (I can hear you
  saying, Good, that's what I didn't do with my son.)
    It's that I took a risk. I became another person for a short
  while. I let myself love Casey without restraint. I refused to
  be cautious. I embraced the moment in a way I was brought
  up to avoid. I dared to believe life could be glorious.
    And I was proven wrong. That's why it's so hard for me
  to write. It takes a leap of faith, and I no longer believe I
  can do it.

Isabelle

Isabelle hits Send and stares at all the shelves and shelves of books that other people have managed to write, despite their life conditions, despite their bad choices, despite their doubts, and she knows somewhere deep inside her that she's trying to explain away her most basic flaw: that she's a coward.

CHAPTER FOURTEEN

The main street of Winnock consists of a stretch of red brick buildings three stories high, leaning shoulder to shoulder as if holding each other up, positioned on either side of the two-lane road that takes people into and out of the small town. Traditional stores, rooted in Winnock for generations, are mixed with shiny new boutiques which cater to the weekenders up from Boston and other Massachusetts cities.

On the east side of the street, in a line, are seven shops. First is Le Breton's Gourmet Foods, open just a year; then Better Living Realtors, and Sewell's Pharmacy with its white beadboard facade nailed over the original brick and a front window packed with ace bandages, stomach remedies, and blood pressure monitors. Next is Bev's Bakery, painted a cornflower blue as a welcome call, and then the dusty, rarely open Antiques and Collectibles, the Granite State Diner with its red neon sign, and finally, on the end, Chatterton's Ice Cream Parlor, where the teenagers from Winnock and surrounding towns hang out, clogging up the sidewalk and adjacent parking lot.

Six stores line the west side of the road: first a bookstore, Leighton's, recently opened, to Daniel's delight, which sits directly across from the gourmet shop, then Don & Tom's

Hardware, in operation since before World War II and stocking everything from drill bits to Tupperware. Bike-orama is next in line—sales and service—the Winnock Arts & Crafts Gallery, the post office, and, at the end of the block, a small local grocery, owned by Gordon Tibbett, which caters to those families who would never buy the foie gras or paper-thin prosciutto or loquats flown in from the Caribbean that line Le Breton's shelves.

The town is just the right size for Daniel. Now he never has to contend with crowds or traffic or unwanted intrusions on his private space. Leaving people alone is an art form here in Winnock, universally practiced. How fitting, Daniel thinks, that Alina, with her unerring instinct for solitude, found her way here.

What he didn't expect is that he would be the beneficiary of that decision. At first he didn't see the isolation as an asset. When Alina pointed out the road into town and told him he'd have to walk the two miles, Daniel felt it as an impossibility. All that open space. Just the thought of it set his heart racing.

But what were his choices? If he wanted to eat, he had to find a way to get into Winnock and buy food. One option was to ask Alina to drive him, but she had made it very clear that she was far too busy to be concerned with his life. "You'll have to fend for yourself" was a blunt and unambiguous message, exactly what his daughter must have felt decades before, Daniel understood, when he abruptly moved out of the family house and his children's lives.

Alina had made it quite clear that she wasn't inclined to help him out in any way. He could ask again. He could explain about his condition, but he had just enough of a shred of dignity left not to plead for mercy.

And so that left the only other option: walking into town on his own.

That first day, that first attempt, felt to Daniel like he was walking to his own execution, even as he knew how ridiculous he was being. What was being asked of him but putting one foot in front of the other along a perfectly delineated path? His rational mind tried to rein in his rampaging anxiety, with no success.

His heartbeat ricocheted into overdrive as soon as he set out. He was immediately sweating and felt dizzy and breathless and had to sit down twice on the blacktop with his head between his knees because he was sure he was going to pass out on this desolate road with nothing beyond it but vast fields of grasses and chaotic wildflowers. How glad he was that there was no one to witness his foolishness, his crippling inadequacy.

But then the road dipped into a large section of woods, and once inside the dense trees—blue spruce and fir trees which towered up to the sky and shut out the sunlight, maple and oak trees whose green leaves shaded and cooled the air—things got a little better. Daniel felt sheltered by the trees. Protected somehow, given a respite from the open space before and after. It astonished him that he was outside a building and yet his rapid heartbeat and ragged breathing had begun to ease a bit.

He made it into town that first day, exhausted from the physical exertion and the emotional distress, and ashamed. It wasn't a walk he wanted to repeat, and yet he had to, and each time the woods provided the oasis he needed to gather himself, to continue on. An astonishment.

Over the weeks and months, the imperative to buy food to keep his body alive slowly worked to bring his spirit alive. He began to sing as he walked. At first it was a hedge against his rising panic, then it became a necessary component for the whole enterprise. He walked and he sang to himself, songs from his youth chosen for their appropriateness or irony, depending on his mood—Elvis Presley's "It's Now or Never," Dinah Washington's "What a Difference a Day Makes," Roy

Orbison's "Only the Lonely." On particularly bad days, he would make himself sing out "We Shall Overcome," even though he felt it was some kind of blasphemy.

The more he walked, the more manageable the task became. The more manageable it became, the more he liked himself, until finally Daniel found he could breathe more easily in the countryside wherever he was.

All the doctors' advice, all the medication suggested, all the fruitless hours of struggling to get his agoraphobia under control, and slowly, over the past two years, his panic has retreated. And he's grateful, supremely grateful, that his days aren't ruled by the anxiety that had a stranglehold on him in Los Angeles, in Colorado, in Iowa.

Maybe his whole previous life in various cities was the mistake. Maybe his alcohol-fueled years, when he was surrounded by plenty of companions whom he once considered friends, had only worked because of the booze and he was really meant to be a hermit.

Maybe he should stop shaving and grow a foot-long beard, let his hair have its own way and fall across his shoulders in busy waves, stop washing his clothes and dispense with all footwear. But he doesn't do any of that. Instead he finds he takes better care of himself here in Winnock than he ever did before.

The walking everywhere has helped him lose twenty pounds. The fact that he has to shop and cook his own food now and that it is simple and fresh makes him feel better. Gordon Tibbett's grocery has become his twice-weekly destination. And Marie, Gordon's wife, who is old enough to be his mother and treats him that way, helps him choose what to buy and gives him tips on how to cook it.

Although their conversation never strays far from the culinary realm, she somehow lets him know she's proud of him— for making it on his own, for turning a corner in his life—and

Daniel has come to depend on these conferences in the middle of the produce aisle to anchor his week and point him in the right direction.

And he sleeps well at night! For the first time in over ten years.

All these things are a revelation to him—the waning of his anxiety, the feeling of well-being, the pleasure he takes in walking everywhere. Could it be that it has taken him fifty-six years and so many mistakes to find the life he should have been living all along?

The only thing he regrets is his loneliness, but he has formed a shaky truce with that. If the price he has to pay for peace, for his newly won freedom from anxiety, is isolation, he will make that bargain every time.

But then there is Alina—so close in physical proximity, just across the meadow, and so distant still.

Despite her admonition that first day that she had no time or inclination to be involved in his life, he tried the first few weeks to extend a tentative hand to his daughter. He would cross the meadow—the DMZ, as he thought of it—and show up at her studio door. Always knocking first, he would step gingerly across the threshold.

The spotted dog, some kind of beagle-bloodhound mix, he guessed, with its long, floppy ears and loose-jowled face, always curled up at Alina's feet, would raise its head and growl, a low, sustained warning that he wasn't wanted. And his daughter, hunched over the potter's wheel, gently guiding a mound of clay up into a cylinder, one hand inside, the other matching on the outside surface, coaxing, urging the spinning clay into a delicate shape, wouldn't look up.

"Knock, knock," Daniel would say softly as he stood a few feet inside the barn, in an attempt to evoke a private joke they had shared at a time when all was well between them. "Knock, knock," he would repeat hopefully.

At three and a half, Alina had become obsessed with knock-knock jokes. She had learned them from the older kids in her nursery school, and she would throw herself into Daniel's arms when he walked through the door in the evening and demand, "Knock, knock, Daddy."

"Knock, knock," he would comply, frantically searching his brain for a new one.

"Who's there?" Alina would ask.

"Ummmm . . . Lettuce!"

"Lettuce who?"

"Lettuce in, it's cold out here." Daniel would shiver with a convincing chill, and Alina would rock with laughter.

"Another one!" she'd demand.

"Knock, knock."

"Who's there?"

"Figs."

"Figs who?" she'd ask, her eyes big with anticipation.

"Figs the doorbell, it's broken."

And Alina would be gone, lost in a puddle of giggles. There was nothing better in the whole world, Daniel felt in those early years, than watching his tiny daughter hiccup with laughter.

But in New Hampshire, the soft repeating of "knock, knock" got him nowhere. Instead Alina, head bent to her task, would ask sharply, "What is it?" as if he were a deliveryman or an annoying salesman come to the wrong house. What did he expect, that she would remember, that she would want to participate in a childhood ritual that was twenty-five years old?

"Do you have a broom I can borrow?" he would ask, chastened. Or "a tea kettle," or "a bar of soap . . ."

"Walk in to Don and Tom's. You can't keep borrowing things from me."

She would never once look up at him. Never call him Dad. And he would feel dismissed. "Okay," he would inevitably say, and shut the door of her studio, leaving Alina to work.

So he waited a while. He settled in. He watched her from across the meadow with longing. He didn't think he was asking for a lot—a cup of coffee and some conversation once in a while. A meal together, maybe.

One day during the waning days of his first summer in Winnock, he was seated at his kitchen table, laptop in front of him as he made notes about his last year at Chandler, when Stefan and Isabelle had seemed to move in counterpoint to each other, Isabelle filling him up with hope and Stefan pulling him into the mire of despair. And he happened to look up, out one of his long uncurtained windows, to see an enormous animal—a moose, he realized after a second or two of wonder, six feet high at the shoulder if he was a foot—wading into Foyle's Pond, seeking the cool comfort of the pool on a hot August day. Daniel had a perfect view as the bull slowly splashed his way toward the center of the water, his full antlers spreading out ridiculously from his head, four feet across. And slowly the animal sank below the surface till only those velvet-covered protrusions, like massive butterfly wings, rested on the water's surface.

Daniel got up quietly but quickly, his first thought that he had to tell Alina, had to have her come see this. How extraordinary the animal! How majestic and impossible—those antlers! And then he stopped himself. He knew what she would say: she's busy, she's seen moose before, she doesn't need to share anything with Daniel. She isn't interested. And so he sat back down and watched the animal rouse itself and tread out of the pond in a stately march, dripping streams of water from its shaggy fur. A singular moose, whose presence revealed a solitary man.

The only thing Alina consented to do, and only because it was a necessity, was to drive him two nights a week to Spring Hill Community Adult School, where he taught a course in "The Novel." The drive was usually conducted in stony silence. After weeks of attempted conversation, Daniel gave up. What was there to say when even his innocuous small talk was met with monosyllabic answers or, worse yet, mutterings and sighs? He could have understood her reluctance to engage with him if he had tried to delve into heavy-duty stuff—if he had wanted to revisit her childhood or impugn her mother or make excuses for his own behavior—but all he was asking from her was a polite conversation about local events or national news or a book she had read or even the weather. Of course he hoped that this impartial conversation might lead to a more intimate one, but he didn't tip his hand. He deliberately kept the topics light, and Alina deliberately refused to engage.

Alina drove Daniel to his class stone-faced. Conversation about the possibility of rain wouldn't change the way she felt about him one iota. He owed her an apology, a deeply felt, wholehearted apology. And that was not forthcoming.

When Daniel found a student to drive him to and from school, both father and daughter were relieved.

Daniel discovered, to his surprise, that he looked forward to those evening meetings. He found that he felt comfortable with his students. They were familiar to him, reminiscent of his mother's friends, taking him back to his days in Erie.

They are middle-aged women, waitresses and school nurses and retired nursery school teachers and housewives who have raised their children and now have time to consider some minor pleasures for themselves, like reading. And like his mother they have a talent for making the best of things and not complaining when they do. Salt-of-the-earth women, some would call them.

And there is a core group who have taken his class each semester. Pauline, small and tightly wound, who always gets the conversation going with her idiosyncratic but definitive opinions, divorced for many years and working at the Granite State Diner for all that time. And Marge, whose soft and pillowy body is perfect for her numerous grandchildren and the infants and toddlers who come to her in-home day care. She is the conciliator in the group and is somehow able to reel in the conversation when it gets heated and contentious. And then there's valiant Sarah, who never finished college but wishes she had, whose husband is at home and bedridden and whom she's nursed without complaint for many years. Sarah comes to each class as a respite, grateful and happy for those hours each Monday and Thursday night that focus on anything but bedpans and medications. Her effort to dress up for the evenings—a little lipstick, small pearl earrings—isn't lost on Daniel. And Bev, whom he sees every morning, her two boys raised and out of the house, one in the military and the other up at Granite State College in Concord, whose no-nonsense attitude endears her to everyone. It's Bev who calls people on not finishing the assigned book or not having something to say. Everyone has to contribute, and Bev is the one to insist on participation. Without ever speaking about it, she and Daniel have formed an implicit team, both committed to reading and discussing and celebrating each two-hour class to its fullest.

Two years into Daniel's stay in Winnock, word has gotten around that "The Novel" is a class worth taking, and its enrollment has grown to twelve students this September, the September Isabelle decides to get back in touch with Daniel.

Daniel runs the class like a book club. Each week the students are required to read one novel and come prepared to talk about it. They have agreed to alternate current fiction—*Memoirs of a Geisha, Cold Mountain*, Toni Morrison's *Paradise*—with the classics he suggests: *Grapes of Wrath, To Kill a Mockingbird, Jane Eyre, Heart of Darkness*, which he thinks will be challenging for the class, but he assigns it nonetheless. A paper is due at the end of the semester, which Daniel reads but doesn't grade. Instead he writes lengthy personal comments, and they are more appreciated than any grade would be. He's aware that these comments constitute "writing," something he couldn't

have begun to do in Iowa or Colorado or all his years in Los
Angeles at Chandler, when simply walking to campus took all
the attention and energy he had.

And Daniel finds now that he's expansive in the classroom,
talking about what makes good writing, using plain words and
plain thoughts that feel comfortable to him. And listening. To
these women who have lived basic, mostly hard-fought lives
and still have optimistic, often thoughtful things to say.

Someone, usually Bev, brings baked goods. There's an old-
fashioned plug-in coffeemaker that Daniel has appropriated
from the school's lunchroom and made a permanent fixture
in his classroom. They take a ten-minute coffee break in
the middle of the class, but the conversation just continues
unabated, far more necessary than the muffins and coffee cake
that accompany it.

It is here, during these four hours in his week, that Daniel's
loneliness abates for a while. During class and during the time
he reads and responds to Isabelle's e-mails.

After her confession that she no longer believes she can
write, Daniel answers her right away.

Isabelle,

Who does?

Daniel

Daniel,

*Don't be glib. I'm pouring my heart out to you. At least take
me seriously.*

Isabelle

And Daniel stops himself from answering back quickly—and, yes, glibly—and thinks about what to say.

It's well after lunchtime now at Bev's, and it's quiet in the empty shop. Bev is in the back, baking; she has the radio on to an oldies station, and Daniel can hear the Beatles' poignant "Yesterday," interspersed with the pinging of cookie sheets against the wooden baking tables and the slam of the large oven doors as Bev takes out her finished goods.

Daniel is alone at his round table beside the front window, laptop plugged into the Internet connection Bev was smart enough to install when it became available. He's nearly as comfortable here as he is in his tiny cottage with its stone walls that cry in the wintertime. What to say to Isabelle?

Isabelle,

Whether your relationship with this transnational emergency worker has worked out or not has nothing to do with your ability to write. That is innate, within you, and already proven.

I am a witness to it. Don't try to con me. I know what you're capable of.

Daniel

Too harsh? Daniel wonders after he's already hit Send. Too late to worry about it. He wrote what he believes about her. She should be able to take it in.

He paces in the small shop. "Bev!" he calls into the back, and she appears, her hands and forearms dusted with flour, obviously in midtask.

"Can I stay a while longer today? Would that be all right?"

"Bakery's open. Anyone can stay as long as I'm open."

"Okay. It's just that . . . I want to see if I get a return e-mail."

"Your student?"

"Yes."

"A special student?"

"She has talent. That's rare, you know."

Bev nods, certain that there's more to this than simply writing talent, but she doesn't pursue it. It's none of her business, even if she's dying to know about this girl.

"Holler if you need something—I'm just in the back."

He sits back down at his computer and there it is—Isabelle's reply.

Daniel,

How can you be so dismissive?

Isabelle

Oh, no. She misunderstood.

Isabelle,

I'm trying to remind you of what is real. Of what you should be grateful for. Of what you can build on. It's within you.

D.

Daniel,

Maybe. Maybe not. But, ultimately, so what? I have no access anymore. Certainly you of all people understand that. Just telling me I can do it doesn't begin to solve the problem.

202 · DEENA GOLDSTONE

I'm sorry if I've disappointed you. I seem to be doing that more and more lately. My parents are scandalized by my life or lack of life. I don't talk to my mother. My father calls to tell me how worried he is about me. My son's father feels most alive when he isn't here.

Only Avi finds me worthy of his attention. So maybe what I was always meant to be is a mother and not a writer.

I.

Isabelle,

Damn it, you're infuriating!!!!!

D.

SITTING ON HER HIGH STOOL behind the front counter of Noah's Ark, Isabelle smiles. *Oh, Daniel.* How glad she is that she's found him again.

anny Hershfeld has been teaching Avi to play Scrabble. Even though he is only five, he got the hang of it immediately. From the time he was two, courtesy of *Sesame Street*, letters, and then words, have been his constant companions. When he was three, he would call from the backseat of the Jeep, safely strapped into his car seat, "Mommy, do we 'got milk'?" pointing to the billboard with the bright blue Cookie Monster surrounded by a hill of chocolate chip cookies and looking forlornly around for his milk. And Isabelle would reassure her son, their eyes meeting in the rearview mirror, that, yes, they had milk in the fridge. "Let's get more!" Avi would chortle, because he had been burned several times by Isabelle's unreliable memory, and she would always answer, "Okay, on the way home," because she couldn't swear that a carton would be waiting for them when they got there.

By the time he was four, Avi was reading simple Dr. Seuss books by himself—*The Cat in the Hat, Yertle the Turtle,* and *Green Eggs and Ham,* a particular favorite because he thought it was hysterical when that strange creature called himself "Sam-I-Am." So when he passed his fifth birthday, Fanny felt he was ready for Scrabble.

Now they have their routine. They meet in the backyard at the wrought-iron table under the persimmon tree—"a neutral zone," as Fanny calls it, for there is no mistaking that each time they sit down to play, they are embarking on a Scrabble battle. Once Avi understood the basic rules, he wanted no more help from Mrs. H, as he prefers to call her. "I can do it myself," he told her, a refrain Isabelle hears every day about most everything, from making his bed to riding his two-wheeler.

Q is often a problem for him because he doesn't know how to spell any words with *q* in them, except *quiet*, but that is a minor issue, since there is only one *q* in the letter box.

Fanny has agreed to an epic Scrabble game while Isabelle drives to the San Francisco airport to pick up Casey, home from Cambodia, where he has been attending to victims of the overflowing Mekong River. It's October, Halloween is little more than a week away, and the weather is starting to be nippy. Isabelle brings a sweatshirt out to Avi when she tells him she's leaving. He takes it but stashes it on his lap, doesn't even look up, too intent on rearranging his little tiles, trying to find a word. His father's frequent comings and goings no longer occupy his world. They are a given, a fact of life, and he doesn't ask to go to the airport anymore for the send-off or the return. There'll just be another one soon, and if he's doing something compelling, as he almost always is, he has no interest in a long ride to the San Francisco airport.

Isabelle made sure she wouldn't have him with her this time, because she isn't bringing Casey back to their house. It's taken her six years and endless discussions with Deepti to have the conviction to say, *This isn't the way I want to live.* She is done with the suddenness of Casey's departures, with no continuity in their lives, with the distinct realization that her needs, Avi's needs, pale in comparison to Casey's need to save the world. Now she has to gather whatever courage she can locate to tell him all this on the drive home. Now she has to deposit him at Art and Louisa's and not look back. Can she do it? She has no idea, but she knows she has to try, and having Avi with her would make that impossible.

"You gonna take all day?" Fanny asks with her smoker's rasp as she watches Avi ponder his letters. She shows him no mercy simply because he's five. The only concession she makes to his youth is that she leaves her ever-present cigarettes in the house.

"Wait a minute."

"I've been waiting."

They adore each other, and Isabelle is grateful that Mrs. H has slipped into the grandma role without ever being asked.

Amazingly, her own mother showed up on her doorstep, unannounced, over a year ago, on July 28, the day of Avi's fourth birthday, her apologetic father alongside, holding their suitcases.

"Maybe we should have called" are the first words out of his mouth.

Isabelle is dumbfounded, blindsided. She has a large group of four-year-olds and their parents showing up any minute for Avi's party, and here are her parents, the last people in the world she expected, or wants, to see.

Her mother, amazingly, looks exactly the same: elegant, beautiful, imperious. She seems never to age. But the same can't be said for her father. His shoulders appear more stooped. He's lost some more hair, and he's wearing glasses now. Looking at the two of them standing side by side, it's hard not to conclude that Ruth has somehow been siphoning off youth and vitality from her husband for her own purposes.

"It's Avi's birthday, isn't it." This from her mother—a declarative sentence, not a question. A challenge. Certainly not the apology for four-plus years of the silent treatment

Isabelle would have liked. "So we're here," Ruth says as she pushes past Isabelle and into the small living room. "Where's the birthday boy?"

"Dad," Isabelle says quietly, "you couldn't have let me know?"

"Your mother made me promise not to." He shrugs. "You know your mother." Then: "She was afraid you wouldn't let her come." And Eli puts down the suitcases and reaches for his daughter, bringing her into a warm, much-longed-for hug. "I've missed you," he says, a whisper into her hair. But Isabelle hears him. She's missed him, too.

In the living room, grandmother and grandson are staring at each other. Finally Ruth speaks: "You look like my side of the family," claiming him because he's an adorable boy, and choosing to ignore the fact that he takes after Isabelle and has the Rothman genes.

"Is that good?" Avi asks.

"Well, yes, of course. Who wouldn't want to look like the Abramowiczes? They're handsome people, all of them."

"I want to look like myself."

"And that you do," Isabelle says, coming in from the front porch with Eli trailing behind her, ever helpful, having picked up the suitcases once again. "You look like Avi Arthur Mendenhall and nobody else," she tells her son. "Unique. One of a kind. Very special. And today the birthday boy!" All of this said as a reassurance to her son and a rebuke to her mother, who takes it as such.

Isabelle can see the hurt pinch her mother's face—oh, that look, she's seen it a thousand times, as if Ruth has eaten something that's disagreed with her. *Well, this has started off badly*, and Isabelle finds herself rushing to rescue the moment, against her better judgment, contrary to the years of resolve she thought she had built against her mother.

"Avi, you are so special that your grandpa and grandma flew all the way across the country to celebrate your birthday with you," Isabelle tells him.

"Lady Momma," Ruth says.

"What?"

"I want Avi to call me Lady Momma. Grandma makes me sound ancient . . . which I am not!"

Isabelle is nonplussed again. How could she have forgotten her mother's overreaching vanity?

"Lady Momma?" Isabelle's voice rises with incredulity and a bubble of laughter.

"And I'm your grandpa"—from Eli as he walks over to Avi, bends forward at the waist like a marionette, and extends his hand to the little boy. They shake hands solemnly.

"This is weird," Avi says, searching Isabelle's face for confirmation.

"Yes," she agrees, "it is. This is very weird."

Her parents stay for two days, two long and difficult days, and by the end of the visit Isabelle has managed to work herself into a serious, inexorable headache that sits right behind her eyes and pounds her with its unrelenting message—*This is a mistake, this is a mistake*—because her mother and father have managed to work themselves back into her life, and Avi's.

AS ISABELLE SKIRTS SAN FRANCISCO BAY, along I-80 and then U.S. 101, she rehearses what she will say to Casey. All her life her nerve has failed her at crucial moments, so she doesn't trust herself. The only hope she has is to rehearse. And oftentimes even that doesn't work.

She grins to herself in the speeding car as she remembers that day at Chandler when she walked across the entire campus from her apartment to Daniel's office mumbling like a deranged street person over and over, "It would be better if

I worked with another professor . . . it would be better . . . it would be better . . ." And even then, when she was standing before Daniel's substantial presence, she was unable to get the words out.

Well, that worked out fine, though, didn't it? It brought her Daniel.

Over the past two years, their e-mail correspondence has ranged far from their initial topic of conversation—her writing. They no longer discuss that, because Isabelle no longer writes.

In the beginning, after Isabelle explained why she rarely, if ever, wrote anymore—"I no longer believe I can"—Daniel would periodically raise the subject again, as if she'd never answered his question, and Isabelle would ignore him. Then he would ask again. Then again, until finally one day she shot back angrily, "Are *you* writing?" And Daniel wrote back one word, "Yes," and the answer took her breath away.

She wanted to ask, *What are you writing? How did you start? Are you happy with it? Can you show me some of it?* But she didn't. Without any credentials on her part, she felt she had no right to question him. Instead she wrote back, "Good," and they went on to other topics.

Daniel tells her about his very small town, Winnock. And his daughter across the meadow who refuses to have anything to do with him. And his class and the women who have come to seem like good friends. And about Bev, who owns the bakery in town, makes heavenly cinnamon buns, and provides him with the Internet connection that makes their correspondence possible.

Isabelle writes to him at first about Avi and how much unexpected joy being his mother has brought her. But then, as they grow bolder with each other, she begins to write about her regret, about how she's spent a lifetime feeling stuck. All but the five months she spent with Daniel. How was he able to make her believe in the future, in her ability to get there?

What was it? she asks him in an e-mail composed late one night, when it feels like she's the only person awake on the planet. Fanny's side of the house is dark. Rain patters gently on the roof and slides down her living room window in slow rivulets. It must be close to 3 a.m., because all the windows of all the houses she can see up and down her street are dark, and mist clings to the streetlights like cotton candy. Then she is able to write, *What was it that happened between us that made every hope and dream seem possible?*

Isabelle, he writes back, *we fell a little bit in love with each other.*

SHE AND DEEPTI HAVE DISCUSSED LOVE a lot. What is it worth? How much should one give up for it? How does one know it for sure? These conversations often take place in hushed voices on the porch of Isabelle's duplex, with Avi tucked safely in bed. In the winter they bundle up in heavy sweaters and sip the aromatic chai tea that Deepti brews in Isabelle's kitchen.

The tiny front porch feels like their private space, designed for just the two of them, Isabelle in her rocker, Deepti in her wicker chair. But one night, well after midnight, Isabelle sees the light from the television go off in Fanny's living room and then hears her neighbor's front door open and there is Fanny, out on her porch, wearing her old chenille bathrobe with a faded rose across the back.

"Fanny, are you all right?"

"What are you drinking? It smells like spice."

"Chai tea, Mrs. H," Deepti says. "I could easily make you a cup."

"Well ..." Fanny equivocates, but Isabelle can tell she'd like an invitation to their porch discussion and so she brings out another chair and an extra blanket, and now it's the three women discussing love in the damp night air.

"I loved my husband, I did," Fanny says with deep regret in her voice, "but what did it get me?"

"Do you wish you hadn't?" Isabelle asks.

"Sure—why ask for pain? I was in pain a lot longer than I was in love. Not a good tradeoff."

The young women look at each other as Fanny stares off into the space of her own past. What's there to say to that? It's hard to argue with the conclusion, and yet neither Isabelle nor Deepti would like to grow old like Mrs. H—solitary, embittered, holding grudges. Deepti especially does not want to live with regret.

"But what else is there that matters?" Isabelle asks finally, after the silence between them has grown into a gulf.

Fanny shrugs. "Who knows?"

IN THE PAST YEAR, HOWEVER, Deepti and Isabelle have had to continue their ongoing conversation on the telephone, very late at night for Deepti, who is at Johns Hopkins Hospital doing her three-year pediatric residency.

The women miss each other with a real ache, but Deepti has promised Isabelle that she will be back. When all her training is done, she plans to practice in the Bay Area. Of all the places she's been in America, that is where she feels most at home.

"Loving Casey is the easy part," Isabelle tells Deepti on the phone one night in the summer as she struggles with what to do when he comes home.

"Yes." Deepti sighs over the phone. "It's everything else."

"Exactly! Everything else gets in the way." And then, after a pause in which neither woman needs to speak and both are thinking the same thought, Isabelle adds, "Well, you know exactly what I mean."

"Yes," Deepti says again, quietly.

It is not necessary for either of them to bring up the great sadness in Deepti's life: Sadhil, the "perfect" one, buckled to his parents' pressure and went home to India for a more or less arranged marriage, leaving Deepti to mourn quietly, as is her way, for years. Now Deepti has grown more skeptical.

"You've reverted to your Indian roots," Isabelle keeps telling her.

"Perhaps," Deepti allows, but she no longer believes in falling in love and living happily ever after. It is an American fairy tale that she let herself believe once and now has turned against with absolute finality. Perhaps she will never marry. Certainly she will never again expect to fall in love. She understands more and more the expediency of an arranged marriage.

So it is Deepti who keeps asking Isabelle the practical questions: "How do you want to live?" "What would make you happy?" and "Can you take the part of Casey he brings home to you and Avi and be content?"

At first Isabelle said yes vehemently and often to that last question, because in those early years, when Avi was just a baby, she was guarding closely her secret hope that Casey would change his ways, change his mind. She never said as much to Deepti, but her friend understood anyway.

Deepti would see the look on Isabelle's face when Casey walked into a room, when he put an arm around her shoulders and she leaned into him and melted. She would watch Isabelle's face relax into pure happiness when Casey put his head back and laughed. So Deepti never believed that the little bit of Casey that Isabelle had access to would be enough in the long run.

When Avi turned four and Isabelle's parents moved back into her life, her mother was never shy to voice every criticism of Casey that flitted through her brain—"He missed Avi's birthday *again!*" "He's been gone for three months *already?*" "Why can't he tell you when he's coming home—does he expect you to just sit there and *wait?*" And Deepti saw Isabelle's dissatisfaction with the arrangement she had with Casey bubble over.

In the past year, Isabelle questioned Casey before every trip, finally laying out what she has come to truly understand: "This is a choice, Casey. There will always be disasters."

And Casey answered simply, without anger or rancor, "And I will always try to help," leaving Isabelle feeling small and wickedly selfish.

Didn't she used to admire that unwavering commitment Casey had always proclaimed to his work, his mission in life? He hasn't changed, Isabelle admits with an honesty she struggles mightily to find. But she has, and probably not for the better, she feels. She's become less tolerant, more prosaic, less benevolent . . . Well, of course, she is the unremarkable, conventional person her mother has always known her to be, and she stupidly wants the adventurer who is Casey to join her in the less than exciting, mundane world she inhabits.

"But that's what you want, Isabelle," Deepti reminded her over the phone this past week. "It isn't wrong—it's what you need. It's what you think Avi needs," she said, to add weight to her argument. "Aren't you tired of being unhappy?"

"Oh, yes—exhausted."

"Well, then."

"Yes, well, then."

WHEN SHE CATCHES SIGHT OF CASEY'S blond head rising above the crowd of people striding rapidly toward the luggage carousels at San Francisco airport, Isabelle's heart seizes with anticipation, heedless of her resolution to stay calm. Oh, it's Casey!

He's smiling, so happy to see her! He puts his arms around her, and instantly every cell in her body meets his long-limbed body in perfect harmony. They hold on to each other. *This may be the last time* explodes into Isabelle's brain even as her body hangs on to his. Guilt overwhelms her.

"Wow, it's good to be home!" are the first words out of Casey's mouth, and with his arm around her, keeping her close, he threads through the crowd and steers them both out to the parking area. He never has any checked baggage, only his backpack and a duffel bag which he carries on. No matter how long he's gone.

And he's talking nonstop. This is how Casey decompresses from his trips. He tells Isabelle about them in exhausting detail, and then he's done. He never mentions his time away again. When he's home, he's home.

Isabelle only half listens. "There was nothing but water, to the horizon line. And here and there you could see the tops of these big old trees poking out. And sometimes you'd see cattle swimming for land, all wild-eyed and frantic, or the carcasses of those who didn't make it floating by, bloated, you know."

The freeway is easy going, thankfully, and Isabelle keeps her eyes on the road, interjecting a "Really?" or "That sounds awful" when appropriate. But she's been with Casey long enough to know that all he needs right now is to talk.

"Everyone was getting around by boats, I mean, there was no other way except these small, handmade boats because nothing bigger could really navigate the river. Under all that water were houses and trees and villages even. All gone. Destroyed by the water."

"Terrible," she murmurs, without taking her eyes off the road.

"The rice fields were completely flooded, of course, and we estimated that, like, probably five hundred thousand people were starving, so what we basically did is hand out as much rice as we could. That was it—feed as many people as humanly possible."

Isabelle nods, but she's trying to figure out how to begin her discussion while Casey continues nonstop. "And then the first cases of cholera were diagnosed and they had to bring in the medical team before it got . . ."

And as she half listens to how many people were affected and what medicines they had or didn't have, she's reaching for the courage to say what she needs to say. It's only when she misses their customary exit off the I-80 that Casey stops talking.

"Babe, where are you going?"

"To your parents'."

"Is Avi there? Are we picking him up?"

"No."

Casey turns in his seat and really looks at her for the first time. "What's going on?"

Isabelle shakes her head, then pulls off the freeway at the next off ramp and parks the car on a street of auto body repair shops and empty, trash-strewn lots, a desolate part of Berkeley she almost never sees. She can't have this discussion while she's driving.

She turns the engine off and stares straight ahead, through her windshield. Casey waits for her, silent. It's one of the things she's always loved about him—his ability to be quiet, to leave her some space. Now it only serves to make what she has to say harder.

"I think you should stay at your parents'."

"Because?"

A good question. "Because" what? Isabelle searches for the words that will answer his question. All the rehearsing in the world hasn't helped. She wants Casey and she can't have him.

She still—stupidly, insanely she knows—clings to some vestige of hope that he might change. She's resolved that she can't keep living like this; she's too unhappy. But that doesn't stop the desire to swallow her words and sleep next to him just one more night, feel the warmth of him against her, open herself to his body one more time.

And yet she has to say what she believes to be true. All those conflicting needs swirl around and silence her tongue.

"Have you met someone else?" is what Casey finally says.

"God, no, that's not it."

And Casey relaxes, leans back against the closed door, immediately relieved. "Okay. Then everything else is fixable."

"No, Casey, it isn't!" And she surprises herself with her vehemence, with a depth of anger that flashes bright, that she didn't even know she possessed. "I'm not okay with all this anymore. I know I said I was. I tried to be. I wish I could be a better, more generous person, but I'm not. I'm selfish and needy and I want you here with us, Avi and me, more, a lot more. You've been away three days for every one you are home!"

"That doesn't sound right."

"Casey, it is! It is! I kept a record because I knew you'd say that!"

"You marked off the days? You kept a time card on me?"

"We want you home with us, and that doesn't look like it's what you want, and so I'm driving you to your parents' because we've got to begin to separate out our lives and this is the first step."

Casey is quiet for a very long time. He simply looks at her, and she stares out the window and won't, can't, meet his eyes. She knows that if she did, she'd capitulate.

Finally, softly, he says, "I'm not any different from the guy you met six years ago."

"I know! I know! But things are different. We have a child and he needs you and I . . . I want more than you are willing to give!" There—she's said it. And it hangs in the air between them, and the worst thing that could happen happens. Casey doesn't disagree. Doesn't try to negotiate with her. Doesn't say he'll change or he'll try.

"I do what I'm called to do." It's a gentle plea, but not at all what Isabelle wants to hear. It hangs there between them, an impenetrable wall, and slowly Isabelle puts her hand on the ignition key and turns on the car and Casey looks straight ahead at a skinny yellow dog patrolling one of the empty lots, nose to the ground, searching for something to eat, and Isabelle pulls out into traffic and drives him to Art and Louisa's and leaves him there.

The next day, a Monday, Isabelle goes into work. She drops Avi off at school, watching him fairly dance across the star stepping-stones to the front door of A Circle of Friends, happy, it seems to her, but she knows the reverberations will come. This separation she's initiated will widen and Casey will be in their lives even less and Avi will feel the loss and she will feel guiltier. What a mess she's made of things.

Her next stop is Full of Beans for her morning cappuccino—today she makes it a double—and then on to the bookstore to open it at nine, the way Meir likes. This morning there's a large box waiting for her at the front door. She knows it's new books, and there's even a flicker of excitement amid the self-loathing she's been indulging in lately.

Over the years she's worn Meir down, and he has agreed to carry *some* new books, those that he deems worthy. True to his prejudices, he never consults the bestseller lists. He picks and chooses from the advance notices he gets from the various publishing houses. He agrees to carry new books by writers he esteems and to consider new works whose supporting quotes from other authors make the book sound promising.

These brown cardboard boxes that arrive unexpectedly and sporadically feel like gifts to Isabelle, and her eagerness to open the box and see what Meir has ordered this time makes her fumble with the keys and struggle to open the front door.

But there! She's in. And she puts the heavy box down on the steamer trunk in the reading area, rips off the packing tape, and slowly, with great anticipation, opens the four folded flaps of cardboard. What riches will she find? What wonderful new book can she read and then discuss with Meir and argue over and read again?

The cover is blue, a bright gorgeous-day sky-blue, with the title across the front diagonally from left to right in thin white script, almost as if it were the trailing wisp of a cloud or the vapor from a plane as it skywrites *Out of the Blue*. And then she sees it, spread across the bottom in elegant black type, the author's name: Daniel Jablonski.

That makes no sense. Daniel wrote a book and he didn't tell her? After all the e-mails and confidences exchanged in the past two years, why would he keep this a secret?

She sits down on the sofa, cracks open the pristine cover, and finds the first sentence. It reads, *Lanie walked into my office without knocking, wearing high-heeled, buttery smooth, caramel-colored boots that made her seem six feet tall. I've always liked tall women.*

No! Those are her boots. The ones she's wearing now, in fact. The ones with the vine pattern along the outer edge that she wore often that last year at Chandler because they were new then and she loved them. And Lanie? Who is this Lanie? And why is she wearing her very boots?

Isabelle sinks into the musty sofa cushions, props the scrutinized boots up on the steamer trunk, and continues reading, devouring each page, whipping it over and eagerly beginning the next. When a small, white-haired man makes the mistake of opening the front door of Noah's Ark and taking two steps into the store, Isabelle barks, "We're closed!" then catches herself and says more kindly, "We'll be open this afternoon, if you can come back. Sorry. I'm so sorry if I startled you," as she escorts him out, turns the front door sign to CLOSED so she can read in peace, and spreads herself out on the sofa with Daniel's book tightly clasped in both hands. And she reads. And reads.

When Meir shows up sometime after noon, she's just finishing up.

"What's with the CLOSED sign?"

Isabelle says nothing, not exactly trusting what will come out of her mouth. Instead she holds out the book so he can read the title.

"Ah, it's here! It was supposed to be a surprise for you."

"Oh, I was surprised!"

"He didn't tell you he was writing it?"

"No."

He takes it from her. "Great cover."

"That's not the point!"

Meir turns it over for the authors' quotes on the back. "Wow, amazing blurbs. You see," he says to her, as if they are in the middle of the first conversation they ever had, over six years ago, "Jablonski isn't finished. He just had a little blip, a couple of bad books, but this one sounds like he's back to his old form."

"Meir! He stole my life! It's all here, in the book. I'm there, or Daniel's take on me, but everything else—what happened between us or what he wished to happen. Okay, it never happened, but he . . . maybe we . . . okay, we might have wanted it to, but Meir, he stole my life!"

She's not making any sense to Meir, but it is very clear that she is consumed by rage. Angry women are not in his wheelhouse—it's one of the reasons he refuses to see his sister,

Fanny. He'll just wait until the Isabelle he knows and loves resurfaces. He'll just move away from her, behind the counter, and busy himself with whatever papers he can find there to shuffle. But Isabelle isn't finished.

She stands on the customer side of the front counter and continues with the same intensity. "He never told me a thing! Never! He'd write me these concerned e-mails and pretend nothing was going on, and all the while this!"

She grabs the book from Meir's hands and bangs it flat against the wood counter. "This! This! This! This!"

Meir wishes there was a hole he could sink into until she calms down.

But she doesn't. The rage Isabelle feels, the sense of betrayal, really, doesn't dissipate in the coming days. In fact, as she seethes, her anger grows. So many things she would shout at Daniel if he were standing in front of her: "You used everything from my heart, everything I am, for your own purposes!" "Didn't we have this implicit pact of trust?" "How could you, Daniel? How could you?"

And then she does something so uncharacteristic that it scares her a little. She packs up Avi's clothes and deposits him at Art and Louisa's with Casey and she gets on a plane to Boston and rents a car and drives to Winnock, New Hampshire, without telling anyone where she is going.

CHAPTER SIXTEEN

Now, four years into his New Hampshire life, Daniel takes the dog, Alina's dog, with him when he walks into town in the mornings. She named him Orphan when he showed up at her studio door one winter morning, motherless, a tiny puppy shivering with cold. Daniel suspects that the name has more to do with Alina than with the state of the dog, but he's never said that to his daughter.

Father and daughter have worked out an arrangement to share the dog, if little else. Orphan ranges freely from Alina's barn to Daniel's small cottage, sometimes sleeping with her, sometimes with him, probably getting fed in both places and yet managing to look perpetually skinny and undernourished.

When Orphan's not with either of them, he roams the woods in search of intoxicating smells to roll in and small game— squirrels, mice, chipmunks, cottontail rabbits—to hunt. And thankfully, he provides the one safe conversational harbor for Daniel and Alina. "I'm taking Orphan into town with me," Daniel might say as he begins his morning walk to Bev's Bakery. Or Alina might knock on Daniel's door after dark, worried because Orphan is MIA. "Is he with you?" she'll ask.

Sometimes they'll tromp through the woods behind Daniel's cottage with twin flashlights, calling the dog's name until they see him burst through the trees, tail whirling with pleasure, a ball of ecstatic energy that somehow manages to melt the deep freeze between the two humans, at least for that moment.

This October morning, as Daniel and Orphan begin their two-mile walk into town, Daniel can't help but notice Jesse Eames's faded red pickup truck parked at a slant, again, in front of Alina's barn. None of his business, he tells himself, not now, nor when the man and truck started showing up over a year ago. Besides, he likes Jesse, a quiet guy who does what he can to get by—finish carpenter, fine furniture maker, hired hand in the spring and summer when there's outside work to do. Daniel's glad, he tells himself, glad that his daughter's got herself a decent man. And the slightly bitter taste of regret? Only that Alina has never felt the need to mention Jesse to him.

But this is a morning to put all that away. The world is ablaze with reds and oranges and the purest of yellows. The maple and oak trees are burning up with scalding color, the last of their leaves clinging stubbornly to outstretched branches and the rest flooding the road and the forest floor with missives the size of dinner plates.

Of course Daniel knows the leaves are dying, that the trees are going dormant for the winter, that autumn is the ending of things, not the beginning, but the foliage show is so gaudy, so aggressively *there*, that it is hard for him to believe the deadness of winter is just around the corner.

And Daniel suspects it's especially hard to believe this year because he feels so much more alive than at any time he can remember. And proud of himself—an emotion he can barely remember ever feeling. For finishing the book. For writing a novel. For honoring Isabelle, as he sees it. For writing something hopeful. Of course he knows that this feeling may well be transitory; the book could be badly reviewed or not at all, it might fail to sell, he may never be able to repeat the experience he had writing it, when the act of creation brought him so much . . . well, joy. But right now, on this glorious morning with the dog at his side and the world around him exploding with one last burst of showmanship, Daniel is hopeful.

Orphan bounds ahead of him, into the trees and out again, barking at something loudly, probably a fox, then circling back and ambling contentedly alongside Daniel, tail in the air, his gait a steady patter. The sky overhead is the brightest of blues. The air is still chilly this early in the morning, and the pumpkins Daniel passes in Steve Wethering's pasture have a dusting of frost along their shoulders. Within a week they'll all be gone, turned into toothy jack-o'-lanterns for Halloween.

When they get to the bakery, Orphan takes his customary place on the sidewalk, directly beneath the large front window, and watches as Daniel goes inside and claims the round table so that man and dog have clear sightlines to each other. That proximity makes each of them feel better.

Daniel plugs in his laptop. Bev brings him a thick white mug of coffee and his customary cinnamon bun. He smiles his thanks as she moves back to the counter and the line of customers waiting patiently for her.

As Daniel opens his e-mail, he vows to himself that today is the day he'll tell Isabelle about the book. He's put it off far too long, he knows, but only because he hasn't figured out exactly how to say what he wants to say. The dedication thanks her, although not by name. He struggled for a long time with what to write, how to acknowledge her, and finally came up with *To I.—who inspires and delights,* because it's naked and true. But he fears that one simple sentence is not nearly enough. He wants her to understand that she brought him alive. He hopes that the book will convey that message, but he wants to prepare her for it.

That first day here in Winnock, when he was unpacking his books and found those eight pages of her never-finished novel, they took him back to a time when he felt the first stirrings of hope. The pages were irrefutable evidence that at least then he had had something to offer. Over the course of the semester they'd worked together, Isabelle had found her gift. He has no doubt of that, and he also can admit in the privacy of his own musings that he had something to do with it.

And of course finding Isabelle's pages couldn't help but take him back to that stifling hot afternoon in May, in his large and messy L.A. kitchen, when he looked up from reading to see her young body silhouetted in the doorway, practically naked in that wisp of a dress. There were so many things he could have said to her that day but never did. And remembering all that prompted him to start writing, endless e-mails of things he wished he had said or wanted to say to her now, e-mails he knew he would never send because they were inappropriate—too needy, too intrusive, feelings he could barely acknowledge to himself, let alone send to her. But somehow they became the foundation for more writing. And then, later, when Isabelle did contact him and they began to e-mail regularly and far more benignly, it felt as though they were building some sort of web of support, a safety net of writing from which the novel came. So without Isabelle, there would be no book. He's sure of that, and he wants her to understand how grateful he is.

But how to do that? Such an unfamiliar feeling for Daniel: gratitude, with its implication that life is good or that something in his life is to be applauded. And so he has put off the e-mail, and now the book is out and he has to alert her, has to share with her how they did this together. That's how he feels:

that the book is a joint project, even though Isabelle never knew she was contributing.

What will she think of the nature of the book—the fact that he's written a fully romantic love story? He can't predict. And all the intimate scenes between the characters? Okay, all the sex, which of course he has imagined and written in great detail. He has only the memory of his lips on her perfect young breast. And from that memory he has created the rest. He hopes she feels adored, because he sees the book as a celebration of her.

All these thoughts render his fingers motionless. The weight of the proposed e-mail sinks it before he even starts. And so he stares out the window and locks eyes with Orphan, who waits patiently, head on his front paws, but can't help him out at all.

The morning crush of customers over, Bev comes with her coffeepot and refills his cup, then pulls out a chair and sits down opposite him. Over the years of morning coffee and evening classes, they've become easy with each other, comfortable.

"Something wrong with the cinnamon bun today? You haven't touched it."

"No, Bev, of course not." And Daniel takes a big bite. "I'm too busy being stuck is all, trying to figure out how to tell Isabelle that the book is coming out."

Bev laughs. "About time. She figures fairly prominently in it, wouldn't you say?" She'd read the book as soon as she had been able to coerce Daniel into giving up a copy of the galleys, blushing in the solitude of her small living room at the sex scenes and marveling at Daniel's ability to bring this girl to life. She knew he'd be a wonderful writer, and he is. She told him so, but he deflected the compliment, always uncomfortable with any kind of praise, the hallmark of a man who hasn't welcomed a lot of goodness into his life.

"It's my memory of Isabelle," Daniel corrects her now. "She's the *inspiration* for the character."

"Hmmm," Bev says as she gets up, not buying Daniel's explanation for a second. "Well, good luck with that."

"Maybe she won't see the book," Daniel calls to Bev's retreating back.

"She works in a bookstore!" is thrown over her shoulder.

Right. There's that. He'd better get busy with the e-mail.

Daniel told Bev quite a bit about Isabelle over the years he was writing *Out of the Blue*. He'd come in each morning with his brain full of what he had been working on the day before or what he was hoping to tackle that day when he got home, and Bev was always a willing audience. To his surprise, Daniel found himself talking about the progress of his writing as he was doing it. In the past he had always felt that it all was so fragile, so mystical almost—this writing business—that talking about the work might shatter all that delicacy into a million irreparable pieces. But somehow, in Winnock, with Bev, he found himself wanting to talk. She knows more about this book than anyone else.

Women—he could always talk more easily to women. His mother first and foremost. Daniel doesn't know where she got the strength to be constantly available to the three needy men in her life: his father, his brother, Roman, who acted out when things got bad at home, and especially to him, who would flee when the latest alcohol-fueled storm of his father's escalated. Gone . . . gone for as long as he could manage. And then later, when he would creep back into the house, he would sniff the quality of tension in the air to figure out whether it was safe to return, or relatively safe.

And he would seek out his mother, praying she would be alone. If he was lucky, he would find her by herself, usually in the kitchen, or sometimes outside reading on the back porch when the weather was nice. Those were the times he would be able to see the toll his father's injury and drinking had taken on her. In repose, while she read, her face would relax into a vision of sadness—slack and lined and careworn. And he couldn't bear it, to see the suffering that she made sure to hide from him most times behind her steady gentleness. And so he would go to her, sit with her, and tell her stories. It was an instinct of his, to fabricate long, elaborate tales which took them both away from the loud suffering that was their life with Gus Jablonski. All Daniel wanted to hear was his mother's astonished reaction of "No!" when he made up something very far-fetched, and then her laugh—that was the grand prize—at the preposterous nature of whatever he said was "true, Mom, completely true." Somehow those stolen moments with his mother would make things instantly better.

Daniel understands now that he has always gone to women. Despite all her shortcomings, Stephanie was a listener, too. She would sit, uncomplaining, for hours in a high-backed wooden booth at the Lakeside Diner in Erie, nursing cup after cup of coffee, and listen to Daniel, barely past his twenty-first birthday, spin the real stories that would one day become his first book, about his father. The irony, never lost on him, was that it was only after he had left Stephanie that he could write them down.

And now in his new life in New Hampshire, Bev's steady presence gives him much the same gift. She listens. She's thoughtful. Well, to be fair, she pretty much dispenses that same thoughtfulness to everyone. She takes in her customers' stories as they buy her sourdough bread and carrot cake and hot cross buns, nodding as she bags maple scones for David Leighton, who opened the bookstore a few years back and is now showcasing Daniel's new novel prominently in the window, or making sympathetic sounds when Marie Tibbett worries about a grandson whose asthma has gotten worse.

Who listens to Bev? Daniel wonders. Maybe Sarah, whose husband has finally died and who seems liberated now, reborn into life after a decade of caretaking. Bev must talk to Sarah. They drive together to the Monday and Thursday class. He supposes there are other times when they see each other, but he doesn't know for sure. He's curious about Bev's life away from the bakery and those two nights a week he sees her in class, but she reveals little, preferring to listen. As it is, he's content with the package deal he does have—Bev, the Internet connection, and the best cinnamon buns in 100 miles—all in one place.

AS DANIEL IS STRUGGLING WITH FINDING just the right words for his e-mail to Isabelle, she is struggling to find her way from Boston to Winnock. They gave her a map at the airport Budget Rentals with the route highlighted in yellow marker, but she's useless when it comes to maps and directions. Taking 93 north out of Boston was fairly easy, and she made the transition to 495, but once she hit 3 and got past Nashua, New Hampshire, she had trouble on 101A after Ponemah trying to navigate the East Milford interchange to get to 101 proper. And then she missed the turn at 123, which was where she had to be, and once she doubled back and found it, she had to stop twice and ask if she was on the right road. It seems to be impossible to find the practically nonexistent town Daniel has decided to settle in, and her anger grows with each mile she travels. Almost nobody has heard of Winnock, and she's beginning to think Daniel may have made it up.

Now that she's on a smaller, more rural road, purportedly the road that will take her to Daniel, her concentration is maniacally focused. She's even too angry to rehearse what she will say once she's in front of him. She feels possessed. It doesn't help that she took the red-eye to Boston, didn't sleep on the plane, got into her Dodge Neon without stopping for rest, and drove straight through with only the awful coffee from Speedy Mart Gas propelling her forward.

She almost misses the turnoff to the O'Malleys' farmhouse. The teenager at the gas station told her to look for a small hand-painted sign stuck into the ground right at the turnoff that reads CERAMICS FOR SALE. What he didn't say was that the wooden shingle was practically covered up by ropes of ivy gone wild.

Isabelle sees it just at the last second and manages the right turn with a slight skid. Quickly she slows the car, because the road ahead is unpaved dirt and narrow, and tries to slow her breathing, as well. To calm down, now that she is here. To figure out what she is going to say. Suddenly the reality of confronting Daniel seems overwhelming.

She drives up to the large white house on the slight rise. There are no cars parked there because the O'Malleys are in Boston, but she gets out of her rental, grabs her copy of *Out of the Blue,* which for some reason she has kept on her lap through the whole circuitous route to Daniel's home, and knocks on the front door. And then knocks again more loudly and calls out, "Hello!" but no one comes. She hadn't thought of this possibility—that no one would be home. That she could have traveled all the way across the country to encounter empty space, devoid of people.

She steps back, off the front porch, and surveys where she's landed. The white clapboard house in front of her, with its wide wraparound porch, is imposing and inviting at the same time. A line of wooden rocking chairs immediately springs to mind, even though the porch is now empty. Probably not where Daniel lives, Isabelle concedes to herself.

She backs up onto the gravel driveway to see a red barnlike structure to her right, then a meadow; then the forest seems to start. Daniel's small cottage, sheltered by the birch trees, isn't visible from the main driveway.

"Daniel!" she yells. Then, louder: "Daniel, where are you? Daniel! Daniel!" She's screaming in frustration now, in hopelessness. Could she have come all this way for nothing?

And suddenly the door of the barn opens and a tall, scowling woman about her age is standing there, clearly unhappy to have been interrupted. Her hands and the front of her jeans are caked with wet clay and she has a dirty towel slung across her shoulder.

Alina takes in this obviously distraught young woman who clutches her father's latest book to her chest and knows she's facing trouble. Here is a melodrama waiting to happen, and she distinctly wants no part of it.

"He's not here."

"But he will be? Tell me he will be."

"I don't keep track of his comings and goings." And Isabelle immediately knows who she is.

"You're Alina, right?"

"Yes."

"I'm Isabelle."

Alina shrugs; the name means nothing to her. She and Daniel don't share personal information.

"I came all the way from California."

And then they're at a stalemate. Isabelle seems to have run out of things to say and to be deflating by the second—her shoulders slump, her arms fall to her sides. Then she bends over and rests her hands on her thighs, as if she's too weary to stand upright, and Alina yields a bit. The same instinct that allowed her to take in Orphan as a tiny puppy kicks in. Isabelle seems so lost.

"He usually walks back from town." And she points. "That road there."

Relief floods Isabelle—he's here, somewhere here. Her trip wasn't an act of complete insanity.

"Thank you. You see this book ... the novel he wrote ... what he wrote about me ..."

Alina waves her hand in dismissal—the last thing she wants is to become entangled with her father's affairs—and turns back to her barn. "You'll have to take all that up with him." And she's gone, back to her work.

Town—so that's where the town of Winnock is. And from the years of e-mails Isabelle knows that Daniel goes there in the mornings for his coffee and Internet and then comes home to work. He's told her all this. What he neglected to tell her was *what* he was working on! Her! Some fantasy of a love affair! As if he had a right to everything she is and every thought and fear that she so completely trusted him with. How could he?!

Furious again, Isabelle sets out on the road Alina pointed out, her feet crunching the brittle carpet of fallen leaves, marching along in the very caramel-colored boots that featured so prominently in the first sentence of Daniel's novel, boots she deliberately chose to wear today. Wrapped in a thick green wool cape knitted by Fanny as a Christmas present last year and valued despite its many flaws and dropped stitches, Isabelle could be mistaken for a warrior of sorts.

Now she's murmuring to herself, head down, rehearsing what she *has* to say, *needs* to tell him: *How dare you? What is your definition of trust? What gave you the right?*

Walking in the opposite direction, home from Winnock to his cabin, Daniel is feeling even better than he did earlier that morning, because he finally managed to e-mail Isabelle. He found the right words, he feels, to present the novel as a celebration of her. Finally!

Unaccustomed as he is to the condition others label "happiness," he can't deny that he feels, at this minute, on this path, with Orphan running ahead of him and the natural world conspiring to flaunt all its beauty at him, that life is good.

He hears in the distance Orphan's frenzied barking, and even that racket is somehow comforting—Orphan ferreting out an animal, Orphan being the adventurous dog that he is. But the barking doesn't stop. Doesn't change pitch or taper off. He's got something.

There have been times over the years when Daniel has had to pull Orphan back from a seriously annoyed black bear he's managed to drive up a tree, and once from a standoff with a snarling bobcat. That one was scary, the large cat cornered and ready to spring. Orphan wouldn't have gotten the better of that confrontation if Daniel hadn't intervened in time, so now he picks up his pace.

As he runs down the road toward home, the barking gets louder, and then there he is: Orphan, hunkered down, his hindquarters in the air and brutish, manic barks cascading rat-a-tat, one after another, filling up the woods with insistent noise.

What he has cornered is a woman, a young woman, whose back is pressed up against the long, irregular furrows of a sugar maple trunk, and who looks to be flapping long green wings at the frenzied dog. A young woman who is . . . Isabelle? Isabelle here? For a crucial second, two, Daniel's brain can't quite compute what his eyes see. He stands frozen.

"Daniel! Get this crazy dog away from me!"

"Isabelle?" And he doesn't move, simply stares at her as if he's hallucinating, as if she might vaporize into a whirl of dust at any moment. He's conjured her—he must have—from all the thought and love he put into her e-mail.

"Daniel—the dog! Get the dog!"

And Daniel grabs Orphan's collar. "It's okay . . . Easy, Orphan, back off." And the dog does. He presses himself

232 · DEENA GOLDSTONE

against Daniel's leg, not quite sure yet that he shouldn't be protecting him from the tall, winged interloper. But the barking grinds down to a low-pitched growl.

"This is your dog?"

"Well, Alina's, but we tend to share him."

And then again, with more indignation, "This is *your* dog who terrorized me? Perfect! Just perfect!"

"Isabelle—"

"Stop saying that."

"Amazing." And then he sees his novel in her hand. "Did you read it?"

"Of course I read it. Why do you think I'm here?"

"To tell me how much you liked it?" And Daniel is grinning, delighted, but Isabelle is not.

"Daniel, you took what is *mine* and hijacked it for your own use!" Isabelle's voice shakes with emotion.

Daniel shakes his head. What can he say? Very quietly he tells her, "Isabelle, listen to me. I've taken what you meant to me, what you mean to me, what you did for me, and written about it. That's entirely different."

"Bullshit! What's your main character called? Lanie. Sound anything like Me*lanie*? Remember her? Remember the novel I was writing with Me*lanie* as my main character?"

"Yes, Isabelle, I do."

"And your title! You couldn't even find your own title? Do you remember "Outlaw"? *Out*law? So you name your book *Out of the Blue*?"

Daniel can't help it; he starts to chuckle.

"This is funny to you?"

"No, Isabelle, I just think that last accusation is a bit far-fetched."

"You appropriated every feeling I've ever shared with you, every thought in my head, everything I've ever told you, and you used it. You used it! You stole my life!" Such a horrible accusation.

And Isabelle starts to weep. Oh, no, how can she be doing this? She stuffs the back of her hands against her cheeks to stop the tears, but they run across her fingers and down her face nonetheless. Oh, she's exhausted. And mortified. And lost. She knows she's completely lost.

Daniel just watches her. It's heart-wrenching, but he knows he mustn't touch her. Not yet. She has to hear him, and so he waits till the weeping slows.

"The book is a love letter, Isabelle. To the woman who saved me. To the woman who came into my life when I was on the edge of self-destructing and gave me hope. You, Isabelle. You did that for me."

She shakes her head, either because she doesn't believe him or because she can't take it in or . . . ? Daniel doesn't know, but somehow he does know that he can move to her now. He can take her into his arms and let her cry against his shoulder, and so he does, and he holds her as tightly to him as he has longed to do from the day she first stepped into his office.

They stand together in the glorious woods, with the surrounding world shouting at them to have one more go at living before the winter. And so Daniel takes Isabelle's hand and leads her back to his spartan cottage and lays her on his narrow bed and covers her with a blanket and lets her sleep. He sits by the fireplace and watches her.

CHAPTER SEVENTEEN

Isabelle wakes to find elongated shadows stretching out across the raw wooden floor. And Daniel asleep in his easy chair, a book open on his lap, his feet crossed at the ankle and propped on the stone hearth of the fireplace. It's so quiet she can hear the last leaves rustling on the birch trees and her own beating heart.

It must be late afternoon. She's slept for hours. Quietly, so that she doesn't wake him, Isabelle turns onto her left side so she can take in the entire room—the two sets of long, uncurtained windows on opposite walls, which look out onto the trees, the plain wooden table where Daniel must work. She can see stacks of paper and his laptop, an orderly pile of books, a ceramic mug—Alina's?—stuffed with pens. The fireplace, built into the back wall, is beautiful with its large blocks of stone in shades of yellow and rust. Everything neat and swept clean of clutter, so unlike the unsupervised mess of his L.A. house.

It's peaceful. Could it be this serenity that has worn away Daniel's sharper edges? He seems less afraid, calmer, as if he's expanded more fully into himself, she suddenly understands. And oh, how she's missed him! The physical presence of him, large and solid and awkward all at the same time. And how she's longed for what he implicitly gives her: his belief in her possibility, his trust in her uniqueness.

"Daniel . . ." she whispers across the silent room, too softly for him to hear, she's certain, but he opens his eyes anyway, stretches his arms above his head, and arches his back. He's too old to sleep in a chair. And then he turns to her and smiles.

"Are you hungry?"

She nods. She's famished. She can't remember the last time she ate. Yesterday morning, maybe?

"Will you drive?"

"Oh, Daniel . . . still?"

He grins. "You can't expect miracles."

"I'll drive."

ISABELLE PARKS HER RENTAL CAR in front of Leighton's Books and Daniel takes her up to the front window so she can see the display announcing *Out of the Blue*—copies of the book artfully arranged alongside a small poster identifying him as a local author, irrefutable evidence to Daniel of his resurrection. Here it is—the book, for all the world to see. He waits for Isabelle's reaction. Did she hear him earlier? Can she see the book as a tribute to her?

"It's a beautiful cover," she finally says, and Daniel nods. He doesn't push for more.

"Let's cross the street."

They head for the Granite State Diner, the only game in town. Bev's shuts down midafternoon. She offers only breakfast pastries and a few simple sandwiches for lunch. By three o'clock the CLOSED sign is hung on the door.

And as they walk past Le Breton's Gourmet Foods, the realty company, and Sewall's Pharmacy, Isabelle slips her arm easily through Daniel's and he smiles at her. He'll take it. She's on her way to forgiving him.

At the end of the block, the diner's neon sign beckons. The

whole long name, THE GRANITE STATE DINER, is spelled out in heavy red cursive above the front door, and they walk toward it, arm in arm, two tall people matching strides easily.

"Good thing I wore my boots," Isabelle says with a sly smile. "I can keep up with you."

Aldo, who bought the diner from the Olmsteads when Mac Olmstead retired, is standing behind the counter as they walk in, wearing his signature outfit, a short-sleeved white T-shirt, whatever the weather, stretched tight over his ever-expanding girth and an even larger red-and-white–striped apron tied around his middle. Years ago, when Aldo migrated up to Winnock from Bayonne, New Jersey, it was easier to see the firefighter he used to be. He was trim and fit and had a lot more hair. Now countless meals of his own cooking have filled out his form—an advertisement for the tastiness of his food, Aldo tells everyone who will listen.

"Professor. Take a booth."

"Professor," Isabelle teases lightly as they slip into the second of a line of red vinyl booths hugging the windowed outer wall. "Wow," she says as she scans the small space, "you've taken me to the quintessential diner."

"Right out of Norman Rockwell," Daniel agrees.

With its black-and-white checkerboard floor, long straight counter with red vinyl stools, open kitchen where anyone can watch Aldo and his son, Luca, cook—a competitive show in and of itself—and the requisite wall of windows and booths underneath which look out on the street, the Granite State Diner is a classic.

"Yankee pot roast ... fish and chips ... meat loaf with mashed potatoes ..." Isabelle reads out loud from the menu. "We're in a fifties time warp."

"Only one of us here is old enough to remember the fifties."

"I watched *Happy Days* reruns," Isabelle insists, head still bent over the list of possible dinners. How can she choose? She wants pretty much all of them. And then she feels Daniel's eyes on her face and looks up. "What?"

"I can see the years of motherhood in your face."

"Meaning I look older and haggard."

"Meaning there's a sort of . . . gravitas there now."

"That's good?"

"Yes, good. Beautiful, even."

"Oh, Daniel." And she sighs in pleasure and they grin at each other stupidly, just so glad to be sitting opposite each other, contemplating a meal together—the simplest of things, until Pauline interrupts, order pad in hand.

Daniel knew Pauline would be working tonight. She works every dinner shift except the Monday and Thursday nights she comes to his class. From the very first discussion she presented herself as direct and unstoppable, so he expects exactly what she says. "So who's this now, Professor?"

There hasn't been an instance in all the years Daniel has lived in Winnock that he's brought a woman to dinner who looks like she could be a date. This one, however, Pauline sees immediately, is far too young for him, younger than his own daughter in all probability.

"Isabelle, Pauline. Pauline, Isabelle, one of my former students."

"When you taught at college?"

"Chandler, in Los Angeles," Isabelle fills in. "Daniel taught me how to write."

Daniel shakes his head, deflecting the compliment, muted as it is.

"And so you're a writer, too, then?" Pauline asks.

"No." Isabelle looks carefully at Daniel as she says, "He didn't teach me how to *continue* to write."

"My fault," Daniel says, and then, to override whatever

next question Pauline is itching to ask: "Now, what are the specials tonight?"

Pauline points to the large blackboard next to the cash register, where "Chicken Pot Pie with Morels," "Three-Alarm Chili," and "Clam Up and Eat the Chowder" have been carefully lettered in chalk by Luca, whose job it is to cook the daily specials.

Daniel orders the chili, because he's come to know that Luca is a gifted chef. There's been talk of his going to the New England Culinary Institute in Montpelier, Vermont, but Daniel suspects that Aldo wants to hang on to him.

Isabelle orders the Yankee pot roast because she's here in Yankee territory.

"Excellent choice," Pauline tells her as she writes it down. And then, because she can't leave without more conversation: "Do you know the Professor teaches a bunch of us, women only, it turns out, every Monday and Thursday night over at the adult school?"

"I've heard," Isabelle says. And then, teasing Daniel again, "It gets him out of the house. A good thing."

"We read novels and discuss them. Sometimes new books, sometimes the older ones that most of us never read in school, or else if we did, we've forgotten." She shakes her head at the passage of time. "For all of us it's been a while since we sat in a classroom, but that doesn't stop us from having opinions."

"And yours among the most vehement, Pauline."

The tiny woman shrugs. "I know what I like."

"That's a good start," Isabelle says, but she's looking into Daniel's eyes as she says it.

When Pauline leaves to deliver their order to the kitchen, Daniel leans forward across the table and Isabelle does, as well, and he says very quietly, "There are a lot of eyes watching us."

Isabelle peeks at the few customers sitting at the counter, the two other couples in the booths down the line from them, even Luca behind the counter as he begins to ladle out Daniel's chili, who all cast covert glances in their direction. Daniel with a stranger, a young stranger, an attractive stranger. My!

"Does it bother you?" Isabelle asks as quietly as she can.

"No," Daniel says, and he sits back. "I've come to understand that people here are well-meaning."

Isabelle sits back, too, and looks at him, really looks at him. And he allows it. He doesn't flinch or deflect her scrutiny. "This place suits you."

"I believe that's so."

"There's a part of you that isn't struggling anymore."

"Ah, Isabelle . . ." There it is again: her ability to see into his heart.

Isabelle drives them home along the same road she walked earlier that day, when she was consumed with anger. But not really at Daniel, she now knows. She needs to read the book again. She suspects it's beautiful and that she'll be proud of it. She'll tell Daniel that later. She'll try.

It's pitch-black, the trees forming a tunnel of darkness, punctuated only by the car headlights as they sweep the scenery in front of them. They're the only people on the road. They could be the last two people on the earth. Even the moon is hidden behind the tops of the trees.

Neither Isabelle nor Daniel speaks. They've never made small talk and they don't now. He hasn't asked about her son, and she hasn't told him about her encounter with Alina. There isn't room in the car for anyone else, just the two of them and the unspoken question between them. What will happen when they get back to Daniel's cottage?

Daniel leads the way in, stooping a bit to fit beneath the low doorway. Isabelle follows. He turns on a small table lamp, which fills the low-ceilinged space with a soft warm glow, and they look at each other, waiting. And then Isabelle turns off the light and the room is lit only by moonlight reflecting off the surface of Foyle's Pond and Daniel reaches for her.

They stand that way, with their arms around each other, her head against his neck, his hand in her hair, and they wait. For permission—no. For courage—maybe. But mostly to make sure this is right. They've given each other so much over the years, been each other's lodestar. Are they risking all that now?

Isabelle moves first. She steps back from his embrace and takes his hand and walks them toward Daniel's bed. Slowly they undress. Unhurriedly. There's a different kind of urgency working here. It's an undercurrent, a hum of desire, the imperative between them so different from her need for Casey's body and the oblivion their sexual energy creates. No, this is something else.

She wants Daniel because she's always wanted him and will always want him, she knows. Not to the exclusion of all else but to anchor her in some deep way.

They stand naked in front of each other in the dark room, their bodies silhouetted against the long windows, and it is Daniel who reaches out and brings Isabelle into his embrace.

She feels enveloped, safe, his substantial body so different from Casey's lean muscles that it could be a different country. And when he kisses her now, she has no doubts, and he feels it, feels her body's energy flow toward him, and he smiles in the dappled darkness.

"At long last . . ."

"Oh, Daniel—it's been forever."

And they lie next to each other on Daniel's unadorned bed and touch the parts of each other they've yearned to touch and stroke each other until Daniel moves on top of her and enters her at the exact moment she thinks she'll die if he doesn't and there's a tenderness to it. And a gratitude that carries them through.

"Oh my God," she whispers as they finish, and Daniel rolls them both onto their sides, their faces inches apart, their arms still wrapped around each other.

" 'Oh my God' in a positive sense?"

"Daniel—you know."

And he does. He knows that they've waited six years for this night and that it has been worth the wait.

DANIEL WAKES JUST AS THE SKY is lightening to the sound of Orphan scratching at his door. Carefully he disentangles his limbs from Isabelle's, grabs his jeans, the dog's bowl and food, and steps outside the cabin. It's freezing, but he knows that if he lets Orphan in, he will wake Isabelle, and it's too early.

He sets out the dog's food and stands there watching him all but inhale the dry kibble, his tail going like an out-of-control metronome, happiness exploding from his body. Daniel knows exactly how he feels.

He looks up at the sound of a car door opening, like a crack in the still morning air, and across the meadow Jesse Eames is getting ready to hoist himself into the cab of his red pickup, but he stops and turns instead to see Alina running from the open door of her barn, barefoot, in a white bathrobe, her hair flying around her shoulders, into his arms. And Daniel watches as Jesse grabs his daughter, and she kisses him, and his father's heart swells with even more happiness. So Alina loves this man. How glad he is for that.

Quietly he opens the door into his own cottage, slips in before Orphan can follow, and discards his jeans as he crosses the cold wood floor. Isabelle is turned on her right side, toward the wall, away from him, and he slips into bed behind her and spoons her body with his.

"You're cold," she murmurs, but returns to sleep and he holds her and breathes deeply, savoring this moment as he has every second since he saw Isabelle in the woods the day before.

THEY WAKE TOGETHER WHEN THE SUN is clearly up, thick stripes of yellow light across the floor, bed, wooden table, and turn toward each other. Daniel strokes Isabelle's hair away from her face, smiling, and she burrows into his chest.

"Morning."

"I don't want it to be morning," she murmurs. "I want to go back to last night."

"Well, maybe," he says as he begins to run his hand down her long back, "this morning will be better."

"There's a thought. Better than last night? Is that possible?"

He grins at her. "Flatterer."

And he kisses her gently, and then not so gently, and she moves her body into his, matching his rhythm—slow, deliberate, careful. She wants to be present as their bodies respond to each other again, not swept away. Present. With Daniel. As she is. As they are with each other.

LATER, WHEN SHE'S SITTING at the cleared-off wooden table and Daniel is at the stove making her scrambled eggs and toast and coffee, and Orphan is curled up, snoring, on his bed next to the hearth, Isabelle tells him she's leaving later that day.

"I figured," he says, not looking at her.

"Avi's only five," she says in explanation, and Daniel nods. "Maybe you'll come visit us in Oakland."

Daniel puts their plates of scrambled eggs on the table and sits down opposite her.

"Maybe."

"I'll pick you up at the airport. All you'd have to do is get yourself on a plane. No driving necessary," she adds, although they both know that the likelihood of Daniel getting himself on a plane is slim to none.

"Or you'll come back here."

"I'd like to." Now they're both in the wistful realm of "if only's." Then, because she doesn't want to leave anything unsaid, she adds, "I'm going to read the book again. I suspect I'll have a different reaction."

He grins at her, instantly happy. "Well, you'll let me know."

"I will let you know—about the book, about everything, just the way I always have, only now I feel . . ." And she hesitates, struggling to find the words to describe what has happened between them. "I feel . . . more *entitled* to do it. Like these two days have given me permission."

"To . . . ?" he asks carefully.

She looks down at her plate, hesitates a minute, gathering her courage, then looks straight at him and says with conviction, "To love you."

Daniel nods, his heart too full to speak. And so they smile at each other, shyly, and Daniel takes her hand, which rests on the table, and brings it to him, opens her fingers, and presses his lips into her warm palm. Isabelle.

October 29, 2000
Daniel,

Last night after I put Avi to bed, when the house was quiet and I had gathered up my courage, which somehow you always give me, I took out your book and began to reread it with a much more open heart. Daniel, it's a beautiful book, as breathtaking as either of your first two. And the rawness is there, which makes the words jump off the page. And I feel honored to be the "inspiration" for Lanie.

How wise you are to understand that my anger was only

about my own disgust at my own inadequacies, my own small and unproductive life, and jealousy, yes, jealousy, that you were able to write a book and I wasn't. So petty and unfair of me.

But tell me why you made your character such a mess. Did you used to drink that much? And smoke that much? And self-destruct that much?

Lanie might have saved Gus—interesting that you named your character after your father, but that's a different conversation—but I don't think I ever did that for you. I might have nudged you closer to where you eventually ended up, but it was completely without a plan and only because I needed so much from you that I grabbed greedily, and the result was a lifeline for both of us.

So my version of events would be quite different, but yours is beyond great. The book is a wonder!

Love,
Isabelle

Isabelle,

Then write your version.

Daniel

Daniel,

Arrrgggggghhh!!

I.

And then, because Daniel doesn't want Isabelle to feel he has discounted the rest of her e-mail:

Isabelle,

And don't think your words of praise haven't made my day, my week, my month, and my forever.

Love,
Daniel

And so slowly, with great trepidation, without telling him at first, Isabelle begins to do just what Daniel commanded: she starts to write her own version of the time they spent together and beyond. Just as Daniel had.

Part Three

SUMMER 2014

It is Alina who calls Isabelle and tells her to come. That Daniel needs her. And of course she goes.

It isn't hard these days for Isabelle to arrange her life so that she can quickly fly to New Hampshire. Avi, who is nineteen and in college at UC, Davis, is spending the summer between his freshman and sophomore years working as a white-water guide. Years ago Casey took him to Alaska so they could experience Mendenhall Lake, at the foot of Mendenhall Glacier. He couldn't resist, Casey told her: "Two Mendenhalls going to see two Mendenhalls—a natural!" And Avi had been dumbstruck by the stark beauty of the landscape—the seven-thousand-foot-tall mountains capped with snow and the pristine, iceberg-studded lake. This summer he's back to lead boatloads of tourists down the rapids of Mendenhall River.

Casey has always understood something about their son that Isabelle might have missed: that he is happiest where the terrain is rugged, that he hates to be contained. Whatever he ends up doing with his life, it will be something without a desk or a schedule. Not unlike his father.

Their relationship these days consists of travel to remote places: hiking through the austere mountain ranges of Pays Dogon in Mali, riding the rapids of the Rio Upano in Ecuador through the Amazon rain forest. They are always planning their next adventure, each trying to best the other in finding the most remote and original trip to take. It is here that they make their connection, here that they are most alike.

But it is the ways in which Avi is unlike his father that reassure Isabelle about his future. Avi examines and mulls and thinks things through. He wants to know the why of things, and especially of people, in a way that has never appealed to Casey.

She's seen him weigh and appreciate Casey's calling, but having lived with the consequences of it all his life, he also understands the inherent self-centeredness in it. He loves Isabelle but wishes she were easier on herself—less self-critical, less heavy-duty. They've had that conversation a number of times, always ending with her son saying, "Just chill, Mom, you know." And she does know, but can't often get there.

Avi has no idea what he will eventually do with his life, but he isn't worried. Right now he wants experience for the sake of the experience, and right now untamed Alaska and the rapids of Mendenhall River fit the bill. So it won't matter to Avi whether his mother is home in the Oakland hills or in the tiny town of Winnock, New Hampshire. He will be in the wilds of Alaska, exactly where he wants to be.

In terms of the bookstore, Isabelle is confident that Julian can easily take care of Noah's Ark while she is gone. He practically does that now. There are so many days Isabelle never makes it into the store. She is constantly grateful for the day, five years ago, when Julian, a longtime customer, came in and asked for a job. His partner of almost seventeen years, Craig, had just died, and Julian was coming apart at the seams.

"I can't stay at home and stare at the walls anymore," he told Isabelle with an apologetic smile, "because they're starting to talk back to me."

Isabelle's instinct told her to say, *Yes, come and work here,* and she did so without hesitation, just as Meir had taken a chance on her twenty years before. And Julian has rewarded her by dedicating himself to Noah's Ark in a way that would have made Meir very happy. The two men would have gotten along, she's certain, although they would seem to be polar opposites—Meir large and sloppy to Julian's fastidious thinness, Meir antisocial as a life creed and Julian living for his wide circle of friends. But both men would declare that they loved books in a visceral, unquestioning way, and that passion would have united them.

Often when she tells Julian one story or another about Meir, she misses him with a sharp-edged sadness, as if his death eight years ago had happened only yesterday. Well, his presence is there, in every shelf of the store, every book she sells, the shop his legacy, which Isabelle honors every day. As does Julian.

Michael will be the one to miss her, but she knows he won't protest. When she met him, nine years ago, Daniel had been such a constant presence in her life for so long that it was like he was a relative, someone to be inherited along with the rest of Isabelle's family—her impossible mother, her three fractious brothers, her gentle, regretful father. And Daniel.

Michael, with his generous heart, embraced them all. Before Isabelle, he had been a man without a family. His Russian immigrant parents used up all their energy, it seemed, getting the three of them to America when Michael was very small. Their premature deaths he attributes to a kind of wearing out of body and spirit as soon as Michael was safely in law school. His first wife was long gone, seeking more excitement than a staid law professor could provide. So he welcomed Isabelle's family, however difficult, and they responded in kind.

How is it, Isabelle often wonders, that she ended up married to a man her parents like? Both of them. Even her mother, the harder sell by far, lets praise for Michael slip through her lips every so often.

And Deepti and Parmeet will look in on him, bring him Indian food for dinner and make sure he remembers to eat it. Their gratitude to Michael will never be repaid, they feel, because he introduced them four years ago.

When Parmeet Joshi was recruited by Boalt Hall from his position as professor of international law at Gujarat National Law University, he came with accolades and honors. Michael expected a sort of legal celebrity, given Parmeet's published work, the papers he had delivered at conferences all over the world, but the man he met was quiet, a bit shy, and self-effacing despite his scholarly standing. He knew immediately Parmeet would be a good match for Deepti.

Michael loves Deepti almost as much as Isabelle does. They share the slightly subversive humor of genuinely nice people and a love of late-night conversations. Before Parmeet entered the picture, they would sit on the sweeping deck of Michael's hillside home and continue talking well after Isabelle had gone off to bed.

It was to Michael that Deepti could air her worries about the financial difficulties of her pediatric practice, given the population she served in East Oakland—low-income patients, mostly on Medi-Cal.

And Michael would talk to Deepti about the politics of his law school. The in-fighting, the warring camps within the faculty. Isabelle could never keep the factions straight, but Deepti regarded all the inner workings of the school as a real-life soap opera. She was fascinated, and so Michael could go on and on, story after story.

From all those late-night conversations and all the dinners the three of them had shared over the years, Michael felt he knew Deepti well enough to say to Isabelle, "I want her to meet Parmeet."

"A fix-up?"

"Well . . ." Michael equivocated. Then: "Yes, okay, we can call it that."

"Great! Deepti needs a fix-up!"

And Michael was right again; his instinct for people was solid. Deepti and Parmeet were married less than a year later, diffident people glowing with happiness, Deepti, past forty, was almost as shocked that her life had taken this unexpected turn as she was joyful. So Michael was a matchmaking genius, everyone acknowledged that, and perfect for Isabelle.

IT ALL BEGAN AT FULL OF BEANS in 2005. Most mornings when Isabelle rushed in, almost always late, it seemed, Michael would look up from his latte and laptop to see this tall woman with graceful hands talking to Alfredo as he made her cappuccino. These two people had an understanding. He gave her an extra shot of espresso and she always asked about his kids, whom he was eager to talk about. Since he had six, there never was a dearth of conversation.

Michael liked how well Isabelle listened—everything stilled, her hands quieted, her eyes on Alfredo's face followed his expressions as he talked. And Michael liked the questions she asked, as if she was genuinely interested. There was also something about the way she seemed perpetually out of breath, eager to catch up to a life that seemed always just a little bit out of reach, which appealed to him. He couldn't have articulated why, but somehow he knew that he could provide ballast that might help Isabelle settle a little, maybe even allow her to sail forward in a more measured way.

Sometimes, after listening to a story from Alfredo about one child or another, Isabelle would contribute a story about her own son, and Alfredo would laugh knowingly. "Oh, yes," he'd say, "a wise child. You have your hands full." And Isabelle would smile ruefully and nod, and it was evident to Michael how much she loved this "wise child" of hers.

So she had a child but didn't wear a ring. Perhaps there was hope.

Most people's eyes would slide right past Michael Davidov. He exuded a solitary air, a seriousness that encouraged people's eyes to seek out the next person, who might be more interesting to look at and who was definitely more engaging in the moment. And there was something vaguely old-fashioned about him, a reticence that was slightly foreign, a legacy from his immigrant parents, who clung to their Russian roots even as they tried to adapt to America.

Well into his thirties when he met Isabelle, he had made peace with his nature. He was content to be seen as just another Berkeley professor in a well-used jacket, button-down shirt, a large briefcase on the chair beside him, going over notes before his morning lecture. Conventional. Easily forgettable.

But Michael's secret was that he grew on people, that the more one got to know him, the more compelling he became. Underneath the seriousness were a wicked intelligence and the kindness that was Michael's defining characteristic. And as he watched Isabelle day after day, the certainty grew within him that if he went about it the right way, this lovely, breathless woman might just see the good in him.

Then came the day that, on an impulse, he followed her. He packed up his laptop quickly, grabbed his briefcase, and walked behind her down College Avenue, two blocks to the corner, where she stopped to unlock the front door of Noah's Ark. He waited a minute, two, and when he saw the OPEN sign appear on the glass front door, he made his move.

The bell on the door jingled as he entered the shop. The front counter was empty, the store silent. Didn't he just see her—Isabelle is what Alfredo called her—unlock the door and come in?

"Hello?"

"I'm coming," is called from the back, and Isabelle appears carrying the third incarnation of the original Mr. Coffee, heavy with water, up to the front counter. "Sorry," she says, a touch out of breath, he notices, and apologizing as a reflex. "Can I help you?" She is busy plugging in the machine and not really looking at him.

"You carry used textbooks?"

"Some. What are you looking for?"

"*Economic Consequences of Intellectual Property/Copyright Decisions,* by Belarsky and Margrove."

Isabelle shrugs. "I don't think so—it's a law book, right? But you could take a look." She points. "Back wall."

And Michael makes his way through the overstuffed shelves to the back of the shop while Isabelle climbs aboard her tall stool behind the front counter and, to the reassuring accompaniment of the gurgling water, begins to sort the mail.

And then Michael is back, standing in front of her with the textbook in his hand, and she looks at him fully for the first time. He could be descended from a long line of rabbis, is her immediate first thought: dark and serious, a prominent nose, large, compelling brown eyes, a face of angles, a masculine face that is not the least bit handsome. A face that in its Jewish soulfulness feels familiar to her.

"We had it—wow, great! What are the odds?"

"I had a hunch. You know, I've walked past this store maybe hundreds of times and today I just had an instinct—time to come in." He smiles at her and his face transforms, all the gravity banished, and he looks almost boyish. She smiles back.

"What do you teach?" she asks as she rings up the heavy book.

"How do you know I teach?"

"You could be the poster guy for 'professor.' "

Michael does a quick inventory of his body and clothes. "Oh, no—that bad?"

"It's not bad at all. You teach at Boalt?"

"Yes, intellectual property law. Well, I guess that's self-evident, too." He holds up the newly-paid-for book.

"What is that—intellectual property?"

"Copyright, patents—the work of the mind. How the law protects writers, artists, inventors."

"Interesting."

"Do you really think so? Most people's eyes glaze over when I mention what I do."

"Well," she says, grinning at him, "I have a special place in my heart for writers." She gestures around the store with its thousands of books. "Obviously. It's great to know that someone out there is interested in protecting them."

And Michael blushes at the compliment, and she sees it and is charmed that so little praise could elicit so much appreciation. What a nice man. She almost tells him that, then thinks better of it. She tells him later, though, often, and always gets the blush.

They begin to say hello to each other on the mornings their paths cross at Full of Beans. Sometimes Isabelle will sit for a minute at Michael's table and chat before she rushes off to open the bookstore. Finally Michael asks her to dinner, and Isabelle finds herself saying yes without any attendant excitement or rush. A nice man, good conversation at dinner. Why not? She can't remember the last time she went on a date.

For years after she asked Casey to move out, his presence in her life and Avi's, even as it diminished, was enough to occupy Isabelle's emotional landscape. At first, she couldn't find a way to have a casual connection with him, an "appropriate connection," she would say when discussing Casey yet again with Deepti.

And Deepti worried about her. In their late-night conversations, Isabelle in Oakland and Deepti in Baltimore as she finished up her pediatric residency, she would ask Isabelle the crucial question often and in different guises: "What good has your separation done if all you do is talk about and think about Casey?"

"He doesn't live here anymore. We're not having sex anymore . . . at least mostly we're not."

"Isabelle!"

"I've only weakened a few times."

"Isabelle!"

"I know."

And she did know. Deepti was right, but it took her years to truly disengage, to genuinely not *want* Casey anymore. It happened slowly, excruciatingly slowly, like peeling off a bandage from a badly scraped knee, millimeter by millimeter, but now, five years after their initial conversation in the car, Isabelle can say to Deepti, "I'm done with him," and mean it.

Perhaps that's why she said yes to Michael. She really doesn't know. He asked, she said yes. It seemed reasonable to agree. How different their beginning was from those heady days with Casey when Isabelle was swept away.

She and Michael talked and talked, not in the hectoring way Nate had often had with her, or the needy, self-revelatory way her father often used. But conversation for the pure pleasure of examining things—ideas, concepts, stories. Michael loved to tell stories. Isabelle felt he was a thwarted writer, and Michael didn't disagree.

"It was never an option," he told her early in their relationship. They were sitting in Gregor's Russian Restaurant in San Francisco, with its starched white tablecloths on square tables, eating melt-in-your-mouth beef brisket and crisp potato latkes with applesauce, and Isabelle was taken right back to Sunday dinners at her nana's—her father's mother. Her mother's mother never cooked anything.

"I didn't need to be reminded of all the sacrifices my parents made to bring us here," Michael told her. "It was obvious. My father had been a research chemist in St. Petersburg, and he was lucky to get a job as a janitor when we arrived. So getting a good education and choosing a solid and prestigious career—that was my end of the bargain to uphold."

They always seemed to be inside rooms—restaurants, theaters, classrooms, where she went to watch him teach, then her own living room, then Avi's room as Michael made a real effort to get to know him. At the beginning that was hard going. It was impossible, really, for Michael to follow Casey, who crowded whatever space he was in, who made the world exciting, who was the ultimate romantic figure, all his focus totally on the moment at hand. And when Avi was the target of that attention, the little boy filled up with pride and a devotion to his dad that left little space for any sort of substitute.

Michael understood early on that he couldn't compete, and so he let Avi come to him in his own time. And it took years. Years when Avi and Michael were polite to each other but little else, then teenage years when even Avi's politeness was in short supply. Michael lost faith during that time that they would ever find a way toward each other, and his sorrow about it spilled over into his day-to-day conversations with Isabelle. She couldn't find the words to comfort him, because she wasn't sure Avi would ever see in Michael what she had come to cherish. But finally, when it was almost too late, he did.

Six years after they all began living together and four years after Isabelle and Michael married, when Avi was seventeen and a junior in high school, he began to switch his attention from his largely absent father to his steady and available step-father. Maturity? Casey's increasing absences? Michael's faith-fulness? Isabelle guessed a little of all of those contributed to Avi's turning to Michael, who was simply grateful. He had been waiting a long time.

Now the two men have a bond that's largely unspoken but very strong. They both love Isabelle. They see the good in each other even as they acknowledge how very different the stu-dious Michael and the adventure-seeking Avi are. It's under-stood by both that they would stand beside the other if ever their presence was needed. And that their small family, which they've cobbled together, would be honored.

For Isabelle, her turning point came a couple of months after she and Michael began seeing each other. It was an early morning in March and she had gotten up with enough time to have a cup of coffee and skim the *Chronicle* before her day began in earnest. It had taken her years to have the discipline to actually do it—get out of bed early—but it made such a difference to have a half hour to herself before getting Avi up, which always took some doing, and driving him to school, and stopping by Full of Beans and hopefully spending a few minutes with Michael, and then opening the store. Meir came in later and later these days, now that he'd passed his eighty-first birthday. All the attendant ills of his heedless lifestyle—high blood pressure, Type 2 diabetes, and especially gout, which somehow delighted him, since it was such a literary affliction—were taking their toll. And so she found herself leaving the bookstore later and having less time at the end of the day. A quiet half hour in the morning somehow made all that possible.

As she gathered in her newspaper, which never seemed to make it up onto her front porch, as she would have liked, she noticed that Fanny hadn't turned the TV off the night before.

She often forgot these days. If Meir was eighty-one, Fanny would be eighty-five. And she had slowed down, too. Not her mouth or her opinions, but her knees kept her mostly at home, and her cough seemed constant and more debilitating.

Isabelle peered in the front window. Yes, the television was going, blasting away, really, since Fanny's hearing had diminished along with everything else. But she wasn't stretched out on her BarcaLounger. She must have made it to bed but forgotten the TV. And then Isabelle saw her, sprawled on the floor, facedown, her arms above her head as if in surprise, positioned between the living and dining rooms, motionless.

"Fanny!" Isabelle screamed as she pounded on the window. "Fanny!" And then she ran to get the emergency key Isabelle had long ago insisted upon, despite Fanny's resistance to anything so practical.

As soon as she opened the front door, she knew immediately that Fanny was gone: there was a void, a startling absence in the house. "Fanny . . ." she said softly as she knelt beside her body. "Oh, Fanny . . . alone, you died alone . . . Oh, no."

Michael came as soon as she called him and put his arms around her and held her as she cried and called the police and the mortuary and turned her head into his shoulder so she wouldn't have that awful image of Fanny wrapped in a body bag, being carried out for the last time.

And it was Michael who sat with her and helped her tell Avi what had happened. For Avi, at almost ten, this was his first significant death. And Michael knew something about that, having seen both his parents through theirs.

It was Michael who went and retrieved Fanny's ashes and stood with Isabelle and Meir, who could barely stand, so overcome with grief was he, as they sealed the ashes away in the mausoleum at Mount Sinai Cemetery in Orinda.

I love this man, Isabelle found herself thinking, when

her thoughts should have been of Fanny and all their years together and all her neighbor had given Avi and herself. And she did think of that often in the days and weeks to come, but at the moment, as pale spring sunlight filtered into the dank room from the narrow skylight and Avi leaned back against her legs, needing to be touching her, and Michael put a hand on Meir's arm to hold him up, she suddenly realized that she loved Michael Davidov and that he probably loved her.

With Fanny gone next door, Isabelle's half of the duplex never again felt like home to her; there was always a sense of loss associated with it now. And when Michael asked them to move in with him, she discussed it with Avi, who shrugged his shoulders and refused to offer an opinion. "Whatever, Mom," was the best he would do.

Michael lived in the perfect house to begin anew. It had been rebuilt by the previous owner on the site of their original stucco house, destroyed by the inferno that was the 1991 Oakland hills fire. Over three thousand homes were incinerated that Sunday in October, and many people hadn't had the heart to rebuild. But not the Constantines—they had had the courage and the stubbornness and the money and the vision to construct a house completely of concrete, glass, and steel. Anything that could burn was eliminated from the building plans. It was all form and line and open spaces, tucked into the hillside with grand views of the bay. The garden was planted with spiky succulents.

Michael bought it ten years later because of its unrepentant modernity. After his divorce he was looking only to the future, and he felt the house made a statement that he was ready to embrace. Isabelle understood that immediately, and it comforted her. She was also ready to look only forward, as long as Michael was by her side.

Daniel was the one anchor to her past life that she had no

desire to cut loose. After her precipitous visit to Winnock in the summer of 2000, their e-mails became more intimate and far-ranging and funny. They knew each other in a more fundamental way now. The days together, the sex, had opened up areas of feeling and connection that had been incipient but never realized. Now they both felt more *entitled*, as Isabelle had put it. They e-mailed many times a day if they felt like it, or sometimes days or weeks would go by without contact, but it didn't matter. Once they began again, it was as if no time had passed. There were no requirements they honored, no prescribed way they had to be with each other, only acceptance and an almost visceral understanding of the other. When they needed to, one or the other would pick up the phone and call.

Daniel started that custom one day in the spring of 2001, about six months after Isabelle's visit to Winnock. What had happened during the previous week was so unexpected, so unsettling, that an e-mail couldn't contain it. He needed to hear Isabelle's voice. He needed her immediate, unfiltered response to translate what he had just experienced into some emotional language he could understand.

Stefan had shown up on his doorstep unannounced, after almost a five-year absence. All he knew about his son were the few crumbs of information Alina grudgingly doled out when he asked, "Have you heard from your brother?"

"He's in Youngstown," Alina told him the first time he asked.

"Why Youngstown? What's he doing there?"

And Alina shrugged, conversation finished as far as she was concerned.

When Daniel asked for an address or phone number, Alina would shake her head. "He e-mails me."

"Then could you give me his e-mail address?"

"Let me ask him first." But she never would. And gradually

Daniel gave up asking, in much the same way he gave up communication with Stephanie when she proved so difficult. To
Daniel, it always felt like every move forward he tried to make
concerning his children netted him nothing but resistance,
and so when he opened the door of his cabin early one April
morning to see Stefan loping across the awakening meadow
still wet with dew, he was stunned.

"Stefan!"

"Hey, Dad. How's it goin'?" his son called as he neared, as if
they had seen each other the previous week instead of almost
five years ago. He looked pretty much the same—scruffy,
unkempt, wearing old jeans and a zip-up sweatshirt with the
arms missing.

"What are you doing here?"

"Visiting you."

Daniel took Stefan into town with him and they sat at his
customary round table in Bev's Bakery and Stefan started talking and didn't stop. Fairly quickly Daniel understood that his
son had "found God," or a reasonable facsimile as far as Stefan
was concerned.

"It's like this, Dad. When the car broke down in Youngstown,
it wasn't some kind of random thing."

"What were you doing in Youngstown?"

"On my way back to Colorado Springs. That's where I was
going."

"Oh, Stefan . . ." Daniel murmurs.

"But there was a plan in place that was so much bigger
than me."

"Really?"

"See, I had to stay there and get the car fixed, but I didn't
have the money for a new transmission, of course, and so I
had to find some sort of job to make the money, you know,
and there we had the same old problem of me finding a job, so

what could I do? I hadda sorta start asking people on the street to help me."

"You mean as in panhandling?"

"Well . . . that's an old-fashioned word, Dad. Not so good."

"Okay, how's *begging*—is that better?"

Stefan put a hand on Daniel's shoulder, calm, not rising to the bait as he would have in years past. "Wait a minute, Dad, here's where the story gets better."

Daniel sat back in his chair and looked around for Bev. Maybe she could come over and bring them some more coffee or talk to Stefan about something else entirely, because Daniel distinctly didn't want to hear the rest of this story. But Bev was busy with customers, and so Daniel had no choice but to say, "Well, I hope so." And that sparked another nonstop monologue from his son.

"So I'm walking back and forth in front of this sort of restaurant holding a paper cup. You know, so people could put coins in, or if they're really nice a dollar bill here and there, and this guy comes up to me and the first thing he does is put some change in my cup and then he says, 'Have you eaten lately?' You get that, Dad, he's interested in whether I've had something to eat."

"A kind person."

"Yes!" And Stefan's eyes were shining. "Exactly! So I go with him into the restaurant and he buys me lunch and then he takes me back to the place he works and shows me this sort of dormitory with lots of cots lined up in rows and tells me I can sleep there if I need to. And I did. I was, like, exhausted 'cause I'd been sleeping in doorways and out in parks, you know."

Daniel was now even more uncomfortable with where this was going but he said nothing, and his son continued talking.

"So when I wake up, this guy, his name is Peter Fairchild,

comes to get me and takes me to this meeting room, there in the building, and that's when I find out that I have been rescued, in more ways than one, by this charity called Trustings." And here Stefan spoke the next sentence like a mantra: " 'We trust ourselves, we trust each other.' Have you heard of it?"

"Should I have?"

"Well, maybe not here in rural New Hampshire, but in any big city, sure. We're nationwide!"

Daniel nodded, and that was enough for Stefan to continue describing what sounded suspiciously like a cult, or at least an offshoot of the seventies version of a cult, est, founded by that charlatan Werner Erhard.

Stefan had been living there since, taking "classes," learning about the "personal blocks" to his success.

"That's what they talk about a lot, Dad—what are our personal blocks to our success? How we all have unresolved issues, you know, things that keep us from the ultimate. That's what we're all striving for—'the ultimate'—don't you think, Dad? Like your personal blocks are pretty obvious."

"Really?" If it were anyone else but his son, Daniel would have been up and out of Bev's Bakery in a heartbeat—he doesn't listen to this kind of psychobabble—but he didn't move. He told himself that his son was reaching out and he had to stay put and listen.

"Well, your agoraphobia, for one. That's a pretty big block."

"And there's more, I presume?"

"Well, yeah, and that's why I'm here."

"To list all my blocks?"

"No, no." And here Stefan actually chuckled. "To help you get past one of your major blocks."

"And that would be?"

"Alina."

"Oh." And just her name jolted Daniel, and Stefan saw it,

and so sat back and was quiet for a minute, to let the air clear before his final statement.

"I'm here to broker a deal between you and Alina," he said quietly, but with confidence. "That's what we call it—'broker a deal.'"

LATER THAT DAY DANIEL FINDS HIMSELF sitting in Alina's white-on-white living room, with Stefan on one side of him and Alina standing across the room, leaning against the fireplace, her arms crossed defiantly. Stefan is the only one of the three who is cheerful. Unnaturally so.

"Think of your own personal blocks like those blocks of stone that make up your fireplace, Alina."

She says nothing. Her scowl deepens.

"They're big," Stefan continues, unfazed by his sister's obvious hostility. "Sometimes they're boulders, much too heavy to move by yourself. So we help each other move our personal blocks. Dad is your personal block—"

"Oh, please, Stefan," Alina finally says. "If you expect me to participate in some kind of—"

"Let's let Stefan finish," Daniel says gently.

"Oh, thanks, Dad! I knew you'd see the sense of this!"

"I wouldn't go that far, but you came all this way, so I think your sister and I should give you a fair hearing."

"Okay, so Dad, you're Alina's personal block and she's yours, and the only thing to do is for each of you to say why and then put your shoulders together to move the blocks." Stefan says all this as if it's self-evident. He's smiling with accomplishment, so pleased with himself.

"Ladies first," Daniel says.

"Stefan, this is complete drivel," Alina says without a moment's consideration. Case closed. Discussion over, as far as she's concerned. And she walks swiftly across the room, reaches for the door into her studio, ready to be gone from this tinder-box of emotion.

But Stefan stops her. "Please," he says, placing a hand on her arm, "we need to talk as a family. You need to tell Dad why you're so mad at him."

And Alina turns slowly, very slowly, and looks at her father, a large man with his forearms on his thighs, his hands hanging between his knees, his eyes searching out hers.

"Stefan, you don't want to do this." Her voice is low, heavy with warning.

"All three of us. It's our work. It's what we have to do. Tell Dad why you're so angry."

Alina shakes her head, but Stefan pushes. "Tell him! Go on! He can take it. You need to give it! Talk!"

"I'm not just angry at him, I'm furious, I'm livid, incensed, enraged, irate! Okay, you got it? You heard it? Now leave me alone." And she tries to push past her brother, to escape into her studio, to be done with all this, but he won't let her.

"You need to tell him why."

"Why?" And it's then that her tightly controlled demeanor cracks and words gush forth from her mouth like an explosion. "Because he left us! That's why. Isn't that enough for you? Abandonment!" She's yelling now. "One day he was there and the next, gone! Without any explanation, without a thought for what we might have been feeling. You don't remember because you were too young, but I remember! Every day, every hour I would pray to God—yes, I used to do that—please, God, if I am very good and cause no trouble to anyone and honor you and do my chores, then he"—and here she points at Daniel, sitting motionless, absorbing every vitriolic word she's hurling—"he will come walking up the front path to our apartment house and open the front door and sweep me up into his arms and tell me it was all a mistake and he will

268 · DEENA GOLDSTONE

be there forever and forever and he will never leave. But no! All that mattered was what he wanted. All that mattered was his life! We were just kids—we were expendable! He didn't think of us when he upped and left, and we didn't matter all those years after when we never heard from him and he almost never visited and he certainly never came and got us, now did he? Is that enough 'why' for you, Stefan?!" And with that, Alina shoves Stefan aside rudely and flees into her studio and slams the door shut.

Daniel hasn't moved. Head down, shoulders bowed, his eyes on his shoes now, a picture of defeat.

Stefan comes over to him, sits beside him on the sofa, puts a hand on his shoulder, and says softly, "That's not the whole story, Dad, I know that."

And it's then that tears fill Daniel's eyes.

WHEN DANIEL DESCRIBED THE SCENE in all its scathing detail to Isabelle, she was silent for quite a while. The phone line crackled with empty air while she tried to find the right response, both honest and as comforting as she could make it.

"She needed to say all that," Isabelle said finally.

"Obviously."

"What did you do?"

"Listened."

"Did you respond? Did you try to show her your side of things?"

"She wouldn't have been able to hear me."

"No, you're right, not with all that anger blocking the way." Then: "But maybe one day she'll be able to."

"Maybe."

"It's what you can hope for, Daniel."

"Yes."

But the only thing that changed after Stefan's visit was that

Alina and Daniel became even more careful with each other, more buttoned up, both aware now of the tumult roiling away beneath Alina's calm surface. Each working hard not to trigger an eruption, something that had mortified both of them.

ISABELLE WAS MORE THAN SURPRISED, then, when, years later, the phone call she received was from Alina. But there was no decision to make, and Isabelle packed her bags and asked Michael to drive her to the Oakland airport and kissed him good-bye and thanked him for being so understanding, because she clearly knew how much he didn't want her to go.

"I'm going to miss you," is as much as he allows himself to say as they stand at the airport curb beside his murky-green Volvo. She is his center and his reason to get up in the morning and his delight at the end of the day when he finishes his work and comes home.

"I know," Isabelle says. "I'll miss you, too." And she means it. Despite the fact that she is going to Daniel, she will miss Michael.

"You can do this," he tells her, and she nods, even though she isn't sure she'll be able to. This time, on this trip, Daniel is the one in need, and she has to make sure she doesn't buckle in the face of it.

As soon as the plane is at cruising altitude and the seat belt sign is turned off, Isabelle settles into her seat. She's never completely confident that the tons of metal she's encased in will make it up into the air, so she holds herself in anticipation until the plane has leveled out. Finally she allows herself a deep breath and lets Oakland and her life there drop away. Her thoughts turn to the last time she saw Daniel, so much easier to contemplate than what awaits her now.

In 2003, almost exactly three years after her first trip, she visited Daniel again in New Hampshire. Avi was eight and

Michael wasn't yet in her life. She had spent the past three years trying to do what Daniel had urged her to: write her own version of their connection. But she wasn't at all sure she was on the right track. All she'd been able to get down on paper were snippets and isolated scenes and paragraphs that didn't seem to go anywhere. How would all these disparate parts coalesce into a real story?

What she needed, she decided, was to pace across the wooden floor of Daniel's cottage and read it all aloud to him and sneak glances to see how he was taking it in and then sit and wait for his verdict with her eyes on his face, the way she used to when she was his student. She wanted to be that student again, and so she flew to Winnock one more time.

She found a quietly confident Daniel, a bit tentative about the warm reception he had received for *Out of the Blue*—after all, he'd been through this dance before—but accepting enough of it to be able to continue writing.

He was working on a series of short stories about a fictional town in New Hampshire that was inspired by the place he now called home. And it was going well, and he welcomed Isabelle with a lightness of spirit that she was thrilled to see.

This time their days together were completely different. They had an ease with the other, a certainty about the place they occupied in each other's life. They wanted nothing more than for all that to continue. And nothing else.

Daniel would stay in Winnock—that was clear. It was where he could breathe deeply and live simply and write without the anxiety that he knew was always crouched in a corner somewhere, lying in wait for him. He saw it as almost a physical being, a sleek black panther, deadly and silent. One false move and the cat would pounce.

Isabelle would stay in Oakland and raise her child where he needed to be, close to his grandparents and at home base for his wandering father. She would work out her relationship with Casey somehow, someday, and help Meir run the bookstore, and struggle to write. That's how they would live their day-to-day lives, but they had each other whenever they needed. If they could count on that, they wouldn't ask for more, because neither of them was certain that more would have been better. "As is" seemed perfectly fine.

They spent Isabelle's visit in Daniel's small cabin, which had been transformed since she was there last. Now it felt like someone had made it a home. There were beautiful white pine shelves and cabinets built into the walls surrounding the stone fireplace. And Daniel had filled them with the books he loved.

"Jesse's work," Daniel explained. "He lives with Alina now, it seems." And then Daniel grinned at her. "He talks to me, even if she doesn't."

And Daniel had bought a sofa, deep blue and very comfortable. There were rugs on the floor and white curtains at the windows. And a real set of dishes stacked on the shelves in the kitchen. A handmade quilt of five pointed stars on the bed they shared. Orphan even had his own monogrammed dog bed, courtesy of L.L. Bean.

And Isabelle was able to walk across the cabin floor and read her pages out loud and watch Daniel's face for a reaction and sit down in a kitchen chair when she was done and ask, "Well? Tell me."

"Why does this story matter?" Daniel's voice is gentle.

Isabelle sits motionless and contemplates what he has asked her. She doesn't have an easy answer. And he waits. The wind outside fills the quiet. The birch tree limbs rub against each other in a sort of moaning.

Daniel is comfortable simply watching her try to find an answer and so he doesn't say anything, and they sit like that, across the small room from each other, until finally Isabelle says, "Because I want to show how the most unlikely people can save each other's lives."

"Yes," he says with a sort of relief, "that is exactly it. Perfect!"

On her last morning there they wrap up in heavy jackets—there is frost in the air—and wind woolen scarves around their necks and walk into town for Bev's cinnamon buns and coffee.

Isabelle had heard so much about "the women" but had met only Pauline the last time she was there, small, feisty Pauline, who had served them their dinner and her unedited opinions at the Granite State Diner. But it is Bev she is curious about, because Daniel has spoken more often about her and she seems to be the heart of the class.

Through the woods they retrace their steps from Isabelle's last visit, laughing about how angry she had been then.

"Angry at myself," Isabelle says now.

Daniel takes her gloved hand in his and doesn't disagree.

The trees are bare now, all the gorgeous leaves underfoot fading into the forest floor. It's more desolate than the last time Isabelle was there, with winter around the corner and the blaze of autumn behind them. But they are content, and Isabelle feels the need to amend her thought.

"But not now."

He nods but doesn't look at her. They stride ahead, hand in hand. A bright red cardinal in the muted landscape hops from one barren tree limb to another, always a few yards ahead of them, leading the way, and Daniel tells her softly what has been so hard for him to tell others. "I'm proud of you."

And she rests her head on his shoulder for a moment as they walk. The comfort they give each other.

CHAPTER NINETEEN

This time when Isabelle arrives at Boston's Logan Airport, Bev is waiting for her. She will drive her to Winnock and Daniel.

It was almost eleven years ago that Isabelle first met Bev, when Daniel took her into the bakery for coffee and a sweet roll on the morning she was leaving. They were celebrating, it felt like, because Daniel had given her what she needed to go home and continue to work: his belief that what she was writing was worthy. That's what she had come for, even if she hadn't been able to articulate it beforehand.

They walked into Bev's hand in hand, Isabelle's cheeks reddened from the cold, a little out of breath from keeping up with Daniel's pace on the long walk, and Bev knew immediately that here was Isabelle—tall, graceful, young, oh, so young, although Isabelle was thirty-one at the time. To Bev, who was almost twice her age, Isabelle was blissfully young.

They sat at Daniel's table in the front window and Bev brought them both ceramic mugs of steaming coffee, and Daniel introduced them.

Almost in unison, they said essentially the same thing: "Oh, I've wanted to meet you," from Isabelle, and "Finally, we meet!" from Bev. And then the women smiled at each other and knew instantly that they would be allies, that they both cared about Daniel and that such a feeling would unite them, not divide them.

Daniel asked for his cinnamon bun and Isabelle ordered a cranberry scone, and Bev rested her hand lightly on Daniel's shoulder as she left, a silent signal of approval that Isabelle noticed.

"You'd better pay attention to her," Isabelle said once Bev was back behind the counter.

"I always pay attention to smart women."

"This one in particular, I think."

"Isabelle," he said, sitting back in his seat, grinning at her across the table, happy to be able to tease her a little, "are you taking care of me?"

"Yes, I'm pointing you in the right direction. You think you have a monopoly on that skill?"

And Isabelle was right. In the following year Bev and Daniel found their way to each other, slowly, with hesitation, because they carried with them two lifetimes of experience that might have been impediments but in the end weren't. They turned toward each other at just the right time. Daniel was sixty-two and deep into the pleasure of writing his Winnock stories. Bev was fifty-nine; her husband had been dead for more than a decade, and she had all but given up on the possibility of loving someone again. Daniel stepped through the very small and rapidly closing window of hope.

Isabelle's first thought when she sees Bev now, waiting for her at the baggage claim, is how much she has aged, her lovely chestnut hair overtaken by gray, the lines on her face deepened into wrinkles. Time has honed her strong face into angles that weren't nearly so prominent a decade ago, but Bev must be close to seventy, Isabelle reminds herself. Daniel is seventy-two.

And of course Isabelle is no longer the young girl who came to Daniel repeatedly for directions to a life she wasn't even sure she could manage to live. She is almost forty-two, and her child is all but grown. She chose wisely and married well. She has helped her brother Aaron through many rough years marked by estrangement from their parents and alcohol abuse. She has run a business by herself and successfully. And she is now a bona fide author. A small press in Berkeley, Indian Rock Books, published her novel, *My Side of the Story*—a title that made Daniel laugh outright. And although it reached a very small audience, she is working on a second. She is a woman in the middle of her life, with skills and accomplishments she would never have predicted when she first walked into Daniel's office.

"Isabelle!" Bev cries out when she sees her, in relief, in pleasure. The two women hug, then Bev pulls back and they look at each other, taking a measure of the other. *Are you ready for this?*

"How is he?"

"Angry," Bev says. And Isabelle nods. Of course.

Quickly they move toward the exit doors, through them, and out to the parking lot.

"Every e-mail I get is about how impossible it is to finish this latest book, how stupid it was for him to begin it, how incompetent he is to write what he wants to write."

"And nothing about the cancer, or what the doctors have said?"

"No. Not after the first news."

Isabelle watches Bev as they reach her minivan. She takes Isabelle's suitcase and puts it in the car, lowers the hatchback, avoids Isabelle's eyes.

"Tell me, Bev."

And Bev does, with tears spilling down her face. "We're

talking about a short time left. He has a particularly aggressive kind of lung cancer—that's what the doctors have told him."

Isabelle puts a hand on Bev's arm, in sympathy, in support, so she can continue.

"He's on oxygen now, and it's hard for him to leave his cabin, which of course, knowing Daniel, he wouldn't do anyway. I wanted him to move into town with me when he first got sick so he wouldn't be so isolated out there, but would he?"

Isabelle shakes her head; the answer is obvious. "Of course not."

"He has to finish his book, he told me. He can only write out there."

"That sounds like Daniel."

"But something's shifted in the last weeks." Bev shakes her head slightly, almost as if she's talking to herself. "I'm afraid he's defeated." And then Bev looks directly at Isabelle. "I can't abide the thought he'll die without finishing that damned book."

As they drive north out of Massachusetts and into southern New Hampshire, Isabelle marvels at how vividly green everything is. It's early summer and there is lush, verdant foliage everywhere—towering pine trees, green-leafed maples and oaks, mountainous shrubs with emerald leaves and white flowers (maybe a kind of rhododendron; she isn't sure), and eight-foot-tall blueberry bushes.

"I'm not used to all the green," she tells Bev. "We're in a drought in California, and the whole state is this gray-green color, as if some alien being has sucked the chlorophyll out of every living thing. And look at that." Isabelle points out the window as they pass a large area of wetlands with an old covered bridge spanning part of it and a great blue heron picking its way along the grassy flats, high-stepping on spindly legs. "We're rationing water out west, and here you have ponds and rivers. Water everywhere." She knows she's chattering about nothing because she's afraid to ask the questions she needs to ask: *How much pain is he in? What will I find when I see him? How have you managed, Bev? How can Daniel be dying? How can that be?* And so she stops talking.

In the charged silence, with so much left unsaid, Bev steers them toward more benign territory. "Tell me about your son."

And Isabelle smiles at her. *Yes, I can talk about Avi and feel a little better.* And so she tells Bev about his summer work in Alaska, about how incongruous it is that she raised a child who only wants to be outside doing something dangerous when Isabelle pretty much considers freeway driving to be as dangerous an activity as there is in her world.

"He's confident and thoughtful," Isabelle says in summary. "What I would have given to have those qualities at his age."

"Wouldn't we all," Bev agrees. Then: "Now tell me about Michael. I know even less about him."

And so Isabelle describes Michael to her—his goodness, what her father would call his steadfastness. How he's almost courtly in the way he takes care of her, opening doors, bringing her a sweater when she's sitting outside and the evening turns cool, taking her feet in his hands at the end of a day as they sit on the living room sofa telling each other their stories of their day and rubbing the tiredness away as they talk, attending to her without making a big deal of it. Small gestures that speak of a great kindness.

She tells Bev that they talked about having a child together, but they married when Isabelle had finally committed to her writing again, after she had been back to visit Daniel, when she had met Bev.

"Of course, I remember," Bev tells her.

And Isabelle was afraid that another child would displace her writing once again, as Avi had, and Michael understood.

And never blamed her when they put away the question of having a child.

"You can see how lucky I am."

"He sounds like perfection."

"He worries. A lot. It drives me crazy. And he doesn't like people much, at least not in a group. One-on-one isn't so hard for him. He'd rather read in his study than take a walk. He refuses to buy himself new clothes. His initial reaction to anything new is *no*, but he thinks about it again, I'll give him that. He eats a limited number of foods, and to get him to a new restaurant is a major campaign. He doesn't understand the concept of risk. He—"

And here Bev stops her, laughing. "Okay, okay—he's a human being."

"A mixed bag like all of us, but I make him happy, Bev, I can see that. Really all he wants is for us to be together. And I feel the same way."

And Isabelle tells her how, over the years they've been married, she has come to rely on Michael more and Daniel less. That there's been a sort of easing between Daniel and her—not a lessening of affection but an appropriate burrowing into their own lives.

"I've seen that," Bev says.

"And of course he's had you."

"But when you finished your book and then got it published"—a grin crosses Bev's face when she thinks about it—"he'd stop people in the street, perfect strangers, wherever we were—Daniel talking to people he didn't know and didn't have to talk to!—and tell them to go buy the book. Immediately! He wouldn't stop talking about it until they promised. He was so proud of you."

"I know that."

"They've been good years," Bev says, summing up the last decade for both of them.

"Yes," Isabelle agrees, "they've been very good."

The women ride in silence, memories of the past decade giving them some solace. Then Bev tries to explain, certain that if anyone can understand, it will be Isabelle, "All those difficult years Daniel spent before he came here, they helped create a . . ." And she hesitates, trying to find exactly the right word. "A grateful man."

"I saw that man the last time I was here. He was so genuinely happy to be here, to have his panic in retreat, to have his class to teach."

"Oh, the women loved him."

"I'll bet." They grin at each other, and then Isabelle adds quietly, "To be able to write again."

Bev nods and then pulls them back to the mission at hand, "But not now." The three words are clipped, like the top of a hinged box snapping shut.

And then Daniel is between them again, in the car with them, the Daniel of today, who is dying and angry and desperate to work but unable to.

"Can you work a miracle, Isabelle?"

Isabelle doesn't answer; there is no answer. The two women turn away from each other, look out their separate windows, take in the fading of this radiant summer's day as they drive toward the difficulty ahead of them.

Alina is waiting for them as they pull up outside the barn late in the afternoon, shadows cutting the gravel driveway in half. She's there to stop Isabelle from marching into Daniel's cottage without speaking with her first.

She looks undone—that's the only word Isabelle can come up with as she gets out of Bev's car and takes a good look at the woman waiting for her. Undone, desperate, the impending loss of the father she has never reconciled with eviscerating her.

But there is, of course, no acknowledgment from Alina of what she's feeling or the difficulty of this trip for Isabelle, and there's no small talk. Not even a *How was your flight?* or *Was there a lot of traffic?* or the common courtesy of *How are you?*

"He doesn't know you're coming," Alina says by way of greeting as Isabelle approaches.

"And why is that?" Isabelle asks.

"Because he would have told me not to call you, not to have you bother to fly across the country to see a sick old man die."

Isabelle looks at Bev. Is that true?

"Sounds about right," Bev says.

"What are you going to say to him?"

"I don't know, Alina. What do you think?"

Daniel's daughter shakes her head. "I've never known what to say to him."

Bev and Isabelle share a quick look: something to be discussed later.

"You need to do it, Isabelle. You need to figure out why he put the book away and you need to get him to finish it."

"I don't know if I can accomplish—"

"It's the only thing that matters to him!"

Another quick look between Bev and Isabelle: the only thing? What about the three women who have come together to tend to him? How can Alina really believe that none of them matter to him?

"Let me see how things go," Isabelle says, and Alina nods, satisfied.

AS SHE WALKS ACROSS THE GORGEOUSLY blooming meadow separating the barn and Daniel's cottage, Isabelle searches frantically for something to say, for the *right* something to say, but comes up completely empty. There's no way to make this better, and there's no way that the Daniel she's known and loved for twenty years would stand for one false sentiment from her. Words fail her. Her heart is pounding. She's afraid of what she will find. She's afraid she'll be inadequate in the face of it.

She doesn't knock but opens the wooden door softly, stooping a little as she crosses into the cabin. She sees him immediately. He's asleep on the blue sofa, covered with a blue-and-white afghan that Bev probably knitted. An oxygen cannula rests in his nostrils, and the clear plastic tubing is looped around his ears to hold it in place. The line travels to a large green canister positioned by the fireplace.

He's gaunt, having lost so much weight that the bones of his shoulders seem to push through his skin, and there's a shadow over his face, a caul, which tells her he's dying. She moves soundlessly and takes a straight-backed kitchen chair and positions it alongside the sofa, so that when Daniel wakes, he will see her sitting there. And then she waits.

The light from the long windows begins to turn purple as the day moves into evening and the sounds of the country, which are so unfamiliar to her, fill up the air—the ruffle of the water against the banks of Foyle's Pond, the harsh call of a bird of prey, maybe a hawk. And then, in the distance, the howling of what must be a coyote and the answering call from another farther away. Mournful and unnerving.

Isabelle sits without moving and watches Daniel sleep. His breaths take effort, but they are consistent and rhythmic. She's grateful to find her panic subsiding in the quiet room, pushing ahead of it the worst of her fear. He's still Daniel. She still loves him. If she can hold on to those facts, she might be able to do this. And then he opens his eyes, when she is as ready as she's ever going to be.

"Isabelle," he says, but not with affection. "What are you doing here?" An accusation. He's not smiling. In fact, she can see he's angry, but she won't be intimidated.

"I couldn't take one more e-mail telling me how impossible

282 · DEENA GOLDSTONE

it is for you to finish your book. On and on, e-mail after e-mail. I'm here to do something about it."

He pushes himself up onto an elbow, moves his legs over the edge of the couch slowly, with difficulty, so he's sitting up and facing her. "A wasted trip, then."

"Don't you think it's a little too soon for that judgment?"

He shakes his head. He's not engaging with her. He struggles to stand up.

"What do you want? I'll get it for you."

"I was going to make a cup of tea."

"I'll do it."

And Isabelle takes the kettle from the small stove, fills it with water. "Since when did you start drinking tea?"

"Since I got sick."

And the fact lies there between them. Daniel watches her set the kettle on the burner and turn the flame up to high, her back to him. She's buying time. She doesn't know what to say, how to approach him. He can see that, but he's not helping her. He can't bear it that she's come all this way to watch him die. He wants to do it in private, alone, unobserved, and now Isabelle is here. Why should she have to experience all this with him when she has decades of life ahead of her? Years and years before all this sickness and dying and regrets and sorrow have to infiltrate her life.

"Talk to me about the book," she says now as she turns to face him, leaning her back against the kitchen countertop.

"No," Daniel says firmly. "I've put it away."

"Well, can I read the pages you've done?"

"No."

"Because they're terrible?"

"Awful."

"Okay, I've read awful before, years and years of awful. You forget how long it took me to finish my first book. I'm a pro."

"No, Isabelle. I've stopped writing."

"That's what I'm here to fix."

"It's unfixable."

Isabelle shrugs. "Maybe. Maybe not."

"I'm dying, Isabelle!" It's a cry, and the words hang in the air, suspended between them. Isabelle can almost see the letters written across the dimming afternoon light: *I'm dying . . .*

She waits, then walks back to him, sits down in the kitchen chair opposite him, and takes one of his hands. He doesn't object, but he doesn't look at her. The skin is papery and thin, bruised-looking, but it is Daniel's hand, large and warm.

"But not today, Daniel," Isabelle says softly. "Today I'm here."

"Go home, Isabelle."

"WE HAD TEA," ISABELLE TELLS ALINA AND BEV when she gets back to the barn, just as twilight descends. The women are sitting on Alina's white sofa, a bottle of wine and two glasses on the table in front of them. The light from a table lamp is pooling amber, providing just enough illumination for Bev to embroider a riot of flowers onto a plump pillow—reds, yellows, purple, the colors startling in the severe whiteness that is Alina's house.

It is Bev who gets up, finds another wineglass, and pours Isabelle a glass. Alina seems incapable of that simple act of hospitality. "Come sit with us," Bev says, and Isabelle finds herself suddenly exhausted, all but collapsing into a white slip-covered armchair positioned next to the couch.

"He told me to go home."

"But you're not, are you?" This from Alina, an edge of panic in her voice.

"He wants to finish his book. He didn't say so—in fact he said the opposite—but I know him well enough to know that."

"Yes, of course," is almost a murmur from Bev.

"Then what are you going to do?" Alina needs to know there's a plan—something, anything that might work.

"I don't know. Come back tomorrow and the day after and the day after that."

And at that reassurance, Alina relaxes a bit. She allows her back to sink into the soft cushions of the sofa, reaches for her wine. "He's being impossible," she says. "Stubborn and contrary."

Runs in the family, almost pops out of Isabelle's mouth, but she restrains herself.

"He pushes people away," is Alina's final judgment.

"Let's see," says Isabelle. "We'll take it a day at a time."

AND THAT'S WHAT THEY DO. Each morning Bev drives the two miles from town and deposits Isabelle on the gravel driveway before she races back to open the bakery, later than she'd like, but everyone in town knows that Daniel is sick and Bev is taking care of him and so there is a patient line of customers snaking along the sidewalk, waiting for the OPEN sign to appear in the front window.

Some mornings Isabelle will have a cup of coffee with Alina before she makes her way to Daniel's cabin. In those early-morning conversations she hears about the resentments Alina can't free herself from, the legacy of Daniel's transgressions as a father, which his daughter still needs to air.

"Did your mother make it hard for him to see you?" Isabelle suggests as a counterpoint to all the accusations.

"That's no excuse."

"No, but maybe an explanation."

"Not enough of one."

And the topic is closed for that day, and Isabelle makes her way across the meadow to do battle with an even more worthy adversary.

Daniel makes sure he's up and shaved and dressed by the time Isabelle gets there. Now he has a reason to get out of bed, not that he tells her that. Instead he starts each morning's conversation with, "Let's make this your last day here."

"Mmmm," Isabelle will usually say, then busy herself making tea for them both. Even though she'd like another cup of coffee, she drinks tea with Daniel.

"Doesn't your husband want you home?" Daniel says this morning, a week into Isabelle's visit, when they've had time to develop a routine.

"I'm sure he does."

"I'm glad you didn't marry that global do-gooder."

And Isabelle laughs: such a reductionist labeling of Casey. But not inaccurate.

"Me, too, but that was never an option." Then: "I married the right man."

And Daniel nods but doesn't say anything. From what she's told him about Michael, he agrees with her.

This morning he's feeling strong enough to go outside with her. They switch his oxygen to a portable canister with wheels and take it with them. Daniel manages to walk to a bench Bev has set up for him at the edge of Foyle's Pond, overlooking the meadow. By the time he settles himself down on the bench, his chest is heaving with the effort of walking and breathing at the same time. And he is coughing, a hacking sound that's hard to hear. Isabelle waits for it to quiet, for Daniel to return to himself.

They sit in the sun, the lush panorama of wildflowers in front of them—the mountain lupines, which come back every year, the sunny black-eyed Susans, and the delicate white lace of the tall yarrow heads that sway with every whisper of a breeze.

A portion of the meadow closest to the barn has been converted into a vegetable garden in the years since Isabelle has been here, with a handsome wood-and-wire fence enclosing it to deter the deer and other woodland creatures—Jesse's work, she's sure. And inside the fence Isabelle can see obsessively straight rows of seedlings, a bamboo teepee for pole beans, a trellis for cucumbers and one for peas, mounds of zucchini and yellow squash plants just starting to sprawl, squares measured out for basil and peppers of all kinds. Everything as neatly composed as Alina's living quarters.

And she is there, on her knees in the garden, weeding carefully around the fledgling plants. She doesn't look up, doesn't acknowledge them, as consumed in this task as she is when sitting at her potter's wheel.

Daniel watches his daughter while his breathing slows and stabilizes. He manages to get out the one word that defines his daughter, he feels—*fierce*—and Isabelle nods in agreement and sits quietly beside him, waiting for his heaving chest to quiet before she starts the conversation she wants to have.

"Talk to me about the book."

"Don't you ever give up?"

"You taught me not to."

"Totally unfair answer." His voice is gruff, and he turns away from her.

"Fairness has nothing to do with what we're doing here. Tell me."

"No."

And then there's a hard-edged silence between them. Daniel's *No* is unequivocal, and Isabelle sits there scurrying around in her mind, trying to find a lateral strategy, a way to sneak up on the answer she needs.

"Does Bev know what it's about?"

"Not this one. If she had known, she wouldn't have called you."

"Alina called me, not Bev."

And that piece of information startles him. She can see it.

He watches his daughter move from plant to plant, lovingly clearing the soil around each one, before he says, "I wouldn't have thought she cared enough."

"Oh, Daniel, sometimes you can be so dense."

ISABELLE MAKES LUNCH FOR THE TWO of them. Daniel eats very little, and unlike Bev, she doesn't push him to eat more. She just wraps up the untouched food and puts it back in the refrigerator. Then he settles down on the sofa. Isabelle covers him with Bev's afghan and settles herself into one of the old armchairs. She reads to him until he falls asleep—today it's from Colm Tóibín's *Brooklyn*, a novel she's recently read and thinks he'll respond to. It's a plain-speaking work and very moving—both attributes Daniel admires.

This is his favorite time of the day. Isabelle is here. She's asking nothing from him. He can listen to her voice and drift. He knows she will be there when he wakes.

While Daniel sleeps, Isabelle walks. At first she varied her route, exploring the land around the O'Malleys' complex, but once she found the beaver dam, she felt compelled to return to it every day. Now she makes her way through the shade of the dense forest growth, across the bright sunlight of open fields, often scattering flocks of wild turkeys, which cackle in protest as she passes, then down the two-lane road and up to a much larger pond than Foyle's whose name she doesn't know.

The beavers are always there—a family, she's decided, and everyone pitches in. The parents take on the trees surrounding the pond, chipping out a wedge of wood from the trunks with their large orange front teeth, gnawing over and over again until it looks like a woodsman has been hacking away with an ax. When a tree topples of its own weight, right into the water with a resounding and satisfying splash, Isabelle feels like cheering.

The younger beavers' job seems to be bringing up stones

from the bottom of the pond and fitting them under the fallen trunks, solidifying the base of the dam. The entire family of four is responsible for diving to the bottom and scooping up sediment. Their tiny paws look amazingly like human hands as they push and pat the mud into place, cementing the branches, twigs, and larger tree trunks together. More twigs and limbs are brought into the water and positioned just so. More mud is brought up. The barrier grows. Each day Isabelle can see how much progress has been made in the intervening twenty-four hours. It's astonishing to her how hard the beavers work and how ceaseless they are in their activity, and especially how they know exactly what to do, with no hesitation.

She could watch them for hours, but she always makes sure to wear a watch and to be back in the cottage before Daniel wakes up, so that when he opens his eyes, he will see her sitting there.

She'll make him tea then and they'll talk about some safe subject—the coming fall elections or the Boston Red Sox's season now that Daniel has become a fan. They're the kind of team he likes—tough, aggressive players—but despite winning the World Series in 2013, the team seems to be off to a bad start this year, and Daniel has concerns.

Isabelle knows a little about baseball; Michael is a San Francisco Giants fan, and she's picked up some rudimentary knowledge from half listening to the broadcast games he seems to keep on all spring and summer. She knows enough to listen to Daniel's indignation with the way the Sox are going and sympathize.

One day he asks her to describe the bookstore. He wants to be able to "picture it in my mind." He wants to be able to place Isabelle there when she's back in Oakland. And so she describes the corner it's on—College and Crescent, within walking distance of the Berkeley campus but not too close.

How the front door is glass and she's left the old-fashioned bell Meir had attached to it to announce a customer. How the front counter is tall and she sits on a high stool behind it.

"Is that where you e-mail me?" Daniel asks.

"Mostly, on my laptop."

And Daniel nods; he can see her there now, doing it.

She tells him the story of how she convinced Meir, years ago, to carry some new books and display them at the very first table you see when you walk in. She describes the small, cozy sofa to the right of the front door, slipcovered now in a deep burgundy twill, and the steamer trunk they use as a coffee table and how people can sit there and browse through a book, even put their feet up on the trunk, since it's well worn, and relax into the reading experience.

She tells him about the changes she made after Meir died eight years ago. How she painted the walls of the shop, which probably hadn't been touched since Meir first bought the store, a warm cream color and replaced the rickety old metal shelves with custom-built wooden ones. How she hired an old-fashioned sign painter to etch onto the large front window of the store, the one that fronts on College, NOAH'S ARK, BOOKS in shiny black letters shadowed with a sliver of gold, and underneath the store's name, MEIR SCHAPIRO, FOUNDER.

She tells Daniel how she's kept all the books she inherited. She couldn't throw out a single one, even though many of them were so esoteric she knew no one would ever buy them. But she just dusted them off and reshelved them. They were Meir's children, it felt like, and there was no abandoning them. So the shelves at the back of the store remain a shrine to Meir's belief in the unpopular, the obscure, the arcane, the unloved. Once in a while she'll sell one of those books. In fact, that's how she met Michael. And Isabelle tells Daniel that story, which she can tell he appreciates.

In those free-ranging afternoon conversations, Isabelle and Daniel move back into the easy intimacy that they once took for granted. The talk flows without pause. They interrupt each other without hesitation, tease each other occasionally, know exactly what the other means even when the other is searching for the right words. It's so easy to talk, so easy to amuse, so easy to understand exactly the point.

But today when Daniel wakes, he's furious. He's pulled himself from a dream he immediately wants to forget. Images linger—a stark and empty hillside, merciless wind, and the sky dark with heavy clouds—a goddamn Victorian novel! He's dreaming a scene that belongs in *Wuthering Heights*. He's had the dream before, various versions of it. There's always a gaping hole in the earth, bottomless, a closed coffin which somehow he knows is his, and cries of grief coming from a source he can't locate in the dream. Not very subtle. Even his dreams have gotten mundane and predictable, and he's disgusted with it all—himself, his situation.

He tries to sit up, impatient with the beautiful afghan that gets tangled in his feet, impatient with the oxygen line, which wound itself around an arm as he slept, impatient with Isabelle, who tries to help.

"This is all taking too long!"

She knows he means this long, slow march to the end, but she asks him anyway. She wants him to start talking to her about it all. "What is, Daniel?"

"This dying business. It's taking too long!"

"Maybe there's a reason."

"Yes, the universe has a sick sense of humor."

"Maybe you're not done yet. Maybe you have things to do."

"Oh, spare me, Isabelle, you sound like some New Age blissed-out *airhead*! 'Things to do'? Yes, I have things to do, but they all involve living, and all that's fucking ahead of me is dying! So stop serving up nonsensical pabulum like I have 'things to do.' "

The vehemence of his words, the blatant attack on her, backs her away. She'd like to walk right out on him, but she feels she can't. The best she can do is move across the small room and sit at the kitchen table. Turned away from him, she watches the rustle of the birch leaves, bright green against the paper white of the trunks. She's disappointed in him— wounded, if she's honest. Daniel, of all people, knows how often she calls into question her own intelligence, feeling in her darkest moments that she doesn't have the uniqueness, the smarts, she would like to, and that is exactly the soft spot he went for. Unfair, uncalled for, even if he's sick.

And he knows it. He sits on the couch silently cursing himself and fumbles to apologize, something he's rarely moved to do in this life.

"You need to stop pushing me," is what he comes up with.

She shakes her head, not looking at him. There are tears there for the first time since she's come—this is all so hard, he's in so much despair—and she doesn't want him to see them.

"Will you make us some tea?"

And she gets up and busies herself with the kettle and the stove. She takes some deep breaths.

He watches her, silent. There's an emptiness between them, and she lets it fill the room. She has no idea what to say.

Finally he starts talking. "I started the book way before I knew I was sick."

"I know that."

"But maybe some part of me knew it."

"Maybe." And then she turns to face him and asks carefully, "What were you writing about?"

"Old age. Dying. Even though I felt completely fine. Explain that."

It's a genuine question, and she thinks about it a moment before she answers. "You'd just turned seventy. You knew what was ahead of you, and you wanted to work it out in your writing before you got there. That's what you do, Daniel—you figure it out as you write."

And she brings the two mugs of tea over, sits on the sofa with him, hands him his. They take a sip, and then Isabelle thinks of what she's going to say next and a small smile plays at the corners of her mouth.

"That's what we writers do," she tells him, amending her earlier statement.

And he grins back at her, giving in, she feels, agreeing.

"Yes," he says, "that's what we writers do."

CHAPTER TWENTY

N ow, in the afternoons, instead of listening to Isabelle read to him from someone else's work, Daniel lies on the sofa and talks to her about his unfinished novel. About how his character, whom he has named Jack Dyson, came to him.

There had been an op-ed in the Sunday *New York Times* about the approaching fifty-year anniversary of the Berkeley Free Speech Movement, that moment in history when for the first time college students took over a campus and demanded their right to a voice. The point of the piece was to contrast the activist students of the sixties with the self-involved students of today, their concerns narrowed to their own personal dramas, brought to them on tiny cell-phone screens. But Daniel's attention had been caught by a brief mention of a former activist who had been one of the acknowledged student leaders and had then spent the rest of his life in the margins.

It was easy to Google Bob Gelfant and learn that here was a man who had led students into Sproul Hall in 1964 to begin the Berkeley sit-in, who had quit college to travel to Columbia University when that campus exploded, then to Kent State in 1970, where four students had been killed by the police. After that he had gone underground and continued to organize and protest and defy the laws he felt were unconstitutional. He was rumored to be part of the Weathermen, but whether or not that was true, he had slipped out of sight.

Daniel wondered what this man, who would now be in his seventies, thought of the sacrifices he had made for his ideals, whether his youthful choices and their consequences haunted him.

"I decided that my guy, Jack, had been on the run for at least twenty years," Daniel tells Isabelle now. "Along the way he had acquired a wife and two children, and they all assumed new identities every time they moved, and that was often because they could never stay in one town too long. He managed to evade arrest for decades. The question for me was, what would such a man think of his life at the end of it? When he was facing his own death."

"You wanted to write about regrets."

"Yes," Daniel said, "because even if a man is following an inner imperative, even if he feels he has no choice in the matter, there are losses along the way. That was the question I was exploring in the book."

"What were Jack's primary losses?"

"One of his daughters, the oldest one. She blames him for her mess of a life. Those years of hiding and fear—she believes all that furtiveness ruined her and that it's his fault."

"Ahhh," Isabelle says, and then keeps quiet. She waits for Daniel, and he finally says, "Echoes of my own life. You can say it, Isabelle, I'm not an idiot."

"Do they reconcile? In your book, do the father and daughter reconcile?"

"I don't know. I didn't finish writing it."

"I'd like to know," she says, and leaves it at that.

. . .

THE NEXT AFTERNOON, AFTER ISABELLE has made them lunch and cleaned up and Daniel has made his way to the couch and quieted the round of coughing the exertion has cost him, each of them settles in. Daniel wraps the afghan around his legs. Isabelle pulls an easy chair up alongside and continues their conversation of the day before.

"What would this Jack Dyson have to do to win his daughter's forgiveness?"

"I don't know that he could. His daughter is angry beyond all measure. And a mess. Did I mention she's a complete mess?"

"Several times."

"Well, that's the problem."

"How much of this have you written? How many pages do you have?"

Daniel waves his hand in the general direction of the wooden table where he works. Isabelle has no idea what he's doing.

"What?"

"It's in the cupboard there—the pages. Two hundred and some."

"And?"

"Oh, Isabelle, don't be dense. Go get them and read them and then we can have an intelligent conversation."

She leans over and kisses him. "You are a dear and infuriating man."

"Right, right," he says, but he's smiling.

ISABELLE TAKES THE PAGES HOME with her to Bev's, where she's staying, and settles down to read in one of the two small love seats framing the fireplace. It's quiet in the old Victorian house because Bev spends the evenings with Daniel, cooking him dinner, which he barely eats, putting him to bed, and staying with him until Daniel insists that she go home.

While she's gone, Isabelle plans to get a good look at Daniel's novel in progress. The manuscript rests on her lap, but instead of picking up the first page, her hands lie idle. She looks around the overstuffed living room, decorated with all the handicrafts Bev is constantly making—knitted throws of mohair and wool, patchwork pillows, a beautiful circle quilt hung on one wall like a tapestry.

Daniel would feel claustrophobic in here, was Isabelle's first thought when she walked in almost two weeks ago. It's such a feminine space, the room narrow, as these late-nineteenth-century houses tend to be, and overcrowded. Daniel is such a large man. There would be no breathing space in these little rooms for him.

Okay, Isabelle tells herself, *focus,* but she can't make herself pick up the first page and begin reading. She's afraid, she knows. What if it is as Daniel said—awful? It's not as if he has an unblemished record as a writer. There were those two books in the middle of his career that never worked, that were universally labeled failures. What if there's no hope for this work in progress? Could she lie convincingly enough to give him some measure of happiness at the end of his life? Should she? Wouldn't he know she was lying? Wouldn't he be devastated if he truly believed this work was irredeemable? Why did she even start this? Why couldn't she have just come and spent time with him and left him in the good hands of Bev?

Of course she knows the answer. She owes him this. The read. The honesty. The attention to a work that might not be all that it could be. He did that for her when she was a student with dreams of writing and no confidence who walked into his campus office and all but prostrated herself in front of him. And when she was struggling with her book and sent him chapters to read, and he sent her back pages and pages of thoughts and suggestions and encouragement in just the form she needed to continue. So now she must read these pages and be honest in her response and find a way to tell him, no matter what she thinks, so that he feels compelled to finish the book. *Wow*, she tells herself, *talk about a tall order.*

She picks up the first page. *When you're dying*, she reads, *it's pretty late for regrets. Jack Dyson would be the first to tell anybody who needed to know that here he was, dying, and he had jettisoned all his regrets. But he would be lying. He had one last, great regret, and he feared he was going to die with it wedged in his heart.*

"Oh . . ." Isabelle murmurs to herself in the silent room. And she stretches out, her back against one arm of the love seat and her feet hanging over the other. She gets as comfortable as she can on the small structure and reads on.

A little after nine o'clock Bev opens the front door and Isabelle looks up. She hasn't moved in hours.

"How is it?" Bev asks without any preamble, almost as anxious about Isabelle's reaction as Daniel.

"How is he?"

"Already cursing himself for giving you the pages."

"Of course."

"Well?"

"I'm only about a third of the way in . . ."

Bev sits down on the opposite love seat, trying to read Isabelle's face. "And?"

"This is vintage Daniel."

"Meaning it's good?"

"Meaning it's very good."

And Bev collapses back into the overstuffed pillows. "Oh, thank the Lord."

"Yes," says Isabelle softly, "on this one, even I would thank the Lord."

Isabelle reads well into the night and sleeps very little. The more she reads, the more convinced she becomes that Daniel must finish this book. Not only because it's quintessential Daniel—beautiful and tough—and deserves to be finished, but because it has a certain energy within it, a pulse, a life force even, that she knows will carry Daniel with it if she can get him to engage.

The next day he's sitting outside on the bench overlooking the meadow, portable oxygen canister parked by his side. She can see him waiting for her as she strides past Alina's garden and through the wildflowers.

"How did you get here?" she asks him when she's within shouting range.

"I fucking walked—what do you think?"

"By yourself?"

"Please, Isabelle, I'm not at death's door yet."

And she grins as she sits down next to him on the bench. "Apparently not. Apparently you still have the ability to write great pages."

And he's more pleased than he even imagined he'd be by her validation. "It's worth something, the book?" And he shrugs, as if to say it all doesn't matter much in the scheme of things, but she's not in the least bit fooled.

"It's worth finishing. You have to, Daniel."

"I don't know."

"I know. It's wonderful."

THEY FIND A RHYTHM THAT WORKS for them. At the beginning Daniel sits on the couch, or lies down if it's later in the day, and talks. His thoughts are randomly arranged, jumping from scenes he wrote early in the book to pivotal arguments between Jack and his teenage daughter much later. Sometimes he'll ask Isabelle to read from the manuscript pages; he needs to remember exactly what he wrote or to hear it out loud to see if it holds.

When he's ready to write, Isabelle opens Daniel's laptop and types. She makes sure to get down exactly what he says. The next day, after she's printed out two copies of what he's dictated, they read it together and hash it out—what works, what doesn't, what's unclear, what's redundant, what slips easily into the novel as written and what doesn't. Daniel takes a pen and edits the hard copy. Isabelle makes tea. They take a break and talk about other things, then they begin again.

One day, as Daniel is describing a memory Jack Dyson has of his daughter when she was only five, when there was still love and trust and silliness between them, he stops in midsentence and simply looks at Isabelle until she lifts her head from the computer and meets his gaze.

"What?" she asks.

"We began in a room. We end in a room."

And Isabelle doesn't disagree. She simply nods. "Yes." Then, with a grin: "We're room people, you and I."

"Womb to room."

And Isabelle laughs out loud.

DANIEL HAD LEFT OFF WRITING in despair when Jack's daughter slipped into the underworld of the homeless. Rachel's disappearance from the book, Jack's impotent agony about it, seemed to be too much for Daniel to unravel.

Eventually, after they have discussed all manner of things and Daniel has rewritten the earlier pages, they reach that section and Isabelle asks questions meant to lead him gently to the next sentence, the next paragraph, the next page of text: *How long does he search for her? Is she living with a group of people or on her own? Does she stay in Portland or move to another city in Oregon?*

Sometimes Daniel will answer quickly, spontaneously, and then they'll have a direction, a path to explore. Sometimes he'll just shake his head and moan, "I don't know. I should know, but I don't!"

But they continue to talk, and gradually Daniel finds his way forward. One afternoon he sees Jack encounter Rachel as she pushes a shopping cart across Burnside Bridge in Portland. The scene comes to him fully formed—he sees it in his mind's eye. And that day's writing goes easily. He talks quickly; Isabelle types as fast as she can. Both of them are drained but elated at the end of the day.

But more often the days move slowly. The talk between them is desultory, with lots of expanding silences. But they continue. That's what has been established: that they will continue as long as Daniel can. No one is backing out now, and so the pages accumulate slowly.

As the book edges toward its finish, Daniel becomes more convinced that Jack and Rachel never reconcile. "Too neat," he tells Isabelle. "I'd rather end with an acknowledgment of the calamity that life is."

"Okay," she says, in as neutral a tone as she can manage, but Daniel hears something in her tone. Of course. Their intimacy has always been grounded in their work, and they are so finely attuned to each other.

"Meaning you don't agree."

Isabelle shakes her head. "That ending will work, but . . ."

"Spit it out, Isabelle."

"My heart is aching for them to find each other again."

"That's the difference between us. I've lived thirty years longer and I know that what the heart wants isn't always possible."

Isabelle nods and says no more.

BEV ARRIVES AT THE CABIN in the late afternoon, after all her baking for the next morning is done. Sometimes she gets there when Daniel is still sleeping, and then the two women have a chance to catch up, sitting on the bench outside the cottage, at the edge of the pond. From there they can see the barn and sometimes Alina if she makes her way outside to the garden.

"Does she ever come to visit Daniel while you're with him?" Isabelle asks as the two women watch Alina harvest pole beans for dinner, snapping them off the tall vines, which now cover the teepee with a blanket of green.

"No."

"And she's never once come in while we're working."

"Alina leaves him be. Nothing's changed since his diagnosis."

"But now, Bev? How can she do that now?"

"I don't think she knows how to do anything else. Neither one of them is big on interpersonal skills."

SOMETIMES BEV WILL DRIVE ISABELLE back to town if there's time, but often, as the days of summer lengthen, Isabelle will choose to walk the two miles. It's a time to decompress from the intensity of Daniel and their work together and the urgency of the ticking clock.

Lately, as she walks, Alina and her newest rescue dog join her for part of the way. Alina uses the excuse that the puppy, a Lab-spaniel mix named Trixie, needs the exercise. But it is very clear to Isabelle that the daughter wants information about her father, and so she starts off these walking conversations with a progress report.

"He was in a better mood today," she might say, or "He had more trouble walking later in the day," or "We're getting close to a solid draft."

Alina doesn't ask questions. She simply listens. She both wants and is afraid to hear how Daniel is doing. At first Isabelle respected the distance Alina keeps, but after several weeks of largely one-sided conversations, she's had enough.

"Ask me questions," she demands one day. "There must be so much more you'd like to know."

Alina shrugs but says nothing, so like Daniel in her gesture that Isabelle almost comments on it.

"You'd be interested in what he's writing about." Isabelle knows she's being provocative, but she can't help herself. She's angry at this grown woman who acts like she's still that five-year-old whom Daniel left. "Would you like to know?"

"Hmmm."

"The book is about a father who's tormented by his daughter's rejection of him."

"Seriously?"

"Yes."

"He thinks I'm rejecting *him* when he's the one who abandoned *us*?"

"Alina, that was decades ago. Don't you think your reaction today, as a woman well past forty, might be a little more . . . *nuanced*?"

"What does he want from me?"

"Forgiveness."

"Because he's dying?"

"Because we all have regrets."

Alina shakes her head. "That's not a good reason."

"Because Daniel is a wiser, better man than the one who left you."

Alina shakes her head again, not looking at Isabelle as they walk, not buying a word of what Isabelle is selling.

Finally Isabelle says softly, "Because he loves you."

And Alina looks stricken, as if Isabelle has just given her news that the world is ending. She has no idea what to do with the information.

"Go in to see him," Isabelle says gently as they walk. "Sit with him. It doesn't matter what you say or even if you say a word." There's no response from Alina, but Isabelle continues on, breaking down the task as if she's talking to that grieving five-year-old. "Open the door to his cottage, take a kitchen chair, bring it close to his bed. Be with him. That's all he wants."

Alina whistles for the dog, snaps the leash on the puppy, shakes her head finally—*I can't, I won't*—and starts back toward her barn.

AS ISABELLE HAD HOPED, at first the energy within the book, the enthusiasm she brings to the collaboration, carries Daniel along and he feels better. And she is cheered and hopeful that they will be able to finish, and even he is optimistic. But as the weeks accrue, it becomes clear that Daniel is failing. Breathing has become more of a labored activity. The pain medication he was given no longer works. He needs help walking from the couch to the kitchen table. When he coughs now, it seems as though he will never be able to stop.

Bev takes him into Nashua to see his oncologist. They return grim-faced. As soon as Isabelle sees them get out of Bev's car, she knows the news is not good and there will be no working today.

She waits while Bev brings Daniel into his cabin, her arm around his waist as he leans heavily on her shoulder. Isabelle has to turn away from the image of Daniel as an invalid, so thin he appears skeletal, clutching Bev in order to remain upright. Perhaps he was all these things yesterday when she was with him, but being separated by many yards, watching Bev tending to him instead of doing it herself—all that conspires to show her Daniel as he now is.

And then she remembers—an image flashes across her mind—Daniel as she first saw him that January day at Chandler. It was his physical presence that stunned her, she remembers so well. So tall and imposing—he took up so much space in the small office. Without exerting any energy, he was intimidating, at least to her, a sheltered, unsure college student who was lost in the world. Daniel felt like a boulder, anchored to the earth in a way she had never before encountered.

Isabelle walks away from the cabin, stands behind the bench, and holds on to its back. She takes a number of deep breaths to slow the rush of panic that assaults her—the comparison of who Daniel was and who he is now.

Finally Bev comes out, having gotten Daniel settled on the couch, and finds Isabelle staring out across the meadow.

"He'll sleep for a while now, I think," Bev says, her face white with fatigue and worry.

"Do you want me to stay?"

"No, I already closed the bakery for the day. I'll stay."

"How do you do this, Bev? Day after day?"

Bev shakes her head and sits down. Isabelle joins her then on the bench. She's searching the older woman's face for an answer, even a clue to her grace and strength.

"It's been so many months for you."

"It doesn't feel that long." And Bev sighs, leans back, and begins to talk. "I married a man I loved with a sort of total fervor. It was a crazy love, I see now, but then I thought that was how you were supposed to feel. We met in college and he was this big, handsome, outgoing guy who made everyone around him feel more alive. I felt like the luckiest girl in the world."

Isabelle doesn't say a word. She's never heard Bev talk about any of the details of her life before Daniel, and she's hungry for whatever Bev will tell her.

"Right after our first son was born, Ned fell into a depression that completely incapacitated him. He couldn't get out of bed. He wouldn't eat or shower or get dressed. I had a newborn to take care of. Now, I don't feel like that's enough of an excuse for what I did, but then I didn't see any alternative. The doctors all told me ... and so I hospitalized him for several months, and then he came home. And then it happened again. And then we had some good years, and then the medications stopped working and he was back in the hospital again."

"I didn't know," Isabelle says softly.

"We had our second son when it looked like Ned could manage it—the new medication had been working for a while. We understood better what was wrong with him. I felt like I could see the warning signs even when they were subtle. We could live with this thing, this chronic depression, and contain it. But we were wrong."

Bev stops talking. Isabelle puts a hand on her arm, lightly.

"You don't have to—"

"One night when he was driving home from a working dinner with a client," Bev continues, as if Isabelle hasn't spoken, "a winter night—it had snowed that week but the skies were clear—his car went off the road and he was killed. We will never know why. Did he hit a patch of ice, or did he fall asleep while driving, or did he deliberately turn the wheel at the exact point on the road home where his car would sail into the air and plummet into a ravine fifty feet below?

"We'd been married twenty-three years at the time. Twenty-three years of taking care of a man with a chronic illness . . . That's how I can take care of Daniel." And finally Bev looks directly at Isabelle and smiles. "It's what I do."

Isabelle is speechless.

"Come on," Bev says in her no-nonsense tone, "I'll drive you back while Daniel sleeps."

And the two women get up together, start toward Bev's car.

"He agreed to hospice today," Bev tells Isabelle as they walk. "The doctor arranged for it. A nurse will come out twice a week to start, and then more often as she's needed."

"That's where we are, then." Isabelle isn't asking a question.

"That's where we are."

ISABELLE CALLS MICHAEL WHEN SHE GETS back to Bev's house, as she has done almost every day she's been away. Sometimes the conversations are lengthy, as Isabelle attempts to bring her husband into the world she's inhabiting now of Daniel and illness. But most of the time the conversations are short, just a sort of checking in. *Are you all right? Yes, are you?*

Today she reaches Michael as he's driving to a faculty meeting. There's been a lot of hubbub about budget cuts from the state legislature. They don't have a lot of time to talk, but really, all Isabelle needs is to hear his voice.

"How is he?" Michael asks, because he's become almost as invested in Daniel's condition as Isabelle.

"Today's the first day we didn't work together. Today Daniel agreed to hospice care."

There's silence on the line. Isabelle knows Michael well enough—they've been together almost a decade—to know that he's trying to figure out how to say what he needs to say gracefully. She waits.

"You've turned a corner, then," is what he comes up with.

"All the work we've done, the years Daniel put in on the book before I got here . . . I don't know now if we can finish."

"Wait and see. Don't jump to conclusions, especially when they're dire."

She takes a deep breath, then answers, "Okay."

"How are you, Bella?" The tenderest of nicknames for her, used only when he's the most worried about her.

"Sad, Michael. I'm so impossibly sad."

"Do you want me to come?"

"Yes, of course, and no. Let me see."

"Okay."

There's more silence. Isabelle can hear that Michael is in the car—the sound of the motor, a car horn outside his open window.

"Where are you going?"

"A meeting about the proposed budget cuts. What will we do if they go through? Can we raise tuition again? Usual stuff. Not life-and-death."

"Oh, tell me about it," Isabelle says, and he can hear the relief in her voice. "I want to think about something besides life and death."

And so he does: Governor Brown's stand, the uproar at Boalt about how tuition hikes will eliminate more minority students. All familiar dilemmas, but Isabelle is so grateful to spend a few minutes listening to Michael's measured voice describe the pros and cons of each side's position. The world has a sort of order. Each side has a point. Michael is always fair in his evaluations. He talks her through a possible compromise he's going to propose; maybe they can use it as a basis for discussion. Michael is hopeful they'll come up with something. Problems have solutions. It's all very comforting.

CHAPTER TWENTY-ONE

Michael was right: a corner had been turned. Now Bev sleeps at the cabin, because she doesn't think Daniel should be alone at night. And now she gets him up in the mornings and dressed and walks him over to the blue sofa, his chest heaving with the exertion of just those few steps. She settles him there in preparation for Isabelle, who arrives early so Bev can go to the bakery and open it up.

Daniel usually has a good hour in the morning, and that's when he and Isabelle work. There are no more long days filled with digressions. They both feel the urgency to finish, and they are so close. If he's having a good day, or if he wakes from his nap with something on his mind, they might work a little in the afternoon, but that's never certain.

This morning as Isabelle is tucking the afghan around Daniel's legs—he's always cold now, despite the summer weather—she asks him, "What do you want to title it?"

"Regrets of a Dying Man."

She looks up quickly at his face. Is he serious? But Daniel is grinning. He's teasing.

"It might sell a copy or maybe two," Isabelle says as she sits down beside him, nudging his legs over so she has room, "since it promises so much entertainment in the reading. *Regrets*—sure, I want to read about someone's regrets. And *dying man*—right up my alley."

"Then there'll be another regret from this dying man— that his final book didn't sell a whit. But, hey, I'll be dead, so who cares."

Since his last visit to the doctor, Daniel seems to have found an unabashed dark humor. Isabelle suspects that the amped- up pain meds have something to do with this new attitude, or maybe it's because everything is out on the table: Daniel's body failing him at an ever-increasing rate, the hospice nurse coming regularly, the finish line looming for all to see.

"No, really, have you thought about a title?"

"Let's finish the book first, then I'll worry about a title."

"Okay, fair enough."

"And if we don't get there, you title it."

"If we don't get there, I might just title it *and* rewrite the ending," Isabelle says as a challenge.

But Daniel doesn't take the bait. Instead he puts a hand on her knee, the immediate connection of their touch, so he can say quietly and deliberately, "There doesn't seem to be any separation anymore between you and me and the book, Isabelle. Whatever you do with it when I've gone will be fine."

"No, Daniel." And Isabelle is moved beyond words that he trusts her so completely. She stands up and moves to the easy chair she always uses when they work. She doesn't want him to see the tears in her eyes.

"We'll finish," she says, and it's a promise she desperately hopes to keep.

She props her feet up on the sofa now, opens his laptop, bends her head over it, and gets to work. "Why won't Rachel talk to Jack when he finds her living in that abandoned building?"

"Why should she? Nothing's changed for her."

310 · DEENA GOLDSTONE

"What if he explains himself to her? Why he acted the way he did. How it was based on principle."

"You think that would cut any ice with a semideranged street person who hasn't seen her father in years?"

"Maybe not. But maybe with a less deranged but equally stubborn daughter—"

"Leave Alina out of this."

"She walks with me sometimes when I'm going back to town. Did you know that, Daniel, she and that new dog of hers?"

"Trixie."

"Yes, and I know she's desperate to ask questions about you. She wants to know how you're doing, but she doesn't say anything. She simply walks alongside me and takes whatever nuggets of information I give her."

"Crumbs—she's content with crumbs."

"Why, Daniel? Why are these women—Rachel, your daughter—content with so little?"

"Have you seen Alina's rooms? Have you been inside her barn?"

"Yes."

"She won't even allow herself any *color*."

Isabelle laughs. "Maybe she just likes white."

"She'd argue with you if you said this, but she doesn't think she deserves much of anything."

"Because you left her?"

"Because she mattered so little that I could leave her."

"But that's not the way you felt."

"Leaving her was the hardest thing I ever did in my life."

"You should tell her that."

"Should I shout it across the meadow?"

Isabelle throws up her hands. "Surely you could find another way."

"I don't think anymore that it would make any difference."

"It would. I guarantee you, it would."

"Well, the next time she comes to visit me, I'll broach the subject."

"Impossible. You're both impossible. Has either one of you heard of the notion of forgiveness?"

And they're off, discussing forgiveness, arguing a bit, talking about Daniel and Alina and then veering off into the fictional territory of Jack Dyson and his daughter, until Daniel stops midsentence and switches gears. "When I'm not making sense anymore, I want you to go home. Take the manuscript and the laptop and go home. I won't have you see me at the end. Promise me that."

"All right."

"Whenever that is—if it's tomorrow. Whenever. If I can't find the words I want to say, then I'm not here."

WORDS, WHICH BROUGHT THEM TOGETHER ORIGINALLY: Isabelle's words on paper, then Daniel's words to her. And all the new words Isabelle wrote during the semester to please him. And then their e-mails to each other—words on a screen, words they cherished for so many years.

And now it's Daniel's words that bind them inextricably together. Will there be time for him to find the right ones to finish the book? Can Isabelle speak the right words to help him?

For twenty years words have been their lifeline, and now Isabelle can see, almost day by day, that Daniel is slowly losing the ability to produce them. Speaking takes more and more exertion, so Isabelle moves to the floor next to the couch to better hear whatever Daniel manages to say, however softly. Soon, she knows, the effort of producing the breath for even a few words will be too much and he'll fall silent.

The hospice nurse orders a hospital bed, and Daniel leaves

it only to make his slow walk to the bathroom. While they work, Isabelle sits on the bed, at the foot, and types in every syllable Daniel manages to get out. During the pauses, while Daniel is either thinking of what to say next or gathering his strength to voice his next sentence, Isabelle keeps a hand on his ankle. *Don't leave me yet. I'm here.*

And then the day comes when Daniel leans back against the many pillows propped up behind him and is finally able to say, "Done."

True to his earlier decision, he ends the novel with the messiness of life, without the rapprochement between father and daughter Isabelle had so hoped for.

Her head is bent over her computer when she hears him declare the book finished, and she remains frozen there, afraid to look up and meet his eyes. She knows before she hears it what he's going to say next. But he waits for her, for her eyes to find his, and finally she looks up and meets his gaze.

Daniel is smiling. Relieved, she can tell. Happy. At this moment, happy.

"Go home now."

She nods, ignoring the tears that fill her eyes. She comes to sit beside him on the bed and he reaches his arms out for her and she embraces him. Oh, he's hardly there—so thin.

She tells him, her lips at his ear, "You have made all the difference."

And he leans back again against the pillows, exhausted, content, smiling at her with such love that her heart seizes. "Yes," he tells her, "you have."

And then, because tears are streaming down her cheeks, he says, "Don't cry," and raises a large hand and wipes away as many of the tears as he can, and she takes his hand in hers and holds on. She can't lose him. She is losing him. How can this be?

"I have a title," he tells her, and she nods. She can't speak.

"Regrets of a Grateful Man," he says, and despite herself she smiles at him through her tears, as he had hoped.

SHE LEAVES HIM BECAUSE HE TELLS her she must and she honors that last request, closing the door to his cabin for the last time and walking, simply walking, because she doesn't know what else to do. Sobbing and walking, blind, and desperate to outwalk the grief, but it doesn't happen.

She walks through the birch forest behind the cabin and across the open field above that and then along the two-lane road which curves and winds its way eventually to Winnock. Without thinking, she finds herself climbing the rise of the small hillock that leads to the pond where the beavers live. And it is here that she stops and stands and simply cries out her heartache into the stillness of the late-summer air until her chest hurts and her throat is raw and she has run out of tears.

Finally she sits on the ground, arms wrapped around her knees, a tight bundle rocking back and forth in misery. The beavers are there, the same family she has come to know—the diligent parents, the two smaller adolescents. Their work on the dam is finished, she can see, and the pond is full and secure. But they have a new building project. Some sort of structure is going up above the waterline, made from the same kind of sticks and branches and mud. It's a mound, almost like a wooden igloo. A home—it must be their home for the coming cold weather. Isabelle has hardly registered the change, but the days have begun to shorten, the evenings hold a hint of chill. While it wouldn't be the end of summer back in California, here in New Hampshire fall comes sooner, and the beavers know it, and they are preparing to survive. Of course.

And Isabelle sits and watches them as she has for all the weeks she's been here, engrossed in their industriousness, their determination to get on with it, and when she stands up and prepares to walk back to town, she is calmer. Resolved.

It is when Isabelle comes through the birch trees toward Foyle's Pond that she sees the white Toyota parked in the gravel driveway and recognizes it. Nancy, the hospice nurse, must be with Daniel. And there she is, just leaving Daniel's cabin, closing the door softly.

Nancy is the most composed person Isabelle has ever met, tender even, and Daniel likes her, Isabelle knows. They all rely on her now—Bev, Daniel, and Isabelle—to answer questions, to make Daniel as comfortable as he can be, to show up whenever they need her. A small woman in her late forties, with strong hands and an unadorned face, she makes her way across the meadow toward her car, parked in front of the barn.

Alina is out in the garden harvesting yellow crookneck squash and foot-long zucchini, shaded now by the massive faces of bright yellow sunflowers, eight feet tall. When Nancy waves, Alina straightens up and returns it, then stands amid the overflowing garden, watching while Nancy gets into her car and drives slowly down the O'Malleys' unpaved road and out toward the main highway.

Isabelle doesn't move. Something makes her stay where she is, hidden by the trees. She's waiting, but she doesn't know why.

And then Alina dusts the earth off the knees of her jeans and walks across the meadow with her long and determined steps. She doesn't hesitate at the door of Daniel's cottage. She simply opens it, bends her head to enter, and closes it behind her.

And when Isabelle walks past, to get to the path through the trees that leads to town, she can see, through the two tall windows next to Daniel's bed, that Alina is doing exactly what Isabelle had hoped she would do. She's taken a kitchen chair and positioned it beside the hospital bed. She is sitting beside her father and she has his hand in hers.

SURPRISE ME · 315

Isabelle turns away—this intimacy isn't hers to witness—and starts on the path into town that she first walked alone so many years ago, the day she came looking for Daniel. The very path they walked many times together after that. The path that will take her back to the bounty of her present life in Oakland, with Michael, who is waiting, eager for her always. The man she chose. The man who makes all the good things in her life possible.

IN THE SPRING OF THE NEXT YEAR, the first copies of Daniel's final book arrive at Noah's Ark. Isabelle has been waiting for them, and she opens the cardboard box with eagerness, Julian by her side.

"Ah," he says as she hands him the first copy, "a gorgeous book."

The cover is a photo of Daniel's cabin on the bank of Foyle's Pond, sheltered by the birch trees. It was taken in late afternoon, and shards of waning sunlight are sprinkled across the water. The title, Daniel's title—*Regrets of a Grateful Man*—is printed in clean, crisp black type across the tops of the trees, and his name is spread across the water at the bottom, almost as if it will disappear in an instant.

"Maybe Deepti is right," Isabelle muses as she takes a second book from the carton and holds it with two hands. "Maybe souls migrate." Memories flood her. They will for the rest of her life, she knows. "Isn't Daniel's soul here, in this book?"

It's a rhetorical question, which Julian knows enough not to answer. Of course Daniel's soul is in his writing. Why else write?

Isabelle opens the book to the back flap, and there is Daniel's face looking back at her. This is Daniel in Winnock. Daniel smiling. Daniel with some measure of peace. She sees that Bev is credited with the photo, and she immediately knows that it was taken during the ten good years they had together. And that makes her happy.

It was Bev, of course, who called her the night Daniel died, less than two weeks after Isabelle returned to California. She tells her Stefan arrived a day after Isabelle left. He lives in Michigan now, and is married to a woman with two young children.

"He works as an orderly in a hospital," Bev says, "and Daniel was very glad to see him. They talked for days—well, Stefan talked, and Daniel mostly smiled at him and nodded. They both were happy with that."

There's a silence as Bev gathers herself, and then she adds, "We were all with him at the end—Stefan, Alina, and of course I was there." Bev pauses again before she makes her final statement. Her voice is confident; this is what she will remember. "I know he felt surrounded by love."

"Oh, yes," Isabelle says softly in response, "he was loved."

ACKNOWLEDGMENTS

Three determined women have guided my writing career: Lynn Pleshette recognized the writer within me before I ever allowed myself to believe in that possibility. Marly Rusoff guided my transition from weary screenwriter to wide-eyed fiction writer. And the intrepid, courageous Nan Talese reached out her hand to me and made it all happen. I am grateful beyond all words to all three.

I also want to thank the Sundance Institute and Michelle Satter, in particular, for inviting me to be part of their Screenwriting Lab. It is in the glorious mountains of Utah that I have learned what it is to be a mentor to young screenwriters from the world over. My experiences there have translated into a better understanding of Daniel here, in this book.

And finally, of course, without the unwavering love and complete support of my husband, Marty, and my daughter, Eva, this book would never exist. They have all my love.

A NOTE ABOUT THE AUTHOR

Deena Goldstone is the author of the short-story collection *Tell Me One Thing* and a screenwriter of feature films and television movies. She lives in Pasadena, California, with her family. This is her first novel.

The text of this book was set in Walbaum, a typeface designed by Justus Erich Walbaum in 1810. Walbaum was active as a typefounder in Goslar and Weimar from 1799 to 1836. Though the letter forms of this face are patterned closely on the "modern" cuts then being made by Giambattista Bodoni and the Didot family, they are of a far less rigid cut. Indeed, it is the slight but pleasing irregularities in the cut that give this typeface its humane quality and account for its wide appeal. Even in appearance, Walbaum jumps boundaries, having a look more French than German.